Dairy Maid

A Manley Dairies Erotic Novel

Lacy Tate

ROCKY RIDGE BOOKS

Warning: this book contains graphic references to sexual activities, including female/female contanct, and is not suitable for audiences under eighteen years of age.

This book is a work of fiction. All characters, places, and incidents are the product of the author's imagination or are used fictitiously, and any resemblance to actual persons, living or dead, companies, or locales is entirely coincidental.

Published by:
Rocky Ridge Books
PO Box 6922
Broomfield, CO 80021
www.rockyridgebooks.com

Anything worth doing is worth overdoing.
~Lazarus Long/Robert Heinlein

Dairy Maid

A Manley Dairies Erotic Novel

Lacy Tate

Chapter 1 Career Change

THE PILE OF MAIL on Ginny Harper's table had been growing, mostly with envelopes bearing pink windows. "Third notice" blared from some of them; "Immediate action required" in red ink decorated others. She'd stopped opening them a while back—she couldn't do a damned thing about them. Flipping burgers just didn't pay that much, and she hadn't been able to get a job as good as her old one since she'd been laid off.

Running out of choices, that's what she was doing. Maybe a miracle would happen and she'd find a job good enough to get her back on her feet, before she was out on her ass. Ginny'd come home to a notice pinned to her door, demanding back rent on the little apartment that had been home since she came to Pennington.

Ginny sighed. Maybe it was time to swallow her pride and take off her clothing. She didn't want to be an exotic dancer, although there were plenty of "help wanted" ads for that position. A dozen clubs down by the river were hiring, and maybe she could pick up enough moves that the horny men would stuff her G-string with fives and tens. *Don't kid yourself, girl, you aren't such a good dancer that they'll stuff twenties in there.* But maybe she could make ends meet.

Goodness knows she had the physical attributes for it. Five foot eight and built cute is what her last boyfriend called her, although how Double-D boobies qualified as cute when they were so damned big mystified Ginny. But they did make her waist look even smaller than the twenty-four inches it measured, and then her hips... Oh, her hips. Starving herself didn't make them any smaller, although thirty-seven inches weren't big hips, they just looked big compared to her nipped-in middle, and at least they weren't big enough to totally balance out her tits. Dolly Parton only younger, Ginny called herself, and she didn't put the long blonde hair on a wig stand at night, either.

Ginny plopped herself and her newspaper down at the tiny kitchen table. Her braids bounced when she landed on that cushiony bottom. She'd have to wash her hair just to get the smell of French fries out. Man, if she could only find a job that didn't involve cooking grease.

Spreading the newspaper at least covered up the horrible piles of bills. Maybe she could run away, change her name, start over. Her boyfriend wouldn't miss her—he'd said *no way* when she suggested moving in with him, just to save on rent, not to get engaged or anything. He'd sneered about *why buy the cow when the milk was free?*

"Well, honey-pie, this milk ain't free no more," she told the heartless bastard. If that's how he felt about her, he could date Rosy Palm and her sisters for a while. Except he'd been dating her best friend at the same time as her, something *neither* of the slime balls had mentioned until things got tough. The little shits deserved each other.

Honestly, no one was going to miss her except the bill collectors.

Skipping past the headlines which would only be bad news anyway, Ginny flipped to the want ads. Maybe all the good jobs were on line, but that meant a trip to the library since her internet was cut off a month ago and she'd sold her computer. She had a quarter for a paper, though, and maybe luck would smile on her today.

Dancer, dancer, driver, driver... Ginny didn't think her little car would stand up to the wear and tear for long if she had to drive her own vehicle. She skipped past that, hunting—Dairy maid. Huh. She didn't know a thing about cows, but what else did she have to do? She could spend five seconds to read.

"Dairy Maid—attractive, personable hostesses needed for hands-on dairy operation. Light work, no shoveling. *High pay for the right candidates. Room and board included. Call 555-0167.*"

No shoveling? Ginny was all for that—desperation for honest, high paying work hadn't gotten to the cow-poop stage. Room and board? Her stomach grumbled, reminding her that she was down to her last few cans of soup and one box of mac and cheese. The notice demanding *Pay up or move out!* crinkled under the newspaper. She pulled out her phone, her one last luxury, and dialed.

"Manley Dairy, how may I help you?" The deep, masculine voice on the other end sounded manly all right. Ginny would have batted her big blue eyes at the speaker if she'd heard that voice in a bar. But stop it now; this was about a job, not a date.

"Hi, I'm Ginny Harper, and I'm calling about the dairy maid job in the paper…" Oh, damn, she sounded like she was in a bar—her voice had gone way down and smoky-like, in spite of her little scolding.

"Hellooo, Ginny," he said, and damn, he sounded like he had meeting-in-the-bar thoughts too. But maybe that's the way he always sounded. "I'm Dirk Manley, the owner. Tell me why you're interested."

She didn't want to sound too desperate, but she'd been raised to be honest. "I need something better than a fast-food job, I think I'm attractive (*hell, she* knew *she was attractive!*) and personable, and I'm willing to learn new skills and really earn my pay."

"I do like a hard worker." Dirk chuckled, and the sound went right to her pussy. "Would you be able to meet for dinner tonight, and we can do a proper job interview? I have a couple of other candidates to interview as well, and perhaps I can answer everyone's questions at once."

Dinner! Wow! "Er, what sort of place? I'd like to dress appropriately, sir." Ginny thought about her clothes right away.

"Lovely attitude, Ginny. I bet you're a great worker." Dirk chuckled again.

Maybe I better call him Mr. Manley, just so I don't go stupid in front of him. "I try hard, sir." It hadn't kept her from getting a pink slip at her office job.

"Just something medium, we'll have dinner at Paul's Place. See you at seven?" His voice promised more than a job interview.

Dairy Maid

"Seven it is. See you then." Oh boy! Ginny *loved* Paul's Place! They had the *best* stuffed jalapenos, and really, everything there was good. She hadn't been there since she and the heartless dick parted ways.

Ginny ran to the shower, pulling elastics off her braids. She had to get the smell of old burgers out of her hair. She stepped into the spray, loving the feel of the water pulsing on her poor tired back. A handful of strawberry shampoo turned to a head of foam under her busy hands, and the scalp massage felt so good, even if she did have to give it to herself. That was one thing she really missed about her scummy ex—he did give the best back rubs and foot rubs, and well— other rubs. Ginny smoothed a handful of lather down her neck and toward her titties.

It had been so long since anyone had played with her titties. Round and plump, with rosy pink nipples that perked up to the sky, with the sweet soft weight of her breast mostly below. She always thought her upturned nipples were saying *Hi!* to her lover, and if he bent down to lick *Hi!* back, she just loved it. Ginny thought about Dirk Manley's deep voice and stroked lather over her nipples. They started to swell, turning darker pink and showing through the soft white foam.

Rubbing her palms over the pink nubs sent little zips of electricity through her. Funny how titties on your chest could be connected to your clit—Ginny had to fold over with the wonderful feeling that suddenly bloomed in her crotch. If she slipped a hand between her legs, she'd find swelling there too—her clit went stiff, trying to peek out between her lips. Not yet, not yet. Ginny twiddled her nips, pinching one, gasping with the delightful shocks.

She cradled one huge tit in each hand rolling her fingers over the skin, feeling the little bumps inside. Milk glands, she supposed, lots and lots of milk glands. And all there to make milk, which she'd never done. Wonder what that felt like? Could you feel each little gland doing its job? You could sure feel them feeling good.

4

She pulled at each nipple, first one, then the other, loving the stretch and the pressure. The cows had it good—people at their beck and call whose job was to pull their teats. Did the cows love it? They came when it was milking time, she heard. Maybe came to the barn, not *came* came. Yeah, how would you know about a cow's orgasms? But bet they liked someone pulling those giant nipples, making huge gushes of milk come out with each pull. Her nipples weren't that big—they only stuck out about a half inch when she was horny, like, oh now. She pinched both sides at once, suddenly needing to touch her pussy.

One hand to cradle a giant tit, one hand to spread her pussy lips and dip a finger in. Milk up top, sweet honey below. She dipped a long middle finger inside, feeling the juiciness coat her digit, and then tickled her clit, all hard and sensitive, and feeling like another nipple. Wouldn't it be funny to give fluid through that?

With quick little rubs, Ginny brought herself to climax, the huge waves crashing through her cunt, making lightning in her clit, and shocks in her hard pink nipples. Oh, a good hard cum! Her cums were always better when she played with her titties. A tiny bit of fluid squirted out of her pussy—she felt it run down her leg after the orgasm faded—it was all the way to her calf before she stopped coming. On shaky legs, she finished washing her hair, washed the bit of rain away, and reached for a towel.

Ginny was never quite sure why she squirted when she came, but it always felt really good. Dumbass ex-boyfriend liked that she could do it, it made him feel all studly, but he didn't like the liquid itself. Idiot. Ginny put on a lacy pink bra. Wouldn't it be fun to squirt milk when she came? She adjusted her Double-Ds inside the cups. If she could, and she came like she just did, bet someone could have a nice big drink.

Dairy cows didn't know how good they had it.

Chapter 2 New Boss, New Friends

When Ginny arrived at Paul's Place, she met Dirk Manley and three other job candidates. Three very pretty girls all sitting at the table, looking frightened when Dirk pulled out Ginny's chair. "No need to be concerned, ladies. I have several job openings, so let's all be friends now, shall we?"

Oh, gee, Dirk was sensitive, too. She started to like the man she hoped would be her boss.

He made introductions: "Ginny, this is Heidi, this is Selita, this is Jordyn."

Each girl nodded as her name was spoken. Heidi had brunette hair cut to her shoulders and an upturned nose—she had really nice cleavage showing from her purple scoop-neck shirt, and it wouldn't be a stretch to call her attractive, no, not at all, this was one big, beautiful woman. Heidi smiled at Ginny—Ginny smiled back. She was desperate for a job, but she suspected these girls might be too. She wouldn't do or say anything to make Dirk think she wasn't "personable".

Selita had smooth tawny skin and large dark eyes that went perfectly with her straight black hair. She'd put a rhinestone clip on one side, exposing her beautiful cheekbones. Ginny looked at Selita, wondering if she'd even had to put on more than mascara to look that gorgeous. Darn. Ginny'd put on a full face, wanting to make the best impression possible. Maybe she'd used too much blush, but she wanted to look all healthy and milk-maid-y. Selita looked more like a fashion model than a milk-maid, slender and elegant, with little tea-cup titties that would be hidden by the palm of a man's hand. Ginny didn't like the contrast—all of a sudden she felt disgustingly busty and rustic, and a little self conscious.

But it was Jordyn who nearly made Ginny swallow her tongue—Jordyn was like looking in the mirror. Except she'd swept her wheat-colored hair into a side pony-tail, with curls at the ends that reached down to tickle one nipple while Ginny had left her hair spilling down her back. Jordyn's big blue eyes and pouty mouth were a lot like her own, and if her tits weren't quite as big as Ginny's, they still bumped against the table's edge to keep Jordyn from getting too close to her plate.

Dirk smiled at all of them while they greeted each other. Bet he'd like his employees to get along! Ginny would be charm itself to every-one.

Dirk himself was everything his voice had promised, with a rug-ged jaw and wavy brown hair combed over one eye in a rakish way. He wore a polo shirt and cologne that smelled expensive, like he'd never, ever whiff of *eau de Bovine*. He didn't look at all like a farmer to Ginny—he looked like he should be on a yacht somewhere. Maybe he looked different in overalls. About forty years old was not at all too old in Ginny's book—so what if she was only twenty-five?

Stop it! She scolded herself—*this is a job interview, not a date!*

Once Ginny was seated, the waitress took their order. Ginny asked for the stuffed jalapenos and a hearty chicken-asiago salad with pine nuts and cranberries. The lettuce would make her feel good about the meal, but it was the chunks on top she wanted, and Paul's Place put lots of stuff on top. No one else ordered as heartily except for Dirk, who wanted a steak.

He watched approvingly as Ginny offered the plate of peppers to her companions, but no one else took one. "Enjoy those now, ladies, because our own kitchen doesn't make them."

Heidi changed her mind and tried one, the cheese sliding out sideways when she bit too hesitantly. She giggled and scooped the gooey white cheese to her lips with two fingers, licking them and then blushing for her manners. Ginny liked her a lot right then—that was exactly the sort of silly thing Ginny herself would do—a girl has to enjoy her food, and when the food tries to escape…!

Dirk grinned at Heidi, clearly enjoying the little show, but Selita raised her eyebrows. *How gauche,* those perfectly plucked arches seemed to say.

"I could share my recipe," Jordyn offered. Right then Ginny decided that if they both got jobs, Jordyn would be her new bestie.

"Thank you, Jordyn, but our cooks are quite accomplished: you'll enjoy the food, but our kitchen avoids dishes that are very spicy, or garlicky, or peppery. Some of our clients have very particular palates, so unless we know their tastes, we avoid anything pungent."

Ooh! The hostesses get fed from the guests' menu!

As they ate, Dirk explained a little about the dairy. "It's almost like a dude ranch. A dude-dairy, if you will, where guests come to fulfill their fantasies. Your job as Dairy Maids will be to provide them with the most exquisite delicacy the dairy provides, which you will be instructed on how to make. Ginny, I believe you said you were eager to learn new skills?"

"Oh yes!" she agreed quickly. "I'm not a very good cook, though—" She cut herself off quickly, not wanting Dirk to think she wasn't qualified.

"You will receive all the help you need, dear," he soothed. "Your current skills in the kitchen don't matter."

Heidi looked a little relieved. Jordyn looked concerned; maybe she'd thought she had an edge there. Selita delicately ate an olive, not reacting to the idea of preparing tidbits for the guests. The olive looked rather helpless between her long, ruby-tinted nails. Ginny didn't think dairies and long nails would go together very well.

Neither did Dirk, apparently. Before they'd even finished the meal, he'd said as much. "Selita, while you are a charming young lady and very pretty, too, may I add, I don't think you're going to fit in at Manley Dairy very well."

She looked panicked, but only for a moment, until Dirk pulled a card from his pocket to give her. "Our uniforms of white cotton and little blue checks are going to look silly on you—the staff uniforms at my friend Maxwell's place will be much more becoming, and you wouldn't need to relocate unless you wished. It's here in town. I'll give him a call to recommend you. I'll let him know that I think you'd do very well for him."

Selita pocketed the card with thanks, and fell to eating her dinner with more gusto. Maybe she hadn't wanted to move.

Ginny asked, "You did say room as well as board. Could you explain that?"

Dirk finished his bite of steak. "Certainly. Our dairy is a few miles outside of town, as you may imagine, and we have what might be called dormitories. Each staff member has their own bedroom with a shared bath, and a common living area with couches, a pool table, a large screen TV, and bookshelves, though the contents run heavily to pink-covered romances. No kitchen, but I already explained why— the dairy takes responsibility for feeding you. You have the run of the grounds on your free time, but if you meet a guest, you're back on duty until the guest is satisfied. Our staff doesn't find that to be a problem—the encounter is usually enjoyable. We do like our staff to mingle with the guests; it makes for a very happy dairy."

A happy dairy sounded a whole lot better than a hot kitchen and flying grease. When would the job offer come?

Dirk pushed away his plate after another few bites. "We do ask that you remain in uniform at all times, even when not on duty, but you'll be comfortable. We'll give you a year's contract, although it comes with a probationary period, because not all new staff adjust well to their duties. If, after a month, you haven't mastered the neces- sary skills, we'll release you from your contract with a month's pay and wish you well. If you work out, we'll finish the year, and renew the contract as long as you are happy with us. We pay bonuses for pro-duction, so it's in your best interest to remain in uniform to qualify."

He looked from face to face. Ginny tried not to look over-anx-ious. A month's pay even if she didn't work out! Bonuses for produc-tion! She could do that. And she didn't have to worry about rent, or electricity, or water, or all of those other things that clamored to be paid for. She liked the salary he named too. She could pay off all her bills and even start to save some money again! Oh please, let him offer her a contract!

"So, Heidi, Jordyn, and Ginny, would you like to be Manley Dairy's newest Dairy Maids?" He looked from one to another with one hand reaching to a briefcase by his feet. "I have contracts with me, and I'd love for you to start right away."

"Yes! Yes!" they chorused, and they all scratched their names onto the sheets of fine print that not a one of them paused to read.

"It's okay even if we don't know anything about cows?" Ginny asked timidly, handing her contract back to him, and afraid he'd drop it if he said no.

"It's really okay," Dirk reassured her. "The three of you will train together and we'll teach you everything you need to know."

Chapter 3 New Bras and a Taste Treat

JORDYN MET GINNY at the front gate of Manley Dairy the next morning. They crept in together, like maybe they were supposed to go the back way, but a smiling Dirk Manley met them before they'd gone very far.

"Come, my new dairy maids, allow me to escort you to your quarters and get you settled." He offered a sweeping bow.

Ooh, gallant, too! Was there a rule about dating the boss? Ginny told herself again to quit dreaming—she needed a job, not a boyfriend. She'd settle for a rich husband though, and from the elegant grounds of Manley Dairy, she'd bet Dirk was doing pretty well. Lushly green lawns rolled away from the gate and a pond with ducks lay between the buildings. A main farmhouse had to be where Dirk lived, and three cheery red barns of different sizes circled it. Another barn lay farther beyond the circle.

He looked a little more like a farmer today, dressed in tight, faded blue jeans and a plaid shirt, open at the neck, and showing some nice skin. Ginny tried not to stare, but when a hunk of six feet two and broad shoulders is offering you a place to sleep, it's hard not to imagine sleeping there with him. One of the barns turned out to be staff quarters, with two floors of bedrooms and baths, each with a common room.

Jordyn and Ginny picked rooms on either side of one of the shared bathrooms—their bedrooms had the only doors into it. They giggled over their new accommodations once Dirk left them with instructions to come to the side door of the big house in an hour, after they'd gotten settled.

"Is this deluxe or what?" Jordyn came to bounce on Ginny's bed while Ginny unpacked her few things. The bed, a pillow topped queen-size with blue floral bedding, let her get a lot of altitude into the bounces.

"This is sheer wow," Ginny agreed. Um, a lot of wow. Just for being a hostess? "Did you notice the bathtub?"

"Ooh yeah." Jordyn bounced again. "With a whirlpool and a hand shower! My old apartment isn't half so nice or so big. I'm so glad to get out of there." Her boobies bounced up and down too, rising when she came down, lowering when she boinged up.

"Me too." Ginny had left a lot of things behind, including big stacks of bills, so the landlord wouldn't think it worth his while to pursue her. She'd taken all the latest bills, and she'd pay them off, including the rent, but first she'd learn her new job and start earning those bonuses. "I hope we're going to like it here."

"I bet we will." Jordyn flopped flat on the bed, and then jumped up to make it tidy. She sat down on the edge and looked a little sad. "Is it going to be hard to be out here for at least a month without going home or calling anyone?"

"Not really." Ginny sat down next to Jordyn. "My ratbag ex and my even bigger ratbag ex-bestie who was sleeping with him all along sure won't miss me."

"That's awful." Jordyn put her arm around Ginny's waist and lay her head on Ginny's shoulder. "I'd never do that to a friend."

Ginny rested her cheek on Jordyn's head. She smelled of vanilla and spices. "Me either. However, I would arm-wrestle her for Dirk."

Jordyn sighed. "I would too. Maybe we should combine forces instead and steal him from the other girls."

Ginny giggled and squeezed Jordyn's knee, making her jump. "Good idea! Except we should find out if there's a Mrs. Dirk waiting to bop us with a frying pan for trying."

"Oh I hope not." Jordyn settled back against Ginny. She was really nice and warm. "Do you think Dirk hired us because we look so much alike?"

"Maybe. We are kind of cute, don't you think?" Ginny stole a look at Jordyn's full titties under her thin, pink cotton T-shirt and her thighs, lightly tanned skin showing from blue cut-offs.

"We are. If we styled our hair the same, we could look like bookends." Jordyn hopped up to check herself in the mirror, like maybe her cuteness needed adjusting. It didn't. "Do you think Heidi's here yet?"

"Oh, I hope so! Maybe she's up at the house already! And then we can be the three amigas and grab all the bonuses."

"Yeah! Let's go!" They ran to the house hand in hand.

GINNY AND JORDYN organized themselves to look a little more like job trainees than little girls before knocking at the side door. Dirk let them in, smiling. "Very prompt! Excellent." He ushered them into a comfortable farmhouse-style living room, all overstuffed furniture and polished wood.

Heidi jumped out of a big leather chair, her arms out. "Hi, guys!"

A little scared of all the new, and glad to see a familiar face, even if it was only a little familiar, Ginny hugged her quickly. "Hi, Heidi!" She was warm and a comfortable armful, her padding made her softly squishy. Ginny liked that, it felt cozy, like they were friends already. Jordyn sneaked a quick hug too.

"It's always great when the staff gets along." Dirk grinned at them—he had to be enjoying the sight of three young women hugging. Well, if he wanted in on the hugs, he should say so. But he was the boss, look and don't touch. Too bad for him!

"I'm going to show you around a bit, and then we'll get you fitted for uniforms. Oh, and—" Dirk put his hand out. "Cell phones, ladies. We'll cover the cost of your plan for the month, but no calls. If you get lockjaw on day 31 from catching up with all your friends, we'll feed you ibuprofen." He collected all three phones. "If it's a desperate emergency, you can use the office phone, but otherwise, we need your full attention for this first month."

Since Ginny didn't have anyone she really wanted to call, that wouldn't be such a hardship. She'd deleted her ex and her ex-best friend two months ago. She glanced at Jordyn and Heidi—if she need- ed to talk to anyone, they were right here with her. She went back to listening to Dirk.

"It's early in the day yet, so we might get your first training ses- sion in before dinner." Dirk gestured for them to follow him out the back door. He showed them tractors and chicken coops, a barn that had equipment in the stalls that Ginny didn't recognize, but she knew she wasn't supposed to be farming so she didn't worry. "A lot of our clients come in here to fulfill their fantasies." Dirk closed the stall door on a milking machine and a stanchion that looked too flimsy to restrain a big old Jersey cow. But Ginny didn't know anything about cows; maybe they were pretty docile.

They looked at hay fields and a riding corral. "You can ride if the clients aren't using the horses and they haven't been worked too hard," Dirk said. "Or if you haven't been worked too hard."

The pond was fed by a pretty little stream. "Sometimes people like to have a fishing hole fantasy—you know, jump in the pond bare-nekkid." Dirk pulled some bread out of his pocket for the ducks, which came quacking to snatch the crumbs. "Or fish in the stream. It makes them feel all Tom Sawyer. They pay good money for that."

"They're old enough to want a Becky Thatcher to do naughty things with," Heidi whispered saucily. "Was she allowed to swim bare-ass in the pond?"

"Probably not," Ginny whispered back. "I get the feeling we may be seeing a lot of guests' bare butts."

"Hee!" Jordyn flexed her hands at butt height behind Dirk's back. "Wonder if we'll see him in the swimmin' hole?"

Heidi made a "hush, not so loud" motion, and Jordyn dropped her hands to her sides before Dirk turned around from the ducks.

"Uh, where is everyone?" Ginny asked. They hadn't seen but a few people on their tour.

"We have a skeleton staff right now, since it's vacation time. Just enough crew to keep up the grounds and feed the animals." (There had been cows in the field, black and white and large: Ginny was glad they didn't go near.) Dirk led them back toward the house. "And a few for training, Old Horace the cowman, and a couple of our trainers. Guests won't be coming in for another week."

They were met by a pretty woman about thirty years old, when they got back to the house. "Ladies, this is your trainer, Elspeth. She'll get you fitted and kitted." Dirk introduced them and left.

Elspeth was wearing a white peasant shirt and a dark blue checked skirt with suspenders like a cheery farm wife right out of a butter commercial. She even had her curly brunette hair in pigtails, though she hardly looked like a child. She looked like a woman who could work all day and then make love all night—her lips had that naughty upturn, and her eyes promised delights. Her bust strained at her shirt, which had little ripples between the bumps of her flesh. Ginny imagined she was popular with the guests, who probably had trouble keeping their hands to themselves. Maybe she'd coach them on how to keep the advances down and the bonuses up.

"Welcome, my dear dairy maids!" She introduced herself to each young woman with a hug, and when she hugged Ginny, she left damp spots.

"Oh, dear, I went and milked on you," Elspeth apologized. "Sorry, I didn't think that would happen. I think I have a bit of time before I absolutely have to do something about it, so let's get started."

Wasn't there a hungry baby around here somewhere? Elspeth didn't seem concerned. She led them upstairs to a bedroom that had a lot of clothing racks filled with white shirts, red checked clothing, blue checked clothing, and a few of the same dark blue as Elspeth's own.

She eyeballed the girls one by one, and found a tape measure in the top drawer of a large oak bureau. "First we do underpinnings. You no doubt brought bras, but the right sort makes the clothing fit better and you'll be more comfortable, too. Shirts and bras off, ladies."

Eyeing each other and getting undressed slowly made Elspeth cluck. "We're all girls together, please. Who's first?"

Jordyn stepped forward, letting her T-shirt fall on the bed. "Me, I guess."

Oh, her titties had a lovely shape—Ginny didn't want to stare, but it was hard not to—full, high mounds of creamy booby with the largest areolas Ginny'd ever seen; a silver dollar wouldn't cover them. A little rosy bud poked from the center of each one, soft at first but getting firmer in the breeze from the window fan. Jordyn lifted her arms for Elspeth to wrap the tape measure around her.

"Lift your breasts, please,"

Elspeth requested. Jordyn put her hands under all that creamy goodness, letting the tape snuggle close to their undersides.

"Let them down now."

Down wasn't very far—Jordyn had to have lived in underwires since she started growing. What lovely firm breasts she had. Ginny thought they might even be prettier than her own.

Elspeth wrapped the tape around the fullest part of Jordyn's breasts, adjusting it to find the widest measurement. The tape flicked across Jordyn's nipple, making her giggle and hunch.

"Stand straight, Jordyn. You'll get used to it." Elspeth wrapped the tape again, loosely enough not to dent the skin. "My, you're a perfect 36 D, and very full." She fished in a lower drawer in the bureau, extracting a white lace bra. "Try this style."

Jordyn clipped into the bra, a front loader, and slung her titties into their new hammocks. Her skin showed pinkish through the lace. "That fits great, Elspeth!" She admired herself in the mirror, turning this way and that, checking the silhouette. She looked fashion model good, if models came with that size bustline. Any man

18

would be drooling to take a bite, so good thing Dirk was somewhere else.

"That's really pretty, Jordyn." Heidi sounded wistful. "I can't ever find bras my size that lovely."

"I think I have something in my magic chest of drawers." Elspeth handed Jordyn a stack of bras and motioned for Heidi to stand up. "Lift, please."

Lifting was more work for Heidi, because her melons were really melon sized, well, almost, and practically begged for someone to put her face between them. Oh my! Where did that thought come from? Ginny hadn't ever touched a woman in bed, well, not unless you have to count that one time in college, and she'd had so much to drink she couldn't really remember. Well, she remembered it was nice. Really nice. She didn't want to remember how mad her roomie was the next morning.

Heidi kept her boobs up, the nipples poking pinkly over the edges of her hands, until Elspeth motioned, and then set them down carefully. She was so big that letting go abruptly would probably hurt. Bet any man lucky enough to touch those thought he had been invited to a seven course meal. Elspeth measured again, around the fullness, and lifted her eyebrows at the number on the tape.

"Oh, lovely, my dear. You need a forty Double-D, and from the shape of you, I have just the thing." She bent to rummage in a lower drawer. "We don't get a lot of call for this size."

"I know." Heidi's lower lip trembled. "Manufacturers think girls my size don't need pretty things."

"And they are wrong!" Elspeth declared. "You deserve pretty undies just as much as anyone else. You are a gorgeous woman, and we don't dress our staff in ugly things. The prettier you feel, the happier you'll be, and then the happier the guests are." She found a pale peach bra. "I think you'll like this one."

"Oh yes!" Heidi slipped her arms through the straps. "If it fits…" she ended uncertainly.

"It will. I'm an expert bra fitter," Elspeth assured her. "And should this one not fit right after a time, you tell me, and we'll adjust. You have to be comfortable, and not in some old bra that looks like a suit of armor." She ran a finger under a strap to get a kink out. "What do you think?"

"Oh, I like it!" Heidi looked like a frosted sugar cookie in that bra, and before Ginny knew it, she'd bounced up off the edge of the bed to hug her.

"You look good enough to eat!" Ginny declared, and then let go, astonished that she'd reacted like that. "Erm, sorry."

"Don't be." Heidi laughed and hugged Ginny against her lovely cushiony bosom. "I'm a pretty huggy person too."

Oh, good. Well, Dirk had been hiring for "personable," and Heidi's sweetness shone like a beacon. Ginny just knew they'd be good friends, and maybe there'd be more hugs along the way.

"I have this style in three colors, too." Elspeth produced more bras, pink, beige, and white. "None that will show under your blouse." Heidi held out her hands to take the pretty garments. "Now you, Ginny."

Ginny had almost forgotten that she'd been sitting there topless, but now she felt self conscious and didn't want to lift her arms.

"Come on, Gin, you don't have anything that we haven't seen in the mirror," Elspeth chided good-naturedly.

"Or on each other already," added Jordyn.

"Okayyyy!" Ginny lifted her boobs before Elspeth could even ask.

"Now down." Elspeth shifted her tape measure once Ginny'd let her perkies rest at their natural place. "You have lovely tits, girlfriend. Bet your boyfriend thinks they're about perfect."

"Not so perfect that he didn't go sucking somebody else's!" Suddenly, all the sorrow Ginny'd refused to feel came welling up into tears. "He...he...my best friend... OH!" She hid her face in her hands.

"Oh honey!" Heidi came to envelope Ginny in her strong arms.

"He's a rat and doesn't deserve to touch this much yumminess." Jordyn got in on the cuddle.

"What a jerk." Elspeth didn't try to retrieve the tape measure, but patted and hugged the bits of Ginny she could touch. She offered tissues when the worst was done. Heidi and Jordyn let go so Ginny could take some.

"Sorry," Ginny hiccupped. "I thought I was over that." She blew her nose and hoped her eyes weren't too red.

"It sneaks up on you sometimes. We'll keep you busy enough you'll forget him fast." Elspeth gave her another tissue.

"Yeah, and he'll never get to do this—" Jordyn suddenly slipped her hands under Ginny's mounds and twiddled the nipples with her thumbs. "—again."

"You're silly!" Ginny hopped backward from surprise, although it felt really good, and if they hadn't been in a room full of people, Ginny would have let Jordyn do that for quite a while. "No, he won't. *Pthbbb* on him."

Everyone joined her in a hearty *Pthbbb*! and Ginny felt better. Girlfriends made everything better. Ginny lifted her arms for Elspeth to measure, her heart much lighter.

Elspeth had to adjust the tape measure a couple of times to get the right spot. Each time it rasped over one of Ginny's nipples. "Sorry, this shape breast you have to adjust for." Elspeth moved the tape again. "Your fullness changes position when you put a bra on, and it will change again later. Thirty-six Double-D is a challenging size."

Ginny meant to ask why, but the question got lost in the sheer gauzy silver bra that Elspeth handed her. "Oh, pretty!" She dove into it. Elspeth certainly favored front loaders. "It makes my skin look shimmery."

"Oh, I like it!" Heidi and Jordyn agreed.

It also made her nipples shimmer, and that was a lot of light when they were this hard and erect—Jordyn was only teasing and hadn't tried to tickle them into standing up, except—they did. That fabric

21

rubbed in an arousing way, and didn't hide her little artesians at all! Elspeth handed her more bras, gold and white.

"Don't we all look great?" Ginny pulled Heidi and Jordyn up so they could all crowd into the mirror and admire themselves. "Good bye, polyester uniform that smells of ketchup, hello, lace!"

"I wore scrubs that smelled of old people at the end of the day," Heidi said. "This is better."

"I won't miss having to wear nylons." Jordyn shuddered, and Ginny and Heidi shuddered too.

Elspeth laughed. "You do look lovely, but we have a few more layers to fit."

"Shame to cover this up." Ginny smoothed a hand over one sparkly titty.

"Not really a problem." Elspeth handed each of them a white peasant shirt, with little puffy sleeves and an elastic neckline. "And skirts." She offered red checks. "The color says you're trainees, and the guests understand that you may not be able to provide all services yet. You'll be switching to blue soon enough, I think."

Ginny wanted to learn her job really, really well. She'd be so good at this! She slipped into the blouse and wrapped the skirt around her hips, fighting to settle the suspenders around her boobs. Over the peak wasn't working—the straps wanted to slip to one side. To the sides really made her boobies stick out. "Hi, world!" they seemed to say. "We're Ginny's tits, and oh, this is Ginny." She tried again to find a place they would rest properly.

"Like this." Elspeth settled the suspenders. "They do make your breasts show. They're supposed to."

"Dairy theme, I guess." Ginny wasn't sure she liked how prominent her natural attributes were. Guys talked to them instead of her enough as it was.

"Exactly," Elspeth agreed, and helped Jordyn settle her straps.

Heidi made a sad face into the mirror. "This isn't a good look for me."

"No, it's not. The waistline isn't in the right place," Elspeth decreed, and offered a different skirt.

"Much better." Heidi modeled for the other two. "It's so hard to find clothes that fit right."

"If we don't have uniforms that fit right, we'll have them made," Elspeth promised. "We want our staff to look spiffy at all times."

Elspeth didn't look so spiffy right now. Her peasant blouse now stretched even more tightly across her breasts, and wet spots grew large, letting the fabric bulge out over her nipples. "I really have to do something about this, girls." She pulled a blue machine out from under the bed. It had hoses attached to a piston, and things that looked like air horns on bottles at the end of the hoses.

"What's that?" Ginny asked.

Elspeth settled on the bed, leaning against the pillows. "My little blue friend here is a breast pump. Haven't you ever seen one?" She pulled down the elastic of her shirt to expose her breasts. "You can watch. You should watch."

Ginny had never seen breasts swollen so large. Elspeth was a medium sized woman, but her breasts rivaled Heidi's, and the skin stretched tightly enough to shine. Her nipples were huge, like raspberries, and nearly as deeply colored. Ginny had never seen anything so made to suck on. Any man who got Elspeth's clothes off probably took hours to get near her pussy.

"No," Jordyn said.

"Never. " Ginny was fascinated. A machine to suck your tits?

"Yes, my friend used one. Hers was green," Heidi said.

The three trainees in red watched avidly while Elspeth settled the horns over her breasts, making rosy-brown circles against the plastic. Her nipples poked into the center holes. "Hit the switch for me, please," she asked.

Ginny flipped the toggle, making the blue machine hum. The piston rode in and out on its geared arm. *Bzzz shhhh, bzzz shhhh bzzz shhh* came from the mechanism, and *spsss spsss spsss* hissed out from the horns Elspeth first clutched to her chest, and then let go once she was satisfied with the suction.

Ginny watched, fascinated, as little squirts of milk shot out from Elspeth's nipples, which enlarged and then shrank with the suction. They looked more like caramels now, enlarging to fill the little pipe from the horn to the T junction that met the bottle, and then shrinking when the pump eased off. White spray became drops, and drops became drips, sliding down to collect in the bottles hanging from her breasts. Ginny longed to taste the white fluid.

"You just happened to have a breast pump in the right room?" Jordyn asked, her eyes riveted on the show Elspeth put on. She had to be demonstrating this for a reason, and she was definitely in teaching mode.

"Of course. I make sure there's one in every room, and the bottles are always ready. You never know when you're going to need them." Elspeth supported the bottles from beneath. Milk collected at quite the rate when your tits were that swollen! She had to have two ounces in each bottle already. Ginny supposed that anyone who lactated like that had to be prepared. The neckline on her shirt was very handy.

"How often do you have to do that?" Jordyn asked.

Maybe her baby was off visiting the grandparents.

"At least four times a day this week," Elspeth sighed. "It will be easier next week." She adjusted the bottles.

Ah, the grandparents would bring little Boo-boo darling back.

"Does that hurt?" Heidi reached out to touch Elspeth, but yanked her hand back and blushed.

"No, it doesn't. It feels rather nice, actually. Not as nice as when someone does it for you." Her eyes twinkled.

"Even your baby?" Ginny slapped her hand over her mouth. Oh no! she'd said that out loud!

"Hee, you've just discovered the dirty little secret of motherhood," Elspeth giggled. "A mouth is a mouth, and you know how nice it feels when your honey-bunny sucks on your titties." All four women giggled, like they'd been caught sharing dirty pictures. "Doesn't that just get your engine all revved?"

"Oh, yeah," Jordyn breathed. "I love that."

"Me too," said Heidi.

"Hell, yes," Ginny agreed. Old dumbass never did it long enough. Long enough for Ginny meant she could come from just that sucking. Maybe she could borrow the machine. If there was one in every room...

"Err, how much milk do you think you'll get?" Jordyn eyed the bottles, which held close to six ounces now. The right one had a little more than the left.

"Is there another set of bottles down there?"

Ginny bent to check. "Um, no." More than nine ounces per breast? No wonder she was leaking!

"Well, then, eighteen ounces this time. I prefer to drain totally with each milking." Elspeth poked her breast. Maybe she could tell how much was left that way. The flesh gave under her finger, moving slightly. If she'd tried that before she'd started pumping, she'd have exploded!

"Is it a problem if you don't?" Ginny got back up to sit on the edge of the bed with the other women.

"Only that I might make a little less next time, and that would be a shame. I need all I can make." Elspeth looked sadly down at the bottles. She must have a very hungry baby. Ginny envisioned a little chubster, with rolls on his thighs and arms just begging to be pinched by his adoring mama.

The pump hissed again with a different sound. Elspeth waved at the pump, which Heidi turned off. Careful not to spill, Elspeth slipped a finger between her skin and the horn to break the suction with a little *pop!* She set the bottles down carefully, and reached for a tissue at the bedside. She dabbed her nipples, but a little milk leaked anyway, making the nubbly tip glisten. "Darn. Still going." She dabbed again.

"Um..." Ginny had to ask before she lost her nerve. "Have you ever tasted...?"

That grin couldn't get much wider. "Of course. And my quality control officer does too."

Oh dear. Ginny bet that was handsome Dirk, whose lips looked made to wrap around a woman's tit.

The women looked at each other. One more question hovered in the air, and no one was brave enough to speak. Elspeth did it for them.

"Would you like to try?"

Everybody giggled, looking at their toes or the floor, and darting glances at Elspeth's breasts. She was so open and natural lying there, her arms opened wide to bring them in.

"It's okay, my darlings, really it is."

"Well, if you really need to be drained." Ginny whispered, but she didn't come closer to those soft, warm breasts with little pearls of white growing on the tips.

"I really do. You'd be doing me a favor." Elspeth offered one breast in her hand. "You can go two at a time, just leave some for the third." The pearls grew large enough to make a drip that left a little damp trail as it slid off her nipple,

Two at a time would make this less embarrassing. Ginny caught Heidi's eye, and they scooted forward.

"Tell me how it tastes," Jordyn mumbled.

"'Kay." Ginny leaned down, not certain how to go about this.

"Let me help you latch on, Ginny, dear." Elspeth squeezed her breast, flattening the nipple. "Get a good mouthful of me, not just the nipple. You need to get most of the areola in too, so you can squeeze the milk ducts. Sucking just the tip will hurt me."

Ginny didn't want to hurt this lovely woman who was offering her such an intimate gesture. She'd be careful. Slowly she wrapped her lips around, taking in this luscious bit of breast.

"Now press rhythmically, that will squeeze the ducts." Elspeth took her hand away and stroked Ginny's hair. "You too, Heidi."

Ginny could feel Heidi bend down next to her. How funny it was to be nursing at a grown woman's breast. Ginny tried squeezing and was rewarded with a little gush of milk.

She was so startled she nearly let go, but no, mustn't waste a drop! Warm, and sweet, and richer than she expected, it was like drinking cream, but better. Nothing could be fresher than this.

"You're getting the hind milk now, girls. Where the butter fat is, and a lot of the vitamins. Is it good?" Elspeth stroked Ginny's head some more. Ginny nursed out another mouthful, and another.

Answering meant letting go, no way. Ginny mff'd *yes*, and squeezed again. Oh, luscious. She tried tickling the nipple with her tongue to coax out another few drops. Elspeth laughed quietly. "I think you're both getting the knack. But leave some for Jordyn."

"Um, that's okay." Jordyn sounded hesitant.

Ginny lifted her head reluctantly. If Jordyn watched her and Heidi, she should have to do it too.

"Come on, Jordy-girl. It's nice! Better than nice." Ginny got off the bed. She took Jordyn's arm, urging her up to Elspeth's breast. "You're never going to get a better opportunity."

"Nooo, I suppose not." Jordyn allowed herself to be coaxed up to the head of the bed. "You're sure it's okay?"

Elspeth nodded and beckoned. "Very okay. I want you to do it. Look, Heidi's not stopping."

Jordyn lowered herself slowly to the nipple Elspeth held out for her, and within seconds she was nursing greedily. And she'd hesitated! Ginny wanted to laugh, but she just caught Elspeth's eyes in a moment of shared intimacy, and they watched the two women suckling at Elspeth's softening breasts.

"Darn. All gone." Heidi sat up and wiped a hand across her mouth. "I had no idea. Um..." She blushed.

"It's fine, darling girl. I offered." Elspeth pulled her down and kissed the side of her head. "I wanted you to do that."

Jordyn reluctantly sat up. "I think you're dry."

Dabbing her breasts with the tissue before she folded the cups of her lacy beige nursing bra over her boobies to hide them away again,

Elspeth agreed. "Thank you, dears. I hope you enjoyed that. I did. Were you afraid you wouldn't, Jordyn?"

Jordyn squinched her eyes shut. "Um, I was afraid I'd enjoy it too much."

Elspeth pulled the edge over her peasant shirt over her breasts. Handy, that. Ginny was suddenly aware she wore the same style. The white cotton no longer stretched too tightly over Elspeth's bustline, although the wet spots had dried to off white splotches.

"There's no such thing as enjoying this too much." Elspeth hugged Jordyn.

"Yes, there is," Jordyn whispered. "Now I'm horny."

"Isn't that convenient?" Elspeth squished her again, and winked at Ginny and Heidi. "Training is over until after dinner. Take your uniforms back to your rooms, and you have the rest of the time until dinner to cope with such things. Check your bathroom drawers. Oh!" Elspeth jumped up to dig in the dresser. "We like you to be in uniform top to bottom. We have matching panties for you." She shooed the women and their armloads of clothing out of the second floor bedroom. "See you at seven for dinner."

Chapter 4 New Games with New Pals

On the way back to the dormitory barn, Jordyn muttered. "That was milk. Why am I so wet?"

"Those were boobs, and very nice boobs too. We were sucking on them." Ginny elbowed her friend. "I'm wet too. Heidi?"

"Yeah." Heidi didn't sound embarrassed. "I kind of expected it."

"You did?" Ginny hadn't.

"Sure. We get wet when we get sucked on, the guys get horny when they suck us, so why not?" She opened the door to let Ginny and Jordyn in first. "My room's right next to yours. Good! But my bathroom goes to an empty room now."

"I bet someone will be in there when everyone gets back."

Ginny hung her new things up or stowed them neatly in the pretty white dresser. Elspeth had said to check her bathroom drawer. She went in, to find Jordyn staring at a brand new vibrator.

"Don't you think this is taking 'make the new hires at home' just a little too far?" Jordyn stared at the toy, which was pretty big. 'There's two. Do you want blue or pink?"

"Um, I like them slightly smaller and veiny." Ginny did think that was going pretty far for hospitality.

"There's that kind too." Jordyn pointed down into the drawer.

"Goodness!" The whole drawer was full of toys. And a couple bottles of lube. "What on earth…?"

"Just at the moment, I am not questioning providence." Jordyn grabbed one bottle of lube and dashed out, shutting the door behind her.

Ginny selected a toy, one that looked just right, very lifelike with lots of veins and a circumcised tip. She hesitated on the lube. The way she felt, that probably wouldn't be necessary. But you never know. She walked slowly back to the bedroom, still a little shocked at how well her new employer was providing for her needs.

Before Ginny shut the door to the common room, Heidi appeared, a peach colored vibrator in her hand. "Did you get one of these?"

"I think mine was a different color." Ginny tried to be suave. It was hard. Someone might come by. "Get in here." She pulled Heidi in and closed the door. "Jordyn found one to her liking."

"Oh she did?" Heidi giggled. "Our bosses take room and board to new heights." Dressed in her red checked skirt and cute peasant blouse, Heidi looked like innocence about to be debauched, the way she held that vibrator, all ready for business. She hit the switch, making the tapered cylinder buzz. She poked it at Ginny.

Not certain whether to laugh or collapse from shame, Ginny fended her off. With the toy.

"Sword fight!" Heidi brandished her weapon. "I will win!"

"Not if I activate my super buzzing power!" Ginny twisted the end until the thing whirred in her hand, and then she waggled it at Heidi. They clacked their toys together this way and that, with one advancing, the other retreating, now going the other way, until Ginny landed a touch on Heidi's tit. "I win!"

"No, I think I win." Heidi rubbed her toy in the same place. "That feels good."

Ginny tried it. "Yeah, it does." She kept rubbing, feeling the buzz and wondering if it had felt anything like that for Elspeth.

"Uh, I guess I should leave you be..." Heidi kept rubbing.

"You don't have to," Ginny breathed. "Um, I've never watched another woman use one of these things, and I always think I'm doing it wrong."

Heidi appeared to consider this. She switched sides. "If it feels good, there is no wrong." Her face, with its lovely dark eyes and long lashes, said she wasn't doing it wrong.

"Okay." Ginny tried stroking her little buzzer across a nipple and shuddered from the touch. A thousand volts of wow zipped through her—she tried again, and again. Dang, why hadn't she ever used her toys up top? Maybe she had been doing it wrong? No, she hadn't, Ginny decided, buzzing her other side and watching the peach colored wand on Heidi's hand make a trail over her mountains. She was just finding a new kind of right.

Heidi's eyes slipped closed, and Ginny's threatened to, too, but she wanted to watch what Heidi did—that was almost as exciting as the whirr of the toy on her tight little nubs, poking out hard against the sheer silver fabric of her new bra. *Bzzz, bzzz,* and shiver, and again, while Heidi did the same. Fascinated by what Heidi was doing, Ginny mirrored her, trading sides when Heidi did, and damn if that didn't make her knees shaky. *Bzz* again, and *zing,* straight to her clit. Ginny quivered, and Heidi sagged a little.

"Better sit down before we fall down," Ginny whispered, and guided Heidi backward until she plopped on the edge of the bed. "Get comfy." She arranged a pillow behind Heidi's back and let her relax, her vibrator still tickling one huge breast, then the other. Heidi swung one leg up on the bed, her knee pointing to the side, making a triangle with her foot against her other thigh. Her red checked skirt stretched over her thighs.

Ginny sat at the foot of the bed, buzzing one nipple until it felt so tight it might pop. She looked at Heidi's skirt now, and tried not to think about how juicy Heidi must be under there. If she was anything like Ginny, she'd be damp enough to soak her panties, maybe leave a little honey-spot against her skirt. Instead of lifting the cotton skirt to see, Ginny made her free hand go to her own breast. The neckline of that shirt was a blessing now—Ginny pulled it down to let one sweet titty out. She pinched the nipple, rolling it in her fingers, irritated by the way the bra got in the way. She pulled the other side down and unhitched the front fastener, letting her firm boobies out to play in the fresh air. Heidi moaned

31

her approval—she'd been watching though those half-closed eyelids, hadn't she, the sly girl!

And she must have thought it was a good idea because Heidi
pulled down her own white top, showing her sugar-cookie titties to
Ginny, who marveled at how far her nipples stuck out, and how Heidi
shivered when she brushed her vibrator across them. Ginny knew just
how good it felt, because she was doing it too.

Heidi unsnapped her bra, and her creamy white mounds spilled
out, glorious hills of flesh on her chest. Working the vibrator across
one side alone, she began to pinch the other side, catching the flesh
far outside her ruddy areola and pulling toward her nipple. Over and
over, she pulled at her titty, and Ginny knew how good that felt too,
because she did the same. Fresh zings and zips traveled through her
breasts, and buzzed her clit, which was stiff and perky, and wet with
the juices that threatened to gush right past her panties. With one hand
to milk herself and the other to buzz, Ginny wished for a third hand
to play with her pussy, because a couple of good strokes would make
her come.

No, she didn't need that third hand, did she? Not with beautiful
Heidi giving her a show, and her sensitive titties getting so much loving that they just might have their own climax, But still, just one more
little thing to happen, just one more... Maybe she should push her
vibrator in, but, her nipple didn't want to share....

"Are you getting close?" Heidi breathed, and oh yes, Ginny was.

Ginny tugged again at her breast, imagining a frothy white jet
of milk flying from the tip, just the way Elspeth had gushed, and she
nearly came right there. Oh, if she could only shoot milk out now,
she'd splash Heidi with milk, and Heidi would splash her back with
the white streams that would surely flow from those bounteous breasts
when she came.

She squeezed again, the imaginary rivulets of milk dampen-
ing them both, and her orgasm hit, making her pussy clench and
twitch, the shocks rebounding up and through her nipples, waves of

pleasure coursing through her. Moaning with the elemental pulsing, Ginny clutched her breast, and nearly fell over. Heidi cried out her own climax, but Ginny couldn't see what she'd done to get there, and really didn't care. Heidi might be soaked in milk or honey, but Ginny's breasts leaked only bliss.

"Oh. That was good," Ginny mumbled and topped sideways across the foot of the bed. She lay flat with her feet hanging off, her knees splayed. Her pussy clenched again when the air touched the wetness on her pants, cooling it. Ginny shuddered, watching her tits shake like mountains in an earthquake.

"Ooh yeah," Heidi agreed. "Were you imagining sucking on Elspeth?"

"More shooting milk at you," Ginny admitted, and they both giggled.

A third giggle made them look, and there in the bathroom doorway stood Jordyn, bright red and with her hand to her mouth. "Um, didn't mean to interrupt, but…"

"You aren't interrupting, silly!" Heidi held out one arm, and Jordyn sat down next to her. "You should have been here."

"I was, kind of," Jordyn mumbled. "I didn't mean to watch, but I finished really fast and came to get you…" She let Heidi pull her into a hug, and Ginny sat up, trying to figure out how to get in on the cuddling.

"See anything you liked?" Ginny asked, and snuggled up on Jordyn's other side.

"Boy did I." Jordyn blushed again, snuggling one arm under Heidi's back and the other around Ginny's shoulders. "I don't know if I should ask you to cover up or if I can touch."

Oh yeah, both Ginny and Heidi's breasts still hung over their white peasant shirts. Ginny twisted her shoulders to press one titty against Jordyn's chest. "Touch, definitely." She reached to pluck at Jordyn's neckline. "And show us yours."

"Oh!" Jordyn squeaked, but didn't say anything else when Ginny and Heidi pulled her top down below her tatas, all round and enticing beneath the white lace. She'd made herself a prisoner by hugging them, so Ginny and Heidi worked together to unsnap Jordyn's bra and peel the fabric to the sides. If Jordyn's nipples hadn't been hard from watching, they were getting hard from the teasing little flicks Ginny gave them. Heidi cupped her hand under one of Jordyn's breasts and began to rub her thumb around the big pink circle, sliding over the nipple on the downstroke.

"Oh that feels good," Jordyn moaned. "I just came and they're so sensitive."

Sensitive? Good! Ginny cradled Jordyn's other breast and did as Heidi was doing, enjoying the little crinkles forming beneath her thumb. "Did you play with them when you did yourself?" Ginny asked.

"No, I just did it the usual way," Jordyn admitted.

"You missed out on the best part," Heidi told her. "We didn't even touch our cunnies." She peered around Jordyn at Ginny. "I think. I didn't."

"Neither did I." Ginny grinned. "Look, no hands."

"We had hands all right," Heidi corrected her. "Just not there." She pulled on Jordyn's nipple. "Here works just fine."

Hell yes, it worked just fine for Jordyn too. She sighed little noises out with each milking stroke Heidi and Ginny gave her and didn't seem to care that it took them a while to get synchronized. "I think I need a little more to come again," she warned them. "That's still on."

"That" was Heidi's vibrator, buzzing alone and neglected, but Heidi stopped her nipple play long enough to park the whirring shaft against Jordyn's pussy, reaching up under her little red and white skirt to place it. "Good?" she asked, and Jordyn nodded, so Heidi went back to her nipple.

Her skin was so soft, and all the bumpy milk glands inside hid from the world, but Ginny found them, running her fingers over the little lumps that could make creamy white foam. When her fingers reached the nipple, Ginny imagined more streams of milk shooting away into the air to fall down on Jordyn's lap. Ginny'd lick up the spots if they fell on Jordyn's legs or stomach.

Jordyn went still, groaning—Ginny paused mid-tug, but didn't let up on the pressure. If Jordyn were lactating she'd have soaked them all, Ginny was sure—her little whimpers went on a long time before she collapsed, letting her thighs fall open. The tent pole the vibrator made disappeared. Heidi grabbed the vibrator and silenced it.

"Oh, wow." Jordyn panted. "Just wow."

"Absolutely wow," Ginny agreed, holding Jordyn's breast tenderly now. Maybe Ginny would get to be in the middle of the next "milking session."

"Do you think if we did this often enough, we'd make milk too?" Jordyn wondered.

"Probably," Ginny agreed. "It might be right in theme with being dairy maids."

"I think we're supposed to," Heidi told them. "There's a breast pump under my bed."

Chapter 5 Learning their Duties

A TRIO OF subdued young women made their way back to the big house. Peeks under Jordyn and Ginny's mattresses revealed little blue machines that rotored and whirred—no one had been quite brave enough to place the collecting horns against her nipples while the others were watching, though they'd giggled nervously while the pistons pushed in and out. Six thirty came and went before anyone recovered enough to speak.

"Moo?" Ginny mumbled halfway up the hill.

"Moo," Heidi agreed. "We really should have seen this coming. All that talk about 'preparing a special delicacy' and 'cooking skills don't matter'."

"And allowing for the possibility of not working out," Jordyn considered. "Maybe not everyone can get stimulated into producing."

"I didn't think you could start lactating unless you had a baby," Ginny pondered. "And I'm not about to let Dirk or anyone else get me pregnant."

Jordyn elbowed her, giggling. "Hell no, although you were willing enough to let him help you practice getting pregnant."

"That was before we translated half his weasel words!" Ginny wouldn't let Dirk unzip anywhere near her now—what else hadn't he explained properly? "Do you think he has any more little surprises lurking?"

"I bet there's at least one." Heidi pulled the door open. "But we probably shouldn't find it out by screaming at him. Or at Elspeth. She was pretty upfront about everything."

"Not everything. Just her part." Ginny didn't feel very trusting right now.

They slid into chairs around the big dining table, lining up together on one side for the strength that came with numbers. Elspeth came in with a platter of fragrant chicken, crisp and golden, and a dish of mashed potatoes.

"Oh there you are. Right on time. Would one of you bring the salad and the green beans in?" She set the dishes down and began to pour ice tea. Ginny rose to bring in the rest of the meal. Everything smelled good; the only stinky part about this operation was Dirk and his little surprises.

The object of her wrath had seated himself at the head of the table by the time she juggled the big bowl of greens, two bottles of salad dressing, and the beans back to the table. The others had passed the dishes around but waited until Ginny had served herself before picking up their forks, and Dirk surprised them by saying a small grace with his head bowed. Ginny dipped her head, joining in the "Amen." She was grateful for what she was receiving, she supposed; she just wanted fried chicken with a side of explanations.

Heidi led off, a drumstick in her hand. "So the milk we're supposed to produce goes to the paying customers?"

"Yes, indeed," Dirk replied, spooning in mashed potatoes as if he hadn't just jumped over several steps of clarification. "Some of them have restricted diets because of medical conditions, some of them just have a fetish, but all of them are paying handsomely for the privilege of supping on Manley Dairy's finest, so we don't drink it ourselves except in small quantities for quality control purposes." He locked gazes with Elspeth, who just smiled serenely. "We certainly don't have it for dinner."

"You weren't very clear that the delicacies we're supposed to provide for the guests came out of our breasts!" Jordyn blushed furiously around a forkful of tomato.

"There are limits to polite conversation in a restaurant," Dirk objected. "It's very clear in your contracts. 'Lactation' or 'lactate' appears no less than four times in the first two paragraphs alone."

Ginny had scribbled her name on the bottom line without reading more than the header and the dates, and the others had been just as quick. "What other goodies appear in there that public conversation doesn't cover? Are we supposed to let them nurse directly from us?"

"Is that a problem?" Dirk peered over the chicken breast he was about to bite into. "That's a bonus situation. You can pump all the time and turn in the milk at our central dairy building if you'd prefer. Our guests are more than average polite; they do understand that it's a privilege, and if they misbehave, their stays grow extremely short. We don't permit our staff to be disrespected."

"Besides," Elspeth mused, "it's quite lovely to sit under a shade tree with your guest lying across your lap, nursing away. Both sides. Somehow the second side is even nicer than the first. Make sure you swap off which side is first." Her face grew dreamy. "I do love my job."

"What else is part of the job?" Ginny wanted to be utterly clear on this. "All the vibrators and lube make it look like we're supposed to provide sex!"

"Heavens, no!" Dirk looked scandalized. "This is a dairy, not a brothel." He set his chicken down hard, making his fork clatter against the plate. "We're also highly experienced with the sexual aspects to lactating, and we want our staff to be happy. We know full well that stimulating your breasts nearly constantly creates other needs. What you do by yourselves is our concern because your job creates the urges."

"So sex and orgasms and such aren't part of the job?" Heidi asked.

"Of course, they're part of the job—haven't we just said?" Elspeth corrected her. "If you mean 'Is this part of what we share with the guests?' that's up to you. Some of our dairy maids do. Some don't. It's strictly your choice. Some of our dairy maids have very close relationships with the clients, but that is outside the scope of Manley Dairy. We don't presume to tell adults who they can and can't sleep with. We are aware of exactly how intimate nursing is, and how it can lead to more contact."

"Is that a bonus situation?" Bonuses suddenly didn't seem like such a good idea to Ginny.

Elspeth snapped, "No! I am not a madam, Dirk is not a pimp, and you should wash your mouths out with soap before you suggest we are." She shook her finger at the three trainees. "You didn't read your contracts at all, did you? Shame, shame. I'll explain in small words what you agreed to.

"First, you agreed to accept stimulation to induce lactation. I'll be open here—some of that will be sexual. It's all geared to making milk. We don't care if you get off on it. If you do, that will help you along, plus being very pleasant, and if you don't, your loss.

"Second, you agreed to participate in research regarding lactation. We have every reason to want to know more about forcing lactation, and this is the perfect laboratory. We expect your cooperation in every regard." Elspeth took a swig of tea, glaring over the rim of the glass. "Yes, this will involve medical examinations and procedures."

Medical…! Ginny tried not to gulp. She was going to read every single word of that contract. Oh, why had she been so quick to sign? She poked a valley into her mashed potatoes, leaving tine marks.

"A few are optional, but if you're tempted to decline, realize that isn't in your best interests." Dirk paused with green beans hovering before his mouth. "We want to run a profitable, happy dairy, and we've learned a few ways to do that. We do want you to prosper along with us and have a good time along the way."

Elspeth added, "Most of our dairy maids stay with us for years, and usually don't leave unless their milk fails, or they find compelling personal reasons not to renew their contracts."

"What about the ones who can't lactate after all?" Jordyn asked.

"That's no fault of theirs," Elspeth said, her voice much less stern. Almost sad. Had someone she liked had to leave because she couldn't give milk? "If they've tried their best, and their bodies still won't co-operate, we give them a severance bonus and wish them well."

"We talked about that at the restaurant," Dirk pointed out. "But we expect good faith efforts."

Ginny stared at her plate. She hadn't imagined this. Learning to churn butter or something, yes, and she wasn't afraid of hard work, even if she was kind of afraid of cows, but she hadn't expected to provide the milk. And she'd gone and promised, even if she hadn't realized what she was promising. Her fault, all of it—why had she signed something she hadn't read? She knew better than that. And she'd made a binding promise.

"We don't expect you to do everything all at once, ladies." Elspeth's voice was soft. "It is a bit overwhelming at first, we know. We'll train you, and please think, has anything that's happened since you've been here been unpleasant? Aside from this rather tense conversation."

"No," Ginny had to admit, and Heidi and Jordyn echoed her. "Not job duties as I always understood them, but not unpleasant." She'd torn off a quick climax in the bathroom at the office once, but she'd been desperately horny and terrified of getting caught. Now it was part of the job.

"But you've never had a job as a dairy maid before, have you?" Dirk smiled with a hint of his twinkle from the day before. "Outside of certain limits, you have a lot of freedom to choose your tasks."

Heidi and Jordyn exchanged quick glances with each other and with Ginny. They relaxed—Jordyn sipped at her tea and Heidi picked up her fork. "As long as we aren't fucking for pay," said Jordyn.

"Our focus is milk, ladies." Elspeth's voice was scolding again. "No need to be crude."

Okay, that Ginny could live with. She had a month to find out of she'd even get to stay. With her mouth full of chicken, it struck her—

she'd thought "get to stay," not "have to stay!" This wasn't going to be such a bad thing after all.

B<small>ACK IN HER ROOM</small>, Ginny took out her contract and read it through. She should have done this before she'd whipped out a pen, but she hadn't, and now she read, discovering that everything Elspeth said at dinner was true. She hadn't mentioned anything about all milk became property of the dairy, but that was to be expected— what was she going to do with it, after all? Nor could she leave the dairy for a month.

The bonus scale was part of her contract, too. Ginny did some quick math—Elspeth had to be giving more than half a gallon per day, and getting—oh my! No wonder she was so testy about the new trainees refusing opportunities.

Heidi came in, her pump in her hand. "Think we should get started on the stimulation part?" She didn't come past the doorway. "I feel a little weird about this and don't want to be alone."

Ginny uncoiled from the bed, smoothing her skirt and understanding the utility of her blouse much better. She crossed the room to hug Heidi, feeling the ampleness of her breasts through the thin fabric. "Me too. Get comfy. I'll go get Jordyn."

But Jordyn had already gotten started. "You guys can come on in here." She folded her legs to make more room on the bed. Her pump hissed beside her. Ginny watched for a few cycles, seeing how Jordyn's nipples expanded inside the clear plastic. What did that feel like? In a minute she'd know. It was hard to tear her eyes away, but she had to get Heidi in here before she got too settled.

No problem—Heidi'd only gotten her shirt pulled down and her bra unsnapped. Not putting a hand out to caress those huge titties made Ginny groan and fall to her knees to fish the pump out from under the bed. "Jordyn says to come on in to her room."

If she wanted to touch Heidi's breasts so badly, how did their clients feel? Knowing that they could touch, knowing that they were at Manley Dairy so they *could* touch? And taste? And suck? And even get milk? Sweet warm milk, gushing into their mouths, just for the asking? Ginny wanted a mouthful—hell, she wanted to give the mouthfuls. Her little blue buddy was the way to get that—she yanked it out, tubing and all, and followed Heidi.

No staring, she admonished herself, and concentrated on getting her blouse down and her bra opened. Sitting cross-legged on the bed like her friends, she was only too aware of how her labia spread under her panties, and how nicely a skirt could flip up. *Behave yourself, Ginny!* Pulling her white blouse under her breasts let her fingers trail over her skin, the sheer fabric of her bra a barrier that would have to go right now. Unsnapping the front fastener let her breasts swing freely. She hadn't spent so much time with her breasts in plain sight since she'd tried on swimsuits.

"Just aim your nipples straight into the opening," Jordyn advised. Her nipples showed pink beneath the tubing, disappearing when the pump let go, and growing again. "It feels pretty good."

"Funny at first." Heidi hunched over. "Or I did something wrong." She took the collectors away from her breasts and began pulling at her nipples. "If they're already hard they'll be easier to aim."

Good idea. For lots of reasons. Ginny tweaked her nipples, though they hardly needed it, just from watching Heidi. Maybe they'd do this for each other tomorrow. Friends have to help friends, right?

Heidi's sweet little nubs were turning into sweet big nubs, and she gazed down at her hands, a satisfied smile on her face. Sure, she had to be pleased with the way her nipples were stiffening, and Ginny agreed. Aim, hah. It felt good, just like hers did, with each little tug not quite to the pain point, just pleasure, a zip of a rush with each stroke.

Like raspberries, Heidi's nipples jutted from her luscious melon sized tits, their color growing deeper as they hardened. Ginny's, too—and her clit was expanding to match. She shifted her butt against the bed, trying to get a little friction from her panties.

Jordyn noticed Ginny's wiggling. "Oh, just put the collectors on and then you'll have a hand to stick down your pants."

Busted again. "You don't have a hand down your pants."

"Don't need to." Jordyn was so smug. "I'm sitting on my vibrator."

Why hadn't Ginny thought of that? The device's buzz was lost in the humming from the pump. Well, she hadn't wanted to walk into Jordyn's bedroom with a toy in her hand, but considering what happened earlier, wasn't that a bit of false modesty? "I'll be right back. Heidi, should I bring one for you?"

"Sure." Heidi's nipples were stiff enough for her satisfaction, and she guided one hard bud into the collector. It nearly filled the clear tube now—what would it look like when the suction made it grow? And she had two—Ginny watched Heidi slide her other nipple into place. "Flip the switch before you go, okay?"

Mesmerized, Ginny groped to the pump. It wheezed and churned, and nothing happened to Heidi's breasts.

"You turned the wrong one on, silly." Jordyn giggled. "Go on, Heidi and her boobies will still be here when you get back."

Geez! If her tits got as hot as her face, her milk would be scalded before she ever squirted it out. If she could squirt it out. Ginny paid attention to which pump she activated, and nearly ran for the bathroom, thumping heavily against the door. She groped a new toy out of the drawer for Heidi and snagged the one she'd used earlier.

"Are we ever going to get used to all this communal sexy stuff?" Ginny wouldn't look at Heidi when she handed over the toy.

"Well, aside from getting past the heavy blushing and walking into walls and stuff, I kind of hope we don't." Heidi activated the toy and slipped it under her skirt. "It might stop being fun."

"That might take a while." Jordyn reached under her own skirt and did something. The collectors stayed tight to her skin, held with the pump's suction.

Oh, oh, oh, was she making sure the vibrator touched her clit? Or was she moving it away for being too much right now? Damn, was it

44

inside? Ginny wanted to lift Jordyn's skirt to see, but as the resident walker into walls, she ought to just calm down before she did something else stupid.

"Come on, girlfriend." Heidi tweaked Ginny's nipple—how had she forgotten that her own titties were swinging in the breeze? "Don't just stand there. Give us something to watch."

With her nipples already hard and crinkled, Ginny didn't have to spend much time pulling on them, but she did, just because they were watching. And liking what they saw, too—Jordyn's eyelids went heavy, and Heidi's breath got faster. With a couple of fingertip tickles, and then a couple more because they felt so damned good, like electricity and chocolate all in one, Ginny placed the collector on one breast. The plastic was cold against her areola, but that would warm up in a second, and then she placed the second collector with one hand.

"Turn me on?" she asked.

"Too late, we're already turned on," Jordyn mumbled, but she flipped the switch.

Oh, man, Ginny could get used to this. Not at all the same as a mouth: the pump pulled at her nipples, sucking them far into the tubes. She watched them grow and shrink with each *whum* from the pump. Nothing squirted away from the tips, not yet, it was too soon, but Ginny could imagine her breasts heavy with milk and the pump pulling white droplets into a stream to fill up the bottles, just like Elspeth's. Oh, and her friends would be yielding their own creamy liquid, soon, soon, and if she asked nicely, she might be allowed to lick the last few drops from their nipples when pumping was done. Heidi could have one side of hers, and Jordyn the other, and then the third friend would have to let the others have turns....

But for now, her pink nipples grew brown against the tubing and her hands didn't have anywhere else to be since they didn't need to hold the collectors up—suction kept them pressed to her titties. Except those roving hands could go somewhere else; they could go to her pussy, which was getting moister by the minute.

Dairy Maid

Was she ready to slide her hands into her clothing with Heidi and Jordyn watching? Their eyes were on her, and her pussy was asking for some attention. Maybe in a minute—with her nipples getting suctioned huge and allowed to retreat back to her breasts, she wanted more and more to do something.

Um, start with the toy. Her vibrator lay quietly at her side, not doing her a bit of good from there. Turning it on, Ginny reminded herself that Jordyn and Heidi were already getting buzzed, and Heidi had parked hers in a sweet spot right before their eyes. It droned suggestively, making her hand tingle, when it could be doing other places more good.

Here goes nothing. Ginny tried not to lift her skirt much, but she had to go in over her thigh. In—that sounded good, but if she guided the vibrator with its bulbous head under her panties, it would take some maneuvering and her friends would see it and know. Um, okay, just slide it under, let the vibrating shaft stimulate her pussy—ah— right—there—good—good—oh yeah. Right on her clit, skimming the gauzy fabric of her new panties. Wasn't as if they didn't already know what she was doing, right? The more the vibrator hummed against her hungry cunny, the more the pump pulled at her titties, the less Ginny cared what Heidi and Jordyn knew. They were doing it too, and Jordyn was reaching under her skirt now, moving her toy around.

If she wanted to watch, she'd have to show hers, Ginny decided. Maybe soon. Maybe she should have shucked her panties in the bathroom. Maybe Jordyn and Heidi were clever enough to have done that already, and they were getting the full benefit from their vibrators. Maybe Jordyn had her toy shoved in deep, letting it pulse against her G spot, letting it *zzz* against the walls of her channel. Oh, how was Ginny every going to know unless she asked, or unless she raised the hem of Jordyn's skirt to look? But—she squirmed against her own toy, desperate to put her clitty right up to the fun. Dumb underwear. Damned modesty. And now Heidi had her hand under there, adjusting. Maybe getting ready to cum. Look at the way her nipples swelled.

And Jordyn's. Oh man, look at hers, expanding to twice their proper size, and feeling so damned good, getting pulled at every few seconds.

Stop being an idiot and just enjoy it, honestly. On the job training never felt so good. Hell with it—Ginny reached under her skirt again, finding the end of her vibrator. She moved it slowly against her crotch, feeling the stiff nub of clit purring with every stroke. Sometimes a little fabric in between kept it from being too much—she wouldn't try to get the panties out of the way when if felt this good. The pump pulled at her nipples rhythmically—it would milk her over and over until she told it to stop. Good little pump, no two pulls and "Roll over" here.

"Ah, I think I'm gonna—" Jordyn arched her back, thrusting those lovely tits up, their collectors and tubing still pulling at her nipples. She grabbed her vibrator right through her skirt—at that angle it had to be doing a clit buzz, not in. She worked it frantically for a few seconds, then held very still. Little puffs of air came out her nostrils, and her face went slack.

Before Jordyn could go limp, Heidi mumbled, "Me too!" She pulled the collectors closer to her chest, squirming against her toy, her lush boobs jiggling with the movement. "Oh!"

Oh, indeed. Ginny flicked back and forth between her friends, watching them come, and knowing her turn would be soon. Heidi looked so beautiful, concentrating on her body like that, and Jordyn, her tits thrust skywards with the pump tugging away at her. Ginny couldn't stop looking and the explosion growing in her pussy would happen any minute. It was growing, expanding—Ginny helped it along, shamelessly pushing against the round buzzing shaft at her cunt. Her panties, all wet now, rasped against the texture of her toy, and her clit, huge and utterly sensitive needed only—that—little—bit—more—

The pulsations broke through her, squeezing her channel with quick little flutters, waves emanating from her clit, and somehow going straight to her nipples, or had they started in her nipples and gone downwards? The pump didn't care that she wanted to freeze and let the orgasm wash over her—it tugged and released, tugged and re-leased, and with every fresh pull another wave coursed through her. Three, four, no, five surges of pleasure took her—Ginny cried out and squeezed her breasts, somehow getting another burst to sizzle her nerves.

"Uhnn," she whimpered, utterly spent at the end and surprised to still be upright. She pulled the vibrator away from her crotch, not ready for more stimulation to her clit. "Was it good for you guys too?" That orgasm had to have reached everyone, or maybe they just shared one big one. Heidi blinked glassily, and Jordyn was still breathing hard.

"Wow." Heidi extracted her toy from beneath her skirt. "Who knew that could feel so good?" Her nipples still pulsed within the col-lectors.

"Yeah—why doesn't anyone sell these things as sex aids?" Jor-dyn tried removing her collectors, but they were stuck tight with suc-tion. She flipped the switch on her pump, stilling it.

"Oh don't do that, girls," came from the doorway. Elspeth smiled at their puzzlement. "The time spent pumping after an orgasm is very valuable for starting your milk production. Keep going."

Jordyn flicked the switch back to on. "How long have you been watching?"

"Long enough to see that you were doing exactly what I was coming to tell you to do." Elspeth pulled the slipper chair up to the side of the bed. "Looks like you're all one step ahead of me."

"We figured this was part of what we were supposed to do," Jor-dyn said. "It made sense." She tried covering up her breasts with her hands, although the tubes of the collectors escaped her fingers, letting her pink nipples poke through with each swoosh of the pump.

Ginny felt the need to cover up from Elspeth, too—her trust hadn't quite come back, and getting watched while coming sure hadn't been part of her plan. Well, yeah, it had, but by her friends, not by someone who'd already scolded her for not paying attention.

Someone who'd let her sip from her bounty. Someone whose nipple had been in her mouth. Hiding from Elspeth now was a little silly, and she'd said no more at dinner than was the truth. Ginny should have read her contract instead of assuming, but really, this wasn't so bad. The pump pulled at her nipples, and the little zings made her mellow.

"Exactly, ladies. Stay on the pumps for at least an hour at a time, and be sure to rub some ointment on your nipples after. Chapping isn't a problem unless they're wet, but a little soreness at first is fairly common." She pulled tubes from her apron pockets and handed them around. "Do this at least six hours a day until your milk comes in, and of course, every time you climax, that speeds up your production. Even after your milk comes in, it's good." She smiled widely. "Perhaps you don't want to know right now that the clients are generally happy to assist, but they are. Your terms, always, and if you prefer the pump and a toy, or your hand, that's always fine."

"Because it's all about the milk?" Heidi asked, with only a trace of irony.

"It's always about the milk here." Elspeth eyed them a little more sternly. "We have clients who have milk shipped all over the world when they can't be here, because it's the only thing, or one of the few things they can tolerate. We keep some of them alive, ladies. It's always about the milk, and if there's a bit of joy in it for you, be grateful." She rose to her feet. "Carry on. Breakfast is at seven thirty, and we'll resume training afterwards. Good evening, ladies." Elspeth paused in the doorway to toss some last information over her shoulder. "Oh, and I've already scheduled your first medical exams."

Chapter 6 Ginny's First Medical Exam

Medical exams weighed heavily on Ginny's mind—she chewed her omelet slowly. She always hated being poked and prodded, but she'd agreed to be a research subject. What if she wasn't suitable after all? Would this be the last day she'd wear a red gingham trainee uniform?

"Ginny, dear," Elspeth broke into her thoughts. "You'll see Dr. Busby first. Heidi, Jordyn, you can pump while Ginny's with the doctor. And don't worry, girls, nothing will hurt."

Heavens! Did Elspeth think she was a big baby? Ginny cleared her plate and followed Elspeth to an outbuilding.

"This is our clinic. Dr. Busby is a medical doctor with a special interest in lactation. We're lucky to have him." Elspeth swung the door open. "We also patch up minor injuries here."

Hoping not to shed any blood from, say, cow hooves, Ginny entered the small reception room. Two doors led into the waiting area, and when one opened before they even sat down, Ginny's heart nearly stopped. Getting examined was bad enough, but getting examined by a young, handsome doctor would make her blush all the way to her knees. Maybe he wouldn't take her pulse, because it was too fast to count.

"Dr. Busby, this is Ginny Harper. Ginny, when you're done, go ahead and send one of your friends down. See you." Elspeth left, and now Ginny was alone with a walking vision, all brunet and blue eyes looking down on her from his lordly six foot one.

"Come in, Ginny." How courtly, he held the door for her. "I'm going to take a full medical history before I ask you to dis-robe, and please don't worry—I haven't lost a patient of embar-rassment yet."

Damn, he'd noticed.

"Have a seat please." Dr. Busby offered her a chair and began to ask innocuous questions: diabetes, no, heart disease, no.... Ginny relaxed—she was a healthy girl.

"Any medications?"

"None."

"What kind of exercise do you do?" he wanted to know.

Ginny considered. "I'd rather swim than run, because of, well, bouncing issues."

"Understandable." He smiled at her. "On a scale of one to ten, one being 'I can't feel a thing' and ten being, 'I'm going to come when you touch those', how sensitive would you say your breasts are?"

Whoa! What a question! It had to be part of his research. Dr. Busby waited patiently for her to answer. "Um, about a nine, I think." A ten wouldn't have needed the vibrator last night, right? "Maybe a nine and a half?"

He made a tick mark on his file. "Interesting. And a good sign, too, by the way. You wear what size bra?"

He could have eyeballed her and made a guess, but he was being a gentleman, so she answered. "A 36 DD."

"And very nicely proportioned, too." He made another tick mark.

That didn't sound very professional, but... Ginny waited for the next question.

"Please strip down to your panties. I'd give you a gown if you insist, but for what we need to do next, it will only be in the way."

Oh why had she put on another pair of the sheer panties? She might as well be nude for all they covered. He must have noticed her hesitation. "I see all the dairy maids here, Ginny. It's all right."

Peeling down, she mumbled, "You must love your work."

"I do, dear lady, I do." He gestured toward a scale. "With luck, so will you."

At least the scale didn't hold any terrors for her—Ginny was aware how nicely curvy she was, and always judged by the fit of her clothes.

"Your weight will increase a bit as your milk comes in, though if you lactate as abundantly as your breasts are capable of, it will only be for part of the day. And if you don't eat well, lactating will suck the flesh right off you until you either look skeletal or can't sustain the milk, or both, so you have doctor's orders to eat heartily." He measured her height as well. Ginny stood tall, aware that it made her tits stick out. "Hold that posture, please. We'll measure your nipples now."

With a wavy-armed caliper, he took the diameter of her areolas, pressing the points delicately to her skin. "Lovely and symmetrical," he noted, taking vertical measurements as well. "Hold still, please." But that was so hard to do when he measured the length of her nipples—so tickly!—and the width. Once he stopped pinching her nipple with his calipers, he made her turn red again. "Please get them hard; I need to measure that too."

Oh did he now? Well, Ginny would give him something to measure! With thumb and forefinger she rolled her nipples, knowing they'd stiffen right up. Now she wished she wasn't a nine, or maybe nine and a half for sensitivity, because with his eyes on her and her own touch, she was getting much too worked up for a doctor's office. She better stop before she demonstrated she could be a ten! But she wanted to give him a show, rolling each sensitive nub delicately and provocatively.

"Very nice," Dr. Busby said, and his eyes said he didn't just mean the half inch extra her nipples stuck out once she'd twiddled them. His little measuring tool had warmed up against her skin, but the point tickled the tip, and she shivered. Coming now would be so embarrassing, but if he kept swiping the caliper across her nipple anything was possible. "I'm measuring now because as you pump and your milk comes in, they may change. We won't know for sure unless we know your starting measurements." At last he turned away to write in his chart.

A moment's reprieve. Not knowing how she was going to make it through the rest of the exam without slipping out to take care of the little problem she'd given herself, Ginny concentrated on breathing, but Dr. Busby's next suggestion didn't help.

"We're going to measure the volume of your breasts now. A cup size tells me something but not everything." He brought out a clear plastic dome with a hose running out of it. He attached the hose to the sink. "Let's fit this over your right breast first."

Very funny, half a plastic bra that didn't fit. Ginny let the doctor insert her breast and check the seal against her chest. He fit the hose to the faucet and turned on the water, which began to fill the dome and float her breast within. "Too cold? Too hot?"

"No, it's fine." Actually, it felt kind of nice. When the dome was as full as it could be, Dr. Busby turned off the water and detached the hose, letting the water run into a graduated cylinder. Ginny let him float her other breast in the dome, and again measure what fit in.

He handed her a towel and did some math. "Hmm." Was "Hmm" good or bad? She waited anxiously. "You're very symmetrical. Lovely. Your right breast is 720cc and your left breast is 716cc, allowing for some experimental error."

Ginny already knew her tits were big. "And as my milk comes in?"

"They may get substantially larger. Many women do. Or you might only expand a little. My data is still far from complete, so we'll be repeating some tests until your milk supply is established." He smiled at her, or was it at her tits? Yup, at her tits, but at least he had a reason. "Please hop up on the table."

Oh dang. That thing had stirrups. Maybe all exam tables came with them and doctors just never took them off. Ginny hoped her feet wouldn't end up in them, but Dr. Busby seemed like the thorough sort, listening to her lungs and heart, pressing for enlarged glands in her neck. "Lie back please." He extended the platform for her feet. "I'm going to check your breasts now. You've had this done before, I'm sure."

Yes she had, but not by a blue-eyed hunk who obviously appreciated the unimpeded view. He sure had a boner going on, but you'd never know it from his demeanor, just pressing into her breast with his fingertips, moving around the circle of her nipple. He must have touched every square inch of her twice. If he measured her nipples now, what would he get? His hands were sure and practiced, and when he finished pressing his ever widening circles, he clasped her breast in one hand and gave a milking squeeze to her nipple with the other. Twice. Oh—three times! And on the other side, too! He had such large warm hands, and he knew she was a nine for sensitivity—what was he doing? Her clit stiffened and her pussy grew damp. Trying to breathe shallowly, she almost missed his question.

"Have you done any pumping?"

"About two hours last night," she admitted. She wasn't going to admit what else she and her friends had done, but—that was his next question.

"Did you have any orgasms while you pumped?" He stroked her nipple once again while he waited for her to quit stammering.

"Twice," Ginny cut her total one short.

"Very good." Dr Busby smiled down on her. "One session isn't enough to throw off your baseline measurements, so I'm still getting good data, and I've never seen anyone start lactating with only one session—I didn't get anything just now. Keep track, please, because we think there's a connection between coming and milk. All fine here," he reassured her, and undid the reassurance by extending the stirrups. "Scoot down and let's slip those panties off now." He hooked his fingers into the elastic, tugging when she lifted her hips.

"What kind of birth control do you use?"

"I'm on the pill," Ginny admitted.

"Not anymore," was his reply. "That will keep your milk from coming in at all. Was your last dose this morning?"

"Yes." She hunted for the stirrup with her feet; he guided her heels into the depression. "I can't be without birth control though."

"Certainly not," he agreed, hooking a wheeled stool out from under the counter. "Have you considered an IUD? Foolproof, no hormones to interfere. Never have to fiddle with it."

"Oh I wish, but I can't afford it." Ginny longed for no-brainer birth control.

"It can be your first perk at Manley Dairy then." He snapped on some latex gloves and brought out the instruments of torture, er, the speculum, and a long pointed rod she didn't recognize, and a few things she didn't see. "But first, we'll take your temperature."

He could have done that while she was sitting up. Ginny opened her mouth, since he wasn't waving electronic things at her ear or forehead.

With warm gloved fingers, Dr. Busby parted her buttocks and slid the thermometer into her anus. Ginny yipped and slammed her knees together. "What the...?"

Dr. Busby pushed one knee away from the other. "Your temperature needs to be accurate, not the calculated and derived reading from an electronic or oral device."

"Nobody's taken my temperature there since I was a baby." Ginny reluctantly let him part her knees. Her hole was hers—nobody got to touch her there, and he just went and stuck a thermometer in! The small rod felt—well, not bad, but—she didn't want anything in her ass! How dare he!

"I need your core temperature; therefore the thermometer goes into your core." Dr. Busby kept one hand on her ass, probably to keep the thermometer in place, poking from between his fingers. His hand was warm, and the little rod that had invaded her hole didn't hurt, but did he really need this reading? Ginny clenched her sphincter. Maybe if she tightened up and let go really fast she could sort of spit it out?

But no. He held the glass instrument inside her for the full time, no matter how she clenched and relaxed. He withdrew the thermometer slowly and read it. "Ninety-eight point six." He placed the thermometer into a glass of disinfectant. "Was that really so bad?"

"It's just… You didn't say." Ginny would have tried to talk him out of it, and no, it wasn't so bad; it might be kind of nice if they were playing doctor, but when it was for real, she thought a warning was in order.

"I see." He ripped off the ends of a couple packets. "Then I should warn you we need some vaginal swabs. Speculum now."

Fair enough. Ginny tried to relax.

Oh why did a man that handsome and desirable have to be looking up the tunnel of love with no romantic intentions? Ginny stared at the ceiling, feeling, or trying not to feel, what he was doing in there. But when he parted her labia with his fingers and slipped the bills of the speculum inside, she had to shudder. Dear man had even warmed them up, which didn't make her feel much better about the metal sliding up within her, the small intrusion growing larger when he opened the bills wide. All her secrets were spread to him now. All the juiciness that she'd wakened with her fingers on her nipples and that he'd increased with the presence of his reaction to her was laid bare, but he said not a word of it.

No, he was poking around inside with giant q-tips, one after the other. Ginny fought not to close her knees against him. Even when he drew a swab against her clit, circling the sensitive flesh and ending with a swipe directly across its now-stiff and embarrassing head, she stayed spread, but barely. Damn, why did this have to be professional? Anyone who gave her such pre-orgasmic chills really ought to be buying her a drink and kissing her. Instead he had her vagina opened up to the universe, and she had to lie still for it.

"I'm going to put the IUD in, but first I need to do a pelvic exam so I know which way you tilt." He closed the speculum and withdrew it slowly.

Appreciating that her pussy was no longer spread wide to his gaze, Ginny still had to wiggle at the feel of the retreating instrument—now she wanted it back, only she really wanted something rounder, and a bit softer, and longer. A cock. She might as well admit it—she wanted a cock right now, and Dr. Busby had one, probably a very nice one, and it was hiding inside his pants and not likely to come out unless she said something totally inappropriate.

She'd get fingers for now—exploring fingers that would only be looking for medical things. Squishing lube over his gloved hand, Dr. Busby made her imagine that he'd ask more questions, like "Do you enjoy your orgasms? Would you like one now? One finger or two? Or maybe three? How about my cock?"

Damn it, Ginny! Can't you behave yourself for half a minute? She wanted to close her thighs, just so she could get control of her thoughts, but no, he was returning to her side with slippery fingers and one hand to press on her belly.

"Going in now," he told her, two fingers probing into her folds.

Oh, Dr. Busby was thorough, investigating this way and that. His hand lay flat against her stomach, and when he pressed up from inside, he'd found her G spot. Surely coming from a pelvic exam would be the most embarrassing thing ever. Ginny tried not to look up into his smiling blue eyes—that would make her beg for way more than a doctor should give a patient.

He scissored his fingers within her, stretching her internally and getting a small sob. "You do know where your G spot is, don't you?" he asked.

"Yes, and so do you," Ginny breathed. Gripping the edges of the exam table really hard might not be enough to keep her from humiliating herself.

"Right here." He pressed again, his two fingertips sliding against her good place. "It's part of your clitoris, you know. The clitoris is much bigger than this one visible section." He demonstrated what he meant with a swipe from his thumb over her swollen nub, and then he did it again. And again, his fingers working against her inner walls.

Too much—humiliation be damned—Ginny rode out the orgasm with little whimpers, lifting her hips against his hand. Pulsing against his fingers, the pleasure spreading through her clit and pussy, she couldn't care about anything except how good it felt to be coming.

A few minutes later, she opened one eye. Dr. Busby hadn't taken his hands away yet—he still had two fingers inside her. Two very wet fingers, no doubt, and a handful of rain, too.

"All done?" he asked, and stroked her G spot again.

No---one more wave shot through her. Ginny moaned, feeling the walls of her channel contract around Dr. Busby's fingers.

"Now, I think," Ginny mumbled. Would he please not say anything about the mess she'd just made?

He slipped his fingers out very slowly, but didn't try touching her clit again. "Nice muscular flutter," he commented, stripping off his wet glove. Ginny could see the streaks of juices on it. "An orgasm pulls your cervix and vagina into better alignment for the IUD insertion. This should be quick and easy."

Like that was the only reason he did it, huh? Ginny'd seen too many excited men to think he was only interested in practicing good medicine. Well, even if this was shaping up to be the only fun OB-GYN appointment she'd ever had, she wasn't going to invite him to act unprofessional. He loved his job, all right.

Of course, she was kind of liking the way he did his job too.

Until he sat down on the stool again and picked up the speculum. Still wasn't a good substitute for what she really wanted, but this time the metal bills felt much nicer sliding inside her cunny, with Dr. Busby's fingers to open her labia for the instrument to enter. With a click, it opened up within her, spreading her pink passage wide, really wide. Much wider than she thought she needed to be spread, but he picked up a long thin forceps and the pointed rod.

"This is a sound," he explained. "So I know how deep to insert the IUD." He guided the metal within her. "I'm going to pass this through your cervix."

Through that little bitty passage? No wonder it had a blunt point. Ginny cringed.

"Relax, Ginny. Almost in." His soothing voice from between her thighs helped a little, but still. She tried to breathe deeply and not notice how the sound pushed in but how could she not, when something spread that had had never widened before. A tiny bump inside told her when he stopped pushing. "Out now," and he pulled the thin metal through her cervix, which had never been penetrated 'til now.

"Now we'll insert this," he murmured, and guided a white plastic tube into her spread pussy, bumping again to require entry to her womb. "Yes, that's going in nicely, and now the plunger…" He withdrew something thin, but she felt nothing, and then he pulled again, letting her feel the tube leave her cervix. "Since you've come, you probably won't cramp, Ginny. See? Done." He reached in again and snipped. "You'll be able to feel the string to check that it's still there each month. You don't have any problem with touching yourself inside, do you?"

A little late to be asking now, wasn't it? Ginny nodded, and then corrected herself. "No problem." Like he would think she'd boggle at putting her own finger in? Maybe other girls were more squeamish, but this was Ginny's pussy, and she'd touch it any way she liked. And she liked, but maybe this was the sort of thing he wanted to be asked to help with. A little foreplay? *Down, girl!*

Dr. Busby closed the speculum and withdrew it. He patted her exposed crotch with a soft towel, lingering a moment on her clit, but not rubbing. "You're protected now, so throw away those pills and let your body respond to the stimulation. You'll be making milk quite soon, I think, but I have one more test to do." He helped Ginny sit up.

It was a relief to close her legs for a moment, and she hoped he didn't notice her squeeze her thighs together. One more little zing, that was all she could get, but she'd be in private soon. "What kind of test?"

Dr. Busby rested his hand on her shoulder, as if he feared she'd topple over. His hand was nice and warm. A very talented hand, but just comforting now. "This test is a valuable contribution to my lactation studies. I'm trying to correlate time to lactation, degree of stimulation, and ability to climax from nipple stimulation."

All that sounded like another medically-sanctioned orgasm in her immediate future. "What do you want me to do?"

Dr. Busby patted her shoulder and stepped to the sink to put some water into a paper cup. He handed the cup to Ginny who sipped gratefully.

"Try stimulating your nipples to orgasm, with a vaginal probe inserted."

Whoops! Ginny spilled half her water down her front.

"Sorry, that was terrible timing on my part." Dr. Busby brought a handful of paper towels to swab her breasts. She felt very, very dry after he finished, though she hadn't felt all that wet across most of her chest.

"The probe will register your orgasm more finely than I can manage with a stopwatch." Dr. Busby took her now empty cup. "You have your choice of probe size. I have a small, medium, or large."

"Did you plan to watch?" Just having him watch might slow down her orgasm—or speed it up.

Now he flushed. "Yes. I take notes on technique. We do need to know what works the best, both for sexual stimulation and for future milk production. My research is in the early stages, so I can't always tell what I don't need to observe. Maybe in a few years…" He pulled back one corner of his mouth, a grimacing little apology.

"Okay, but I need to pee first." A little, but Ginny really wanted a couple of minutes to compose herself.

Dr. Busby waved her to a door in the corner of the exam room. "I'll get everything set up."

At last, a door between her and the handsome doctor. Sitting on the pot, Ginny let flow, enjoying the rush of liquid through a swollen passage, and flinching a little with the burn. "You're getting quite the workout today, aren't you, puss?" she addressed her crotch. Wiping and washing, she gave her still swollen clit a little squeeze. "You know what to do." Yes she did, and one more tickle to her engorged button would make sure it got done.

She came back out to dimmer lights, an assortment of cylinders in the promised sizes, a machine with dials and an oscilloscope, and Dr. Busby apologizing. "I know the ambience isn't great," he said. "I've been told by some of the other dairy maids that the couch in the waiting room might be more comfortable, but it's too exposed. I could lock the clinic door if you'd like the couch."

"I can cope in the name of science." She smiled at him, taking stock of the probes. The large one might be considered unfair help, particularly if it buzzed. It sure looked like a dildo. Then again, it was her choice, and if Dr. Busby offered it, he considered it good science. She pinched the probes, soft silicone that would feel pretty good inside. "Let's use this one." She held out the large probe, which was about the same size as the toy she'd chosen last night, but smooth and pale yellow, cylindrical rather than life-like. More suitable for science, Ginny decided.

Connecting the probe to a cord, Dr. Busby waited for her to get back on the table. "Do you think you can do this with your legs open? It will help my observations."

"I can try," Ginny decided. "But I might have to change part way through."

"That's fine," he assured her. "Keep your legs open as long as you can, and don't touch anything but your breasts until you just can't stand it any more." He positioned her legs, feet together, knees far apart, making her labia part by themselves. The air on her dampness gave her a chill. "It is a required test, but I appreciate your willingness to do this."

"For science," Ginny said, but it was for her milk, too. If this would give her a better chance at lactating profusely, she'd take it.

Pumping after orgasm was supposed to be good, Elspeth had said, so playing with her nipples had to be good too, and another orgasm shouldn't be scorned either, although she'd prefer if Dr. Busby shucked out of that white coat and pants and just gave her a hand, or a cock. Or maybe he should just put her in the stirrups again and roll that little stool up so he could lick for science. For that she'd position her feet herself, but no, it was a little blob of lube that he spread across the opening to her body, smoothing across her perky inner lips and delving inside to make sure he could slip the probe in. He didn't neglect her clit, though, but he'd probably make a note in his chart about how it was poking out from the folds before she'd even started stimulating her breasts.

The probe was larger than she thought though, or she was more swollen than she expected, because he introduced the tip and didn't slide it in farther. Instead, he swirled it around, almost playfully, at the entrance, and then pushed another inch in. Was she resisting? No, she didn't think so, but he pulled it out and tried again, going a tad deeper this time. This would be a lot more fun if they were doing it for the sexxors, not the science. Out again, and in, and Ginny liked the technique, feeling her passage expand to take the probe. At this rate she wouldn't have to play with her nipples to climax.

At last he had the probe seated to his satisfaction. "Good girl. You can take the big one. Go ahead and start touching your breasts."

Ginny didn't have to be told twice. The probe filled her so, and her pussy clasped around the cylinder tightly. Too bad it wasn't moving, but the in and out would be unfair to the test. Her fingers knew their work well enough. Ginny pinched her nipples, making them poke up from their pink areolas, letting her fingers travel along the exquisitely sensitive nubbins until they sailed off the tips, tickling gently before starting again.

How about both hands for one titty? She wrapped up one creamy mound in her hands, letting her nipple peek out between them, rhythmically squeezing from the outside in to the center, where milk would spurt in little fountains soon. Oh, yes, if it felt this good to get milked, she wouldn't mind at all having the dairy's guests help her. Her hands weren't big enough to cover her breast; one hand alone had no chance at all. Even if it was a hand as big as Dr. Busby's, and Ginny wavered a moment about asking him to do the other side. But no, this was science, and she was going to see how long she could do this for herself.

So good on one side that she had to do the other, getting a nice little pinch and zing when she applied the pressure. Too bad she couldn't get her nipple to her mouth—that would still be playing with herself, if it was her own tongue that lapped at her stiff peaks. Ginny'd danced her tongue against Elspeth's nipple, the memory of creamy droplets in her mouth making her want to squirt her own milk as soon as possible.

Why didn't she have four hands? She could squeeze both sides. She could still squeeze both sides—but she could still get two hard nipples, just with a different motion. Tickling a tip and pulling the other side made her pussy clench against the probe, which didn't vibrate but did push against her cervix and distend her channel. She might not have to touch her clit the way she was going. She squeezed the probe again—she had it, she could use it.

Changing to the light touch of fingertips and a gentle scratching with her nails across the sensitive tips felt so nice. A demanding mouth would feel good too, just the way her mouth made Elspeth feel good. Ginny could imagine being both mouth and nipple, tongue to swirl and tit to feel, especially the way she touched herself.

She clenched again, feeling the probe filling her pussy, and tugged at her nipples firmly. Wouldn't Dr. Busby give her just a tiny hand? No? He stood between her feet, watching her, taking notes. A fine sheen of sweat covered his forehead, but Ginny was more concerned about the fine sheen of juices covering her pink pussy lips, stretched around the probe.

So. Close. One more pull at her nipples. One more. One. More. The fireball that would be her climax stubbornly refused to come out. But Ginny wouldn't close her legs for a sweet thigh squeeze. Twirling frantically at her nipples, she moaned, begging the orgasm to happen, happen now, please....

But the orgasm wouldn't come just for her willing it, just for her breasts getting played with, just for pulling her nipples until they stretched pinkly above her chest. With a moan that was more nearly a sob, Ginny tore one hand away from her nipple to pinch her clit between two fingers and pull that swollen nub the way she pinched her nipples.

Two squeezes brought her to climax, the waves roaring through her pussy, which crushed the probe tightly, bringing more of the exquisite ripples. She cried out wordlessly, her head thrown back, feeling the reverberations from clitoris to nipples, milking the pleasure for all it was worth.

"Oh! Oh!" she cried. "Yes, oh...!" Clenching the probe increased the crashing through her pussy—she squeezed until the instrument within her should have been crushed to half its size and still the waves came. Ginny pressed on her clit again, trembling, and rode out the orgasm.

When she could breathe again, she let her hands fall limply to her sides. "That was awfully nice."

Dr. Busby agreed, "Lovely. But we're not done." He set aside his clipboard and gripped the probe. "Can you come again?"

The probe was a dildo after all, the way he worked it in and out of her pussy. Too surprised to argue, Ginny clutched the sides of the exam table, letting the doctor push the probe deep inside her and pull it out again, long squishing strokes that were going to help her to another orgasm.

"Do you feel it building?" Dr. Busby gasped. "Tell me!" He thrust the probe roughly back into her cunny, banging against her tender cervix. "Come again!"

"I—" she gasped. "I think—" But no, Ginny couldn't think, not with another climax that wanted to shake her tender parts. She'd come again, but Dr. Busby wasn't waiting for it.

He cupped her swollen mound with his long fingers, and slipped a thumb between her plump lips, finding her clit with a flick. "Come now!" He pressed down and fucked her hard with the probe.

"Agh!" she shrieked. His demands yanked the orgasm through her. The walls of her pussy clutched the probe again and her clit twitched with the rough pleasure he demanded of her. He jammed the probe deeply into her pussy and held it while she clenched and wailed, unable to do more than feel the exquisite shudders pulse through her.

"Very good." He withdrew the probe slowly, and didn't take his thumb from her clit until the rounded tip was free of her pussy. "You certainly are a nine and a half. For a moment I thought you'd be a ten. I've never encountered a true ten. Perhaps with practice...?"

"Some other day," Ginny panted. "I may not sit again for a week after that." She eyed the probe on its electrical cord. Was it even attached to a machine? Did it do anything besides fill her pussy?

Dr. Busby set the probe down and read dials on the instrument panel with evident satisfaction. "You probably suck it right out of a man if he's lucky enough to...." he mumbled. "Oh. Sorry." That was loud enough to be pitched for her ears. "I have one more treatment to administer before we're done for today."

"What's that?" If it involved touching her pussy again, she might cry. That many orgasms left her swollen and content, and she didn't want to disturb that feeling.

"We've learned that certain chemicals applied to the cervix will bring on your milk faster. Especially if the outer layer has been disturbed, as we've done with the probe and the IUD." Dr. Busby sounded like he'd had to memorize that speech—he didn't look like a man who could string that many words together on the fly, with the way he was breathing hard and the distinct bulge at his groin, even through the white coat.

"What chemicals?" Ginny didn't like the sound of that. "And apply how?" She was *done* with that speculum.

"Prostaglandins. And we'll just squirt them right in your cervix." He gazed hungrily at her pussy. Ginny became aware that she was still splayed wide, but she was too languid to close her legs. "Shouldn't take long. Not after that experiment."

"Using what? A syringe?" After too many orgasms to count, she wasn't about to let anyone, not even Dr. Busby, stick her inside with a needle. She snapped her knees together in a hurry at the thought.

"Nothing that horrid." Dr. Busby shed his white coat and reached to his belt. "I made the prostaglandins, and the applicator is my penis. I'll make it quite nice." He let his thick cock out.

Ginny stared at eight uncut inches, everything she'd wanted an hour ago. "No, you won't. That's just a cheap excuse to fuck me." She wrestled her feet out of the stirrups. Dr. Busby tried pushing her knees apart but she squirmed to sitting.

"No, it's not. It really does help bring milk on." He took a step back.

"No doubt, but it takes nine months to finish working." Ginny winced as her overworked cunt pressed against the table. "You don't fool me."

"I'm not trying to fool you." Dr. Busby held his hands up in surrender. "I want your milk to come in as badly as you do, and this helps. If it's me you object to, we can call Dirk in. He makes prostaglandins like any healthy male, but I'm here, and we've already done all the other tests and it would be a shame to call him away from his work."

"I'm sure he loves his job as much as you do!" Ginny snapped. She popped off the table, trying to look spry and hard to catch if he grabbed at her. She hobbled to the chair with her clothing.

"The only other man at the dairy today is old Horace, the cowman." Dr. Busby's cock had wilted to half mast. "Surely you don't want his prostaglandins."

Ginny tugged her panties across her swollen pussy. "I certainly don't want his, or any prostaglandins at all!"

"No prostaglandins is going to delay your milk, and damage my study's credibility!" Dr. Busby kept her from hauling her blouse over her head. "Please!"

"What it's going to do is make you have to whack off instead of coming inside me." Ginny yanked her shirt away and put it on. "Oh boo hoo." She snapped the skirt around her slender waist."I can be your control group, no prostaglandins."

"Please? How can I convince you?" Dr. Busby begged.

"What you should have done once the probe was out was lean over and kiss me and say, 'Ginny, I know this is horribly unprofessional of me, but you're so sexy, I can't help myself, and I really, really want you. I'm so hard for you.' I would have gone for it. Or tell me ahead of time." She jammed her feet into her navy blue flats. "If it really was for science. I went along with everything else, didn't I?"

"You did, and thank you, and yes, it is unprofessional of me but you are terribly sexy and I do want you but it really is for science."

Ginny left Dr. Busby babbling with his dick hanging out of his pants. Prostaglandins indeed!

She got back to her room scarcely less angry than she'd left the clinic, and yanked her pump out. Heidi and Jordyn lay sprawled all over Heidi's bed, their pumps suckling tirelessly at their breasts. Looked like they'd been enhancing the effects of the pumping, judging from the toys lying on the bedspread and Heidi's skirt hiked up high enough to show she wasn't wearing any underpants. That would give her a head start with Dr. Handsy.

"Who's next?" Ginny plugged her pump in and plopped on the bed. "And watch out, the doctor has a helluva bedside manner."

"Why? What happened?" They sat up abruptly.

"He has all these tests, and they got him so worked up he wanted to spray prostaglandins all over my cervix," Ginny snarked.

"What's wrong with that?" Jordyn asked.

"Spray them out of his dick into my vajayjay to 'make my milk come faster'." She added air quotes. "Said he'd 'make it nice'."

"Erm, really, what's wrong with that?" Jordyn asked. "Was he rude, or some old troll?"

"No, he's very handsome and he seemed nice, and if I'd met him some other way we'd be humping like bunnies," Ginny grumped. She had to aim her collectors twice before she got them seated over her traitor nipples. "But I don't like liars."

"He wasn't lying," Jordyn said. "Semen does have prostaglandins, and they do make your milk come. At least from the preliminary research."

"How do you know?" Ginny went cold. Was he telling the truth after all? She'd been so rude....

"Internet." Jordyn jerked her thumb at her open laptop on the desk. "We were looking for ways to—" She stopped, staring at Ginny, whose mouth had dropped open. "You turned him down, didn't you?"

"Yes." Ginny's cheeks burned. "I did."

"Girlfriend," Heidi said, getting up and smoothing her skirt. She found her panties on the floor, flashing her damp pussy and generous bottom as she put them on. "You are an idiot."

Chapter 7 Shaving Each Other

Dinner was a cheerful affair for everyone but Ginny. Heidi had come back from her appointment with a rosy glow to her cheeks and apparently a pussy full of prostaglandins, and Jordyn, too, had returned with a happy face. She and Heidi exchanged private smiles, like they knew something Ginny didn't know and would never know. They'd pumped all afternoon, but Ginny had retreated to her own room after lunch, and played with herself more because she had to than because it was fun. At least until the second session. Then she'd brought a second, thin toy in, and tried to recreate the feeling of getting her temperature taken. Her hand wasn't nearly as big as Dr. Busby's.

And now they all sat at the dinner table, listening to Elspeth and Dirk discussing previous vacation sessions' activities and clients.

"We have barbecues and dances; a few of our dairy maids are quite good musicians. And we'll have competitions in various fields, too." Elspeth put her fork down to use both hands to adjust one breast. "Sorry about that. I think I need to get my main pump serviced. We haven't had a Dairy Maid Olympics in a while, Dirk. We ought to schedule one for this month. The guests find them quite enticing."

Dirk chuckled over his forkful of coleslaw, which the girls wouldn't be permitted to eat after this week of training, and especially once their milk came in. Ginny had taken seconds. "Yes, let's. They also enjoy the gambling. Girls, when this event comes along, if you're lactating by then, find a backer who will bet on you for your strongest events. It builds good will."

"I'm not much of a runner," Heidi admitted. She glanced down to her abundant breasts.

"That's not what we're competing on. Distance squirts, volume per breast, that sort of thing. You might be quite good at them." Elspeth patted Heidi's shoulder.

Ginny stared at her plate. Had she messed up her chances at winning by refusing Dr. Busby's treatment this morning?

"For tonight, girls, we want you to do one more pumping session of at least an hour," Dirk told them. "Try to have another orgasm if you aren't completely worn out. I hear you're all doing quite well so far."

Ginny didn't quite sigh. She could be doing better.

"You each have another appointment with Dr. Busby in the morning," Elspeth informed them, and robbing Ginny's barbecue of all flavor. She shouldn't have yelled at Dr. Busby—he was only trying to help. "Heidi, you first, and then Ginny, your turn, and then Jordyn."

Heidi and Jordyn cast arch looks at each other. Ginny couldn't share in it.

"Do I need to be on call again?" Dirk looked hopeful. Jordyn hadn't said anything to Ginny about her source of prostaglandins, and she hadn't been blushy around Dirk at dinner. Neither had Heidi. "I didn't get called this morning, though. Buzz must be quite the man." He scanned around the table, hoping for good news.

"Um, maybe I could get a treatment this evening?" Ginny dared to ask. She might be able to catch up. Not to mention have a nice time with her handsome boss, who clearly would have sex with his employees if the reasons were right.

It was Dirk's turn to sigh. "I wish, but I'm by prescription only for pre-lactating dairy maids. Hold that thought for morning?"

Ginny excused herself and went back to her room, where she flopped across the bed, cursing herself for a fool. Maybe she could apologize and get back on track. Heidi and Jordyn couldn't be so far ahead she couldn't catch up, could they?

"Aw, don't mope." Heidi sat down next to Ginny and started rubbing her back. "It's not the end of your hopes. It's just one treatment, and you'll be giving milk soon, I'm sure."

Jordyn sat down on her other side and helped Heidi rub. "You pumped a lot, and came a lot, and you'll do more. It'll be okay."

Ginny mumbled into her crossed arms. "I was really rude and he was trying to help, and now you guys have had a treatment and I haven't."

"And a good time, too, even on the exam table." Jordyn giggled. "He knows how to use that cock."

Ginny slumped further, as if she could get flatter on the bed with her big breasts under her. Bad idea—she was tender from having her nipples tugged at for hours today. Maybe she was tender from her milk glands starting to wake up. Either way, she wasn't comfortable and rolling over sounded like a good idea.

Tits up, she had to look at Heidi and Jordyn, who looked abashed. "Sorry, I shouldn't be snickering." Jordyn ran her hand over Ginny's breast. "Maybe we could make it better for you? It's better to have natural stimulation if it's available, Dr. Busby said. And we're your pals."

It felt good, but Ginny was less than an hour away from her twelfth orgasm of the day. "Really? He didn't tell me that." Maybe he would have if she hadn't yelled at him.

"Oh yes," Heidi agreed. "We'd take care of you."

"Aw, you guys." Ginny thought she might cry. "Thanks. Can we just give me a minute to stop sniffling?"

"Sure, hon." Jordyn left her hand on Ginny's breast without moving. "You know what, if we have to see doctor again in the morning, I want to do a little, uh, personal grooming. I would have waxed if I'd known we'd be getting looked at."

Heidi jumped up straight. "Oh yeah. Me too. Um, what do we have? I'm kind of, well, natural right now, and my little leg razor isn't enough."

"They've been so good about meeting our needs; maybe they left something for this too?" Jordyn hopped up to rummage through the bathroom.

Ginny could hear her thumping through drawers and banging around under the sink. "Douches, geez, and—Oh! They think we need those?"

"Those what?" Heidi called, but Jordyn didn't answer.

"Found it!" She came back with a black zipper pouch. "This should do it." She dumped an electric trimmer and an assortment of guide combs out on the bed. "Wanna be a four? Or a one? Or down to bare skin?" She waggled her eyebrows.

"Um, I'll do a one. I don't want to itch growing back. What about you?" She looked at Jordyn.

"Bare, for sure. I like that best anyway; I just didn't have the money for a wax before we got here. Ginny? What about you?" Jordyn fitted the correct guide to the trimmer and plugged it in.

"Um, I like bare best," Ginny fibbed. She actually was terrified of waxing and didn't like the way the coarse hairs caught on her panties when they were short—that made her think about her cunt all the time. But here at the dairy, what else was she supposed to think about? She wanted to feel like one of the gang again after screwing up so spectacularly this morning, and if the price was her pubic hair, she'd pay with every last strand.

"Okay, let's get Heidi first. Peel down, girlfriend. Ginny and I will get you purty." Jordyn hit the switch, making three threatening buzzes. "You want to do the honors or shall I?"

"Um, you can." Ginny was a little concerned about getting up close and personal with Heidi's pussy. She wasn't at all sure she could keep her mind on business if she was trying really hard to get a good look at all the folds and how the little man in the boat poked from his hood. Accidentally pinching Heidi's tender pussy lips would set her back again, and what if she forgot herself and licked? Just thinking about it make Ginny want to stroke her tongue along Heidi's inner ruffles and nibble on her clit. And now Heidi was peeling off her panties and oh, my, everything else. She lay down next to Ginny.

"Come on, Lazy Bones, whatcha gonna do for me while Jordyn does the barbering?" Heidi held out her arms to Ginny.

"Erm, what would you like?" Ginny asked hesitantly. She slid into Heidi's warm embrace, trying to not put her arm right on top of those luscious melons. If Ginny wasn't mistaken, their areolas' color was deeper after a day of pulling and pumping, and her nipples were crinkled and stiff.

"I want three kisses. Two from Ginny, one from Jordyn, and I am so sick of that pump. I want you to suck on my nipples instead."

"Why only one from me?" Jordyn asked slyly.

"Because each of you is gonna kiss what you can reach." Heidi spread her legs wide, as if she was back on the exam table, and pulled Ginny down to her face.

Their lips met, sweetly nibbling, and Ginny sucked in a huge breath to be kissing Heidi anywhere. Her lips were so soft, and her tongue was so wet—Ginny hadn't dared dream about thrusting her own tongue into Heidi's mouth. Just getting hugged against those huge cushions on her chest was as much as Ginny had hoped for, and now was she not only getting the deepest, sexiest kisses, her hand was being moved onto Heidi's breast.

"Play with my nipples, Ginny," Heidi breathed, and went back to kissing her, pushing her tongue against the seam of Ginny's lips. Oh, yes, she'd open for Heidi, and let her invading tongue come in and make itself at home. Feeling daring, Ginny probed back, thrusting her tongue into Heidi's mouth and finding a welcome there, and a gasp when she pinched Heidi's nipple, so swollen and hard.

"Pretend you're milking me," Heidi breathed. "Pinch and stroke, like you're chasing all the milk out my nipples, yeah, do it just like that. Her other hand was busy with the breast Ginny didn't have hold of, and she moaned under Ginny's lips.

Dairy Maid

The buzzing was loud from between Heidi's thighs, and Jordyn moaned with them. The sound changed with each swipe of the humming machine across plump outer lips that were losing their covering of curls. Ginny peeked—Heidi hadn't been kidding about 'natural.' Her mound started out with a curly brunette bush that was falling away with each pass of the trimmer. Jordyn puffed the trimmings away, leaving a closely clipped velvet covering.

"Suckle me, Ginny." Heidi pushed Ginny's head down after a particularly lavish kiss, one that Ginny could feel all the way to her clit. "Suck my titty; you know you want to."

Hell yes, Ginny wanted to! And she didn't have to be told twice. She knelt over Heidi and placed her lips against that rosy nipple. She wanted to suck, but first she wanted to lick, little experimental tickles that quickly grew to trying to engulf every bit of Heidi's areola. "Not just the tip," Elspeth had told them, so Ginny took a big mouthful of Heidi's luscious breast, and began to suckle in earnest.

The little glands under the skin rolled beneath her lips, and she could feel the bumps around the nipple get hard. And the breast under her hand felt just as good—she cupped the other enormous titty best she could and began to pull at the nipple, starting way down and easing up. Trying to match her movements with mouth and tongue, Ginny could barely believe she was nursing on Heidi. No wonder men came from all over to visit the dairy! They wanted to do what she was doing, and drink the warm, rich milk that would surely begin to flow from these huge breasts.

Ginny checked what Jordyn was doing, without ever taking her mouth away from Heidi's breast. Watching them shamelessly, that's what she was doing, and Heidi's mound must be all tidy, because Jordyn turned the trimmer sideways and pressed it against Heidi's pussy. That would feel like a huge vibrator. Heidi moaned with the pleasure.

When Ginny peeked again, Jordyn was kneeling between Heidi's knees, still keeping the trimmer vibrating against Heidi's clit, and she was fingerfucking Heidi. Ginny strained to see—how many fingers?

In and out she pushed her hand. Looked like two fingers, and every now and then she stopped. The way Heidi moaned and bucked, Jordyn had to be hitting her G spot just right. Ginny switched breasts, leaning over Heidi's bare body to place her lips against her second fleshy target.

Oh, my, did Jordyn just add a third finger? Her hand was curled differently, and Heidi wasn't keeping her hips still at all; no, she was bucking and thrusting against Jordyn's hand and running her fingers through Ginny's hair, guiding her head.

"I'm gonna cum!" Heidi moaned. "Oh!" Her body shook with her climax, and Ginny wiggled her tongue against Heidi's nipple to amplify the waves that had to be roiling through her from her clit on out.

"Think you can do it again?" Jordyn did something with her thumb, shoving it under the vibrating trimmer. Heidi cried out—yes, she could. Ginny took long broad licks against Heidi's nipple, wanting to make this as extended a climax as she could.

"Oh, oh!" Heidi cried out, thrusting her breast harder into Ginny's mouth. Ginny sucked greedily on the stiff nipple, flicking madly with her tongue. Gripping Heidi's other huge breast, she milked the nipple hard. "OH!" Heidi nearly screamed, and Ginny could imagine her pussy fluttering and clenching around Jordyn's fingers, her sweet juices flowing and dripping down to her ass.

If her ass was wet, she'd be slick enough to slide a finger in... Ginny would do that for her but right now she had two glorious breasts to pleasure. But the thought went straight to her clit, as if suckling those bounteous breasts hadn't already made her hot and wet. Now she throbbed and couldn't keep her ass still—if Heidi was climaxing, Ginny wasn't too far behind, and if she could only get a little more action on her clit, she'd be there. But she couldn't do more than wave her ass in the air, trying to rasp her clit against her panties. Her turn would come—right now it was just a tease of a touch.

"Oh." Heidi collapsed against the mattress, spent. "You guys... Wow, Ginny. Heidi. Just, wow." She pulled Ginny up for another kiss, this one soft and lips only, with just a tiny flick of tongue. "That was so good." She shuddered, making her lovely, lush body jiggle, and bucked away the trimmer. Jordyn shut it off.

"Ooh, that was good." Heidi reached down to stroke her crotch. "My pussy feels so nice now."

That made both Ginny and Jordyn giggle. They'd been working very hard to make Heidi feel nice. They met each other's eyes, and Jordyn brandished the trimmer at Ginny.

"You know what I mean, you silly girls. And yes," Heidi gasped, "that was intense. Just wait 'til we shave one of you two. Well, both of you. I'm not going to be the only one."

Jordyn produced a hand towel and swabbed at Heidi's wet pussy, brushing the little hairs away. "You do look so pretty. And your clit's much easier to find now — it's showing."

Heidi reached down again, pushing one finger into her slit. "I suppose it is." She drew her finger away slowly, shivering.

Ginny had to look; she came to kneel next to Jordyn, who wasn't kidding. The deep pink nub poked out, right from the top of her cleft. The smell of Heidi's freshly come pussy wafted to Ginny's nostrils, sweetly musky and all woman. Longing to taste, Ginny wanted to reach out, but Heidi had to be very tender right now. But — Jordyn still needed to be shaved.

"Your turn." Ginny took the trimmer from Jordyn's unresisting hand.

Jordyn stood up long enough to peel away her clothing, which was getting seriously rumpled. She'd pulled her top down to let her tits out, but when the blouse hit the floor, followed by the bra, Ginny's mouth almost watered. Heidi was beautiful, and Jordyn was beautiful in a different way, with her round ass and nipped in waist, and of course those high, round mounds on her chest tipped with pink. Stiff, ready pink — Jordyn's nipples would poke right into Heidi's mouth.

"Lie down, Jordy-girl." Ginny smiled expectantly. She'd never had such a good excuse for looking at another woman's pussy, touching even, and making her come. Now she knew they were welcome to touch each other, she wasn't at all afraid to kneel between Jordyn's knees and explore.

Jordyn settled into the pillows, lifting her knees and parting her thighs. Her skin was creamy and soft: Ginny ran her hands down Jordyn's inner thighs, which pointed like arrows to the apex of her body. Her pussy lay open at the point, with a short and not yet curled covering of blond fur. Shaving that coating away was Ginny's next task, but she had to pet it first, feeling the half-inch-long hairs crisp against her palms. Soft and yet stiff under her hands, that hair invited Ginny to stroke Jordyn's mound from the base of her stomach down to nearly her rounded butt. The mystery of her hole hid between those scrumptious cheeks.

Her petting let Ginny feel the very edges of Jordyn's inner lips dragging against her palms, wet, but still catching at Ginny's skin. A few more passes and Ginny's hands would be slick with cunny juices, but Ginny would grow bold enough to spread those plump lips and explore with eager fingers before her hands grew much damper. Jordyn moaned, but from Ginny's tentative strokes or Heidi's more forceful kisses, Ginny couldn't tell. Maybe both—Heidi leaned tit to tit against Jordyn, cradling her in strong, round arms, and her face in kissing range.

There had to be a lot of tongue going on up there, but Ginny couldn't see and frankly didn't care, as long as Jordyn was too happy to say anything that sounded like "stop." Ginny didn't want to stop— she wanted to do more than caress the outer surfaces of Jordyn's mysteries. Using her thumbs, Ginny gently stretched Jordyn's slit wide enough to see what was inside.

The deep rose of Jordyn's pussy, with all its folds and hidden places, lay open to Ginny's eyes. Inner labia, firm with excitement, cuddled within her fleshy outer lips, also swelling with lust. Jordyn bounced when Ginny drew a fingertip from clit to hole along the ridge of labia, forcing Ginny's finger to the opening of Jordyn's hot box.

Should she press inwards? Should she wait? Ginny couldn't take her finger away from the hot channel that would surely clench around her digit as if it were a cock, a very short and thin cock. Surely that wouldn't be enough to please Jordyn, but no, Ginny knew that a finger used well would be delightful. She just had to use her fingers well. Fingers were not all she had, either, but she could feel the slickness, and stroked the wetness from Jordyn's opening all around her pussy.

A woman's secret places were fantastic, and she hadn't even dared venture within. Not yet—Ginny didn't want to snatch every new feeling without treasuring it. Jordyn was trusting her with her most intimate place, and Ginny would bestow nothing but pleasure for being given that gift.

The electric trimmer knocked against her knee, reminding Ginny of why she knelt on the bed between another woman's knees—she was supposed to be the barber here. Good-bye, pubes. Ginny flicked the trimmer on, making it buck in her hand. Holding it steadily, Ginny pulled it downward from Jordyn's belly. A swath of hair fell away, exposing pale skin from belly to slit. Ginny pulled the trimmer again, exposing more of Jordyn's mound.

A master sculptor releasing beauty from stone had nothing on Ginny, who revealed the glory of Jordyn's mons. One stroke at a time, soft skin greeted Ginny's eyes as its hair fell away under the blade. Ginny whisked the trimmings away, and shaved Jordyn's pussy clean. Even down into her crack. Ginny pushed Jordyn's legs high enough to bump against Heidi, who had risen to her knees to take one of Jordyn's nipples in each hand. She pulled rhythmically at Jordyn's full breasts, milking her even if no spray flew. Ginny shuddered—that thought had pulled electricity through her own tired cunny.

Jordyn was made to give milk, with those high, firm teats tipped with pink. Heidi was made to draw it out of her, with those strong, tireless fingers to pull at stiff nipples. White mist would spurt from her breasts, if not tonight then soon, and Heidi would squeeze the miraculous liquid from her. And Ginny would put her lips to Jordyn's breasts to drink, once her lactation started. Oh, how Ginny hoped that would be soon! But she had her own mission—Jordyn's puss still had raspy spots.

The blade of the trimmer made quick work of the patches once Ginny recalled herself to her task. The skin left bare was soft under her fingertips. Jordyn's crack got attention—Ginny spread her wide with one hand and darted into the shadows with the trimmer, removing any daring hairs that hid within. Travelling along the border between wet pinkness and dry paleness, Ginny shaved away any bit of roughness. Jordyn's crotch felt like a baby and smelled like a woman.

A woman in need: Jordyn's outer lips had touched each other when she'd started shaving, looking like a soft and fuzzy peach, with its cleft promising sweet juices. And as Jordyn's excitement built, her cunny swelled and opened. With her juicy center revealed, surrounded by clean-shaven skin, Jordyn's pussy demanded to be caressed. Licked. Stroked. Penetrated. Fucked. Pounded, over and over. Forced to climax, because nothing but the purest pleasure should touch her wet, musky cunt. And Ginny would make sure that pleasure happened.

Alarmed at her own decisiveness, Ginny dropped to her belly between Jordyn's legs. She hovered for a moment over Jordyn's flesh, knowing that the intoxicating aroma of excited woman would become a feast under her tongue, if she could but bend her head that last inch.

"What am I waiting for?" Ginny asked herself, and the answer was "For nothing at all." Jordyn's pussy lay open for the tasting, and that's what Ginny did. Tentatively at first, and then more strongly, Ginny lapped at the banquet spread before her.

The tip of her tongue touched Jordyn's clit, which stuck out impudently at Ginny. "Dare you lick me?" it seemed to ask, and Ginny did, with tiny flicks that made Jordyn yip. The tip of her tongue became the flat of her tongue, taking long swipes from juicy hole to stiff clitoris. A girl could get drunk on pussy juices. Ginny limited herself to tiny tastes at first, but that impertinent clit bumped against her lip once too often.

Ginny wrapped her lips around and began to suckle. The nubbin grew even stiffer, and its owner cried out, but Ginny only tickled the tip with her tongue as she sucked.

Jordyn bucked her hips against Ginny's mouth, dislodging her but giving her other ideas. She nibbled on the engorged inner labia like they were rare fruit, sweet and juicy, and plunged her tongue at last into Jordyn's channel. Hot and grasping, Jordyn's pussy seemed to demand Ginny probe it more deeply, running with moisture into her mouth. Ginny swallowed and lapped again, finding more liquid with every plunge within.

Cupping Jordyn's thighs let Ginny pull herself face first into Jordyn's depths, which ran with honey and spread more widely. But this wasn't enough—she returned to flick against Jordyn's clit, and one hand stole to the passage it guarded.

Palm upward, Ginny pressed a finger into Jordyn's cunt, feeling the dampness that her efforts had drawn from the other woman. Ginny's own walls had felt her touch, but somehow Jordyn's were all new. Each ridge and fold was a fresh experience—Ginny slipped within until she could go no farther.

That nubbly place had to be the G-spot—Jordyn lifted her hips and all but screamed when Ginny curled her fingertip against it. Muffled though—Heidi must be holding her prisoner with her mouth as surely as Ginny did. Caressing inside again, Ginny increased her efforts of tongue against clit, lips providing pressure, and did her level best to suck an orgasm right out of Jordyn.

Tiny moans became keening wails—Jordyn flung her hips against Ginny's hand. She must need another finger. Two digits to thrust inside now, twice the experience of Jordyn's hungry pussy trying to engulf her hand, and more wild lapping at a clit swollen enough to protrude well beyond cunt's edges. Ginny squeezed her lips around the stiff button, swiping back and forth with her tongue.

Jordyn's moans became a full cry and then silence, as her pussy twitched and clenched with her orgasm. Two fingers inside taught

Ginny the true meaning of muscular flutter—Jordyn squeezed and contracted around Ginny's hand. Her clit twitched under Ginny's tongue, which stayed flat and comforting against the convulsing nub.

She stayed with Jordyn throughout her climax, her nose pressed to Jordyn's mound and her hand and mouth experiencing all the pulsing and contractions. Jordyn's orgasm seemed to last forever, and when it faltered, Ginny pressed two fingers up into the G-spot to coax out a last wave. Jordyn cried out again and wiggled wildly as if in search of more something—which Ginny gave with quick slurps at Jordyn's clit.

"Fuck!" Jordyn screamed, and yes, Ginny would, fucking Jordyn with her hand and mouth. She thrust stiffly into Jordyn's canal with another long swipe of tongue. Jordyn cried out again, pulsing, and finally went limp.

Ginny placed tender kisses around the rim of Jordyn's pussy and across the delicate skin of her mound. Her womanly parts were so beautiful and capable of so much pleasure; they deserved kindness after being pushed to crashing climax. Her moist places were so like the inside of Ginny's mouth that they must belong together, and only Jordyn's complete collapse meant they should be separated. Ginny withdrew her fingers from Jordyn's inner channel and licked the drips away. With a last kiss to Jordyn's clit, Ginny sat up and met Heidi's eyes. Whatever the other woman had been doing to Jordyn's breasts and upper body matched Ginny's lower attentions well.

"I think we fucked her into the mattress," Heidi observed, and celebrated it by kissing Ginny. Heidi's tongue probed deeply into Ginny's mouth, and she lapped away the juices from Ginny's lips. "Yay us.

Yay us indeed. Ginny delved between Heidi's lips, giving Jordyn a show if she could manage to open her eyes. Sharing Jordyn's juices with Heidi seemed like the most natural thing in the world. Once her milk came in, she'd share that with her friends too, and they'd live in a haze of horniness, joy, and sweet fluids from their bodies.

Jordyn might catch her breath here soon. And then it would be Ginny's turn to lie down under the inventive attentions of her friends.

With Heidi's soft lips pressed against her own, and her wonderful, wet tongue pressed into her mouth, Ginny would let Jordyn take quite a lot of time deciding she could move again. Ginny squirmed her upper body to get her own big breasts interwoven with Heidi's enormous tits—they couldn't get close enough to hug otherwise. Oh, but Heidi was soft and warm! Her flesh was a good balm for Ginny's swollen breast and well-tugged nipple.

With the one corner of her mind that wasn't intent on holding on to Heidi, Ginny wondered who would play with her breasts and who would shave the soft curls away from her mons. They should be fair, right? Heidi had a turn at Jordyn's breasts, and Jordyn had a turn at Heidi's pussy. Would Jordyn want to shave Ginny too? But Ginny wanted to kiss both her friends. And was Heidi squeamish about another woman's crotch?

"I want some." Jordyn's panting had calmed enough to let her rise and join the snugglefest going on above her. She wormed her own large breasts against Heidi and Ginny and tried to join the smooching.

Only being able to cuddle Jordyn let Ginny unwrap from Heidi, and she craned to meet Jordyn's mouth. Her hand slipped down Jordyn's back, against soft skin and the valley of her backbone to the swell of her ass. What a beautiful ass Jordyn had—and now Ginny had a hand cupped over one scrumptious buttock. She squeezed gently, making Jordyn moan. Heidi leaned in to claim her own kiss.

Jordyn turned to meet Heidi's mouth. Jordyn deprivation! That wouldn't do—Ginny wanted the intimacy of wet flesh, and if her mouth was elsewhere, Ginny would find what she wanted somewhere. She leaned down enough to slide her hand further under that round, bouncy bum. Her fingertips reached the wet cleft between Jordyn's legs from behind. Jordyn scooted her knees a little farther apart to give her better access. With a wiggling middle finger, Ginny dipped into the juice dripping from Jordyn's pussy. She could tickle the opening of Jordyn's canal while she dropped her mouth to the other blonde's shoulder.

"Greedy girl." Heidi whispered against Jordyn's mouth. "You just had a turn." She licked a wet trail against Jordyn's mouth and lifted her hand to grab first one girl's tit and then the other. She lingered on Ginny's breast, pinching her nipple and rolling it from side to side. Ginny felt the wetness oozing between her legs—a droplet tricked down the inside of her thigh.

Ginny couldn't help it—she'd enjoyed Heidi's breasts and Jordyn's pussy, and she was desperate to have her friends do something for her. She moaned, thrusting her finger upward into the cleft of Jordyn's cunt and leaning into Heidi's grabby hand.

"Let's lay this little slut down before she explodes." Jordyn planted a last kiss on Heidi's lips. "She needs to cum, and we need to make her."

"And she's still all fuzzy." Jordyn winked at Ginny. "But not for long."

Would they just get to it? Ginny threw herself flat to the mattress, her breasts poking high into the air. "Somebody do something!" She spread her knees wide, feeling the *whish* of air over her inner lips as they parted. All that juicy pink would stay moist as long as her friends played with her.

"Prepare to be bare!" Heidi brandished the trimmer, which buzzed forgotten against the bedspread. "This is one hellagood vibrator, except it doesn't fit inside, you know?" She shaved the curls away from Ginny's mound, straight down the middle and twisted the handle to touch directly against Ginny's clit. She held it there.

Ginny would have bounced up to sitting, but Jordyn held her trapped against the mattress. "No, no, no!" Jordyn singsonged. "All your hair are belong to us!" She followed that silly statement with a deep and melting kiss, with lots of tongue. So what if Ginny's tit was pinched beneath Jordyn's chest—Jordyn was probing her mouth with deep licks. And she moved, oh good—Ginny's titties were so tender from all the pumping. She had to make milk soon—a couple more days of pumping would either toughen her up or kill her completely.

But if it felt the way Jordyn's hand felt... Milking her breast while kissing Ginny with an open mouth, Jordyn played with Ginny's nipples, making the sparks fly south to her pussy, which lost another swath of hair under Heidi's strokes. Again and again the razor hummed over her most tender flesh, and again and again Jordyn pulled at her nipple.

"You have such pretty breasts, girlfriend," Jordyn moaned between kisses. "I love the way your nipples go up. And they're so hard. I can't believe how hard they are..." She rolled one in little quick strokes, spreading the fire. "These were made to suck on." Scooting lower so she could reach with her mouth, Jordyn glanced at Heidi. "Tell me how pretty her cunt is. Nice as her boobies?"

"Every bit as nice!" Heidi moved the vibrating trimmer against Ginny's clit. "She looks like a rose in the snow, with all those pink ridges against white skin. A rose with nectar in the center." She pushed a finger inside—Ginny wanted to snap her legs shut and hide her rose, but Heidi slid in and out, leaving the trimmer resting sideways against her clit. It felt so good—almost too good—almost too much—but Ginny didn't want Heidi to take away that probing finger, not when it stroked inside her and made the shudders come. She wasn't ready to cum yet—but close. So close. The waiting was sweet torment—but any torture that involved Jordyn's pouty mouth on her nipple was torture Ginny would accept.

Jordyn had a big mouthful and was flicking her tongue against Ginny's stiff nub while she sucked. One day Jordyn would do that and get a mouthful of milk as a reward for the tingling and quivering she gave. Brat girl took her time with each long stroke, curling the tip of her tongue in complete circles around Ginny's aching hard nipple, and sucking rhythmically.

"How long did it take you to cum for Dr. Busby? Heidi asked. "Did you twiddle your nippies and show him what a little tart you are? You are a juicy little tart, sweet and tangy and tasty."

Ginny moaned. She wasn't going to tell them about Dr. Busby—they already knew she'd been a fool.

"Sweet little tart—did you use the smallest probe?" Heidi slid a finger into Ginny's pussy, fucking her at slow speed. "Or wasn't that enough for this juicy little cunt?"

One finger was a lot the way Heidi did it—she pushed all the way and drew out with a hard stroke against Ginny's G-spot. And she kept doing it, all the while the trimmer hummed against its target.

"No...I..." Ginny couldn't talk, not with the way her pussy was ramping up for a great big orgasm. She was ready to spasm against Heidi's finger, ready to cream all over her hand. She hadn't said she was a rainmaker and Heidi was about to find out the hard way. And she didn't want to find enough brain to make words with the way Jordyn squeezed her breast, and oh damn, Jordyn had moved over to lap and suck Ginny's other breast. Her poor nipple should explode in a shower of milk for what Jordyn was doing to it, and the nipple that wasn't being sucked was getting pinched and pulled until it should make a flood of its own.

"Oh, then you used the medium probe?" Heidi was such a wicked girl! She pushed a second finger into Ginny's pussy, stroking her inner walls with twice as much surface. "You like something bigger in your cunny—you like getting filled up." Fingerfucking Ginny faster now, she moaned, "Dr. Busby would have filled you up. He's got a nice fat cock, so long and thick. He gets all excited, pushes it in...."

"He'll give it to you tomorrow." Jordyn lifted her head. "We'll make you feel good now." She reached down and rubbed the trimmer against Ginny's mons and right on her clit.

"Oh yeah." Heidi bunched her hand. "I'll give you something big now." Three fingers was big, and even bigger the way Heidi did it.

Ginny couldn't believe how much she was stretching, but with the vibration on her clitoris and Jordyn's tongue gone back to licking her breast, it was exactly what she wanted. "I used the big probe."

87

"I bet you did—it had to fill up this sweet pussy." Heidi doubled her efforts and swirled the buzzing trimmer around. Ginny's clit throbbed with the climax that was just out of reach. "Did he fuck you with it for an extra orgasm? Just like this?" She jammed her fingers deeply into Ginny's cunt, hitting the sweet spot with every pass. "I bet he nearly died not being able to put his prick into you. Only ramming this juicy hole with the probe. He's a dirty boy, wanting to fuck you, and you're a dirty girl, 'cause you want to be fucked."

Ginny didn't care about getting fucked right now—she wanted to cum and she didn't care how it happened. With both women working on her, she should go up in flames any second. "Heidi!"

"Yes?" With a big leer, Heidi took the trimmer away from Ginny's naked pussy and put her face down. Oh damn, that was Heidi's tongue, snaking in between her now hairless lips, finding her juicy spots and her clit. With a small shriek, Ginny gave herself over to the pounding waves of her orgasm, the ripples pulling through her pussy, making her nipples pulse along with her clit. Her inner walls gripped Heidi's fingers over and over.

"Do it again," Jordyn rasped, but talking made her stop sucking. Ginny didn't have enough control of her hands to push Jordyn down—she had to lift her chest and offer her nipple to Jordyn instead. Fortunately Jordyn took the hint, slurping Ginny's breast deeply into her mouth.

And Heidi did do it again—she sucked Ginny's clit between her lips, flipping and flailing her tongue against that sensitive morsel of flesh.

Ginny never quite stopped cumming—one orgasm merged into the next, pulsating through her clit and into her cunt with every new flick from Heidi's tongue. And Jordyn added her own delights above, playing with her nipples. If she passed out, would they stop? And if they didn't stop, would she keep cumming? Another lick from Heidi answered that question—Ginny clenched again, the sparks all but flying from her cunt. Heidi would catch them with her probing fingers, three of them poking into Ginny's channel.

Just when she thought her clit would blow up, Heidi stilled with her tongue pressed flat to Ginny's clit. Holding still for the first time since she'd bent to lick, Heidi let the waves die away. When Ginny went limp, Heidi took her tongue away, carefully enough not to wake any more twitches from Ginny's exhausted crotch. She kissed Ginny's now-hairless mound, and let one finger caress the outer lips, shorn of fur.

"You're so pretty down here." Heidi pulled Ginny's lips apart with her thumbs to survey the pink folds. "I ought to suck you every day."

"Okay." Ginny was up for that, but maybe not until tomorrow. "I get to do you guys too."

"Wouldn't dream of stopping you." Jordyn kissed her cheek.

Heidi let go below and came up to join the cuddle. Her lips were wet. Ginny licked at them, tasting herself on Heidi's mouth. "That was wonderful."

"Good times," Heidi agreed. "Suppose we ought to pump some more?" She squeezed Ginny's tit, and then Jordyn's.

"Time spent pumping after orgasm is valuable," Jordyn quoted. "But I think I'm too tired."

Ginny left Jordyn and Heidi cuddled around each other. After pulling the blankets up around their shoulders and taking the towel back to the bathroom, she went to her own room and affixed the collectors to her breasts. Her friends had a head start on her after Dr. Busby treated them with prostaglandins—she had to catch up. Even if her nipples were ready to fall off from too much touching. She had to explore her naked pussy just a little—the satiny skin where hair had been was a delight under her fingertips. She finally left her hand cupped over her pussy, just because it was soft. Ginny fell asleep to the *whum whum* of the pump suckling at her.

Chapter 8 A Shocking Examination

WAITING IN THE exam room for Dr. Busby to return with her chart, Ginny thought over all the things she needed to say. And the things she needed to ask. She'd peeled her clothes off at his nod, and sat gingerly on the end of the table.

"I'm very sorry about yesterday," she ventured, hoping he'd look up from the papers. "I was rude and you were only trying to help."

Dr. Busby did look up, but he didn't look his lustful self of yesterday. "No offense taken, Ginny. I didn't explain well, and you didn't understand the science, so let's put this behind us. In fact—" He stopped to pencil a note into her chart. "—you accidentally did me a favor."

"I did?"

"Yes. I hadn't set my experiment up correctly. My baseline was unstimulated women with random applications of prostaglandins, when it should have been stimulated women without prostaglandins. You saved me from a serious scientific error."

"Oh. Good. I guess." Yay for science, but what about her? Ginny suddenly feared what he'd say next, because that didn't sound like "We'll start your treatment a day late."

"Yes, indeed. Tell me how many hours you pumped yesterday." He looked up at her, as if he was assessing the honesty of her next answer.

She wouldn't make him doubt her. "A total of thirteen, because I fell asleep with the pump on."

"Oh, my. Are you sore?" He looked concerned.

"A bit," she admitted. "But not enough to stop me today." She shifted on the table, which didn't have enough chill to soothe her real problem.

"Did you pump this morning too?" He made another note.

"Yes, about a half hour." Ginny had iced her nipples after that, and coated them with the ointment she'd been given.

"And how many orgasms did you have yesterday?" Dr. Busby wanted to know.

She should have been counting. Ginny had to think. "Um, fourteen? One was pretty huge and lasted like, forever, so should that count for more?"

"We'll have to count that one as two, I think." He smiled with that notation. "How did you become so stimulated?"

As if he didn't know, at least part of it. "Four of them I had here, so nipple stimulation, and G spot stimulation and getting fucked with the probe. Clit stimulation." She blushed, thinking how that had happened. "I used some toys."

Man oh man, had she. And now she couldn't sit properly. Ginny shifted her weight to her other cheek, hissing when the movement pressed her crotch into the table.

"You seem uncomfortable," Dr. Busby noted.

"I'm...kind of swollen," Ginny admitted.

"Lie back, let's take a look." With one big hand on her back, Dr. Busby supported her gradual descent to lying flat. He guided her heels to the stirrups.

Normally she would mind being exposed this way, but today it was sweet relief. She let her knees fall away from each other. The air soothed her inflamed tissues. Dr. Busby pulled the stool up to the base of the table to take a good look.

She felt gentle fingers touching the newly shaven skin of her mons. They pressed lightly, traveling all around the outside of her vulva, seeking damages. Dr. Busby *hmm'ed*, Then he parted her labia, as if they weren't already blooming, and stroked the inner ridges. Ginny shivered as he flicked them—they were stiff and poking out, and she'd been glad to take off her panties. Even their fine cotton crotch had been too rough for her overstimulated flesh. He handled her clit, pinching a little, as if he was assessing for hardness. Damn, it was hard, all right, hard like she'd had hours of foreplay and no release, and him moving it around, assessing it, wasn't getting her closer.

"Did you have an orgasm this morning?" He reached to the instrument table. Ginny was afraid of what he'd pick up.

"One, but it didn't make things go down." And she'd had to use a smaller toy than she usually liked. Her favorite was too big.

"Hmm." He slid the bills of the speculum into her pussy, the cool metal soothing against her overheated walls. When he spread the instrument wide, more cool air rushed in, offering her a moment's relief. "Does this hurt?"

"N-no." It did feel strange.

He clicked the instrument, forcing her open farther. "This?"

"It's a little uncomfortable." She gripped the edges of the table. Was he going to open the speculum another notch?

Click. "And this?"

"Yes, a little." Ginny hoped he wouldn't do that again.

"Then I'm sorry for this, but you aren't spread enough for me to see." He clicked once, twice, and Ginny yelped. "You did say you wished to be warned." With a long swab, he prodded here and there. "This is solvable. We'll send you home in better shape."

Ginny blinked back tears. Why did he have to open her up at all? Why couldn't he just bring her to the sort of orgasm that would make her soften again? Whimpering, she thought more. Because if a normal old orgasm would help, her climax this morning would have solved the problem. But here she was, red, swollen, and in need of relief. The speculum stretched her to the point of pain, and it wasn't even very wide.

Dr. Busby pressed another button and the speculum collapsed, much to Ginny's relief. If he'd fuck her with it closed up, maybe the cool metal would help? But he slid it out of her, letting her pussy lips come together again.

"This is usually a problem of overdoing, Ginny." The doctor took a tube of something from the instrument table. "We'll give you a soothing gel for now, and a complete treatment before you go. I have to do a few other things first for accuracy."

He stroked the gel onto her overheated vulva. He was so careful to work it onto her folds and creases, although when he coated her clitoris, she flinched. He didn't let that stop him—he spread the gel around her nubbin and into the hood. With another glob of gel, he pressed two fingers into her vagina, working the medicine around to cover her thoroughly. If he enjoyed his job now, it didn't show on his face.

But Ginny felt a little better for having the gel on her. And his hands. Except he noticed a problem that she was hoping would resolve before medical help was needed. "You're tender around your perineum and anus. Probably from your vaginal juices dripping. We'll treat that too."

"It's just a little—" Ginny objected. She was uncomfortable but not to the point of wanting his intervention.

"A little can become a lot." The doctor frowned at her crotch. "This isn't unusual in our dairy maids, Ginny. I'll give you something for it."

Oh all right. She was lying there with her thighs wide apart. Might as well. He came back with a different tube.

Again he spread ointment, something thicker and greasier, over her chapped skin. It did feel good, and she tried not to leap away when he massaged some into her anus. She really didn't like having him touch her there, but he was insistent, and held her thigh down while he worked that large finger into the rim of her ass. "You'll feel better for this. Apply it three times a day."

She was going to have to shove stuff up her butt three times a day? But it did feel okay, except that seemed like a very large finger.

94

"You might only need one of these, but I'll send a couple with you." And with that, the doctor peeled a wrapper from a small white pellet.

"I don't need—" Ginny protested, but he'd pinned her thigh again.

"You are not the best judge of what you need," the doctor told her sternly. "You've already caused intractable engorgement, delayed your lactation, and keep trying to refuse treatment you need. I'm beginning to wonder if Mr. Manley was right to hire you for a dairy maid at all."

What if Dr. Busby gave her a poor report and Dirk sent her away? Ginny mumbled an apology and let her legs spread.

With thumb and forefinger he parted her cheeks and touched the suppository to her anus. "Relax."

She tried, oh she tried, but he still had to force the butt bullet in, and followed it with that large finger to seat it correctly. She whimpered as his finger twisted within her hole. He didn't withdraw until he was satisfied, and it seemed to take forever to satisfy him. Her pussy twitched and contracted with his movements, and only seemed to get more swollen.

"Stay where you are for the moment. We'll do this next while you're supine to keep the pressure off your crotch. " Dr. Busby went to fetch his calipers. Bringing the strange tongs back, he again took measurements of her nipples and noted the results. "This seems to be the erect measurement from yesterday."

Probably. "They didn't want to go down either." Not after she'd pumped for hours by accident. "And my breasts feel hard."

"I wouldn't doubt it." He started a breast exam on her as he'd done before, probing with flattened fingers against the swollen mounds on her chest. "Did your bra feel different?"

"I couldn't wear it," Ginny confessed. "It rubbed against my nipples too much."

"That's actually a sign of progress." Dr Busby went around the circle of her breast again and switched sides. Exploding under his fingertips felt entirely possible, and she was damned tired of signals going from tit to clit. Did she get a vacation day? Ginny tried to enjoy his manipulations of her breasts, but that plan went up in a yelp when he gripped one breast in each hand and tugged on her. Her flesh slid through his fingers—he was milking her!

"Ow!" Ginny whined.

"This is the only way to assess if you've begun lactating. You'll toughen up in a few days." Dr. Busby milked her again, stretching her nipples much farther than she liked. "It might take a few strokes to achieve letdown." He pulled at her breasts in unison, pinching outside her areolas and bringing his fingers up to the base of her nipples. She gasped, but he did it three more times, tugging harder than she thought he needed to. "Nothing yet. It's a bit soon though." He let go.

Finally! Ginny stifled a sob. She was trying to be a good dairy maid and get her milk started, but she didn't like this part at all.

"Stand please." He helped her off the table and led her to the sink, where the plastic dome waited. "We'll check your volumes again." He fit the device against her chest and ran the water in. It felt good to float her breast. She tried not to be sad when the water flowed away—they'd do the other side. She kept her feet wide apart to avoid feeling the greasy ointments all over her crack and cunt.

"Well, Ginny, your breast volume has increased already from yesterday. You're now at 745cc and 741cc. All that pumping is getting you started." He dried her breasts with a soft towel.

"How long before my milk comes in?" Ginny asked timidly. She didn't want to offend him again.

"It might be as early as two more days," Dr. Busby said. "But that's just based on your percentage increase, and isn't a guarantee." He hefted her breasts, one large globe in each hand. "I do wish I could weigh these accurately." He didn't seem inclined to let go, and his thumbs wandered over her sensitive nipples. Ginny would take some more stimulation if that would help convince him she needed the prostaglandin treatment.

But he suddenly came to himself and let go, almost fast enough to let her tits bounce. "Let's take care of that engorgement problem, and Ginny, do keep the pumping to a maximum of six hours a day. I never thought I'd have to restrict a young lady's orgasms, but not more than ten a day, or you'll encounter this engorgement problem again." He patted her butt to shoo her to the table. "Back in the stirrups, dear."

Ginny waddled to the table, trying very hard not to rub anything between her legs. The gel hadn't done very much to help yet.

Once she lay on her back with her feet in the air, Ginny wondered what sort of treatment he'd give to relieve her swollen pussy. Her clit felt the size of a grape, and it hadn't stopped throbbing since, well, yesterday when Heidi sucked her. And that thought made her throb some more! She missed the *snick* of the cuffs at her ankles, but jumped away when Dr. Busby velcroed a restraint around her wrist.

"What?" she cried.

"I wouldn't do this if you hadn't already demonstrated that you interfere with treatments, Ginny." He wrapped the strap and secured it. "I can't have you moving around for this next treatment or it may not work."

Ginny really wanted it to work—she couldn't waddle like a horny penguin for the next two days, or two weeks, or worse. "I won't." She tugged against the restraint and tried to free it with her other hand.

"Quite right you won't." Dr. Busby caught her free hand and forced it to her side, where he quickly secured the strap. "But I don't trust your word for it given how you've complained already at everything I've done, which has all been for your own good."

He really was trying to do right by her, and she had complained a lot, but still was strapping her down necessary? "I'll hold still."

"Don't promise what you can't deliver, Ginny." He whipped another strap around her knee, making her leg stay close to the stirrup support. "You might not put your hands down, but everyone reacts to this treatment." He fastened her other knee to its support. "And I have no patience to talk you into doing what's in your best interests after you've decided you don't much like this treatment either. So straps it is."

Ginny felt like a complete fool, for every one of his words was right. She had complained and argued, and her reward was getting what she needed anyway, except for those prostaglandins, although he might do that after her swelling treatment. Maybe he'd let her up for that. Enough to cooperate with him, which would be more fun for both of them. Unless he had a kink for bondage, in which case a little role playing with her treatment might be okay.

She was spread so wide! He could step right between her legs and see everything she had, pulled far apart to expose the entry to her body and all her rosy ruffles, Her clit, swollen far beyond mere horniness, poked out at him like a tongue. Maybe licking was part of her treatment? She couldn't see what he was getting from the drawer.

"Oh, and Ginny, I do keep a ball gag in the office. Can you keep your whining to a minimum?" the doctor asked over his shoulder. "Shall I get it out, or will you stop putting barriers before your needs?"

A ball gag! Ginny gulped. "I'll be quiet." She shouldn't have been so snotty—he was the doctor and he did know what she needed in his area of specialty. She must have angered him more than she thought!

"You won't, I suspect, but you at least won't be complaining." He turned back to her spread pussy, holding an instrument she didn't recognize. A long handle with what looked like a purple knob on the end. He plugged it into an outlet on the table.

"W—what is that?" Surely he wouldn't mind explaining?

"Ginny, you need to relax. This is a violet wand, and yes, I'm going to use it on your vulva. It will help, or I wouldn't be doing it." He flicked it on, and the ball began to glow. It hissed and a spark darted away from the knob to ground against her inner thigh.

"Ow!" Oh, no! What if he gagged her for reacting? But that hurt!

"Sorry about that." He twisted the dial. "I'm going to bring this near your vulva. I don't think I should promise that it won't hurt, given that you just got a shock."

Ginny wanted to wriggle off the table, and run out the door screaming. She struggled against her bonds. She wouldn't even stop for her clothes; she'd just flee, and never come back. The shock on her leg was bad enough, but to have that land on her poor wet clit?

"Must you?" she whispered.

"Must I get the ball gag?" Dr. Busby shot back. "One more comment from you and I will." His eyes narrowed. "Or I can let you up and get dressed, and you can pack your bags and leave, because obviously you aren't willing to do what it takes to be a dairy maid. Then you can hobble around until your crotch subsides on its own. That shouldn't take more than a few days."

Days! Ginny wanted to wail. And be on her own, broke, with no place to live, and all because she couldn't be still. "I'm sorry. I won't question you again."

"Then let's begin." He brought the wand near her exposed pussy, stopping before he came close enough to touch, and twisted the dial again. Then he came closer.

Ginny wanted to squinch her eyes shut, just so she wouldn't see great sparks attack her. Her poor clit would get zapped like her thigh! Didn't what stick out farthest get struck with electricity first? But she stared at the glowing violet bulb, unable to control her shaking.

He turned another knob, and brought the instrument even closer. And reaching down from the top, he used his free hand to spread her pussy lips as far apart as they would go, pressing his fingers deep into her swollen flesh. Her inner lips poked out, and her clit had no protection at all.

The wand hummed, but didn't spark again. Ginny's vulva also hummed—the electricity danced on her flesh, buzzing her as if she was a live wire. She felt all effervescent, like tiny bubbles from champagne were popping against her labia, and the bubbliness traveled with the wand, down one inner ruffle and up the other side. Ginny relaxed—this felt almost good. Strange, but good.

"Very good—stay still," the doctor intoned. "Your clitoris now."

He moved the wand and the bubbles grew—they weren't champagne bubbles any more, they were soda bubbles. Her clit twitched—Ginny would have pulled away if she could, but the straps held her. She might be able to get used to this. Maybe. But it was insistent and she whimpered. If it was stronger it might make her come. If he put two fingers into her pussy and zapped her, she might come. But he didn't enter her, only waving the wand ever closer to her clit.

She couldn't help it—she squirmed.

"You risk touching the wand directly when you do that," Dr. Busby told her. "Then it will hurt, regardless of what I do." He moved the wand back down her inner labia, circling the opening of her vagina. He didn't try to press the wand in, but made it *zzzz* along the ridges and back to her clit.

Her clit hummed with the emanations of the wand. She whimpered, the sound coming out of her nearly closed throat. He didn't chastise her, and circled her clit again. The electric current made her shiver, and what if she touched the bulb? She tried to hold still.

"Doing well, Ginny." Dr. Busby gave her a bit of encouragement. Her joy in that disappeared when he adjusted the wand to a higher setting, its buzz growing louder and more threatening. He returned his hand to her mons, again pulling her labia wide.

He made a slow pass again at her clit, his eyes intent on her flesh. She couldn't tell what was happening down there—the *zzzzz* the wand provided overwhelmed anything else she might feel. Squirming again was a real possibility. Ginny bit her lip and tried not to cry.

"Nnnnnh!" she tried not to say, but the sound squeaked out all the same. The buzzing in her clit overrode anything she could do to stop. The sensation had grown overwhelming, but not anything that would bring her the joy of a climax. The bubbles feeling had gone from the tiny spheres of sparkling wine to an enormous fizzing.

"Nearly there, Ginny," Dr. Busby tried to soothe her. The zap from the wand went around her clit, touching first one side and then the other, then back, front, and top. It hovered over the tip of her clit, buzzing her hard.

She could last, she muttered in her head, she could last and she'd be fine after, if she could just endure this. This *zzziipp* of electricity would break her. The strangled sound came from her throat again.

"Doing well, Ginny," Dr. Busby murmured again. "Almost done."

And then her world exploded. The glass globe pressed into her clit, jolting Ginny off the table. She couldn't control her limbs, bouncing under the jolt of electricity. It rammed through her clit and her vulva, spreading through her body. She contorted, hauling against her restraints. Not by choice—choice was gone and all she could do was jerk beneath the wand.

She screamed. He didn't relent. The wand stayed pressed to her clit.

And at last, he withdrew his instrument. Ginny couldn't believe it at first—sense took a while to return. But she could lie still.

She hadn't climaxed. Many things had happened to her cunt, but an orgasm wasn't one of them. Ginny sobbed with what she'd gotten and what she hadn't.

"There, there," Dr. Busby murmured. He came to wipe her face with a tissue, blotting up the tears that trickled away from her eyes. "All done now."

The sobs and hiccups from her experience didn't let any words out. Ginny sniffled and pulled at her wrist straps. He released her wrists and then went down to her legs to release them as well. He paused between her legs, parting her labia once more and smiling at what he saw. He held her vulva open, pinching the inner lips, which were much softer now. Even her clit was softer under his fingers, but if he didn't stop rolling it like that, they'd be back to the beginning. Ginny whimpered but didn't speak, and with a last stroke down the length of her clitshaft, he released her.

"It's over, dear." Dr. Busby reassured her again. "And it worked. You're much less swollen, and should be back to normal in a few more minutes." He helped her sit up, putting pressure on her pussy, which had no objection at all to being sat on now. He cuddled her to his chest. "Shh, you're fine now."

And she was, but she let Dr. Busby hold her close all the same. He'd had to be stern with her, but he was right, and she felt so much better. Ginny was content to lean against his broad chest, and hope her closeness made him think of the next treatment she needed. Something with a proper orgasm, preferably.

"Now get dressed, dear. You're to have no more orgasms until tomorrow morning, and you're to pump no more than six hours total today. We don't want to have to do this again, do we?" He pressed his lips to her hair, a gesture Ginny barely appreciated.

"But don't we need to apply prostaglandins?" She could do without the orgasm if she had to, but Heidi, and soon Jordyn, would have that advantage.

"No, Ginny, dear. You're my control for the experiment." He patted her shoulder and squeezed her more tightly against him. "No semen is allowed to enter your vagina until this experiment is finished. If you have intercourse, you must use a condom. You'll be swabbed at intervals, so I will know if you've disobeyed, and if so, you'll be dismissed from the dairy immediately. But I know you won't make that necessary. Will you?" He kissed her hair again. "And if you'd like to get together after office hours, don't worry. I have a supply and will bring them along."

"Don't worry about it," Ginny said faintly. Sometimes she fucking hated science.

Chapter 9 The Milking Machine

ON THEIR FOURTH day at the dairy, Elspeth had news for Ginny, Heidi, and Jordyn. "It's time to progress to your next level of training, girls." She surveyed them over the lunch table. "You've been doing a wonderful job of pumping and getting your breasts ready to lactate. Dr. Busby has cleared you all to advance."

Ginny shifted uncomfortably in her chair. She hadn't enjoyed her appointment this morning at all. She'd had to use the next size dome to measure volume, because her breasts had swelled so much—she was planning to ask if she could be refitted for bras. And then he'd swabbed her pussy and checked under the microscope for sperm, as if he couldn't trust her word. Who would she have gotten semen from? She was too mad to ask him, Dirk wouldn't risk the experiment, and old Horace smelled of cows.

"Our vacationing staff will be returning over the weekend, and our guests will start arriving Sunday evening, so we want you to be familiar with the equipment now." Elspeth rose and motioned them to follow. She must have pumped earlier, because her breasts weren't fighting with her blouse yet. What kind of bra did she wear that stretched so much? Ginny wanted one.

They followed Elspeth to one of the small "barns," actually a clean and tidy outbuilding with a tile floor and four of the benches they'd seen on their orientation.

"The building is warm, so you'll be most comfortable if you

strip rather than bunching your clothes up underneath you." Elspeth watched them disrobe and lay their folded red-and-white clothing on the benches around the room. "We use this barn for demonstrations, but no guests will be coming by. You'll be quite private."

Ginny didn't want to peel down—she felt too exposed, even with the reassurances, but Heidi had already removed everything but her peach panties, exposing all her bountiful flesh. And Jordyn wasn't hesitating either—her peasant blouse and skirt were already off. Ginny reminded herself that her friends had already made better choices for training than she had, and her clothing came off fast.

Elspeth motioned to the benches. "Let's affix the breast basins first. Ginny, Jordyn, you need the blue rimmed size." Guess she could tell by straight eyeballing. Or not. Elspeth lifted Heidi's breasts thoughtfully. "And you'll need basins with the purple rim. Oh, you're swelling beautifully." She squeezed Heidi's nipples. "Your milk should come in very soon." Heidi wriggled under Elspeth's hands.

None of them had made a drop yet—Ginny felt a little better about that, even if her friends were enjoying the "treatment" as much as they were getting benefit from the chemicals in the semen. She clicked her basins onto the bench.

"Now lie down on the bench and place your breasts into the basins. Your nipples, obviously, go through the center holes." Elspeth helped each of them settle into the basins, which supported the weight of their breasts, even if their nipples and a fair amount of creamy white breast did poke out the bottoms.

Ginny found what had to be handholds and gripped them. They'd be good for leverage. She was glad her breasts didn't hang down unsupported—they were too big and swollen to dangle, not that she ever let them flop for long before.

"And now your headrests. You'll get very tired if you have to support your head for the entire time." She levered the headrests forward and clicked them into place. Ginny was grateful to be able to lean against the padded bar, even if the frame did go over her head and close to her shoulders. What had Dirk called these? Stanchions? She was almost comfortable, except for her legs. She'd knelt over the bench with her thighs together, but that wasn't a good position to maintain for long. She parted her knees and found that she wasn't fighting the end of the bench so much that way.

"Excellent!" Elspeth encouraged them. "Now I'll place the milkers over your nipples."

Ginny turned to watch. Jordyn was in the middle, and Heidi beyond her, and an empty bench beyond that. The room was lined with what looked almost like small bleachers. Did they give milking demonstrations? How interesting could that be?

Elspeth picked up two stainless steel cylinders from the rack on the wall. They had some kind of rubber gasket at one end and a hose trailing from the other that disappeared into some machinery. It all looked very dairy-like. Ginny hoped no one would see her.

Kneeling at Heidi's side, Elspeth clicked the cylinders to the underside of the breast basins. "I'll put bottles on to keep the pressure sealed, not because I expect you to lactate yet, girls." She screwed small containers to the mountings on the cylinders. Heidi looked quite ready to be milked.

"Moo?" Jordyn joked. She must have thought the same.

"Moo," Heidi replied, looking a little less amused. "At least I'm not alone."

"Wonder if the cows think the same when Horace milks them." Ginny didn't know if the cows cared, as long as their udders didn't remain engorged and full.

Elspeth quickly affixed the steel milkers to Jordyn's breasts, and knelt to arrange Ginny's. Wanting to feel how things assembled, Ginny tried to reach the fittings. And discovered her wrists were shackled. "Hey!" Ginny yelped. "We're tied up?"

"No, you aren't tied, and I'm right here, you needn't shout." Elspeth tugged at Ginny's nipple, moving her breast around in the basin. "You are immobilized because this is expensive equipment and we don't want you to damage it or yourselves by moving around while it's on you. When your hours of milking are done, we'll let you up." She clicked the second milker onto Ginny.

How hard was that going to pull on her tits? "But...?"

"No buts. We know how to make women lactate." Elspeth rose and surveyed her three captives with satisfaction. "This works."

"Hours?" That could be a very long time without a break.

Elspeth slapped Ginny's ass, hard enough to sting and more than hard enough to ring through the paneled room. "Dr. Busby said you argued with everything and I didn't believe him. If I let you up now, you go pack."

Ow! Her butt stung with the imprint of Elspeth's hand. Go pack?

"Shut up, Ginny," or some variant came out of both Jordyn and Heidi. "Some of us want to get started." Jordyn glared at her through the stanchion.

"Sorry," Ginny mumbled. She wanted to get started too.

"And—" Elspeth went behind Ginny. "If I hear one word of complaint about this, you go. This is a happy dairy and we don't need a whiner." She hooked her fingers into the elastic of Ginny's panties and hauled them down around her thighs.

What! Ginny bit back the shriek, even though she didn't like her ass and pussy exposed when she couldn't do a thing about it. She tugged at the shackles, but they held her fast.

Elspeth slapped her bare ass again. "And don't wiggle. This is required for the next level of training.Ginny, annoy me once more and you're done."

That hurt! Ginny wanted to be a good dairy maid, but she didn't think they'd have to do anything like this! Or—this!

Elspeth shoved two fingers in Ginny's pussy. "You aren't wet enough." She withdrew and must have found some lube because her fingers invaded Ginny's tender tunnel again, only now they were cold and slippery. Ginny endured the fingerfucking, and once she quit fighting it, it felt good. Elspeth lubed her fingers a second time and thrust them back into Ginny's cunt. She twisted them within until Elspeth was satisfied with her internal slickness. "There. Now you can take the vibrator."

A tiny squeak came out of Ginny's throat before she could stop it. A vibrator? When she was shackled and helpless? But yes—and Elspeth had chosen a big one. She started working it into Ginny's vulnerable cunt, and she wasn't being gentle. It felt huge, and if Ginny tightened against it, it would hurt! She tried, and yelped when Elspeth shoved it in another inch.

"You'll take it, and you'll enjoy it, and you won't say a word that doesn't sound like 'thank you'." Elspeth fucked the toy deeper into Ginny's pussy. "We have lots more applicants than we have openings, and we don't need a dairy maid who won't do the work."

That wasn't fair! Ginny was trying hard, but people kept doing things to her! And not explaining and then being mean about it. But Elspeth obviously thought Ginny was a whiner and a slacker, and she wasn't, not at all. So she tried to relax her pussy to let Elspeth finish getting that toy in before she beat a hole into Ginny's cervix. And she didn't say any of the things on her mind.

Whatever Elspeth was using had a broad flair on the base—not only was Ginny filled *way* full, something rested against her vulva. Bet her clit was going to get a good vibrating too. At least Ginny wasn't alone. She could turn her head enough to watch Elspeth pull Jordyn's panties down. The blue lace made a band around her upper thighs.

Elspeth ran her hand over Jordyn's ass. "You look juicy, dear. Let's get you fitted." She dribbled some lube over a fat metal cylinder with a fanned out base on one third. She touched the tip to Jordyn's cunny, and with a smooth, slow motion, made the vibrator disappear. "Very nice. That should buzz you quite effectively."

Ginny would find a way to wipe that smirk off Jordyn's face.

She couldn't see what Elspeth did to Heidi, but it had to be more of the same, because Heidi sighed and said, "Ooh, yes."

"I'm going to turn the milking machine on now. It will pull at you differently than the small pumps do, so don't be surprised and, Ginny, don't try to pull away. And I'm going to activate your vibrators, which will stay in the whole time. Someone will come by to check on you." Elspeth surveyed the three women, stanchioned and ready for milking. "We want this to be a soothing experience—giving milk should be pleasant. Be still, think about milk flowing from your breasts, and don't worry about whether or not you come—the vibrators are more for comfort and milk stimulation."

Elspeth produced some black scarves from her skirt pocket. "Block out everything except the milking, dears. This will help you focus."

She tied the scarf over Ginny's eyes, and Ginny knew better than to object. She leaned against the forehead rest. This wouldn't be so bad. Just drift, thinking of milk. She would show them. She'd give more milk than her friends. No one could yell at her if she gave the most milk of anyone. Her breasts lay in the milking basins, so swollen and ripe—they'd be ready to give up their precious fluid. Someone would drink it and be nourished.

Ginny barely heard the clicks of the machinery starting, but the milkers began to suckle at her breasts. With a rolling motion from the edge of the nipple openings to the tip of her nipples, a firm pressure squeezed her breasts. Oh yes, she could believe she was being milked.

After a bit, the door clicked, and Ginny was alone with her fellow dairy maids.

"Are you okay, Ginny?" Heidi asked.

"Yes, I'm fine." A little nervous and a lot ashamed, but fine. She shouldn't give Elspeth, Dirk, and Dr. Busby a hard time about everything they needed to do. It was all about the milk, and she'd agreed.

"Good. I thought you might freak out about the blindfolds."

"I just like to know what's going on."

"What's going on is you two are chattering and I'm trying to give milk." Jordyn sounded cross. "Be quiet and concentrate or we'll never lactate."

And Ginny did want to lactate. She wanted to prove she could do what the dairy needed her to do—she would give copious amounts of milk and please everyone. White streams would flow from her breasts to feed the men who relied on human milk for their needs. And if her milk met their pleasures too, there would only be more happiness in the world. She relaxed and let the milkers pulsate around her nipples.

Even the soft buzz from her pussy barely distracted her from the motion of the milkers. It felt good below, but in a quiet way, and Elspeth was right, it was soothing. Her clit and cunt had more of a workout this week than ever before in her life, and now a little massage would make her feel better.

She let her mind drift, returning to her dreams of milk when the milkers started another pulsation on her breasts. Oh how she wanted the fluid to drip from her teats with each stroke.

Funny, it was more like they were cows. Human cows. Hucows. Dairy creatures with milk machines to pull the milk from their breasts, which hung down like udders. Ginny's breasts had been large, but now they were enormous. So big it was almost a shame to have only one teat on each side. If she had more, she could give more milk.

The milkers rolling her nipples nearly hypnotized her—how much time passed she didn't know. The door opened with a puff of cool air, all that alerted her to someone coming to check on them. That was nice—Dirk cared. Or Elspeth. But they were fine. Really fine. Just drifting on rivers of milk.

Steps thudded over the floor, and she couldn't see who it was, but it didn't matter. A faint whiff of cattle clung to their observer, but she was too relaxed to lift her head to sniff. She felt a warm, rough hand slide down her flank, and she might have leaned into the caress.

"Pretty little things, aren't you?" a man's voice said. "Pretty, and docile, and you'll be good milkers soon." He patted her rump. "Let's see, Dirk said condoms for the blonde. One of them. And I can't tell you apart." His steps moved away, and she was sad he left her.

"But not for you, darling heifer. Aw, look at you, just so big and beautiful. Shame to have a machine to do a man's job. We'll just take that out, now, won't we?" Someone whimpered. "There, there, darlin', we'll have you filled up again in no time." Something went *zzz*, and the floor creaked.

"Beautiful, look how broad your back is, and your rump was made to cup with a man's hand, wasn't it, darlin'?" His voice stayed low and soothing. "Handle your teats when you aren't being milked. Let's get you filled back up now, I have just the thing. Big and stiff, perfect for a juicy heifer like you, yes, in we go, isn't that nice?"

Faint, rhythmic slapping came to her ears, making her think of the machine inside her. It hummed her walls and buzzed her nubbin. Nothing exciting, nothing like being mounted, but nice, and she clenched on it, grunting.

Someone was being mounted, she was sure, and she'd like that too. Maybe she'd be next.

"Oh, you're a big, beautiful one. You're the pride of the dairy, aren't you, darlin'?" he crooned. "Huge teats and a soft rump and the juiciest cunt I've ever felt, oh, you're a dairyman's delight." The rhythmic slapping got a little louder, a little faster. "You're just full of milk, and I'm going to add some cream. Don't you worry, precious heifer, my cream is good for you."

The slapping sounded through the soft words that barely made any sense. She should know what he was saying, but milk, that she understood, and she pushed her teats hard into the milkers, wanting to let the fluid squish away from her. Something in her back end twitched, feeling good. Not as nice as the milkers sucking at her, but good. She clenched on the buzzing thing again.

The slapping got fast and loud, and then stopped. The man grunted.

"That was nice, wasn't it, darlin'? Good for you?" Slipping sounds, and another *zzz*. "Well, guess it was good, you ain't complaining none. Let's just put this back where we found it, shall we?"

Something squished. Someone said, "Ah."

Yes, it was all good. She squeezed again on the thing inside her. Felt good. Felt nice. Nice as the pulling on her teats. Milk coming, yeah, milk.

The door opened with a squeak and another puff of air across her flanks. Guess she wasn't getting mounted today.

But she'd get milked again tomorrow. And maybe she'd get mounted then.

Chapter 10 Making Milk

HAVING THE SCARF removed from her eyes roused Ginny. Elspeth and Dirk moved among the three dairy maids, removing machinery from either end. Ginny's breasts ached, not just her nipples, but from their engorged state. If anything, she feared, they were bigger than when she lay down.

"A very good milking session, ladies," Dirk told them, beaming with pride. "You're all making great progress."

"Even me," Ginny thought, trying to sit. She hadn't come from the vibrator, and although she still needed to, she wasn't going to do it under Elspeth's disapproving eye. And if Dirk wanted to watch, he could pay for the view with some prostaglandins, applied directly to her target. She put a hand down anyway, afraid that her previous swelling had returned. Dr. Busby would scold her if it did, but she hadn't done anything her trainers hadn't told her to do.

Her twat was firm, but not overly so—nothing like yesterday. Ginny pulled her panties back up with a small sigh of relief.

"Let's take you back to your rooms, girls." Elspeth handed Heidi her blouse. "You probably weren't truly asleep, but milking can induce a trance, and it's good to sleep properly after that. We'll tuck you in for a nice nap." She slipped a finger under the red-checked strap on Jordyn's skirt, straightening it over her shoulder.

They walked back to the dorms in silence. Elspeth leading the way, and the three dairy maids walking with a slightly spraddled gait.

Ginny removed her skirt and blouse—undies were enough for a nap. Undies wouldn't get in the way of what she needed to do, either. A few brisk rubs and a squeeze to her clit brought the needed orgasm. Now she could sleep. She poked her head into Jordyn's room. She didn't want to nap alone, and she wanted someone to hug her.

Jordyn lay on her back, knees high and wide, her panties around her ankles. Elspeth was inspecting her shaven pussy. "Try again."

Her hand flickered back and forth against her clit, and Jordyn's face was squeezed up with effort. "It isn't happening." She twiddled harder. "It's just not happening."

Putting a hand out to Jordyn's wrist, Elspeth stopped her. "Don't force it. It won't help to fight that hard, and it will only undo the benefits of your morning's milking. We'll just have to bring down the engorgement some other way." She went to the small refrigerator in the corner and pulled something out of the freezer. Unwrapping it on her way back to the bed, Elspeth revealed a flexible cold pad with a blunt spike sticking out of the middle.

A dildo shaped spike. And yes, that's what it was—Elspeth introduced the tip into Jordyn's channel and inserted it all the way to the base. Jordyn yipped but stayed spread, even after the chilly pad touched her vulva.

"This will bring the swelling down, even if you can't come, and as much as you've been coming this week, you may just need a break." Elspeth helped Jordyn pull her panties up, which held the frosty dildo in place.

Ginny flushed. If she'd known she had a remedy at her fingertips, she wouldn't have needed Dr. Busby's violet wand. He hadn't mentioned cold as a treatment. Did he assume she'd already tried this? Her crotch stung with the memory of the electricity, and her hand went instinctively to hold it.

"Do you need a compress too, Ginny?" Elspeth inquired.

"No, I'm okay. I just came." She might again if she stuck her finger into her slit and rubbed her clitty through the fabric, but if she was only supposed to have ten in a day, she ought to ration them. But she didn't let go, and shivered.

Jordyn noticed. "Yeah, it's cold. But it's helping."

Elspeth added, "Dr. Busby has a treatment if this fails."

"Boy does he." Ginny let go of her crotch with an effort. She came to snuggle next to Jordyn.

Jordyn pulled Ginny against her shoulder. They had to bump around a while to find a way to accommodate four enormous breasts, but they finally got comfy.

"Sleep with that in, and see the doctor if there's still a problem when you wake." Elspeth drew the coverlet up to their shoulders. "But you should be fine in a bit. Pump this afternoon for an hour, and again after dinner. Sleep well, girls." She left.

Heidi peeked through the door and then came to join the cuddling. She snuggled up on Jordyn's back, and draped one hand over Ginny's arm. "What's the matter?"

"I'm all swollen and can't come. Elspeth shoved a popsicle in there." Jordyn rubbed her legs together. "Hope it works."

"Hope really hard that the cold works." Ginny didn't want her friend to get the violet wand treatment, even if she did smirk earlier at the barn. "His treatment is pretty, um, shocking."

"Ohh, did you get one?" Heidi wanted the news.

"Yes, and never again." Ginny shuddered. Jordyn pulled her closer. "I didn't like it."

"This morning was pretty weird." Heidi stroked Ginny's arm absently. "Kind of Zen space. Nothing mattered except giving milk."

"Is that why you let Horace fuck you?" Ginny whispered. She recalled the unfamiliar voice and the scent of cows—it couldn't be anyone else.

"Did I?" Heidi seemed startled. "Huh. I guess I did. Why didn't anyone say anything?"

"Why didn't you say anything?" Ginny couldn't have spoken up to save her life this morning, all adrift on the milking. "It was your pussy."

"It was kind of nice. He was slow and gentle. And huge." Heidi sounded pleased. "I didn't come, but I've had another prostaglandin treatment."

"Bitch," Jordyn said, but there was no heat behind it for Heidi getting ahead.

Ginny could only be sad—she wasn't getting any, even from Horace.

"Did he really call me a heifer?" Heidi asked through a yawn.

"Fraid so," Jordyn told her.

"He did say I was beautiful," Heidi mumbled.

"That's because you are." Ginny finished her words before sleep took her away.

WHEN THEY WOKE, everyone headed to the showers. Sleeping in a pile was cozy, but kind of sweaty too. Jordyn stepped into the big shower stall with Ginny. "I'll wash your back."

And wash her front. Jordyn turned Ginny around and lathered her from collarbone to navel. "These are getting so big." Her hands slid over Ginny's breasts. "You have to be ready to let down any minute."

"You too." Ginny smoothed suds over Jordyn's tits. "That milking machine felt good, better than the pump."

"But not as good as a mouth." Jordyn giggled. She giggled again when Ginny reached down to lather her crotch.

The smooth lips of Jordyn's pussy were so soft under Ginny's hand. "Guess the swelling went down okay." Should she attempt to bring it back? After a couple hours of sleep, Jordyn might be recharged enough to come to climax again. But they should probably pump first. Ginny contented herself with parting Jordyn's slit and drawing a finger the length of her wetness.

Jordyn hadn't stopped fondling Ginny's breasts. "My bras don't fit right, and it's only been a few days." She tickled both nipples at once and then reached for the hand sprayer. The stream washed all the bubbles down Ginny's skin.

"Me too." Ginny turned from side to side under the spray. "I was going to ask Elspeth to refit me, but now I'm kind of afraid to ask her for anything at all."

"You should be fine. You did really well once she finished bitching. And they really should tell us what they plan to do." Jordyn aimed the water into Ginny's pussy. "I guess I'm more ready to go with the flow."

Oh that felt nice! Ginny spread her legs to get the spray where she wanted it. Jordyn played the stream of water from clit to hole and back again. "I'm always asking questions." Ginny sighed. "It gets me into trouble sometimes." She suddenly thought of a question that hadn't been answered when she'd asked. "What did you find that made you shriek when you were looking for the clipper?"

Jordyn paused with the water pounding on Ginny's butthole. "Enemas. Do you really think we need those?"

Ginny's hole clenched at the very thought. She took the sprayer away from Jordyn and began to rinse her friend off. "I hope it's for 'just in case.' I really hate having things stuck up my butt."

"Dr. Busby does like to take temperatures there," Jordyn sighed. "Says he's measuring our basal rates so he'll know when we're ovulating. He thinks our cycles matter to beginning lactation."

"So that's why he keeps doing that." Ginny had gritted her teeth and let Dr. Busby insert the thermometer this morning without discussion.

"A question you didn't ask!" Jordyn laughed. "It's nicer when there's a bit of romantic intention, some kissing, all that." Jordyn leaned over to kiss Ginny lightly. "He's a little unclear about science and sex sometimes." She didn't say whether she'd enlightened the doctor.

Once they were clean, they grabbed their pumps and headed to Heidi's room. She was already showered and partly dressed, although her bra looked like it didn't fit much better than Ginny's now, or Jordyn's. All three girls had enlarged substantially after days of consistent pumping.

"Back to the salt mines," Heidi said, fiddling with the hoses of her pump. All three young women opened their bras and affixed the collectors to their breasts.

"I'll be so glad when our milk comes in. We haven't really been outside for a walk or anything since we've been here." Ginny watched Heidi's nipples swell into the tubes. Their color had deepened to a luscious plum. "Maybe then we can do more."

"That would be nice," Jordyn agreed. "Then it could be 'see a cow, have an orgasm, see a bird, give some milk, see another cow, have an orgasm.'"

"If you meet up with Horace again, you could see a cow, give some milk, and have an orgasm all at the same time." Ginny had to razz Heidi a little.

"Oh you!" Heidi tugged playfully at Ginny's long blond hair, which she had styled into low pigtails. "He's really not so old, you know. And he has a very large cock."

So did Dr. Busby. "Do you think Dirk has a big prick too?" Ginny wondered aloud.

"Yes." Jordyn said one word and then went silent and red.

"Tell us more, girlfriend!" Heidi urged her. Jordyn kept her lips shut tight and pretended to fix her pump, but Heidi and Ginny clamored for details.

"After you went and wore Dr. Busby out yesterday, we had to call Dirk when it was time for my prostaglandins," Jordyn finally admitted. "He has a lovely 'applicator' and he applies it very nicely. About seven and a half inches and very thick. He applied it again this morning."

And if she hadn't been such a priss, Ginny might have found out for herself. "Cut or uncut?"

"Cut." Jordyn licked her lips. Who had been applying what to whom?

"Dr. Busby's uncut," Ginny said. She'd noticed that much before she flounced out.

"And who knows about Horace?" Heidi muttered.

"I'm sure he'd show you if you asked," Jordyn teased. Heidi hit her with a pillow.

The pillows flew fast and hard, and everyone's collectors got knocked off before they ran out of weapons. Jordyn fell of the bed and landed with a thump, and Ginny's elastic bands were half out and her hair askew, but they were all laughing hysterically, so what did it matter if Heidi was all tangled up in her open bra?

"We still have another five minutes to pump," Jordyn noted once they'd gathered themselves.

"Pump, shmump." Heidi held out her open arms to her friends. "Come suck on me, and we'll take turns sucking everyone."

Ginny and Jordyn stared at each other for a second, and dove at Heidi as one.

Oh, to have that big, firm tit in her mouth! Ginny had to steady Heidi's breast in both hands. Taking a good look—for aim, she told herself, but she really did love looking at that round, plum-colored nipple in the center of its crinkly areola—she smiled, and then latched on firmly.

Oh, Heidi's breast was as delicious as any cock Ginny'd ever sucked—maybe better, because anything that squirted out of her nipple would be sweet milk, meant to be drunk. Meant to feed the lucky person who suckled her. Ginny pulled hard on her mouthful, then rested and tickled the tip with her tongue. She suckled again, maintaining a steady rhythm. Those generous breasts would nourish the drinker with the creamy white fluid that Ginny swallowed down.

Wha—? Ginny pulled off, staring at the white pearls forming on the tip of Heidi's nipple.

"Is everything okay?" Heidi worried.

"You're—you're lactating!" Ginny slurped at Heidi's breast. "You're giving milk!"

"I am?" She pulled her breasts away from her sucklers and tried to look at her nipples. She squeezed one and a fine spray flew into Jordyn's face.

119

"Yes!" Jordyn shouted, and dove back onto the teat. "Mmf, mff!"

"I'm giving milk!" Heidi shouted. "But let go!"

Both blondes pulled away, startled. Heidi groped for her pumps. "I have to have something to prove it! You can't drink up every drop of my first milk." She stuck the horns onto her breasts and hit the switch.

All three girls stared as Heidi's nipples gave up their milk—white spray became white drops in the collectors and ran down in tiny streams to the bottles. The *whum whum* of the pump became the *spss spss* they'd heard when Elspeth had pumped for them, although milk wasn't flowing into the bottles nearly as fast.

"Maybe...." Jordyn breathed, transfixed. She grabbed her collectors and fumbled them onto her breasts.

Ginny shook herself and affixed her collectors too, hoping against hope that milk would miraculously flow from her breasts as well. Would pumping be enough, even without semen to jump start her? Oh how she wanted to lactate! A tear trickled down her cheek. She was happy for Heidi, but would she ever have this joy too? She closed her eyes, willing her breasts to provide.

The pump suckled at her, getting nothing. Maybe the big milkers would be better—Ginny would spend every minute possible in the stanchion if that would help. And maybe Horace would come to check, and think she was the blonde who didn't have to use condoms. He might help a girl out. He could call her a heifer or even a cow if he could make her give milk like Heidi.

Maybe she'd beg Dr. Busby, promise to be cooperative and charming if he'd just fuck her until she milked. Or Dirk—he'd see the benefit of having a happy dairy maid who gave plenty of milk and think it was more important than stupid old science. She'd play with herself every possible minute, even have that forbidden eleventh orgasm if it would help.

But nothing flowed from Ginny's nipples. And then Jordyn sang out—"Yes!"

Ginny's eyes snapped open.

Jordyn jiggled her breasts with excitement, one huge breast in each hand, holding the collectors on. "Oh my goodness! I'm milking too!"

Damn it! Ginny's nipples expanded into the tubing and shrank again, yielding nothing. "That's—that's great." She wanted to be happy for her friends, but when her own chances seemed so slim, it was hard to smile and be sincere. She watched the milk dribble into Jordyn and Heidi's bottles.

"If it's only four days to milk with prostaglandins, honey, it can't be much longer for you." Heidi divined the problem. "You'll make lots of milk soon."

"We'll nurse on you lots," Jordyn promised. "We have to be the three amigas, so we'll help you bring your milk."

"And let you nurse on us too," Heidi offered. "Maybe drinking the milk helps bring your milk."

Ginny was pretty sure it didn't work that way, but it couldn't hurt, and she did like it. But so did all the guests who came to vacation at the Manley Dairy, and they paid to do it. She couldn't ask her friends to give up their bonuses. "Thanks, guys." She sniffled. "I'm really glad for you."

"And you'll catch up, really you will," Heidi reached out to pat Ginny's shoulder.

They watched, fascinated, as milk pooled in the small bottles on Jordyn and Heidi's collectors, and everyone averted their eyes from Ginny's empty bottles. When Heidi had a little less than two ounces from each side, the trickles stopped coming, though she left the pump on. Jordyn's breasts were exhausted a little later. She'd given about an ounce from each side. Ginny squeezed her breasts hard, hoping to get a drip or two, but—nothing.

"Let's show Elspeth and Dirk!" Heidi cried. She scrambled into her clothing.

So did Jordyn. "Yes, and Ginny, you have to come with us." She poked one of Ginny's swollen breasts. "You need to get new bras so these enormous boobs get good support. I just know there's milk in there waiting to get out. Come on, girl!" She shooed Ginny into her red skirt.

They ran up the hill, Heidi and Jordyn with a bottle in each hand, and all three of them with an arm across their chest to keep from bouncing wildly. Ginny ran most slowly—she had the least to run for, and she kept her milkshake joke to herself.

"Wonderful!" Dirk collected the bottles and made some notes in his laptop."You just finished pumping? Very good volume for a first milk, both of you. Now—what about quality?"

Ginny shuddered—she didn't know how she or any of the dairy maids could affect the quality—didn't boobies just do what boobies do?

Dirk unscrewed the cap from one of Heidi's jars and took a sip. He rolled it around on his tongue as if he were tasting wine, and swallowed thoughtfully. "Nice, Heidi, very nice." He drank the rest and grinned. "You got the hind milk. Now that you're producing, you need to watch your diet even more carefully. We won't feed you any more coleslaw, especially once our next set of guests arrives." He wrote her name and date on the jar and stowed it in the fridge. "Now yours, Jordyn."

Again he tasted, swishing the sample over every taste bud. Jordyn held her breath. Ginny held Jordyn's hand, and thought her fingers might be crushed before Dirk made his pronouncement.

"Lovely flavor, Jordyn. Good consistency for a first milk. Of course, this will change with time, but a very nice start." He sipped the rest of that small sample, and Jordyn started breathing again. Ginny rubbed her bruised fingers. Jordyn's second jar, labeled, went into the fridge with Heidi's.

"Ginny?" Dirk regarded her. She said nothing. "It is a little soon. But don't worry—your friends have both started unusually early. I frankly wasn't expecting anyone to begin lactating until next week."

He gathered them all to sit around the big dining table. "I'll explain what happens next. Ginny, stay with us, you'll need to know this

122

soon, I'm sure." His smile was probably supposed to be reassuring, but Ginny didn't want any more assurances—she wanted to lactate!

"You did right to bring your milk here immediately. You'll take your bottles to the milkhouse after this—that's the low red building with the white gables, and they'll be checked in, and possibly shipped around the world. Your volumes will be recorded and credited to you. First milks are highly prized by some of our guests—we'll have an auction of those two bottles, and your bonuses will be a percentage of the price, over and above the milk scale."

Elspeth came around the corner just then, a stack of folded dish towels in her hands. She must have caught the tail of Dirk's words. "First milks! Already? Who?" She set her load down and went around hugging anyone who looked happy. She paused at Ginny, and then hugged anyway. "Your turn is coming soon," she whispered. Ginny leaned her head against Elspeth's huge breasts, needing the comfort. Elspeth cradled her head briefly and then plopped into the next chair and reached for Ginny's hand under the table. Ginny squeezed back.

"Did you explain about first feedings, Dirk?" she asked.

He smiled. "I was just getting there. Girls, you'll do two first feedings. If you're willing, that is. One is required, because it's part of your training, but after that it's your choice. The mandatory one—" He smiled broadly. "—is me. I'm your trainer for this. One session is usually enough, darn it." He poked his lower lip out and made everyone laugh.

"But since our guests want your milk enough to make reservations months in advance, I have to restrain myself. And the second first feeding, and I suppose that does sound weird, is your first feeding of a guest. Again, this is an auction situation, but we restrict the bidders to guests you've chosen. We'll let you mingle with the guests, and you may give tokens to anyone who strikes your fancy. And once bidding is done, you'll provide the best feeding you can. Whether or not this involves "dessert with whipped cream" (here Dirk made air quotes with his fingers) is up to you."

123

Dairy Maid

"You'll pump every four hours until you've made up your minds about the bidders. We suggest you select four or five. That brings the price up the best. Too few and they don't get frenzied, too many and they get dejected." Elspeth squeezed Ginny's fingers again. "And then they start to think that second feeding might not taste much different."

Who would have thought there was a strategy to nursing? Ginny began to appreciate Elspeth more.

Elspeth rose from her chair. "Come upstairs, girls. Looks like we have another bra fitting to do, and a uniform change!"

They followed her up, exchanging shy glances. Heidi and Jordyn already had the prospects of pleasing their guests. Ginny wondered miserably if some guests wanted to dry-suckle. She'd rather give milk, but if she was still dry, that would be an opportunity…

"Off with those red trainee skirts, my dears," Elspeth said, and didn't extend her orders to Ginny.

Ginny sat back on the bed, knowing this wouldn't be about her. Her friends unsnapped their waistbands and undid their suspenders, shedding red as if it were soaked. Heidi's large, dimpled thighs took Ginny's gaze—she'd had her head between them to lap at sweet pussy juices, so hadn't she helped bring Heidi's milk in?

Jordyn lifted her arms, raising the hem of her white shirt. Her pink lacy panties flashed below. Ginny knew what lay under the lace. She'd pressed her tongue into that hairless pussy and flicked until Jordyn screamed. And she'd do it again as soon as Jordyn would hold still for it. But would she even want to, now that her milk was here and the guests would be vying for the opportunity?

Ginny felt left out already, and her friends had done nothing to make her feel excluded. She wasn't being fair, she knew, but she wanted to lactate too, and would they have time to help her or the desire to play with her?

"Pale blue checks now, girls." Elspeth handed out new skirts. "This marks you as beginning milkers. Our guests won't expect huge volumes from you, and they'll know to be especially gentle since you're new."

"You're dressed in dark blue," Jordyn pointed out as she fastened her suspenders. "How do we get to that color?"

Elspeth smiled, straightening Heidi's waistband and smoothing the rump of her skirt, something she did rather slowly and provocatively. "You have to be in the top rank of producers. Once you can pump five ounces per breast every six hours, you'll get medium blue checks, and if you can average nine ounces per breast every six hours, then dark blue. I meant it when I said I need all the milk I can make, because it's not easy to maintain that level of production." She paused to adjust one of her breasts within her bra. "There are only a few of us in dark blue."

Ginny hated her red checks all the more. She'd go back and pump for two more hours once they were done.

"Now for bras." Elspeth turned Heidi toward her and slipped the elastic neckline of her blouse down her arms. Her huge breasts hadn't deflated much for yielding their milk, and stuck proudly out from her chest. "All of you need refitting already!"

"I haven't worn but two of my new bras yet," Heidi complained good-naturedly, letting Elspeth measure. She modeled her new size in the mirror. "I didn't know there was such a thing as an E cup."

"Some bra makers call them DDD," Elspeth commented. "I think the biggest in my chest of drawers at the moment is an H. We had a dairy maid who wore an L cup, but she left us about six months ago to get married."

"To a guest?" Jordyn wondered. There didn't seem to be a lot of other ways to meet men out here at the dairy.

"Oh yes." Elspeth smiled. "I was her dairy maid of honor. We hosted the ceremony here, because so many of the groom's friends need human milk. It was a charming wedding."

Great. One more thing that was beyond Ginny's hopes if she didn't start lactating. She poked her balky breast and hoped no one saw.

Jordyn's new bras had lacy flowers to match her underwear, and sported an E cup as well. "Oh, yes, this is more comfortable." She cradled her huge breasts, lifting them up and sighing. "Much better. Come on, Gin, your turn." She let go of her tits and offered a hand to Ginny, who rose reluctantly. She was the last dairy maid in red.

Elspeth pulled Ginny's neckline away from her chest and peered in. "Oh yes, dear, your cups do runneth over. Let's get you fitted."

The tape measure chafed Ginny's well-exercised nipples, but she didn't say a word. Instead she tried on the first bra Elspeth handed her. She tried to seat her breasts in the cups, but something pinched. "I don't think this is quite right."

Elspeth frowned. "No, the separation isn't what you need." She dug in the chest. "Try this one."

Much better. Ginny's breasts felt well-supported, and the bra was very pretty, even if it was huge. She'd never imagined needing an F cup. "This feels really good." She admired herself in the mirror. Her tits had certainly expanded in a few short days.

"Looks good," Heidi said from her spot on the bed.

"Let's see if it comes off good." Jordyn came to undo the front clasp that suddenly felt very fragile.

"Why?" Elspeth was confused. "Of course it does."

Ginny's breasts spilled out of their shimmery white prison. Jordyn cupped them, her hands overwhelmed with creamy flesh tipped in pink.

"Because we promised Ginny we'd suck on her nipples and help her milk come in," Jordyn explained, her eyes on the hard nubbins her thumbs could barely reach. "And we haven't yet. Heidi, let's keep our promise."

"Of course." Heidi came to stand at Ginny's side.

Her friends steered Ginny backward—she bumped into the end of the bed and sat with a flop. They scooted her up to the pillows and made her lie back. Looking up at them was like looking at a solid wall of breasts. Then they cuddled up to her, one on each side, and took hold of her breasts. Her nipples stared up blindly at them.

"'Scuse us, Elspeth, we have some sucking to do." Heidi put her mouth down on Ginny's breast and began to turn lazy trails around the nipple. Her tongue was pointed and very wet. Ginny moaned.

"I'd better see how you're doing," Elspeth commented. "That's a good latch, Jordyn."

Oh yes it was! Jordyn had a big mouthful of Ginny's breast and was suckling away. She held Ginny's breast in both hands, and nursed greedily, much like Heidi did, once she'd drawn lots of wet tracks over the bumps and crinkles of Ginny's areola. Ginny moaned again, and stroked her friends' hair. She hoped they wouldn't bump heads leaning over her like that, and sucking on her needy breasts. Would one of them shout for joy of getting a taste of milk?

Elspeth watched them with approval. Her nipples had grown hard—they showed clearly though her bra and blouse. Her eyes went hooded, and her lips parted. "You're doing very well, girls. Suck those nipples. Suck them hard."

Ginny smiled. Her friends were following instructions beautifully, and not only were her nipples hard, so was her clit. And she couldn't reach it! Heidi and Jordyn were so intent on suckling that they weren't trying to slide a hand under her skirt. They'd find a juicy, horny pussy under there if they did.

Elspeth watched them with one hand to tweak her nipple through her clothing, and the other starting to rub her crotch through her skirt. Why was she just standing there pleasing herself when she could be helping? Ginny crossed her legs and gave a good squeeze with her thighs. It wasn't much, but it was nice, and her friends would make her come if they suckled long enough. Ginny hadn't quit being a nine, or maybe a nine and a half, for nipple sensitivity. But she had gotten spoiled about getting her cunt played with too. She squeezed her thighs tighter again.

"You two are a little too single-minded about sucking her," Elspeth chided. She climbed on the bed with them and shoved Ginny's knees apart.

That was more like it. Elspeth pushed Ginny's skirt up around her waist and hooked her fingers into the panties' elastic band. Ginny helped by lifting her hips and then her feet, and those pesky panties got out of everyone's way. Ginny parted her knees and gave Elspeth a good look at what she'd uncovered.

Running a thumb up Ginny's slit let Elspeth dip into the juice pooling between wet, red lips. She was very slick, and Elspeth brought that moisture up to the needy clit that poked out of its hood. A small noise grew in Ginny's throat, and it sounded like 'More."

Elspeth dipped the juice up from Ginny's pussy, painting circles and lines onto her stiff clit, with another hand on her own nipple. Ginny's nipples were getting the royal treatment, with suckling and licking, and when Jordyn nipped lightly with the very edge of teeth, Ginny cried out and doubled up, pushing her clit harder onto Elspeth's hand. Shocks reverberated from nipples to pussy—Ginny cried out again, yearning for more pressure, more movement, more—

And Elspeth gave it. With a practiced movement, she slid two fingers into Ginny's pussy and rubbed more small circles on that demanding clit. She found the G spot, and Ginny's world went swimmy, with the waves of pleasure that blossomed in her cunt, growing like a spreading rose, all the way to her breasts. Oh! That should push milk out of her nipples—her body couldn't contain anything as marvelous as this orgasm—Ginny climaxed around Elspeth's hand.

"Suck, girls, suck!" Elspeth commanded them, as if they weren't already. Would Ginny's nipples explode the way her cunt was exploding? Little *oh, oh, ohs* came from her throat. And then Elspeth sucked too.

She put her face down between Ginny's legs and slurped her hard clit between those expressive lips, suckling as if she expected milk to gush from there. Jordyn and Heidi squeezed her breasts, redoubling their efforts on her nipples. With three to suckle on her, Ginny yielded up everything in a crash of joy that consumed her body and blanked her mind. White sparks showered through her vision and she hoped white showers would spurt from her breasts, but that hope was very faint in the incandescence of her orgasm. And then all she could do was feel, as the climax rattled her again and again, shooting from the nipple Heidi suckled to the nipple Jordyn laved, and down to her joyful nubbin between Elspeth's lips and the hot spot she pressed within Ginny's pussy.

At last the orgasm faded—her three friends had provided her with a triple delight that lasted triple-long. Ginny collapsed into a boneless heap, unable to even hold her hands up to stroke her sucklers. A low sound trickled from her throat.

Elspeth sat up slowly and withdrew her fingers, which gave Ginny one last pleasurable contraction. Heidi and Jordyn let go as well, and the three of them gazed down on Ginny's heaving chest. Her breasts jiggled with each breath.

"Perfect, girls. That should bring Ginny along quite nicely," Elspeth pronounced, wiping her mouth. She dug this room's pump out from under the bed and placed the collecting horns on the moving targets that were Ginny's nipples. "Now, you lie here and pump, and you two—" She waved Heidi and Jordyn toward the door. "Go get some sun. You have approximately two and a half hours before you need to meet here with Dirk for training." She winked. "And whatever you do, don't go hide in that nice little glade among the hickory trees by the pond, even if it is the perfect place to get frisky with each other." She flipped her fingers, *shoo! shoo!* at them, and they bent to kiss Ginny quickly before running away hand in hand.

"And you, Ginny—" Elspeth bent to kiss her as well, with the tang of pussy on her breath. "—I believe you're doing just fine."

Chapter 11 Return of the Dairy Maids

The vibrator slid from her cunt, its buzzing exit marking the end of her milking session. The rhythmic, rolling pressure on her teats halted. She blinked in the sudden light—her blindfold no longer covered her eyes.

Ginny wanted to stretch. Once Dirk released her stanchion, Ginny stood up and reached out for the rafters, uncoiling her limbs. It felt wonderful, but—! She checked her bottles. Empty. Again. Would her breasts never release their milk? After two hours on the milking machine, they should have filled the containers, but not a drop yet.

She stole a glance to her friends' produce. Heidi and Jordyn both had filled their bottles around the three ounce mark. At this rate, they'd be trading their sky-blue newbie skirts for a deeper color very soon. They'd come along to keep her company as much as to get the better draining from the professional equipment. For them, two hours on the machine wasn't necessary and only confused their production statistics. But they were very good friends.

"Sore, Ginny?" Dirk reached out with a blob of ointment on a fingertip. "You've expanded so much I'm surprised you haven't let down by now."

"I'm not sore, but I'm just really tired of not lactating." Ginny cradled her breasts, lifting them for Dirk to apply the ointment to her tired nipples. She'd gone up another cup size since Thursday. Three days, bigger boobs, and no milk. She sniffled a little. Jordyn and Heidi came to hug her, carefully arranging their enormous tits around her.

"Soon, honey, soon," they murmured.

Ginny hoped they were right. "Um, it would be sooner if I got a prostaglandin treatment." She smiled brightly at Dirk, hoping he'd see the wisdom of laying her down right there on the bench, or in that little glade by the pond, or in her bedroom. Anywhere he'd go bare. She'd gotten nowhere with Dr. Busby on that, and she couldn't bring herself to ask Horace. Even now that he could tell Ginny from Jordyn when they were milking, he still preferred Heidi. A little trail of come trickled down Heidi's inner thigh now.

"Sorry, Ginny." Dirk hefted her breasts, judging their engorgement for himself. "Dr. Busby'd turn me into a steer if I wrecked his experiment, and I like being a bull."

Maybe the guests wouldn't know about her restriction. But the doctor would swab her, and that would be the end of her career, even if it brought her milk. And then she'd be fired, out in the world, gushing milk, and no way to benefit from it. She'd have to keep pumping until it happened. Ginny sniffled again.

He let go of her breasts. "A little friendly get to know you with a condom on, we could do that if you liked."

Now she really was going to cry. "I think we should multitask if we're going to do it." Since when did a man insist on using a condom? Usually they whined about having to wear a raincoat.

For answer, he handed her a bra. "Go get some real sleep, Ginny."

The three dairy maids walked back to the dorm, and curled up together for their nap. "It can't be much longer, Gin," Jordyn whispered after diddling her to the orgasm the vibrator left her primed for.

Heidi had already come from Horace's attentions but didn't mind cumming again. She had one hand in her crotch and her other hand in Jordyn's. "Real soon, baby. JJ and I were just early." She doubled over, moaning, and Jordyn fell face first into Ginny's breasts, panting hard.

They woke to laughter and excited chatter in the great room. "How was Mexico?" "Wonderful! How was Scotland?" "He liked cream for his parritch! Haha!" and other snatches of conversation came to them. They jumped up to dress and see who had invaded their quiet dorm.

"Oh, look! Newbies!" A lovely brunette with an extraordinarily huge bustline noticed them. "Come out, honeys, and meet the rest of the crew." Two suitcases lay at her feet, and a profusion of other beautiful women, all dressed in casual clothing, and every single one with breasts that tested their shirts to the max, clustered in the communal room. "I'm Kitty; who are you?"

The girls stammered their names, and a storm of "I'm Patti" and "I'm Emily" and "India" and "Mindy" and "Sailor" and "Taylor" and "Brianna" and more washed over them. Who was who? They'd have to figure it out soon! Have to know who was hugging on them so hard.

"It's fine to see you, sweetcakes!" India roared. She was a luscious black woman with a profusion of waist length braids. "We need some good boobies around here! Big ol' milky boobies!" She honked Jordyn's breasts with both hands. "We can't hardly feed all the hungry men!" And when she turned to Heidi, it was a big grin. "Good thing you two are spewin' the white stuff. Lactate away, girlfriends." She hugged Ginny hard. "Damn, girl, those are the biggest, hardest tits I ever did feel. When they gonna give some milk?" She yanked Ginny's suspenders down and pulled her elastic neckline below her tits. Of course she could tell the state of Ginny's lactation from the color of her skirt. Dammit! "We gotta see these big ol' boobies, chickie."

Ginny didn't know what to do! Sure she'd peeled down for Dr. Busby, Dirk, and Elspeth, but they were staff. And for her girlfriends, of course, but they were buddies and if they saw, or touched, or sucked, it was all between friends. She wanted to throw her hands over her breasts, but there was nothing on her chest that two little hands could cover up, so she didn't even try. Instead she stuck her chest out proudly. Maybe she'd put this India's eye out with a hard nipple.

133

"Ohh!" A general moan went around the room. "Gonna be a contendah!" "How much milk is in there!?" "Son of a bitch, those are big." "Bigger than you, honey," and "Mmm, those need to be tasted!" Hands plucked at her bra, opening the front clasp that put up no fight at all.

Ginny looked at her friends for help, but they were getting peeled too. Jordyn's gigantic breasts lay open to everyone's eyes, and Heidi fended off more hands, but ineffectually. Someone hugged Ginny from behind and caught her wrist in one hand. Someone else caught her other hand and *sproing!* Out came her titties! The fabric that had covered her offered no shelter at all.

"Oooh, look at her!"

"Bend over, honeys, we gotta see how them boobies hang down." India pushed Ginny toward the big ottoman. "Lean over. We gotta check." Others guided Jordyn to the ottoman and someone pushed a chair over for Heidi.

"Oh, look!" "Yes, indeed, aren't they pretty!"

Pretty was not Ginny's first thought. Her breasts swung freely, and her nipples had to be down by her elbows. Nothing but the insubstantial air supported their swollen bulk. Beside her Jordyn tried to still her swaying breasts, much to the displeasure of the crowd gawking at them.

"Let 'em swing, girlfriend!" Someone reached an unhelpful hand under Jordyn and pushed, making her swing and jiggle. While she was unhelping, she batted at Ginny, making her tits swing like udders and her face flame. They must look like a row of cows. Heidi's breasts oscillated like fleshy pendulums. Ginny's back bowed under the weight of her breasts, and Jordyn's attempts to still herself only made her tits swing unevenly—she swayed as much as Ginny did. All their new companions knelt, craned, and shoved to see them. Some reached to touch, pinching nipples or pushing breasts into greater arcs. A sea of faces and reaching hands made Ginny dizzy—she would have stood straight if hands hadn't pressed her shoulders.

"Yummy!" and "Gotta taste that!" chorused around them. "I wanna lick!" "No, me!" "Me!" Hey, they each have two! Don't fight!" The experienced dairy maids clamored for a chance at the newbies' breasts.

"Everyone can have a taste!" rang out the voice of reason. India. "Two at a time, girls." The pushing hands became helpful, lifting Ginny upright and then snaking around from behind to cop a feel that roused the sleeping cat between her legs.

The girls surged at them, and Ginny had two lovelies sucking on her titties. Oh, but these gals knew what they were doing! As good as her friends could suckle, these two knew their way around breasts even better, although Ginny would deduct points for not asking and for being strangers. But they knew what to do with their lips and tongues. If her nipples could have cheered, she would have been deaf. Yay for being a nine, or maybe a nine and a half!

Her clit poked out from between her lower lips, demanding to be introduced to the charming people who were sucking on her upper nubs. Ginny dropped kisses on the red head and the brunette who suckled at her nipples. Names? Who needed names? Except to find the owners of such talented mouths again. Taylor? Mindy? Chelle? Who cared when it felt that good?

But they all felt that good. A shuffling occurred somewhere down the impromptu line and then Ginny found a Hispanic girl whose name she couldn't say—Luz?—and a brunette slurping her nipples. Would they get milk? A hand approached from behind and below, finding her pussy. Ginny threw her head back, reveling in the attention.

The hand snaked up and over her panties, tickling her asshole on the way by. But those fingers wanted her juicy cunny—they traveled over, under, and back, touching lightly on places she'd always thought she'd keep to herself—until lately—and slid into her suddenly hot and wet tunnel. One finger slithered in, rotating around and finding good spots with every rotation. *Mmmmm!* Ginny spread her legs.

Strong fingers wound into her long blond hair, reaching through her loose tresses and cupping the back of her head. Her head got yanked back abruptly, and a woman without a name thrust her tongue into Ginny's mouth. She probed expertly, demanding a response. Ginny thrust her tongue back at her kisser—what else should she do when her whole body was being stimulated so skillfully? Ginny would cum any second now.

Two fingers! Oh! What sparks they were stroking from her pussy! Thrusting back against the hand that wanted to fill her cunt, and that now pulled back enough to expand their offering, Ginny demanded the best that hand had to offer. Three fingers—good offer! Ginny humped the hand that filled her. "Suck harder!" she demanded. "More tongue!"

And she got more tongue. And more fingers—they crushed her G spot and fucked her cunt. Another hand invaded from the front—her clit got captured between expert fingers that stroked up and down. And more mouth—tongues flickered against her nipples. More hands squeezed her breasts without her asking, pumping her swollen breasts to the point of pain, pushing her rosy nipples into mouths that didn't give a fuck about introducing themselves. Pleasure and pain mingled. Wild flicking at her extravagantly enlarged tits made her scream aloud, "Yes! Yes! Don't stop!"

They didn't. Oh, no, they didn't. Ginny's climax stole her sight, stole her senses, gave her incandescence and joy. Her nipples flared, talking to her clit and her cunt, taking her eyesight in a white flame and her hearing in a roaring of meaningless noise. Except—it meant *Yes! Fuck me more! Yes!* And they did, even when her knees buckled and she fell onto her tormentors, who insisted on pleasuring her until her senses could no longer cope. She fell, and the hands and tongues followed her down. Down and yet higher, with sparks and screams, with contractions and flames, with cumming and delight beyond words.

Over and over her pussy jerked and contracted, her clit sang and flickered. Eager hands grabbed at her pleasure, demanding to share. A lone finger diddled at her clit, prolonging her cum until she thought she might die happy. "Ah!" she cried wordlessly, unable to tell her coterie that they'd done what she'd wanted. Needed. Required. And still that finger vibrated her clit. "Oh! she exhaled, and the pleasure outlasted her consciousness, the last contractions taking her mind into oblivion. "Oh...."

BUT NO MILK. Ginny came to without a drop of moisture at her nipples.

"It's okay, Gin-gin," a soft voice murmured. Was this Taylor, or Sailor, or Patti? Did it matter?

"Look at how her titties are the same shape as India's," that soft voice insisted. "They'll be perfect together. Our guests will love that. Chocolate and vanilla swirl. Oh, the bonuses!"

Only if her breasts gave milk like India's, Ginny worried. India's voice had that dark-blue commanding tone to it.

"Naw, India and Heidi have the same body type—our guests won't be able to resist. 'Her Fleshness Black' has 'Her Fleshness White' to be a team now. She won't need this one." A derisive finger poked Ginny's tit.

"But she looks so much like Jordyn," another voice insisted. "Bet they were hired for their looks. Blonde and tiny waists. Long hair. Almost the same color."

"Then she better make milk, or it won't matter," another voice suggested. "She's still wearing red. Jordyn's in blue. They have to match or the guests won't believe the twin act."

"Early days yet," a deeply sonorous voice insisted. "She hasn't been here a week."

"Special snowflake!" the tit-poker mocked. "She was out cold from cumming!"

"You used to pass out from cumming, and make others pass out too," the deep voice insisted. "Now you just want head and never give back. Oughta whip your ass for that. And I think I want to whip you just for pissing me off. Make red marks on your butt-tocks. See the lines bloom 'cross your ass. Put some red slashes 'cross your butt 'cause you can't see the good in no one. These girls be sweet. Pure. They want to feed the world with their titties. Not like you, just want the bonuses. Your milk be sour. Like your mind be sour. These girls be good. They gonna nurture. They gonna feed the hungry and love the sad ones. You don't love no one but you, and you don't love you much. These girls, they gonna do good in the world with their milk and their hearts. So you shut your mouth."

"You talk too much, you old black cunt!"

Flesh against flesh sounded—hands against face. A chorus of "Get out of here, bitch!" and "good riddance to bad garbage!" chased the nasty one away.

India knelt next to her. "Don't pay no mind to that sour-puss Rita. She ain't no good an' I don't know why Dirk keeps her. The rest of us, we wanna be friends."

"We want to be friends, too." Ginny let India and another girl help her off the floor. They'd been pretty friendly already.

Chapter 12 The Guests Arrive

Ginny and her friends were on hand to greet the first arriving guests. The men trickled in one and two at a time, in limos and late model vehicles, running heavily to the luxury end of the spectrum. Her cheeks hurt from smiling, and she might have burned out her blush. Of course these men were going to be interested in her breasts—they'd come to spend valuable time one on one with breasts. She tried not to lose her cheer when some of them turned away from her to the other girls, all dressed in shades of blue. She had nothing fluid to offer yet, and her red checked skirt announced that.

A few of the men gave her particularly warm greetings though, and one whispered that he'd love to taste her first milk, should that occur this week. He gave her a sweet kiss on the cheek, and she made a note of his name. Her chest hurt from the hugging and she expected to leave each newcomer's embrace with wet spots on her shirt and his.

But nothing yet.

"What do we do with them?" Ginny asked India, who did indeed sport the same deep hue as Elspeth.

"They on vacation, honey. They here to have a good time." India paused to give a particularly warm greeting to a distinguished older man who called her by name and whispered something in her ear that made her laugh. "Hang out with 'em, go riding with them, hell, play checkers if you want to. And if they want to suckle, you let 'em."

"Even if I have no milk?" Ginny whispered back.

"They help you get milk, and if they get an accidental mouthful, well, they be lucky dudes. And if they want to lift that little cotton skirt, you say yes or no as pleases you. 'Cept you do it with a condom like Doc Busby said." India put one strong arm around Ginny's shoulder. "This is a great place to work, you don't do nothing stupid to get sent away."

Did *everyone* know about her and the prostaglandins? Ginny discovered her blush wasn't burnt out after all.

Dinner that night was in the big barn, where the dairy maids outnumbered the guests, all of whom seemed to be repeat visitors. The distinguished older gentleman selected Heidi, who looked adorable in her crisp blue skirt, and India to sit with him, and the laughter from that table was loud and frequent. The other guests dined with dairy maids, and in one case, they dined on the dairy maid.

Two men had a pert redhead whom Ginny thought she might have met earlier in that jumble of hands and mouths. She sat on the table where plates should be, her white peasant blouse pulled down below her breasts in that way that was becoming so familiar. She had one man on each breast, nursing from her. She stroked their hair as they took long pulls on her nipples, gazing down fondly at them.

"Right here in the dining room?" Ginny would have thought nursing would be a little more private.

"Those two have severe food allergies, and they'd still like to eat socially. It's eating, so why not?" Brianna said. She and Kitty had taken Jordyn and Ginny to sit with them at dinner. "They share everything. When Mindy is dry they'll suckle Patti together." Lovely brunette Patti sat next to them, eating her dinner and waiting her turn.

"And maybe Luz if they're still hungry," Kitty added. "Luz and I are breakfast." She smiled. "They're sweet guys, and they like to taste everyone while they're here."

"What do they do when they aren't here?" Jordyn asked.

"All that milk we take to the milkhouse gets frozen and shipped out to men like them. They get to thaw little white popsicles and drink their dinner. Not nearly as much fun." Kitty took another forkful of their buckwheat noodles.

Dinner tonight was much blander and contained no wheat or dairy. So as not to pass on anything in their milk, Ginny supposed. She understood better what Dirk meant about eating from the guests' menu and why.

"Are all of our guests food-intolerant?"

"No, not at all!" Kitty laughed. "Some of them just like their milk fresh from the source. And a few—" She looked around the dining room. "—will spend some time in the nursery. I'll be babysitting later in the week." She giggled. "My little darling comes in Wednesday. Of course, my little darling is six foot three. Good thing he doesn't get too naughty, because trying to put him over my knee to spank would be a problem if he resisted." At Ginny's shocked look, Kitty elaborated. "Adult babies aren't that rare, Ginny. Adult babies who can afford to come here and get breastfed before naptime are rarer. It's their way of relaxing from the stress of adulthood. It's all negotiated ahead of time." She patted Ginny's hand, which dangled the fork loosely.

Dirk himself passed through the dining room, chatting with the guests and the dairy maids. He kept glancing toward the door, as if he expected someone to come through that hadn't shown up yet. He sat down in the open chair at Ginny's table with the plate he'd filled at the buffet.

"Getting a bird's-eye view of the festivities?" Dirk glanced at the door again, and then at Mindy being suckled.

"It's, um, different in reality." Ginny tried not to stare, but one of the men had left off sucking Mindy and was rearranging Patti's clothing to expose her swollen breasts. He licked one of her nipples. She giggled and hopped up on the table in the spot vacated by the redhead.

"Just remember that nothing happens here that isn't consensual." Dirk dug into his food. "I'm a little concerned—Roger Styles said he might be in tonight, and he's usually in for dinner. I'll have the kitchen keep a plate warm for him just in case he's really late."

141

"Is he coming in from Europe?" Brianna asked, her eyes bright. Looked like pretty Brianna had a soft spot for this guest.

"Paris. It might be midnight." Dirk glanced again.

"Oh. I'll have to pump before then," she sighed.

Hiding under the table sounded like a good idea to Ginny. Would she ever have something to offer a guest?

She and Jordyn were clearing tables in the nearly empty dining room when a tall, handsome man in a rumpled business suit came in and slid wearily into a chair. The noxious Rita, who had been clearing in another part of the room, spied him and ran to the kitchen. She reappeared with a plate and silverware, which she placed before him. She smiled and tried to sit down at table with him, but he waved her away. Did he know Rita, or did he want to be left alone?

Ginny wouldn't intrude on his meal, something all white that he didn't seem very pleased to eat. But wouldn't it be something he'd requested if the kitchen kept it especially for him? Ginny smiled hesitantly when he glanced up at her, but she didn't come forward. If he wanted her company, he'd make a gesture, surely. She finished clearing her tables and went out to stand on the veranda.

It really was pretty here, green fields and yellow fields where the hay had been cut. Pastures where the black and white cows stood. Red barns and outbuildings, which might not be very farmlike inside, but matched the surroundings. The duck pond, where two dairy maids and a guest were baiting a line. The sun lay low on the horizon. It wouldn't be dark any time soon, and she had a task yet to do.

"You must be new here." The late arriving guest spoke behind her. "I'm Roger."

He was even more handsome up close, with a dimple in his chin and straight dark brows over deep brown eyes. Ginny wished she could offer him the hospitality of her breasts. "I'm Ginny, and yes, I'm new."

"What do you see when you look out over this?" He stood next to her, his hands on the railing.

"A beautiful, fertile land, where everyone seems happy." Ginny could see Jordyn and some of the others setting up croquet on the lawn.

"Happiness. Not something often seen." He smiled down at her. "Would you like to go see the cows? I should finish my meal, but I wanted to catch you before you disappeared."

"Yes, Roger, please come finish your meal." Rita appeared on his other side. "I'm the only one still full—I was saving myself for you, and everyone else is drained." She slipped her hand through his arm. "It will be hours if you wait, and of course Ginny can't help you there, poor thing." She beamed up into his face.

"Damn, there is that. And I haven't eaten since I left Paris." Roger's face did look worn. "Maybe later?"

"That would be nice." Ginny didn't know which she hated more right now, Rita or her dry breasts.

"Shall we go somewhere comfy, Roger?" Rita simpered. That girl would lift her skirt for him herself in a heartbeat.

"The dining hall is fine; you can sit on the table." He gave Ginny a tired smile. "Later."

Rita threw a venomous look over her shoulder on the way back inside. "Leave him alone; he's *mine*," she hissed.

Bitch. Maybe she had milk, but she didn't have Roger. Dirk had said everything that happened around here was consensual, and Ginny hadn't heard Roger say to leave him be.

But damn. Rita had the milk, and Ginny needed to pump. She trudged back to the dorm. She sat in the white rocker on the porch with her little blue friend, waiting for Roger to come back and embark on a cow-viewing expedition. She pumped for two hours before she gave up.

ROGER DIDN'T SHOW up for breakfast either. If Rita had her way, she'd be feeding him breakfast in bed and then impaling herself on his cock. She was at breakfast, and glared daggers at Ginny throughout the meal.

"I wore him out," she snarked. "He doesn't need you."

If he didn't, he'd be the one to say. But Ginny's breasts ached with their fullness that wouldn't let down, and Rita sported medium blue checks on her skirt.

"Go suck an egg, beyotch." Heidi came up beside Ginny and stared defiantly at Rita.

"Language, language, girlfriends." India joined the clump of women. "Rita, I'm sure you have someone to feed or somewhere else to be, or some wine to curdle into vinegar. Go, on, git."

Rita "got", but not without a glare at Ginny.

"Don't mind her, but don't get into it with her either. And remember you're hospitality staff and talk hospitable, even to her." India hugged them with one arm apiece. "We don't drop to her level. And Heidi, you and I have an appointment with Mr. Bevington. We gonna play some cribbage and some drinking games." She winked. "And if you can't play cribbage, we skip to the drinking games."

"Drinking games? This early?" Heidi sounded scandalized.

"Honey, he drink from you, he drink from me, we play some games." India escorted Heidi away.

"Isn't there anything we could do to bring my milk on faster?" Ginny begged Dr. Busby while he took her temperature. She kept her knees splayed and didn't argue a bit when he pushed the thermometer into her butthole. Surely being good would get her the answers she needed?

He started to palpate her breasts with his fingertips before he answered. "Not without disturbing the data. Most of the other methods have dangers—there are medications that would promote lactation, but they would change your personality and I would be remiss to prescribe them—they're meant for other conditions which you don't have." He began to pull rhythmically at her nipples, one in each hand.

"I know you're anxious to begin lactating, but really, most of our dairy maids take longer than a week to get their milk. That month's trial is for a reason." He continued to milk her, although nothing squirted or dripped from her breasts. "You're pumping on the small pumps and using the big milking machine, and getting plenty of personal stimulation, right?"

Did that mean orgasms or being suckled on by people? "Uh, yes." She'd been getting both, courtesy of the other dairy maids. And she hadn't stopped being a nine, or maybe a nine and a half—what he was doing made it hard to think because her clit wanted in on the action. She could feel the moisture forming in her pussy. A droplet rolled down her crack to dampen her anus.

"Now that guests have come, you can have all the nursing you can coax them to do. That could be quite a lot." He continued pulling rhythmically on her breasts. "So don't despair."

But Ginny was despairing—her friends were off with the guests, who were delighting in the low ratio of guests to dairy maids and were behaving as if they were drunk, if they were seen at all. More guests arrived, but they were only polite to a dairy maid in red, and even the gentleman who wanted her first milk really wanted her milk, not her dry breasts. And Roger was nowhere to be seen. She was ready to go pump on the big milkers, but she couldn't reach the switch if she was in the stanchion and it wouldn't activate unless the stanchion was clicked closed. She gave up and went outside in search of someone to play with.

She didn't find anyone and wandered around the duck pond. Everyone was deeply absorbed in what they were doing, though Brianna and Kitty looked up from the men who lay in their laps suckling.

Sigh. Ginny found her way to the hickory grove. She peeked through the trees, recalling that there was a little glade that was fairly private. Maybe no one was using it. She was sick of being indoors, but she needed privacy.

All the other happy campers were elsewhere. Ginny sat cross-legged at the base of a large tree and leaned back. She spent as much time with her breasts exposed as she did with them covered up these days. Down came the neckline of her blouse, although her breasts were getting so big she feared the elastic would snap on the way over her mountains. She opened her bra.

Ginny would finish what Dr. Busby had started. Using both hands on one tit, she massaged firmly from her chest wall out to her nipple, trying to move any fluid to its rosy exit. There had to be milk in there—what else could explain how she'd swelled three cup sizes? The fresh air made both nipples stand to attention, and she hadn't even gotten started yet.

She pumped at her breast until her hands got tired, and then switched to the other side with her hands reversed. Maybe she should have brought a towel to sit on. She wasn't even playing with the best parts and already her pussy was getting wet. So Dr. Busby had never met a true ten, had he? If she couldn't lactate yet, she could work on being a ten. No hands for pussy.

When both breasts were well-massaged, Ginny decided to switch tactics. With light touches she swirled around her areolas, feeling how the little bumps rose up under her finger tips. Her nipples crinkled under the teasing, and her clit grew just as stiff. Ginny couldn't help squeezing her thighs together, but she wouldn't reach down. Not yet. Not until she absolutely couldn't stand it.

Because her nipples were enjoying the softer stimulation—it was nice to have something different that the endless tugging, the sucking, and the noise of the machinery. She could sit here in the dappled sunlight filtering through the trees, with the sound of birds chirping and the wind in the branches, doing something as sweetly natural as breathing, and a great deal more fun. She pinched both nipples lightly and felt the *zing* go straight to her clitoris. Felt so good she did it again.

But it wasn't enough to bring her climax, so she switched to the even handed milking motions that should be pushing milk through the little ducts inside. Her busy fingers should be making small fountains leap from each stiff peak. Over and over she milked herself, dreaming

146

of the rivers that had to flow from her giant breasts, breasts that hadn't woken up to their proper function yet. She leaned back against the tree with her eyes shut. She didn't have to see to milk her uncooperative boobs. Her cunt was much better behaved and responded to the nipple stimulation—she could be a ten today, maybe.

A soft cough made her open her eyes. Roger stood at a little distance, his eyes on her—face? Heavens. She would have stared at the bustline herself if she'd come upon a woman milking herself in the woods.

He was dressed in casual clothing this time, a blue T shirt that clung to broad shoulders and tight abs, and jeans that made the most of his natural attributes without being too tight to allow his cock to swell. Which it was doing. She tried not to stare at it, although it was closer to her eye level than his face was. Just seeing him grow erect for her reversed most of the damage to her budding orgasm that the surprise of seeing him had caused.

"Could I help with that?" he asked. "If your hands are getting tired?"

Her hands were getting tired. Ginny licked her lips. "Okay." She scooted forward from the tree, and he stepped behind her, sitting down with Ginny between his long, muscular legs. She refrained from running her hands along them. His stiff cock was pressed up against her ass. He was being as much of a gentleman as a man with a hardon and two handfuls of breast could be, and Ginny was mad enough about last night that she wasn't going to encourage him just yet. She didn't have to lift her skirt for him, and she wouldn't, not unless he did some explaining. She was a dairy maid, and touching her breasts was a privilege, not a right, although he started milking her with enough dexterity that some of her irritation went away.

"I'm terribly sorry about last night," Roger told her, and he sounded sincere.

Making eye contact was hard when the other person was behind, so she tipped her head back onto his shoulder. He smelled *very* good, soap and man and some cologne that should have been named *Testosterone Prime*. She could look up at him out of the corner of her eye. He certainly looked sincere, at least as much as she could see.

"Once I had some milk, jet lag caught up with me and I almost went to sleep in the dining room. Someone guided me to bed and I was out like a light for about twelve hours." He squeezed her tits some more. "I came from Singapore by way of Paris and hadn't slept properly in days. Once I had some breakfast I came looking for you." He grinned, which she felt as movement of his cheeks more than the flash of his ultrawhite teeth. "You're an elusive one."

Bet that bitch Rita fed him this morning too. Bet she tucked him in last night when he was dead on his feet and then jumped in beside him, ready to flash her milky tits in his face when he woke. "I had an appointment this morning and then this seemed to be the best place for a little *al fresco* milking. I wasn't hiding, really." She smiled back. "But I'm kind of shy about showing my breasts in public."

"Good, because I don't want to have to chase you down and then find out you didn't want to be caught." His strong hands milked at her breasts. "How does this feel?"

"It's very nice." Better than nice — she was at about nine and three quarters and what would he think if she came there in his hands?

"Is Rita always that pushy?" Roger asked, and her orgasm backed right down.

Speak hospitably echoed in Ginny's head. "I only just met her." *And want to push her face in already.*

He snorted. "She was remarkably hard to shake. You, pretty Ginny, are to hold my hand at all times in public areas, in case she tries to drag me away for nefarious purposes."

Rita's purposes were nefarious all right — if she wanted to cut Ginny out from this charming man's company, she was going to have to do better than lactate. Ginny relaxed against his chest, so warm and broad and sheltering. She didn't believe for a second that Roger could be dragged anywhere he didn't care to go, but if he wanted her near, she'd stay near. The only way she could get any nearer right now would be to take his clothes off, and that was starting to look like a wonderful idea. His dick pushed against her ass with every stroke on her breasts, but he wasn't making an issue of it, although he was finding it a little hard to speak.

And her without a condom. His clothes had to stay on for now. "What were you doing in Singapore?"

"Buying a factory. We have some widgets to bring to market." His words made little puffs of air in her ear. Ohh! "Stopped in Paris to talk with the designers for another line." He nuzzled her ear. "I should have just teleconferenced that and then I could have met you a day sooner."

"You could turn a girl's head with talk like that." He was probably full of crap, but it was charming crap.

"Good." His lips found her earlobe to nibble. Ginny turned to let him have better access—she loved getting her ears nibbled, and he wasn't missing any strokes on her breasts. He milked on her steadily, and brushed the column of her neck with tiny kisses. Ginny sagged backward against him—and he never stopped squeezing the imaginary milk from her.

Ginny's nipples were so hard they hurt, engorged as they were from her constant stimulation, and his fingers treated them with firmness. If milk would only flow from her, she could dampen her toes with the gushes. But if her milk would come, Roger would have his mouth wrapped around the stiff peaks, suckling the white goodness from her body.

If he didn't want to suckle directly, if he just wanted to milk her as he did now, they could fall to their sides with their clothing out of the way, and his stiff cock could find its way into her juicy cunny from behind. He could thrust his hard meat column into the musky damp of her pussy, and she'd clench around him, cumming over and over. With his hands to pull the climax out of her tits and his fat cock deep inside her, she'd explode in a shower of milk and honey, and say, "Yes, more, yes!"

Roger nipped her neck, finding the big strap muscle and working it as expertly as he worked her breasts, flicking his tongue over her skin. "More than this?"

Had she said that aloud? "Yes!"

He set his teeth into her neck, flickering furiously over her skin and Ginny dissolved into a cloud of pleasure, raining into her panties and crying aloud. "Oh!" pulled from her throat, a pale imitation of the wonder exploding in her untouched pussy. He nipped again and stopped milking her to twiddle her nipples alone through his fingers, and another climax pounded from tit to clit.

She fell bonelessly against him, unable to do more than pant. Roger's hands stilled on her breasts, cupping them for support alone. Applying firm pressure to flatten her nipples even with her areolas, he helped her ride out the last shocks with his lips pressed to her skin. He held her while she caught her breath, saying nothing.

When her eyes fluttered open again, all he said was, "Do you need any suckling?"

Ginny always needed suckling—but did he want to suck when he'd get no milk for his efforts? Or—he might! Ginny could hope that her breasts would respond to him as well as her cunny did, and let down the bounty of their milk into his mouth. "Yes, but—you don't have to." Her breasts might not give him a drop: the disobedient things hadn't given anyone so much as a taste.

"Let me move." He brushed a kiss across her temple as she sat up, and if he bumped his stiff cock across her back, that had to be an accident. How could Roger be this much of a gentleman when he'd already handled her breasts more thoroughly than any man with sex on the brain?

A man who regularly visited the dairy probably wasn't impressed with mere tits. But his dick had been *very* hard. Still was—he sat beside her and lay back into her arms with a huge tent in his jeans. Ginny'd never cradled a man for nursing; they had to wiggle around until she could make a pillow with her arm and a backrest with her thigh, but soon he leaned against her and found her nipple with his lips. He didn't need to be told to take all her areola or why; he latched on like he drank his every meal from a woman's breasts, and he suckled.

He suckled firmly, he suckled expertly, and if her damned breasts would just let down, she could have flooded his mouth with her milk. With lips and tongue he suckled her nipple, never an edge of teeth, and the strong sucks that should have drained her only inflamed her. Coming again was a real possibility—she looked down into his face, so strong and handsome, so perfect for having her nipple between his lips. His eyes were shut, as if any extra sensation might ruin his nursing, and he pressed his tongue against her nub even while he demanded what she couldn't give him.

What she couldn't give him *yet*. Ginny nearly sobbed with the orgasm that was too frequent a companion and for the milk that refused to flow. But she would. She'd do anything to be able to give Roger the milk he should have.

He let go with a kiss to the nipple that still denied him, and opened his eyes. "Other side?" he asked.

"Oh yes," she breathed, hoping that her left tit would be kinder than her right and let down for him. He rearranged himself in her lap and nursed at her unsuckled breast. Elspeth was right— the second side was better, or he'd determined what she liked, and gave it to her with a willingness. Why couldn't her body do the same for him, she implored it. *Give him milk, breasts, oh please give him milk.*

Roger sucked her with gusto for all that it was a dry suckle—he hadn't opened his eyes with the surprise or delight of getting a tasty mouthful—all the moisture on her teat was from his mouth. But, oh, he gave her such a nursing—not even her friends had swirled their tongues so skillfully nor worked her milk ducts with such vigor. Ginny moaned with each clench of his jaws and each swipe from his tongue. She was going to come again any second—she leaned to kiss his forehead and curved her free arm over his broad chest. If she could only feed him with her breasts it would all be perfect.

Except she was still a nine and three quarters—she had to clench her thighs under him and then she was awash in rain, her pussy pulsating with the exquisite shudders that clenched her channel and made her clit throb. But damned near perfect, even without the milk.

Roger wasn't complaining though, not with his mouth full. The battle in his jeans came to a crashing conclusion—his mighty cannon was primed to fire, and its explosion shook him almost to the point of biting. He nearly snapped double and groaned into her flesh. She yipped at the press of teeth but had no reason to cry out from more than surprise. And when the denim at his groin darkened, she said nothing, and rearranged her mouth to neutral before he opened his eyes. She wouldn't laugh at him for creaming his jeans, not when she was sitting in a puddle of rain and was probably wetter than he.

But next time she'd kind of like to get his pants off first.

Roger released her nipple as if he were sated, but instead of opening his eyes after he'd calmed down, he scrunched them tighter. "Haven't shot my wad nursing like that since I was twenty." He pressed his face into her chest, as if he didn't want to look at the spunk mark. "But there was no holding back."

"It's okay." She squeezed him to her, and dropped a kiss into his deep brown hair, which had started out neatly combed and had gone mussy over his forehead. "That's kind of a compliment." She kissed him again. "And you did the same to me. I'm all soggy now."

He chuckled without raising his face. "Aren't we a pair?"

I wish we were. Ginny already loved his thoughtfulness. Even if she was only the newest dairy maid, he'd been kind. But—if he'd been nursing since he was twenty, or even earlier, she had to be only the latest pair of titties he'd suckled. She shouldn't read too much into his interest.

He uncoiled from the ground and gave her a hand up. Ginny rearranged her clothing, suddenly shy about tucking her breasts away, and turned from him. "No." His warm hand on her shoulder made her face him again. "Don't hide. Your breasts are lovely. I like looking at them. And you can't go shy after I sucked them 'til we came." He stroked a fingertip along her face. "You're lovely. I like looking at you." He tipped her chin up for a kiss. "It's not always about the milk."

She let him meet her lips, a soft caress that lasted an instant, just long enough to get past her resolve. She was a dairy maid, and he was her job. Falling in love shouldn't happen.

Too late. *Ka-thud.*

ROGER HELD HER hand all the way back to the dining room. They had to skirt the duck pond, deserted now, and Ginny stopped to play with a cattail at water's edge. Anything to not think too hard about a man she couldn't expect to keep. "I've always seen these and never touched one." She nearly overbalanced but Roger caught her waist before she could splash in. Her expanded bustline had changed her balance too much for such antics. She bent in the middle with him behind her.

"What does it feel like?" She could hear the smile in his voice.

She wrapped her hand around the brown cylinder and stroked it. "It's fuzzy!" She played with it some more, since he held her safe from the water. The wonder of the texture was at the forefront of her mind, the velour of the cattail sliding against her palm and fingers.

Roger emitted a choked noise from behind. "Ginny!"

Oh! She let the cattail spring free. She wasn't really teasing him— it wasn't her fault a cattail was the same shape as a cock and was easy to pet the same way. And that he was holding her like he'd fuck her from the rear while she did it. She came upright and he turned her to face him. "Um, cattails, uh…." She couldn't say anything more, except "Oops." She buried her face in his pecs. Mistake, now she could smell his skin and that marvelous cologne, and feel his chest heave.

"Are you a natural tease or do you just like nature?" Roger gritted.

"Sorry," she mumbled. Now he'd think she was a slut. Well, she could be, with the right provocation, which was usually a loving and trusting relationship, but she wasn't a slut for sluttiness' sake. And not the same thing as needing prostaglandins she wasn't getting. "Sorry," she mumbled again.

"You're going to make me crazy." He pressed a kiss into her hair. "Would have served you right if I'd dropped you into the pond."

It probably wouldn't make her any wetter than she already was. At least around the crotch. "I just like nature. I like ponds and water lilies and cattails, and I'm used to living in a city. I wanted to touch."

"It's okay, Ginny." He held her close, his arms heating her skin through her clothing. "I like ponds too. All the art in my office is of ponds."

"Really?" Ginny seized on the topic. "Monet painted a whole series of pond paintings. Lots and lots of them, hundreds really; he especially liked to paint in summer when the water lilies bloomed...." She was babbling, she knew she was babbling, but if she didn't talk about something neutral she'd push Roger down on the lawn and fuck him where he lay. Even if she died of embarrassment right after climax. She'd die happy.

"And he had cataracts, so it wasn't exactly his style of painting that changed, he was still painting what he saw only he saw all fuzzy..." She flinched. She'd already embarrassed herself enough by running at the mouth that Roger was safe from imminent ravishment.

"Mine are from 1916, so yes, he was definitely seeing fuzzy then." Roger let her go, the bonds of his arms becoming only a firm clasp of her hand. They headed toward the outbuilding which housed the dining room.

"They have some really lovely reproductions now," Ginny sighed. "Giglee prints have such depth of color..." She'd had only the cheap posters in her apartment, and the manager had probably trashed them or taken them to the charity shop with the rest of her abandoned things.

"Mine—" Roger twirled her into his arms for another kiss, a rollicking buss on her forehead this time. "—are not prints." He grabbed her ass and stilled. "We can't go to the dining room like this—we look like we've been rolling in a swamp."

Right, she'd been sitting in a puddle of her own juices. And he'd creamed his shorts.

"Go change and meet me in the dining room." He patted her butt and turned toward the guest accommodations, throwing a smile over his shoulder.

She'd meet him anywhere he wanted. But preferably while clean and tidy. She bolted for her room. And only while half in and half out of her clothing did his words sink in. *Not prints?*

Roger met Ginny at the door of the dining room, smiling as if it had been a year and not ten minutes since he'd seen her. "Go through the buffet line and I'll snag seats." And good to his word, he had chairs for them at the same table with Jordyn, Heidi, and some of the guests whose names Ginny had lost in yesterday's hail of introductions. She had a full plate of turkey sandwiches and salad, while a plate of white rice waited before Roger. Guess he was picky.

Her friends were delighted to see her, interested to meet Roger, and bubbling with news.

"We're going to have our first feeding auction right after lunch!" Jordyn burbled. She cast a happy glance at her companion.

He smiled at her, but his eyebrows were knit.

"Now, now, Cyrus, you know I can't just point at you and say, 'He wins!' It's dairy rules." Jordyn pouted prettily.

Heidi agreed. "There'd be some very unhappy guests if they didn't have at least a sliver of a chance." The distinguished older man next to her didn't look like he gave a rat's ass about anyone's happiness but his own. She patted his hand. "But you'll win, won't you, Larry?"

"I always do."

"Unless you're bidding against me." Cyrus eyed Larry as if he found the other man lacking, and he grew openly contemptuous when he turned to Roger. "You've never bid on a first feeding, have you, Roger?" He smiled like a crocodile. "No one's ever liked you well enough to give you a bidding token."

Roger shrugged. "You might be surprised." He ate another forkful of rice. Jordyn looked appalled at her companion's snideness.

Their conversation continued through the meal, wandering through various topics. Roger had finished his rice and was disinclined to discuss business when Cyrus brought up steel futures. "You seemed quite knowledgeable about Impressionist paintings, Ginny." He turned the subject. "Is that a particular interest of yours?"

She patted her lips with her napkin. "I majored in art history, actually. I wanted to be a museum curator, but I didn't know how hard it would be to break into that field."

Cyrus interrupted Ginny with a belch. "It takes the new ones a while to catch on that we don't visit them here at the dairy for their brains." He threw down his napkin on his plate. "Going to see a man about a dog before the auction." He left, and Ginny was glad to see him go. Jordyn looked equally appalled.

"Back in a minute, Heidi." Larry stood up. "I want a word with Dirk."

Jordyn spoke through gritted teeth. "I thought he was nice." Ginny reached for her hand.

"As long as he's getting what he wants, he probably is," Roger told her.

"And then he turns nasty. How do we make sure he doesn't get what he wants?" Ginny thought she was more likely to get away with that than with beating his knees in with a tire iron. Dirk had said guests who disrespected the diary maids weren't allowed to stay, but this was a case of "he said, she said." Would Dirk believe them if they complained?

"Who else got a bidding token?" Roger asked. "I could have a word or two about—strategy."

"Carl, Milton, and Frank." Jordyn looked worried. "I only gave out four."

"Better yet." Roger put his hand out. All three girls stared. "I can outbid him, ladies. It's what he wants; therefore I can keep him from having it." His teeth showed in a smile that would make sharks leave the ocean.

"But—" Heidi and Jordyn stared at Ginny now.

"If that's okay with you, Ginny." He turned to her with concern. "I feel like I ought to help your friend, since I enabled her choice of bidder to expose his shriveled-up heart."

Was it okay with her? Ginny wanted to help Jordyn, but if Roger went and suckled her near-twin who *could* give milk— "Do it," she said faintly. She had to have a little faith in his interest, and if he was that easily swayed, best to know now.

"No. I won't." Jordyn glared holes into Ginny. "I told you already I wouldn't do such a thing." She smiled helplessly at Roger. "Thanks, but Ginny's been betrayed by a friend once. I can suffer through a half hour of his company if he wins."

"That's it!" Heidi piped up. "Bid up the price, just be sure not to win!" She laughed with her head thrown back and then chopped it off before heads turned. "Cost him a bundle!"

"Perfect!" Jordyn crowed.

Roger went feral and put out his hand again.

Jordyn handed him a blue embossed poker chip. "Thanks, Roger. Heidi. Thank you, Ginny. You guys are the *best.*" She put her happy face back on and pretended to be glad to see Cyrus when he returned. Larry also returned, sitting down beside Heidi, who also had to perk herself up.

Dirk walked up to a microphone that stood beside the buffet table. He activated it with a pop and a whistle. "Good afternoon, dairy maids and gentlemen, and welcome to Manley Dairy, where only the finest dairy products are served in the most delightful way. We hope you're enjoying yourselves—" He had to stop talking in the thunder of applause." Everyone at Ginny's table clapped, although Roger had a sideways glance for her and one arm over her shoulders as he thumped the table with his free hand.

Dairy Maid

"We are fortunate in having two very lovely ladies who have recently come into their milk and are ready to offer their first feedings to our guests. Some of you are first time guests, some are veterans, so I'll explain. This isn't an open auction. Our dairy maids—come on up here with me, Jordyn, Heidi—" Dirk waited for the applause and wolf whistles that followed the two girls up to the microphone to subside. Ginny uncorked a whistle between two fingers, because her friends were gorgeous and ought to be appreciated.

Roger lifted an eyebrow.

"Well—" Okay, that wasn't entirely ladylike. Ginny cringed.

"You'll have to teach me to do that," he whispered.

Whew!

Larry and Cyrus turned their chairs to be able to see Dirk and the girls; they'd been sitting with their backs to the microphone. They both looked hungry, and not for the meal.

"Our dairy maids have given some of you tokens, and raising that allows you to bid. Please, only guests with tokens are to bid. Gents, if you are holding one of Heidi's yellow tokens, please raise it now." Dirk took careful note of the five arms in the air. "Thank you, and now if you are holding one of Jordyn's blue tokens..." Again he noted the location of the bidders. Roger lifted his arm directly behind Cyrus, moving slowly so as not to attract attention with the movement.

"We'll start with our lovely Heidi, gentlemen." Dirk brought her forward, showing off her lushness and putting his arm around her. "Who'll lead off?" He lapsed into auctioneer's chant, and everything else he said after that sounded like "Beebahdah beebahdah beebahdah" to Ginny, but the men apparently understood enough to raise their tokens in the air at the right moments. "Going once, going twice, done!" Dirk smashed Heidi to his side, planting a kiss on her temple. Congratulations, Larry." Heidi smiled widely and said nothing.

"And now Jordyn—who wants to be the first guest to feed from her milky breasts?" Dirk went back to "Beebahdah" while holding her hand. Jordyn wore her "brave face."

The bidding started high and quickly went higher, but without Roger's participation. It started to flag around the same price Heidi brought. Roger raised his token for the first time. Dirk flicked his finger to Roger and "Beebahdah'd" again. Cyrus lifted his token and turned around. His eyes were bulging.

"Damn you, Styles!" he spat.

"Said you might be surprised." Roger calmly increased his bid by a hundred dollars, which Cyrus matched in an instant. Roger only lifted his token again, and then again when Cyrus met him bid for bid. The others dropped out of the duel, for duel it had become, between gray hair and shaking jowls and the firm flesh of a man in his prime. If the weapon was money, the wounds would still bleed. Ginny crushed Roger's free hand and tried to communicate with her eyes to Jordyn that her knight was protecting them both, it would be fine in the end.

"Beeb!" Dirk shouted.

Roger didn't lift his token again. Jordyn's first feeding had been run up to nearly double Heidi's winning bid. Cyrus all but slavered at the thought of winning. Ginny felt ill at the thought of that horrible man with his mouth on Jordyn's nipples.

"Going once, going twice, done!" Dirk declared Cyrus the winner. "Your room accounts have been debited, gentlemen, so need to let anything come between you and that drink you've been longing to take from your dairy maids."

Ginny wanted to cry at the horrid look of triumph Cyrus cast first at Roger, and then at Jordyn, who returned to her seat more slowly than she'd left it.

"Not enough of a man to win, are you, Styles?" he spat. "You're left with the one that can't lactate." He rose and grabbed Jordyn's arm with the air of one whose rightful possession had returned to his hand. "Come on, it's time." Cyrus half-dragged her toward the door.

Roger spoke through white lips. "I'm going to buy his company for pleasure of firing him."

Larry raised a skeptical eyebrow. "He works for General Motors."
Roger smiled grimly. "I know."

Even knowing they'd engineered this, Ginny still felt sick. She almost didn't register Elspeth running, well, bouncing, up to Dirk at the microphone. She thrust an envelope at him. Dirk opened it, the ripping of the paper loud in the mike's pick-up.

"Everyone, please stay where you are." Dirk glared Cyrus into immobility and then scanned the paper. "Folks, I have to report a serious violation of dairy policy. As you all recall, part of your admission here is to pledge nothing but respectful treatment to the dairy maids who so graciously feed you. Violators are charged the full price of their stay plus any extras, and are escorted off the property. Such persons are not welcome here again. Our dairy maids are precious and will be treated so. Cyrus Culpepper, go wait at your car for your baggage." Dirk looked daggers at Cyrus.

That nasty man's face went pale and then red. "I won this auction! I'm going to collect my winnings." Jordyn flinched and tried to pull away, even though her arm indented where he squeezed her. He yanked her hard against his side, making her stumble.

"You should have thought about that before you insulted our dairy maids three times before lunch and once during. Let her go, Cyrus." Dirk put the microphone down and strode toward them. "You know the rules—what you're doing right now is enough to get you thrown out."

Roger was on his feet in a flash—he and Dirk had to scuffle to get Cyrus to turn loose of what he considered his property. Jordyn yelped once, and there might have been a kidney punch involved, but they ended with Roger escorting Jordyn back to the table and Dirk frog-marching Cyrus out the door. One of the other guests held the door open for them and shut it firmly once they were through. A collective cheer broke out.

Roger seated Jordyn and patted her shoulder. "Sorry about that."

Elspeth took the microphone. "Thank you for your support, gentlemen, and I know all of you remaining here *are* gentlemen. We'll be starting the horseshoes tournament in about half an hour and anyone who'd like to go for a ride should gather at the horse barn. Enjoy your stay at the Manley Dairy!"

She hurried over to their table, ready to comfort Jordyn, who was trying not to cry on Ginny and Heidi's shoulders. "What happens now?" Jordyn wiped a tear away. "Do they have to bid again?"

"I don't believe we've had this happen before." Elspeth tapped her lips with a forefinger. "But since someone won the auction, whether or not he gets the feeding depends on his behavior. Cyrus has been billed already, so the auction is complete, and he can't stay because he misbehaved, which is not your fault, so I think you're now on second feeding and can do what you like." She smiled reassuringly. "Please don't think this is usual here; it isn't. We've only had to eject one other guest, ever." She turned to Roger. "Thank you for assisting Dirk, and Larry, thank you for notifying us there was a problem."

The other man shrugged his *aw shucks*. "I couldn't let that pass. Wasn't much else I could do besides punch him in the snoot and get us both ejected." He reached over to run his fingers through Heidi's brunette tresses. "And I'd like to take this gal somewhere a bit more private for dessert."

She turned, and her smile promised that his afters might be very sweet indeed. "You'll be okay, Jordy?"

With a nod and a mumbled "yes," Jordyn shooed Heidi away with her admirer.

"I guess I better go pump." Jordyn hefted her breasts, which had started to leak onto her blouse. "Or—Roger, you bid and you haven't had any milk with your dinner yet, and Ginny, I wouldn't poach for the world, but—maybe if you were there too? It could be like you feeding him but with my tits?"

Ginny trusted Jordyn to say only what she meant. She meant this. "Thank you."

Roger looked stunned. He also looked a bit peaked, and hadn't had anything but rice and water at the table. "Thank you." He gallantly offered each of them an arm. Ginny slipped her hand through the crook of his elbow, knowing Jordyn did the same.

The three of them headed toward Roger's suite. Calls of "Lucky man!" and such followed them out the door.

Once they were inside Roger's suite, Ginny and Jordyn tried to decide how they'd go about this. Maybe Roger knew—he had more experience with breastfeeding than they did. But Ginny didn't really want Jordyn to lie back against her with Roger cradled in her arms as he'd lain in hers earlier. How would she be involved enough?

But Roger knew. He sat on the end of the king bed. "My mouth and your breast should be at about the right height if you stand, Jordyn."

Feeding Roger consumed Ginny—but there wasn't a thing she could do yet, and here was her dear friend, full of milk and compassion. Ginny pulled Jordyn's blouse down to expose her breasts, full and dripping. If Ginny couldn't feed him, she'd make sure he was satisfied all the same. With both hands she unfastened Jordyn's bra, unhooking the plastic clasp with a *snick*. One at a time and slowly, for this was like a dedication, Ginny eased the cups over the swollen mounds of breasts. Jordyn held still, a tiny smile playing over her lips. With her hugely distended breasts free from their fabric prison, she waited for Ginny to be the one to offer her bounty to the ravenous man who watched them. A droplet fell from her nipple.

Ginny wouldn't waste what she herself didn't have. She reached across the gap between their faces and kissed Jordyn, a soft and thankful kiss with lips slightly parted. Jordyn nuzzled back, and her breasts pressed to Ginny's. Roger moaned. She couldn't keep him waiting any longer. Pulling back, Ginny pinched Jordyn's nipple to stiffness— milk ran into her palm. Her darling could latch on now. Ginny licked the fluid from her hand.

She brought Jordyn to stand before Roger, and her breast was nearly the height of his mouth as he'd predicted. Ginny leaned to kiss Roger her blessing, and kissed Jordyn again, another benediction. Jordyn slipped her arm around Ginny's waist, bringing her more completely into this circle. Ginny lifted Jordyn's dripping breast in offering, and stroked her fingers into the dark locks at the back of his head. This was the best she could do for him now. She guided his mouth to the expectant nipple.

Roger latched on, his eyes full of tenderness for Ginny—she could have drowned in those dark pools when he looked up at her. His throat worked with Jordyn's creamy gift sliding down his gullet, swallow by swallow. But his eyes were on her, the one who had given Jordyn's milk to him.

Ginny's breasts ached with the need to offer him this bounty herself. Her nipples stood high and proud on their turgid mounts, chilling in the damp spots Jordyn had pressed into her clothing. But there was no reason for her to unclothe herself save to entertain her Roger, and now he needed the nourishment she could not provide. He fed from the full breast she held for him, but she couldn't feel the press of his lips nor the wet flicks of his tongue. Jordyn could—she buckled slightly, catching herself before she fell.

Ginny knew exactly why Jordyn's knees had failed—Roger had done the same to her, nursing with the kind of skill that spoke of years of practice. He'd made Ginny come with his mouth on her nipples and not another touch—and Jordyn had never said if she was a one or an eight or a nine and three quarters.

Ginny slipped behind Jordyn to support her, arms around waist. She could plant feathery kisses at the back of Jordyn's neck, and peep over her shoulder to Roger's limpid eyes gazing up at them both. The sound of their breathing and of his rhythmic swallowing were the only noises in the room, though Ginny feared everyone could hear her heart beating.

With Jordyn's rounded ass pressed against her hips, Ginny could feel her want more to go with this feeding. Roger, the darling, was too much of a gentleman to take anything he wasn't offered, and perhaps to take some of what he'd be given on a silver plate. Jordyn wouldn't offer—not after her gallant refusal earlier, and Ginny—couldn't. But Jordyn quivered against her, in desperate need. Roger's mouth alone might make Jordyn climax as she so clearly desired, but then, it might not. Ginny wouldn't leave her friend in a bind.

With one hand she kept Jordyn from swaying, possibly tearing her nipple from her suckler's mouth, and with the other, she reached beneath Jordyn's skirt.

Ginny knew what she'd find there—they'd all seen each other naked or nearly so often enough in recent days. The swell of Jordyn's ass rounded down to her lean thighs, a triangular peephole where her ass and legs met. And from the back, her swollen pudenda could be seen poised like the ripest peach on the branch. The smooth skin where she'd been shaven met with damp inner flesh, begging to be plucked.

It was here Ginny put her hand, approaching from the back. Inside satiny panties and down the cleft of her bottom, Ginny trailed a finger, warning Jordyn of what was to come, or perhaps promising her. The two sweet halves of her parted under the touch of a finger, the nectar within dribbling down from tender flesh. Jordyn moaned, and leaned both hands on Roger's shoulders. He never paused in his suckling. Ginny's hand was as insistent as his mouth.

She could curve her finger up into Jordyn's dripping channel, to find the secret places, so nubbly and wet. Inner labia, succulently stiff, made a fan around the passage Ginny sought. She stroked them thanks for guiding her and dipped her long middle finger into the honeypot.

Roger pulled away, a drip of milk trickling from the corner of his mouth. He brushed it away with a sigh, and bent to kiss the nurturing nipple that had fed him. He pressed his cheek against her breast for a moment. With the first edge of hunger slaked, would he nurse her second side with the gusto of appetite or with the savor of the connoisseur?

Ginny would have to ask later—all she could tell from Jordyn was that he did it well. Roger held Jordyn's milk-laden breast with both hands, and even his long fingers couldn't completely encircle that globe. Her nipple poked out at him, white pearls growing on the pink tip. Her letdown had started, and he reached to take her bounty. Jordyn let her head fall forward as if she was too drained to hold it upright, but that was only pleasure, not the crashing climax she had yet to reach.

Ginny reached many things, her finger deep inside Jordyn's channel. Delicately working her middle finger in and out, Ginny swirled and probed within, making Jordyn clench and flutter. She withdrew from the depths to play in Jordyn's slit, teasing the perky ruffles around her hole and bringing the slick of her juices to her pleasure pearl

Jordyn swayed in place, never so much as to take her nipple from Roger's mouth—he gulped greedily at the milk that flowed from her. Oh how Ginny wished that was her breast he suckled, that the life-giving fluid poured from her own nipple into his mouth. He knew how to suck all right; the hour Ginny'd spent with her teats between his lips outstripped what her girlfriends had been able to do, and even surpassed the experienced dairy maids who had welcomed her so vigorously.

Jordyn had to feed Roger for Ginny's sake, and for Jordyn and Roger's sake Ginny had to bring the climax that his skilled mouth roused. With her finger on Jordyn's button, Ginny vibrated the way that she loved, and that would bring her every time. She'd done it to Jordyn, too, and seen her arch her back and mewl her orgasm. The fleshy nub was stiff under Ginny's finger, wet with pussy juices, and ready to cum. Ginny swirled quickly, feeling the firm tip and the soft hood stretched around it. Jordyn cried out.

"Nnhhh!" was her choked moan—her pussy clenched under Ginny's hand and her knees nearly buckled. Her nipples had to be throbbing under Roger's tongue—Ginny knew how that orgasm felt—unless it was different with milk squirting from her rosy nubs. Ginny yearned to feel that, ached for Roger's lips to coax her milk out, mouthful by mouthful. She could only press her huge, tender, but dry breasts against Jordyn's back and tighten her arm around Jordyn's waist.

Roger was suddenly on his feet, clasping Jordyn to his chest. Clasping both of them—if Jordyn was going to fall, she'd have to do it in spite of the two of them holding her up. Strong arms on Ginny's back braced her. He held them both, and Jordyn's head lolled to his chest. He met Ginny's eyes over her head, the deep brown orbs both hooded with pleasure and crinkled at the corners with joy. Ginny'd bet anything he was hard, maybe harder than he'd been earlier, with two of them and his favorite beverage. A man couldn't suck on Jordyn's beautiful breasts and not be hard, she corrected herself, even if he only wanted a drink of milk.

She wanted Jordyn out of the way; she wanted to be the one crushed against his muscular body. She could have that much, even if she couldn't feed him from her own teats. She wanted to make that tight T-shirt disappear, and trace every line of his abs with her tongue. She wanted—she wanted to suck his nipples stiff, even though they'd be dry as her own. But Jordyn was only slowly finding her balance.

Roger released them, letting Jordyn stand unsupported. Ginny withdrew her hand from beneath her friend's skirt, trying not to snap the elastic on the way out. How much had he noticed? Jordyn's orgasm, certainly, but had her Roger been aware of what Ginny'd done to bring it? Her finger was damp with Jordyn's juice. Her friend would forgive a quick wipe on her panties on the way out.

Roger shuffled them so they both leaned against him. He held them tenderly, even reverently, one arm for each. Their blonde heads were nearly of a height, their bodies so similar, save in this one important regard of lactation. If Ginny had to share him with anyone, Jordyn was the one. Her exposed breasts flattened against the blue cotton jersey, while Ginny's remained encased in the lacy bra that was only a pretty prison now.

He pressed kisses to the tops of their heads, one, then the other, then Ginny again. He lingered to nuzzle her and he sighed. "I have never been given such a gift."

Jordyn lifted her head to kiss Roger, a lingering kiss that had more of goodbye than hello in it. "Thank you. That was wonderful." She turned in their arms to hold Ginny. "It's going to be so amazing when you can do that," she breathed. "Soon." Meeting Ginny's lips with her pouty mouth, Jordyn kissed Ginny too, a grateful affair that needed a little more tongue than Ginny expected, but she parted her lips to accept Jordyn's benediction. Roger made a little squeaky noise that might have been "No." But it might have been "More".

Jordyn pulled back. "Thank you both. This was so much better than it would have been with *him*." Letting go of Ginny gave her two hands to tuck her breasts away, and then she slipped out the door.

Roger didn't watch her go---he watch watching Ginny. "You two are quite the sight together, but—" He gathered Ginny up into his strong arms, giving her sole cuddling rights on his chest. "—I only have eyes for you." He bent to kiss her.

Ginny let her eyes flutter shut and her lips spread open. His mouth tasted of Jordyn's milk but under that was all man. With sweet caresses of lips and tongue, he found his welcome in her lips. Oh but he was welcome, to her mouth, her breasts, her—her anything he wanted. She pulled more tightly against him, finding that her enormous breasts, hard with the milk they refused to release, made it impossible to plaster herself against him as thoroughly as she liked. Her hips thrust forward, to catch a brush of the enormous erection trapped in his clothing. Would he let her undress him? Or would he insist on stripping himself? She wanted so badly to see his hard body, to handle him, and to make him cry out. For now Ginny contented herself with exploring the firm muscles in Roger's back— they had all day.

But Roger didn't hurry past the kissing stage—bet he'd take his sweet time with unveiling her. Brushing his lips across her cheeks and nose, he explored her face. The little scar in her eyebrow from a long ago fall got a kiss, as did the corners of her mouth and the curve of her chin. He brought one hand up to stroke her cheek with the backs of his fingers.

167

"You are so—Oh damn!" He jerked completely upright and angry at the unexpected eruption of orchestral music. "Damn it all to hell and back. Sorry, Ginny, but that is the twenty million dollar problem ring tone. Don't go anywhere."

Not that she could—he continued to crush her to his body while he dug in a hip pocket for his phone, which thundered "The Ride of the Valkyries" at them.

He finally got it answered one handed. "Styles." Roger listened for a moment. "You didn't. Oh. They did. And? Fix it." His eyebrows drew together. "I see. The jet's at the Pennington airport; call the pilots and tell them to file a flight plan back to New York. I'm on my way." He jabbed the phone into darkness.

"He can't fix it?" Whoever "he" was, besides the person Ginny hated most in the universe at the moment.

"No, Gin, he can't. And it will create havoc in three other contracts if this falls apart. He should have used the hundred million dollar ringtone, although he's not aware of some of the interlocking pieces. Even so—" Roger hugged her more tightly. "I'm going to bust him down to dogwasher for interrupting us. I wanted to spend this whole afternoon getting to know you better." He gazed down at her before stealing another kiss. "I'm sorry, but I really do have to go, and I refuse to rush through any first experience with you."

Making the unknown him wash dogs sounded nicer than what Ginny wanted to do for the interruption. "I suppose you do." She wouldn't pout—Roger looked so unhappy as it was, and she'd rather wait than hurry. "Come back when you can."

"Oh, I will," he promised, parting with a squeeze. He threw his clothing into a case that had lurked beneath the bed. "But this could take weeks, now that a wheel has fallen partially off, and they're swearing they'll deal with only me. But—" He looked up from the pile of socks he was shoving into the bag. "I'll call you. Okay?"

And no one would answer. "New dairy maids have no phone privileges for the first month, or I'd give you my number." Ginny cursed the dairy's policy, which had seemed rational at the time.

"Huh." Roger threw a stack of underwear at the bag. "I've been coming here for fifteen years and I didn't know that." He zipped the suitcase. "But then, I've never met a dairy maid I wanted to call." He gathered her up for another lingering hug. "I've got to go, but I'll be back, soon as I can."

"Maybe I'll be lactating by then," Ginny dared to hope aloud.

"Oh, sweetie." Roger moaned into her hair. "I hope so." With a last kiss, he was gone.

Chapter 13 The Beginnings of Despair

Her friends didn't have as much time for her now that their milk was in, but they still found time to commiserate while they pumped. Ginny's breasts stubbornly refused to let down even a drop, while Heidi and Jordyn pumped four and five ounces at a time. Heidi had already graduated to a medium blue skirt, and it seemed like Jordyn would be only a few days behind. Those two would carry their bottles to the milkhouse, where they would be credited for the production and their milk frozen into little white popsicles that would be shipped out to milk aficionados. Ginny hoped desperately that Jordyn and Heidi's milk went to Roger.

"It's been more than a week since Roger had to leave so abruptly," Ginny sighed from the couch in the common room; she'd grown weary of pumping in the bedroom with no company. India had paused to sit and chat, and Mindy had sat with her long enough to pump two bottles of eight ounces each, not quite enough for a dark blue skirt like India or Elspeth's.

She missed Roger so much. None of the other clients had been nearly so sweet or helpful, but at least none of them had been like Cyrus, either. Word must have gotten around. She broke the suction on her collectors, releasing the pressure that had made her breasts larger and firmer, but hadn't made her lactate. India stopped her from fastening her bra.

"Honey, let's see those titties." India reached out to squeeze. She milked at Ginny's nipples, and while it felt good, Ginny hadn't worked herself up to an orgasm with the pump and didn't feel like going for it now. If it were Roger pulling at her, well, that would be a different story.

"How long does it take usually?" Ginny'd tried asking Dr. Busby this morning.

"Anywhere from four days to a month," he told her, but when she pressed for better statistics on when most girls started, he'd grown intent on shoving that thermometer up her ass. More intent than usual, and he'd turned her down flat *again* on the prostaglandins. Not that she wanted his, but asking if Roger could treat her had been met with a frosty "No," and the doctor jabbed her vagina hard with his damned swab, hunting for stray sperm that weren't there. Ginny's skirt was staying firmly down until Roger came back, and if they had to use a condom, she'd put it on him and smile doing it.

"I don't know why you aren't a fountain, girl. These are some stubborn titties." India pulled at Ginny's nipples, alternating hands. Ginny felt like a cow, a particularly useless milk cow, destined for hamburger patties. With the size her breasts had expanded to, she ought to be the pride of the dairy. Elspeth's magic chest of drawers had contained lacy 36 G lingerie, but Ginny'd given up trying to sleep on her stomach.

"So I'm taking a long time?" Ginny fretted. "It seems like a long time, because I'm waiting for it to happen, but...." She would respond to the way India milked her, except for being so worried.

"Could be any minute now." India bent down to put her soft, pillowy lips around Ginny's nipple. Still pulling on the other, India suckled firmly. That swishing tongue had to be checking for droplets, right? Her long braids swung down around her face, hiding Ginny's breast in a curtain of bead-bedecked strands. India regrouped, taking a bigger mouthful, nursing firmly on her pink target.

Ginny moaned. Ten was beginning to feel really possible. She wanted to touch India, take a firm handful of her enormous breast and squeeze it. Milk would pour out, dousing her palm and dripping through her fingers. Something in her core clenched at the thought. India could reach back, she had a free hand, and dip her fingers into the pooling moisture between Ginny's lower lips. "Ohh!" trickled from her in a sigh.

India switched sides, pulling Ginny's neglected nipple into the warm haven of her mouth. Teasing for droplets became a steady suckling, each pulse of pressure pumping Ginny's clit stiffer. She'd reach into her own panties to play—to hell with being a ten if it meant waiting—and stroke herself to an orgasm. The scent of her juices wafted up. India had to have noticed. Why wasn't she helping?

Maybe because they were sitting in the living room and people were starting to stare. "Ginny, India, not that we don't like watching, but why don't you take that down to the demonstration barn and we'll round you up an audience?" Patti seemed to be rating their technique.

India sat up. "Some good bonuses in that, Ginny. Six or seven fellas to watch? A milk show's always a draw." She grinned widely. "And our horny little friends can see how it's done."

A show? Ginny put her hands over her breasts protectively. Here with just the girls she was ready to stick her hand down her pants, but deliberately? With an audience? Of men? "What do we do?" she quavered.

India slapped Ginny's thigh lightly. "Just what we been doing, girl." Except we keep going and it gets a little splashy. Watching us suck each other is all good, but after a while we need to do somethin' ah, a little more *visual*. You'll look fine with some milk dribbling down your skin, and hey, it shows up real good on me."

White streams of milk flowing down India's bountiful chest and belly? Oh... "Isn't that wasteful?"

"That's why our audience ponies up big to watch," India agreed. "You coming with me, girl?" She got up from the couch and held a hand out to Ginny.

"But I don't have any milk." Ginny didn't let India pull her off the couch. *Because they had prostaglandins and I don't,* Ginny wanted to wail. If she hadn't been stupid, she could have had some from the usual sources, and then Roger could have given her as many prostaglandins as he liked.

If he'd just come back, maybe she'd risk it, Dr. Busby and his evil Q-tips or no. She might have to leave the dairy anyway, but Roger would know where she went and why. And maybe follow her.

Quit dreaming, girlfriend.

"I have enough for two." India cradled her enormous breasts, bouncing them for emphasis. "And you might start right there. The men, they'll get a rare treat if you do." She winked. "I'll do my best to help you get going."

That's all anyone could do for her. Ginny quailed at the thought of showing an audience how much she didn't lactate, especially compared with a woman in a dark blue skirt. "I... I don't think I could..." She crossed her arms over her breasts. She had to reach a long way to do it.

"Suit yourself, girlfriend. But you'll excuse me if I have to work off some of this fine mood with someone else." India winked and turned to the other girls, who had gathered in the living room. "Any takers?"

"I'll do it." Rita pushed her way to the front.

Huh? They were on slapping terms last time Ginny'd seen India and Rita interact. Didn't seem much different now.

"In your dreams, Rita." India didn't say anything nasty, but somehow "Rita" sounded like "Bitch" all the same. "Anybody else want to do a milk show?" A forest of hands went up.

"Patti, I think you'd do better if you fetched Mr. Dashner to help you watch." India winked at her. "And Kitty, you go find Leon and Joshua. In fact, anyone with a favorite here go find him, and Heidi, what do you say we go down to the demonstration barn and get comfy?" She held out her hand to the big, beautiful woman. "We can give 'em one hell of a show."

Heidi reach out, stunned to be chosen, and the two of them walked hand in hand out the door. Everyone else scattered to do India's bidding.

Only Rita and Ginny were left. "I thought you didn't like her." Ginny tucked her breasts away, all thought of a good time gone.

"I don't, but I'd do a milk show with a dark blue skirt any time. Bonuses get averaged over both dairy maids' milk production." Rita laughed without mirth. For the first time, Ginny noticed that Rita was wearing a pale blue checked skirt. She'd worn medium blue when she'd returned from vacation. Was Rita's milk failing? "India was trying to do you a kindness."

"I...didn't know." Ginny pulled her blouse back over her breasts. India had offered to average with zero, and Ginny'd said no. Now she cursed herself for a fool.

"Well, if those full boobies ever do let loose with the milk, you'll be a flood all by yourself." Rita sat down and put a companionable arm around Ginny's shoulders. She reached over to heft one of Ginny's breasts experimentally. "Maybe soon."

Ginny's eyes prickled with tears that she didn't want Rita to see. How was she ever going to figure out what was right to accept without screwing up? She'd cost herself prostaglandins by yelling at Dr. Busby, and now she'd gone and turned down a milk show with one of the two highest producers in the dairy. When would she ever learn?

"There's other stuff you can do." Rita pinched Ginny's nipple through the fabric, almost hard enough to hurt.

"I'm trying as hard as I can, but so far my breasts have gotten bigger and that's all." Ginny shrugged away from Rita's hand. Really, what a grabby bunch these dairy maids were! Ginny conveniently forgot that she'd been about to have a full fledged lesbian encounter with a lactating black woman she'd only known for ten days, right in front of everyone.

"Did you spend any time on the milking machine today?" Rita asked.

"No, just the pump. They were all in use when I got there." Ginny shivered with the memory.

She'd gone down to the demonstration barn where the big milking machine was. All four stanchions were full. Four dairy maids bent over the milking benches with their breasts in the basins, milkers tugging at their teats. Milk sprayed into the collecting bottles with every pull of the milkers. All four were naked, their wrists shackled by the stanchion cuffs, their foreheads resting on the padded bars. Their rumps were roundly, gloriously naked to the world. Vibrators stuck out from two cunts, while the other two gaped pinkly, twitching for something they needed. Ginny couldn't recognize who they were from this angle.

But right now they were dairy cows in some guest's fantasy. Ginny hadn't dared come all the way in, but had watched while the "farmer" inspected his herd. He strolled between his cattle, running a proprietary hand over a head here and a flank there, stopping to adjust a breast in its basin. Ginny had trouble not thinking of them as udders. He pulled a treat of some kind from his pocket and offered it to one of the girls without a vibrator. She nibbled it from his palm, and he said something to her, too low for Ginny to hear.

The farmer strolled around to the rear of his dairy herd, patting rumps as he went. One vibrator was seated to his satisfaction—he checked, twirling it in position and making a mournful "mmm" come from the other end. The second he pushed farther into its warm cavern. He continued to the counter at the far wall and removed a silver toy with a wide base from the drawer. Dribbling some lube over it, he wiped the surface until he was satisfied with its coating, and approached his herd.

"Coo—ee, coo-ee," he crooned, touching the toy's tip to an empty girl's vulva. "This will bring up your production nicely. Improve your butterfat content." He inserted it slowly, and withdrew it again, not all the way. "This will have to do until we bring you to bull." Ginny watched, both horrorstricken and intrigued, while the farmer slid the toy in and out, fucking his unprotesting dairy maid. Well, why would she protest? It had to feel good. Ginny's pussy swelled and began to dampen.

After several minutes of slowly thrusting into her exposed pussy, the farmer pushed the toy into her all the way to the hilt. He twisted,

checking for position. "There you go, bossy-girl. Keep you contented."
He stroked her ass, and then went for another toy. This one was larger.

One last dairy maid had an empty cunt now, which he proceeded
to fill. Again he frigged the naked, bound girl with the vibrator, spend-
ing more time on this one's clit in between dips inside. Had he played
this game often enough to know what they liked, or was he pleasing
himself? She shifted her weight under his attentions, though the bench
supported her body. He slid the toy in and out of her, her own juices
coating the shiny surface in uneven ribbons.

"Good girl, good girl, he mumbled. "Take it all now." He pushed
the vibrator as far into her as it would go. Ginny's pussy contracted
just from watching.

Again he surveyed his herd with satisfaction, checking the col-
lecting bottles. "Doing fine, doing fine," he said, switching out a full
bottle for another. "Eight ounces and still going, and yes, eight on this
teat too. Good girl." He found a treat in his pocket for her. "You're
getting there, keep going." He stroked a different girl's head. "Time
to bring you to bull."

This one had a vibrator in her cunt when Ginny arrived; now the
farmer removed it. It slid from her with a squishing noise. She said
nothing, she probably couldn't. Ginny knew what kind of trance the
milkers induced. The girl made a little, low sound, and shifted on her
feet. At least her breasts and body were supported as she stood bent
over.

The farmer unzipped his jeans, pushing them down around his
thighs. His underwear fouled on his stiff cock; he had to unhook his
erection from the fabric to push them out of the way. His cock stood
straight out from a nest of reddish pubic hair. Fat and veiny, his dick
had a plum-purple helmet that dripped with precum. A drop fell, mak-
ing a long strand that resisted breaking. He stroked himself twice, his
foreskin peeling back and then covering the head, though if it made
him harder Ginny couldn't see it from here—he looked rigid as pipe.
She put a hand to her crotch, wishing for a huge cock, no, Roger's

huge cock, to fill her up. The farmer lined the head up with the girl's now empty cunt and pushed inside. With a satisfied smile, he began to thrust within her.

*Ginny couldn't stand it—she ran, and when she reached her bedroom, she fucked herself mercilessly with a dildo, until her pussy pulsed, her asshole twitched, and her clit damned near exploded. That could have been her, lying on the milking bench—she'd been one of the eight who'd volunteered this morning for an expensive, compli-cated fantasy, and she'*d been turned down. *Now she was glad—she'd been aroused more than she could believe by the placidness of the girls under the farmer's ministrations. But the only one she wanted to fuck her was Roger.*

"That's too bad." Rita commiserated with the lack of available milking machines. "There's another one in a different barn, did you try that?"

"No," Ginny admitted. "There's hardly ever anyone there and I can't turn it on by myself." She hadn't wanted to take her friends away from their guests just to help the hopeless, dry dairy maid try to milk.

"I can set you up," Rita offered. Maybe she wasn't such a bad sort after all. Maybe she and India were two very nice people who should never be in the same room. Ginny'd met other people like that, just bad chemistry in one direction. "You'll have the place to yourself, since everyone else will either be at the milk show or off playing their own games."

"Okay." Ginny let Rita guide her to the outbuilding with the single stanchion and the milk machine.

No one was there. Nothing stirred in the building, though a dove whirred away at the opening of the door. "No one will bother you." Rita hunted through drawers until she found the vibrators. "Hmm, there's only small ones. They must have taken the others away to be cleaned." She handed Ginny a thin, gold-colored vibrator.

"I hope that will do some good." Ginny didn't want to undress in this spooky barn, even with Rita there. She pulled down her blouse and released her breasts. At least the basins were big enough—she'd expanded into the aqua-rimmed size. Ginny pulled her panties down and left them around one ankle. Trying not to flinch under Rita's appraising eye, she reached under her skirt and inserted the vibrator. Felt good, though she'd had a bigger one only a few hours ago. She clenched on it so it wouldn't slide out, and sat down on the milking bench. The vibrator buzzed inside, perking her nipples right up. Ginny rolled them to hardness anyway—it felt nice when they grew stiff as pencil erasers and noticeably bigger. She was getting expert at lining up her stiff nipples with the holes in the basin. Settled now, she let Rita click the stanchion closed over her head and wrists. Rita camped on the milkers—they began to pull at Ginny's nipples. Maybe this time she'd give some milk.

"You'll come back and get me in an hour, right?" Ginny asked. No one else knew where she was.

"Fat chance, bitch." Rita stood up with satisfaction. "Try four hours, or six, or when I damned well feel like it. I heard Roger's coming in today for a quick visit, and I want you out of the way. Told you, he's *mine*." She slapped Ginny's ass, hard enough to hurt through her skirt and panties.

Rita was gone in a light blue huff, the door slamming behind her. Ginny screamed for help and tugged against her bonds, but no one came to rescue her. Would Rita bother to come back? Would she be stuck here for hours? A day? Days? Her heart thudded at the thought of days in the stanchion, unable to get loose, hungry, thirsty, and with a bladder growing so full that she'd have to piss where she stood. She wrenched at her bonds again, rattling the stanchion that she'd thought was so flimsy for a cow. It was more than strong enough for a twenty-five year old girl bent at the waist with no leverage to loosen the cuffs on her wrists.

Rita might never let her out—Ginny'd be so mad she'd punch the bitch the minute she could catch her. After days in the stanchion Ginny didn't expect to run very fast. Surely someone would come by sooner? She screamed again, her cries echoing within the deserted barn. The vibrator in her pussy hummed its song, oblivious to her plight. Another dove called from the rafters, begging its mate to fly home.

And Roger was coming! How had she been so stupid as to trust a woman who wanted him? Ginny willed herself not to cry—instead she screamed again, and again no one answered. The milkers pulled at her breasts, the pressure soothing in spite of the hammering of her pulse.

The thin vibrator touched her G spot, buzzing that nubbly, responsive place deep inside her. The milkers kept up their rhythmic pulsing, drawing her nipples out with pressure and suction. Her teats pulsed to their unceasing action, lulling her in spite of herself. She screamed again, but more softly now, and with less hope. Ginny rested her forehead on the stanchion's padded bar, and a bitter tear dripped off her lashes to splash on the floor.

Her breasts might let down, that would be the best she could get from this mess. She screamed again, not expecting anyone to hear her, though the hum of the machinery might attract someone's notice. Her teats expanded and contracted at the milker's steady pace, and the vibrator purred within her cunny. In spite of her best efforts to stay alert and yell out every few minutes, Ginny was soothed by the whir of the machines at cunt and teat, and she slipped into a milking trance.

"GINNY, SWEETIE, time to get up." Gentle hands patted her shoulders. Opening her eyes was too hard. Was that her name? The hand patted her more insistently and then went away. The milkers stopped, and someone released the pressure on her teats. The air was cold on them when the milkers went away. She blinked.

"Oh good, you're coming back." A familiar voice greeted her. "Not sure how long you've been on the milkers—I've been sitting with you for half an hour, and I'd let you stay except I don't have very long." Something touched her rump—the vibrator slid out of her cunt. Its absence saddened her. The man left and came back.

A soft touch on her head moved down to her cheek. "Have to get up, Ginny. I can't undo the stanchion unless you can support your head."

She wanted that stanchion gone, she remembered dimly. Lifting her head was such hard work. She'd been resting here peacefully giving milk; asking her to move wasn't fair. But—that was Roger! Ginny found the energy to lift away from the forehead support. Things clicked around her.

He helped her sit up on the bench, gingerly putting pressure on her crotch. He helped her tuck her breasts away, drawing a finger around the red pressure marks circling her nipples, but saying nothing. Roger had to snap her bra and cover her, for Ginny was too dreamy to raise her hands. He sat next to her on the bench.

"I wish there was some way of letting you know I was coming." Roger slipped his muscular arm over her shoulders and pulled her to him. "I can't wait for this month to be over—I want you to be ready for me when I get here." He kissed the side of her head. "You're trying, though; you're working so hard to get your milk."

Right, she was wearing a big red message around her hips that she hadn't begun to lactate. "How did you find me?" Ginny found some words to voice the fears.

He chuckled into her hair. "I asked myself, where's the loneliest, remotest place on the Dairy, and that's where you'll be. But you weren't in the hickory grove and you weren't in the hayloft or the haystack, or at the milk show watching, so I tried here. You are such a darling, giving up the milk show to pump."

Not why she'd done it, but okay. "I'm trying to lactate, really I am."

"I can tell, sweetie. It's an individual thing, when girls start." He squashed her more tightly. "But let's get out of here."

Right. Spooky barn with doves, that felt like a trap. "Where? I need to sleep." Ginny swayed on the bench.

"I know. Milking trance. You were so peaceful I hated to disturb you." Roger helped her stand. "Let's go to the haystack. It's deserted and private. You can cuddle on me for a bit."

He walked her to a field fairly close to the deserted barn, dotted with small haystacks. The grasses weren't bound into bales or squashed into flakes, but stood humped against the brilliant sky. Roger dug a nest for them among the dried stems.

She curled against him, relishing the softness of his T-shirt atop the firmness of his pecs under her cheek. "You smell good," she mumbled, and if *Testosterone Prime* and hay didn't go together, the hint of sweat in his armpits and the natural scent of his skin certainly did. Her pussy reminded her that she'd had low-level stimulation, not enough to cum.

"Roger?" she mumbled. "I think I need...." Ginny buried her face in his shirt.

"Anything," her rescuer promised.

"Make me cum." She was too woozy to be indirect.

"Without leaving semen in your vagina, right. " Roger rolled Ginny to her back. At her "eep!" of dismay, he clarified with a kiss. "Dirk explained about condoms, and I have one, well, two, but that's not what we'll do. For that, I want you alert and interested. Right now you're just a horny mess."

"Uhh." Ginny didn't like that characterization. Even if he was right. And scooting between her legs.

"Sweetie, I've seen dairy maids in all shades of comatose. You aren't in any condition to appreciate what I want to do to you." Roger pushed her knees up. When he pulled her skirt around her waist, the warm breeze wafted across her damp pussy. Where had her panties gone? Oh yeah, she'd walked out of them back in the barn.

But Roger had lifted her skirt, and that was worth any quantity of lacy bikinis. He put that big hand on her smooth mons and drew his thumb up her damp slit. She shivered under his touch, yearning for more of it. His thumb traveled in smooth circles around her clit, bringing her closer to what she needed. But not close enough. Ginny whimpered, nothing as distinct as a word.

The blue sky framed him, a tender expression on his face and his thumb never stopping. "Do you like head?" Roger wondered, but didn't wait for an answer. The sky was suddenly empty and her crotch suddenly full—he knelt and put his mouth to her pussy. Her clit met his tongue, so much softer and wetter than his thumb, and more talented, if such be possible. Swirling over her pearl and finding the places that made her moan, Roger laved her juicy pussy with his miracle of a tongue.

If it felt this good when Roger licked and she was still half in a milking trance, how much better could it be if she was alert? He'd already brought her up another notch of horniness—the low level need becoming mid-level wonderful, with pressure growing in her pussy. She twitched under his ministrations, her cunt flexing.

Suckling gently on her clit for a few moments, he tickled her button with the very tip of his tongue, before moving lower to find her entrance. He slurped at her moisture, exploring his way into her damp tunnel. His tongue probed deeply, touching her opening and promising to fill her. He pulled her stiffened inner lips into his mouth, tugging ever so gently and getting a small cry from her—she meant *don't tease me now!* but coherent words were beyond her.

Ginny lifted her hips to bring herself into his range, and dropped again to aim him. Alert to her needs, he let her offer her clit again to his questing tongue, and at her "Uhnnn yes" he stayed with her even when she relaxed against the bristly hay. With long, firm strokes he probed her, finding the pleasure button over and over again, getting her to writhe beneath his mouth.

So good! Almost too good—the explosion built within her, the waves lapping at her edges but not breaking over her. She dug her hands into the hay, unable to cry out her nearness, her need for that last stroke that would bring her crashing.

But Roger gave it anyway, with a flicker of his tongue at the sides of her clit. Ginny bucked against his mouth once, twice, and then froze. Orgasm was too small a word for the pulsing and clenching of her pussy and clit. Her walls fluttered emptily, her asshole clenched with the pounding pleasure.

He stayed with her, his tongue a warm blanket over the madness in her pussy, and a small move brought her again to climax. Small noises escaped her closed throat, and only when she had to gasp for air did he leave her wet flesh. A last lick made her contract again—she couldn't help thrusting against his mouth to bring one more flickering. He pressed a kiss against her mons and hauled himself up next to her. Modesty awakened—she brushed at her skirt. He pulled it down.

"All good?" Roger gazed down into her eyes, which she couldn't open beyond mere slits. "More?" He wrapped his arms around her when she shook her head minutely. More might just kill her. He cupped her breast, though even a hand as large as his couldn't contain that mound. His thumb swept over her nipple, a last jolt of pleasure running through that rock hard nub.

"Should do something for you," she mumbled. His erection jutted against her hip, and she thought she might be hearing the hammering of his pulse.

"It's okay," he said, but that needy length trapped between them made it not okay. He held still, not thrusting, but the tension in him said he wanted to thrust, *needed* to thrust, or his gentlemanly tendencies would be the death of him. Ginny knew how that felt—hadn't she just begged him to make her cum? And how well he'd done it—Roger deserved a reward. Sweet sleepy kisses weren't enough.

He'd get it, if he didn't mind doing all the work. "Open your fly," Ginny murmured into his mouth. "Straddle my waist."

Hay flew in a storm around him—Roger was over her in an instant, fumbling his massive cock out of his jeans. Would be easier if he took them off, but they were out in the open, even if they were sheltered by the haystack. Best not to strip him out here.

Ginny pulled her blouse down to expose her breasts to his anxious eyes. Poor Roger, so eager, and so hesitant to help her expose herself. His hands fluttered over her breasts, but he waited for her to offer. She unclipped the center clasp, letting her huge tits out again.

"So beautiful," he breathed, as if he'd never seen them before. Sure, he'd suckled for hours, but that was for milk. This was for him.

Ginny wrapped her fingers around his cock—she couldn't quite get her thumb and middle finger to meet, and she shivered. Roger had already told her he wasn't willing to rush, but she didn't hear him complaining as she stroked up and down the length of him. A crystal bead formed at the tip—Ginny would lick it away if he'd come closer. He followed her tugging.

"Ginny, oh…" Roger breathed her mane to the accompaniment of her tongue on him, little flicks that tasted salt and musk. She could kiss the head of his cock now, with her lips slightly parted and her tongue finding new ways to swirl over his glans. Every trick he'd used on her clit she'd give back to him now.

Taking him fully in her mouth needed better leverage than she had right now, but Ginny'd had other ideas from the start. His controlled tension could be unleashed that way—he barely moved his hips, not thrusting into her mouth more than she wanted, and her hand on his shaft kept him still. But she wanted to let him go wild.

His furry balls rasped against her breasts, swaying with his small thrusts. Her tits kept him from getting much closer to her mouth but that's where Ginny wanted him. With a long, wet lick across the reddened head, she eased his prick down between her breasts.

"Oh, Ginny!" Roger moaned when she pushed her giant mounds around him. Her breasts became a warm haven for his cock, enveloping even such an enormous prick with warmth. He flexed his hips, moving inside the flesh tunnel she'd created just for him. "Ginny, oh!" he breathed again. "You're wonderful, you're beautiful, oh!"

His exposed glans poked up toward her face, and scooted away again, the rhythm of his hips nothing like the raggedness of his breathing. His hips were slow, as if he couldn't believe he was really fucking her tits, as if this might all suddenly been a dream and he'd awaken alone, but no, she was there. She proved it with her tongue, swiping across the head of his cock every time it came close enough to her mouth. Roger slipped a helpful hand beneath her head, though he braced himself against the hay with the other, and gazed down at her face and tits with naked adoration.

She could only lick his cock a second at a time, but the seconds grew closer together—he thrust within the crevice she made with her tits. Pushing her gigantic breasts together around him even harder, Ginny wanted him to feel good, just as he'd made her feel with his mouth on her pussy.

Big as her tits were, his prick was a fair match for them, and he thrust faster between her fleshy hills. "I'm going to…" he gasped, and she only flicked harder against his rigid cock, trapped between her fair mounds.

"Yes!" she gasped, and he froze, the head of his cock nearly invisible between her enveloping breasts. Ribbons of pale cum shot from his prick, splashing against her chest. He pulsed against her breasts, over and over, the creamy proof of his climax smearing her skin.

When he could breathe again, he dismounted, swinging a long, jeans-clad leg over her. Roger dropped to the hay beside Ginny and gathered her against him. "That was wonderful," he mumbled between kisses.

Roger drew his fingertips through the puddles he'd left on her chest, as if he didn't quite know how they'd gotten there. "Next time I give you a pearl necklace it ought to be real pearls."

"I liked this one," Ginny whispered, and took his wrist. She guided his damp fingers to her nipple and helped him paint that rosy tip. Together they painted her other nipple with his cum. Roger gave both of her nubs another coating of his fluids, and finished his artwork with kisses.

"We'll take a short nap," he decided, and set his watch to wake them. They left her damp nipples and his now-flaccid cock out to dry, and he curled around her, his forearm supporting her breasts.

"Take that, Dr. Busby," Ginny thought muzzily on her way to slumber. "And *Pthhbbb* to you too, Rita. Roger likes *me*."

THEY WOKE TO BEEPING from Roger's watch, and shyly tucked themselves back into their clothing. "Little Boy Blue," Ginny dared tease Roger, picking wisps of hay out of his hair. "Asleep in the haystack."

"With his Little Girl Blue," Roger jested back.

"Little Girl Red. "Ginny plucked sadly at her skirt. He looked chagrined. He didn't really mean to hurt her feelings about her lactating, or lack of. "But your prostaglandins might change that faster."

"Anything I can do to help," Roger assured her. "I'd suck on you some more right now, but…" His stomach growled.

"Let's go find you some milk." Ginny died a little inside, but anyone he sucked on right now would only be lunch. She hoped. Hand in hand they ambled to the main house, passing another conical haystack. "Any idea why they use French style haystacks?" Ginny mused, at a loss for words in this awkward moment. "Not bales or rolls?"

"No idea." Roger eyed the cone of fodder. "Maybe because they're shaped sort of like breasts? And how do you know they're French?"

"Lots of artists painted them. Millet's were realistic, Monet's were Impressionist. Van Gogh's were all wavy, Post-Impressionist." Ginny didn't think any haystack as wavy as Van Gogh's would stay standing in a wind. "They're prettier than bales."

"But not more efficient." Roger squished her against his side.

"It's not always about efficiency, is it?" Maybe for the head of Styles Enterprises it was, but Ginny suspected Roger missed out on some of the nicer parts of life. Nothing but rice and milk sounded like eating for efficiency, not pleasure.

They came around the corner of the milkhouse. Patti came out the door and waved at elfin but busty Taylor, who was coming toward the milkhouse holding two bottles with around seven ounces each. "Good pumping, hon?" Patti asked. Roger perked up and walked faster.

"Yes! Let me just drop these off and we can meet Jeff and Carl at the swimming hole." Taylor waved her bottles.

Roger dropped Ginny's hand. "May I have those, Taylor?" He *would* know all the dairy maids, Ginny thought.

"Um…" Taylor hedged. "I'm supposed to drop these off for credit."

"Okay, check them in and then I have first dibs." Roger held the door for her.

She returned in a moment and handed him both bottles. "Enjoy!" She and Patti ran off, but not before Ginny caught their pitying looks. Damn it! When were these enormous breasts going to do their job?

"Excuse me a moment." Roger twisted off the top and swigged down the white fluid. A few large chugs and he'd drained the bottle, and dove right into the next one. In no time at all, he'd finished both bottles of milk. He stepped inside the milkhouse long enough to drop off the containers. "Sorry, but I was running on empty." He looked embarrassed.

Too happy at his finding milk without sucking on any other dairy maid, Ginny just patted his arm. "No problem. I just wish I could have fed you myself."

"I'd love that." Roger hugged her, squishing her oversized boobies against his chest. "Soon."

Soon. That's all anyone could tell Ginny, and it wasn't happening soon enough for her. She had ten days to accomplish it. Would she ever have milk for him? She opened her lips under his, tasting the traces of Taylor's milk on his mouth, and willing her breasts to produce what he needed.

"Let's get you some lunch," Roger suggested. "I'll keep you company." They continued toward the dining hall, when Ginny selected a roast beef sandwich. Roger spooned some potato salad on her plate. "Donating calories to guys like me will suck the flesh right off you if you don't eat," he scolded her gently.

"First I have to lactate." Ginny didn't let him add a brownie to her meal. She said nothing about the plate of plain rice he fetched for himself.

"You know so much about art," he mused while they ate. "Which galleries have you visited?"

"We did a class trip to the National Galleries but that's all." Ginny sighed. "There's so many great museums in Paris, but I couldn't afford the trip with the class." She'd gotten her passport and made plans, but then her car died and a roommate moved out, and there went the money. He'd been in Paris recently, she recalled, and hearing about it was easier when it wasn't from someone who'd made that trip without her. "Have you visited the *Jeu de Paume* or *l'Orangerie*?"

"Nope." He ate some rice. "In all my trips to Paris, I've never been."

Ginny nearly snorted crumbs. "Surely you've been to the Rodin Museum?"

He shook his head.

"The Louvre?" No one could go to Paris without visiting the Louvre; Ginny was quite certain that was a law.

"Never." He'd eaten his rice. If he tried dining like that in Paris, surely the chefs would chase him out into the street.

"Why ever not?" She was scandalized.

"I'm there on business, and usually in a hurry." Roger smiled wryly. "And maybe I need a good tour guide." He laced his fingers together to make a chin rest, and regarded her steadily. "Eat. I like to watch you."

Ginny poked an escaping tomato slice back between the bread and the meat. Maybe he thought this was food porn? Except why wasn't he tucking into his own sandwich? She took a bite and chewed luxuriously. It was a darned fine sandwich, toasted and mayonnaised and slathered with mashed avocado. She took another bite and moaned. His eyes fluttered, much as hers did.

After lunch they wandered outside again, hand in hand. Ginny didn't sneer at Rita, who looked ready to spring on her and start pulling hair, but Roger did clutch her hand more tightly and hurried her away. Ginny was glad to go—Rita's nefarious purposes definitely included wickedness toward her.

Dairy Maid

They ended up at the cattle barn, where they at last admired the black and white beasts that lay in the sun, chewing their cuds. One cow faced them, her enormous udder poking four teats in their direction. "How much milk does a cow like that give each day?" Ginny thought a dairy maid ought to know such things.

"Not sure about this one, but the range is from four to twenty gallons," Roger told her. "Or not a drop that does me a bit of good." He reached to tickle her nipple through her clothing. "For that I need you."

She *had* to start lactating soon. Maybe she should go pump right now. Maybe she should demand Dr. Busby change his mind on his study. Maybe she should give up. Maybe.... Ginny wouldn't cry.

"Or maybe—" Roger hugged her, one hand on her ass and one threaded through her hair. "I just need you and milk." He kissed her deeply, his tongue probing between her lips, and Ginny tried to believe that he could want her, milk or no. His questing kisses chased back the tears, and she felt herself opening to him, moisture forming in her pussy. It would run down her leg—she still didn't have any panties on, and there might be a handy stall in that barn where she could pull down his jeans.

But Roger wasn't inclined to stop what he was doing, which needed little nibbles on her neck and squeezes on her ass. Ginny squeezed back, trying to locate the pocket with the condoms, but stayed, totally entranced by the muscular cheek under her hand. He was already hard again. She nuzzled his ear, trying to stay in the moment, but wanting to move on to nakedness.

"Take yer little heifer up to the hay loft," a gruff voice advised.

Ginny and Roger whipped around to see Horace the cowman with a shovel over his shoulder. Of all the people she didn't want to see right then! If Horace announced anything about condoms, she'd just die right there and he could use that shovel to bury her red-faced corpse.

"Good idea, but I need to be at the airport in—" Roger checked his watch. "—forty-five minutes." He bent to whisper in her ear. "And I'm still not going to rush through any firsts with you."

190

He led her back to the main house, away from Horace's knowing eyes. They could probably see right through her skirt to her lack of panties. Ginny hugged him much more chastely when they reached his Porsche Boxter.

"Hate to go so soon, but I only had a few hours on my way to LA," he muttered between kisses.

"Why'd you come for such a short time?" Ginny asked. Hope rose in her heart.

"I wanted to see you." He found her lips once again. "I'll be back next week. Think of me until then." He got into the sleek black monster and pulled away with a wave.

Ginny watched the sports car go through the dairy's gates. As if she could think of anything else.

Chapter 14 Desperate Measures

Ginny lay on the examination table, completely naked and completely humiliated. Dr. Busby, Dirk, and Elspeth all stared down at her huge, stupid, dry breasts.

"I really don't know why she hasn't begun lactating." Dr. Busby spoke as if Ginny weren't there. He began to squeeze her right breast again with both hands, as if something had changed in the five minutes since he'd done it last. "Her breasts have expanded close to twenty-five percent and all the signs suggest she should be giving no less than twelve ounces every six hours."

Her nipple was crinkled and stiff in the chill air of the exam room, not because of anything he was doing that she was enjoying. No, Ginny wasn't enjoying anything at all about this. Crawling under the exam table and never coming out seemed like a really good idea. An even better idea when Dirk began to massage her other breast in time with Dr. Busby's hands. If Elspeth tried to fuck her with a probe Ginny would leap away and run screaming toward the horizon.

They'd already watched her get her breast volumes measured, which was bad enough, and had exclaimed over her rectal temperature, which was a good degree higher than normal. Elspeth had reprimanded her for shrinking away from Dr. Busby's calipers. Why would Ginny want them to see that her nipples had grown since coming to the dairy when no milk came out of them?

Dairy Maid

Elspeth nudged Dirk to one side and squeezed Ginny's breast with one hand and tugging on her nipple with the other. "The ducts are firm and filled," she assessed, "and her nipple doesn't seem to be blocked."

Ginny shut her eyes. With her luck, unblocking nipples would be painful. Elspeth wasn't being especially gentle, pinching and gripping and trying to squeeze fluid out of her recalcitrant breast. Dr. Busby wrestled with her other tit, although he wasn't pinching.

"I really think we have to reconsider the matter of prostaglandins," Elspeth declared.

"But after three weeks and all the signs?" Dr. Busby objected. "Science will not be well served. She should go another week."

"Fuck science," Elspeth declared, in the only sentiment expressed so far that Ginny could agree with. "Another week and she'll be out of her probationary period. And if she hasn't started to lactate by then, we'll have to let her go. You have enough data."

Let her go? Ginny'd kept a careful eye on the calendar, and yes, she had less than a week. Roger hadn't returned, her milk hadn't come in, and India'd chided her for her long face every time they'd gone to greet incoming guests. Ginny sniffed, trying not to break down. "My milk has to come. Really it does."

"Are you sure she's displaying milk sign?" Dirk asked, and Dr. Busby gave him a grim look.

"I'm never mistaken about these things." The doctor let go of her breast at last. "You've handled her breasts, and you can feel it plainly as I can. She's hugely distended. As for the rest, see for yourself." He put up the stirrups. "Feet up."

No! Ginny wanted to wail, but this was her future about to go up in smoke. She scooted down the table, hating every inch she traveled, and found the stirrups with her heels.

The speculum was an old enemy, breaching her vagina and spreading her wide. Dr. Busby aimed the light into her gaping hole. "You can see, she's the right color, and her cervix is quite distended.

194

Just as she should be for substantial lactation." He moved aside to let Dirk stare into her vagina.

"How many times a day have you come to orgasm?" Dirk inquired, pinching Ginny's clitoris. "You have been playing with yourself and the other dairy maids, haven't you?"

"Of course I have!" Ginny snapped. Was he trying for an echo effect in there? "I come ten times a day, just like Dr. Busby told me to. Although once I came eleven times." Ginny'd been terrified of intractable swelling that day—she did not ever want another touch of Dr. Busby's violet wand on her clit. The dildo-shaped ice pack had been enough to make the swelling go down, to her great relief.

"An extra cum is only a good thing," Elspeth reassured her. She came around to peer into Ginny's vagina.

Maybe Elspeth had yet to meet the violet wand. Ginny didn't correct her.

"Yes, she does look like she should be lactating well." Elspeth prodded Ginny's clitoris thoughtfully. "And I know she has vigorous orgasms." Of course Elspeth knew—the last time she'd touched Ginny there was about two days ago, and they'd both done some moaning. But only Elspeth had sprayed milk at climax.

"There's really nothing else for it, Buzz." Dirk released the speculum and pulled it out of her pussy. "She needs the prostaglandins."

"But my experiment!" the doctor exclaimed.

"But my milk!" Ginny wanted to yell. "And Roger!" but she stayed silent. She'd been begging for prostaglandins, not getting them, and not milking. Surely Roger would understand—he knew almost everything about how dairy maids worked. He'd know this was necessary. And then, Ginny had to admit, he hadn't come back. She shouldn't be pinning her hopes on a client who visited irregularly.

"We'll treat her now and then again this afternoon while she's on the milkers," Dirk decreed, reaching for his belt buckle. "Morning and night until she lactates."

In spite of herself, Ginny shivered. She didn't try closing her legs—she needed this, and Dr. Busby had been ruthless about binding her for treatments.

"She needs natural stimulation while I, ah, apply the treatment." Why didn't Dirk just come out and say "while I fuck her"? Ginny thought bitterly. *It's not like they think I'm more than cattle anyway.* Dirk pulled his penis out of his trousers. It grew hard while she watched—Dirk helped it along with some brisk stroking.

Dirk's cock was everything Jordyn had told her it was, and if they didn't have an audience, *and if she'd never met Roger*, she'd be grinning with anticipation.

"Put that away, Dirk." Elspeth's voice stopped him for a moment.

"Why? She needs the treatment, I have the treatment, and you two get to sucking on her nipples. We'll have her lactating in no time." Dirk lined up his stiff dick with Ginny's hole. Was she wet enough to take that monster?

"After her freshening, then you two can squirt her with prostaglandins until her milk comes in." Elspeth reached over to slap Dirk's cock away from Ginny's pussy.

"Oh, right." Dirk's shoulders drooped. Even Dr. Busby deflated. Like the bastard hadn't been anxious for his turn.

Ginny sat up, closing her legs. "What's a freshening?" she demanded. No one was going to do anything to her she hadn't agreed to.

"It's, um." Elspeth put her arm over Ginny's shoulders, totally awakening Ginny's mistrust. "Think of it as a mass application of prostaglandins. And a way to make a substantial bonus, which you will need if your milk doesn't come in after all, and which is never a bad thing anyway." Cupping Ginny's breast, Elspeth ran a gentle thumb over the soft nipple. Ginny could barely remember last time her nipples had been truly soft. "It's nothing you haven't done before, you aren't a virgin. It's just a combination of old things in a new way." She thumbed Ginny's nipple again and squeezed her shoulders. "You do like doggie style."

Doggie style! What!? "Who?" Ginny asked faintly.

"We don't know yet," Elspeth didn't say a thing to reduce Ginny's panic. "But it won't be these two cheapskates. We'll take sealed bids at dinner. The top five will take care of you while you're on the milkers. We've had dairy maids increase their production halfway through a freshening. Why, you could start right then and there! And then we could have a first milk auction too! And a first feeding auction for later." She smiled brightly.

"Best wait a day or so on that one, Elspeth." Dirk had tucked his dick away again. "But yes, Ginny. A freshening would be in your best interests."

"I think that would work," Dr. Busby concurred. "We can treat you later if needed." He rearranged his junk inside his trousers.

Ginny hunched silently on the end of the exam table. Everyone who knew the dairy best was urging her to do this, even though her heart said *no, wait for Roger*. But every time she'd said no, she'd missed out on something she needed or could have benefited from. And here she sat, six days away from her walking papers, with *No* on the tip of her tongue again. But without her milk, her future, only seven days from now, looked mighty grim.

"All right," she whispered.

GINNY PICKED at her dinner, and when it came time to collect bids, she could barely walk up to the microphone where Dirk offered their guests the chance to make their offers. "Our lovely Ginny needs to be freshened," he boomed through the mike, and didn't explain what he meant. Did this happen often enough that none of the guests needed clarification?

She summoned up a trembling smile that didn't last long, and kept her eyes on the ground. Her swollen breasts obscured her feet and quite a lot of floor in front of her, but she didn't want to watch two dozen eager guests scratch out their offers. The other dairy maids whispered to their tablemates or guests, or smiled encouragement at her. Heidi and Jordyn blew her kisses—Ginny suddenly appreciated how they must have felt when their first feedings had been auctioned. How much easier would it be to only have to give up a taste of milk? Her pussy clenched; that damned thing only knew about the upcoming fucking. Her head worried more about who would win the bidding and how much they'd gloat over Roger. And where was he, anyway? Ginny graduated to cursing the dairy telephone policy before the last envelope was collected.

"We'll tally tonight and announce at lunch tomorrow," Dirk told the assembled guests and dairy maids. "You'll do our Ginny well." He let her return to her table.

Oh yeah, they wanted to do her well. And thoroughly. Ginny could only hope none of them lasted long.

"It'll be all right, Gin-gin." Heidi whispered in her ear. They lay cuddled in the bed, Jordyn on her other side, with her hand in Ginny's crotch. They'd suckled and diddled her for an hour, against her growing dread, and her hope that they'd bring her milk before morning. "You'll get your milk."

"That's what we've been saying for almost a month," Ginny quavered. "And I'm still dry."

"Not very," Jordyn joked, taking her wet hand away from Ginny's pussy. "I know, hon," she said, when Ginny sighed. "But worrying isn't going to help."

"I just want Roger!" Ginny snuffled. "And I can't even call him to tell him to come bring his prostaglandins!" She buried her head in Heidi's neck.

Heidi and Jordyn exchanged a long look over Ginny's head. Jordyn nodded silently, and got up with her handful of rain. She returned in less than ten minutes, and snuggled back up to Ginny. "It'll be all right."

Ginny lay in her friends' arms, listening to their rhythmic breathing, but she didn't fall asleep for hours.

198

STILL NOTHING. Ginny broke the suction on her collectors and fretted again. She didn't go down to breakfast with Heidi and Jordyn, spending the entire morning on the pump, and she sure hadn't wanted lunch. Looking her prospective fresheners in the eye, or greeting the unsuccessful, was too hard to bear. Maybe a warm shower would help.

Wearing nothing but a big clip in her hair and a fuzzy blue towel, Ginny was surprised to return to her bedroom to find Elspeth.

"I've come to get you ready for your freshening," she said. "I think you have what we need already. Don't dress." She disappeared into the bathroom.

Ginny clutched her towel more tightly. Don't dress? What was Elspeth looking for?

She returned tearing open a tall rectangular box. "Got it. On your knees on the bed, Ginny, and shoulders down." She pulled a long nozzle and a bottle out of the box.

"What? Oh, no." Ginny took a step back. "You didn't say anything about an enema."

Elspeth looked puzzled. "Did I need to? Ginny, there's a train on that track somewhere, and we don't want it pulling into the station at an inconvenient moment." She screwed the nozzle to the bottle. "Come on now."

Ginny didn't move.

Elspeth tried again. "Unless you're really accustomed to this sort of thing, I can promise you that 'scared shitless' is a real possibility. Do you *want* to humiliate yourself?" She waved the enema bottle. "This is how we prevent that."

Ginny took a very deep breath and let it out in shuddering gasps. "Damn it all to hell." She dropped the towel and climbed onto the bed. With her ass up and vulnerable and her cheek pressed against the bedspread, she waited for the touch of the nozzle. For fuck's sake, ever since she'd come to this dairy, someone wanted to stuff something up her ass or into her pussy. She wouldn't cry at this invasion—she wanted to clench tightly enough to keep it out, but Elspeth had a greasy fingering circling her puckered hole and pressing in. Nothing Ginny could do would keep that invader out, though she tried.

"Ease up, Ginny," Elspeth told her. "It's going in, like it or not." She worked her finger in and out of Ginny's asshole twice more, spreading the lubricant. "It will hurt if you don't relax." She didn't sound like she cared if it hurt. "Press down, like you're trying to go."

Like that would happen—Ginny couldn't bear down, but she did stop clenching so tightly. Elspeth's finger went away, and the cold nozzle touched her hole. "In we go."

The long, thin nozzle breached her hole, pushing her open and sliding within. Ginny gritted her teeth while Elspeth seated the nozzle, pressing it all the way into her anus until the shoulders of the bottle touched her cheeks. The cold started—Elspeth had to be squeezing the fluid into her rectum. The chilly liquid gushed into her—Ginny mewled her discomfort, but Elspeth only slapped her buttock lightly.

"Don't be such a baby." She lifted the bottle, which *shlooped* to suck more air in and reflate the flexible sides. And then she pressed the nozzle back in. The length slid through Ginny's anus, making her clench on the slender probe. A second dose of liquid gushed into her, bringing cramps. Elspeth reflated the bottle, and reinserted the nozzle in Ginny's ass. She reached under to rub Ginny's belly. "We want to get that fluid up high. In fact, I should probably have brought the long tubing and bag for a high colonic, but the troops are getting restless. They're gathering in the demonstration barn right now."

Oh, no, Ginny did *not* want a high colonic. She had some idea what that entailed, and no one, not even Elspeth, got to shove something that far up her ass. She massaged her stomach, trying to bring relief.

"All in now." Elspeth withdrew the nozzle. Ginny's hole clenched once it was out. So many things she couldn't control had been done to her—this latest outrage almost made her question staying at the dairy. The liquid sloshed within her.

"Now lie on your left side, and stay there until you absolutely can't hold the fluid any more." Elspeth gave her a gentle shove. Ginny lay on her side, her knees pulled toward her chest. "Did you shave your pussy?" Without waiting for an answer, she pushed Ginny's knee up to inspect. "Oh good."

Yes, Ginny thought crossly, she had shaved in the shower, lest she feel like a hedgehog. She slammed her knee back down, bringing another wave of cramping. With her eyes scrunched shut, she rode out the pain.

"Doing okay?" Elspeth asked. Ginny didn't think she was hearing much pity—Elspeth was the one to do this to her. "Just remember, it's all about the milk here. Even this."

Even this. Ginny suddenly knew that if she didn't get to the toilet, like, NOW, her bed would be very, very messy. She dashed to the bathroom, taking only enough time to shut and lock both doors. She didn't want Elspeth coming in to supervise. Not one moment too soon, she parked her offended ass on the pot.

She rocked back and forth to comfort herself with one arm across her breasts to keep them from flopping, and the other she pulled against her stomach, trying to ease the cramps. The fluid rushed from her hole in great gouts, taking with it everything she didn't want to accidently release with an audience. Over and over she squirted, the contents of her guts all but flying out of her.

Gradually the squirts dwindled and nothing further came out. The cramps receded, leaving her with a fine sheen of sweat. Ginny snuffled, hating the dairy and everyone who worked for it. Milk was way overrated. What would happen if she just screamed her opinion through the door and refused to come out?

Reluctantly she cleaned herself and flushed the evidence away. She could get through this, she could get through anything. Even the audience down in the barn.

Five of them. And she didn't know who. Only that none of them was Roger.

Dairy Maid

ELSPETH ESCORTED Ginny down to the demonstration barn, huddled inside her fuzzy bathrobe. Ginny wasn't feeling sexy inside all the terry cloth, with no make-up ("You'll only smear it," Elspeth had said) and not even underpants. ("You're only going to take them off.") She'd styled her hair into loose braids to keep it from flying into her face. In her last glance into the mirror, Ginny thought she looked about fifteen years old and hoped that would make her fresheners feel like old pervs. Except they only had to look at her body to know she was all woman. And maybe part Jersey cow. Ginny wrapped her arms around her breasts to keep them from jiggling on the brief walk.

An excited buzz of voices came through the open door. Ginny tried not to listen. She didn't want to hear what they might say about her fresheners or her body or what was about to happen. Each of her foolish decisions earlier had led to this moment, and she wished fervently that her milk would magically come in, preferably in the next twenty seconds.

"One last thing." Elspeth halted her in the anteroom where she'd peeped on the "farmer" and his "herd." "Bend over. You need this." She showed Ginny a slender butt plug that had been hiding in her pocket.

"Why?" It had better be good—she was already riding the thin edge of panic.

Elspeth squirted lube from a small packet onto the plug. "Ginny, I know you think I'm just adding humiliations, but this is something you need." She rubbed the lube over the blue silicone. "Look, the men get crazy excited during a freshening. They pump wildly, they don't always mind where they're thrusting, and if your ass isn't already full, you're liable to get a stiff dick in there with no lube. Do you want that?"

"No," Ginny said, almost too faintly to hear herself. The world went swimmy at the thought of some unknown man's barely slippery dick shoving into her poor virgin ass. "I don't." She bent at the waist and bit her lip hard when Elspeth found her asshole with the plug.

Even though it wasn't very big, Elspeth had to work it in, shoving the toy into her ass a little farther with each push. Finally the wide shoulders slid past her protesting ring and the thin neck held her hole open only a little. Ginny sniffled and dashed her terrycloth sleeve over her eyes. Oh why had she agreed to this?

"It will be okay, Ginny." Elspeth hugged her tightly, as tightly as she could with two huge sets of breasts between them. "Your milk will come and you won't have to do this again unless you choose."

Dairy maids *chose* to do this? Ginny didn't think any of the lactating women could be as desperate as she, and what else would convince them a public gang bang would be a good idea?

"You can do this," Elspeth encouraged her. She took the robe from Ginny's shoulders, leaving her totally bare, save for the blue toy poking from between her cheeks. "It's time, sweetie."

The blood pumped cold through Ginny's veins. Roger called her sweetie. Lord, but she hoped he'd never hear about this. With tiny steps she entered the demonstration barn proper, Elspeth's hands firm on her arm. They entered to thunderous applause—Ginny stared at the knotholes in the wooden floor rather than pick out any one spectator.

Dirk was making some sort of announcement, but the roar of blood in her ears drowned out the words. Maybe he was telling everyone who'd be fucking her in a moment's time. Ginny didn't want to know. She wouldn't look behind her, she wouldn't acknowledge their names or faces, and she'd slap any man who referred to this day in the future. If she had a future at the dairy. She shuffled to the milking bench, Elspeth leading her on.

Dirk and Elspeth lowered her belly down to the bench, and settled her breasts into the aqua-rimmed basins. Her enormous breasts filled the clear plastic bowls, her nipples, anything but hard now, poked through the openings at the bottoms. If she thought about how the milkers were tugging at her nipples, maybe she wouldn't be too aware of what happened inside her cunt.

Dairy Maid

The stanchion clanged into position around her head. The cuffs trapped her wrists. The milking bench pressed into her thighs, forcing her legs apart. She could fight her bonds, and they might let her up. Or they might not. Her fresheners might like it even better if she writhed to evade their stiff meat poles even as they strove to plunge into her cunt. But if she fought back, and won, her milk would never, ever come.

Maybe she'd slip into a milking trance. If they gave her a moment or two of suction and pumping, she might escape the bonds of now, be forever unaware of the plunder of her body. Dirk brought the silver milkers to her and knelt to affix them over her nipples. "You'll do fine, Ginny," he whispered. "You'll get your milk."

It was all about the milk. Always about the milk, even if it looked like sex. She had to hold tight to the thought of getting her milk. She couldn't feed Roger without her milk, only watch forever while he drank from others. Or watch once more while the clock ticked away the last of her month at the dairy if she stayed dry.

Oh, dear, sweet… Even her thoughts went blank. Dry. She was so afraid that her cunt had to be bone dry. Someone would push into her and it would be pushing an emery board prick into a sandpaper tunnel. They'd scream and boo. They'd refuse to touch her. Her milk would never come. "Elspeth?" she croaked, and her instructor came to hear what she had to say. "I'm so dry."

"Bet you are, sweetie," Elspeth whispered. "I'll fix it."

A moment later, the milkers hummed into action. Then gentle fingers probed into her cunt, bringing moisture with them. Ginny flinched, but they only stroked slickness across her pink parts and inside her channel. Something hard, a nozzle? slid into her and more chilly wetness flooded her pussy. She clenched without willing it, without enjoying it, but the audience ooh'd and ah'd.

She clutched the handlebars until she thought her knuckles would explode with tightness, and shut her eyes. Dirk made another announcement, names she tried not to listen to. Someone stepped up behind her and spread her pussy lips with his hands.

"Fine woman," the unknown pronounced, and the pressure at her cunt had to be the fat head of his cock.

Five of them, she had to endure five of them. Ginny whimpered.

"She's enjoying it already and I haven't even gotten in!" he announced to the crowd.

A door slammed open, running steps sounded. The pressure at her cunt disappeared. A crash.

"Don't anyone even try to touch her!" a voice roared. A familiar voice. A beloved voice.

Roger!

Just kill me now.

Chapter 15 The Freshening

"She agreed to a freshening to bring her milk, Roger," Dirk explained. Ginny still couldn't bear to open his eyes.

"She's been working hard to lactate!" Roger's voice held a note of fear. "This can't be the only way."

"We've assessed her and haven't determined a better course than prostaglandin applications," Dr. Busby, the traitor, told him. "You know how this works."

After fifteen years of dairy visits, Roger'd probably seen dozens of freshenings. Just none of them starring Ginny.

And after seeing this one, he couldn't possibly still want her. Another possible future went *poof!* in her head.

He knelt by her head. "Ginny, sweetie, you can't need your milk this badly." Stroking her cheek, he tried to make her look at him.

"She can't back out now, Roger." Dirk's voice boomed through the barn. "She's bound by her word. The audience is assembled. We don't stop in the middle of these things; you know that."

"Then don't stop it!" Roger was on his feet, shouting. "But no one else freshens her. Only me!"

"She's bound for five applications. One man isn't adequate for five." Elspeth spoke out. "And we have winning bidders."

"I'll reimburse the winners and ruin anyone who disagrees!" Roger snarled at the audience, who had gone silent with the shock. "But no one else touches her!" He backed around Ginny until he was at her rump. He leaned against her exposed ladybits, shielding her from the audience's eyes but also moving the blue plug in her ass. She didn't dare squeak.

"But five applications, Roger?" Dirk queried. "You can't do that many in the allotted time."

"Maybe ordinary men can't, but I can," Roger insisted.

Ginny's eyebrows went up. So far she hadn't seen anything to back that statement up, but now was a piss-poor time to mention it. Roger had suckled her breasts and cum in his pants without a single touch.

"Really." How many voices had said that, or something like it?

"Really." Roger stayed positioned behind her like a fig leaf, but his voice dared anyone to disagree.

"All well and good, but how would you prove that?" Elspeth sounded genuinely perplexed. "If you don't cum inside her, she doesn't get the semen and prostaglandins, and if you do, then there's no proof you came."

"I know a way," Dr. Busby spoke up. "I have equipment that registers orgasms." The audience gasped.

"Bring it on," Roger declared.

"There may be a slight problem," Dr. Busby said. "Normally these probes are used vaginally. Not possible with you, of course. But they will work if inserted anally."

"Anally." Roger's voice faltered. Ginny's heart faltered with him. "If you clowns need proof that I'm doing what I say I'm doing, then you don't know me very well."

"We know you, Roger," Dirk said. "But we have five men who have arranged to do what needs doing."

"And I now own enough of General Motors that Cyrus Culpepper is out of a job," Roger insisted. "Exactly as I said I would. Do you think I'd do less than I claimed for Ginny?"

But the mood of the crowd had grown ugly—murmurs were growing, starting with the five fresheners. "Prove it or move aside, Styles. We have some freshening to do."

Roger gulped. "I can prove it. Get the probe, Buzz." He remained at Ginny's rump, shielding her from others' eyes, and laying a possessive hand on her back.

Dr. Busby was back in a moment, carrying a probe on a cord and his oscilloscope. "This will register your climaxes. Drop trou and bend over, Rog."

Roger bent over Ginny's back, a parody of doggy style. It did bring his face near hers without exposing her private parts. "This is only worth it if you want me more than you want them."

"I don't want them at all—just my milk," she whispered back. "I'm sorry. I want you, but not like this." She'd been where he was now, not even an hour ago, with Elspeth sliding the enema nozzle into her bunghole. And again a few minutes ago, when Elspeth inserted the butt plug that Roger was squirming against now, and making shift inside her ass. She hoped Dr. Busby brought one of the small probes.

"This is what we've got. Any orgasms you don't have now I'll make up to you later, Ginny," Roger promised. "But I'll try to make it good." He flinched and hissed through his teeth. Maybe Dr. Busby brought one of the medium probes. The audience murmured that he was wearing too many clothes. What had Roger let himself in for? "Showtime."

The whip of fabric over her head had to be his shirt, and he shifted behind her, no doubt shedding his trousers. Oh, her poor Roger. Ginny almost forgot about 'oh poor her' until she felt the head of his cock at her entrance.

He'd managed to get it up in spite of the audience and the occasional heckling. And he was every bit as big as he'd looked between her breasts. Ginny's pussy needed every drop of lube Elspeth had squirted into her, and even then, his prick didn't fit right away. Roger rocked against her, demanding to be admitted inside. Her cunt expanded a fraction with every insistent shove—the head of his cock felt the size of a baseball. She tried to relax to him, to let his dick inside, and another half dozen thrusts let him slide home.

The audience moaned for him, watching him penetrate her—the last four inches brought gasps from some of the women. Perhaps from some of the men, the ones with pencil-dicks, or pencil-dick minds. Ginny was getting fucked by a real man.

He had hold of her waist, his hands braced against the swell of her hips. Pulling himself against her, his fingers dug into her flesh. She'd have bruises tomorrow, but in a good cause. She trusted Roger—if he left a mark it was needed, for leverage, for access, for—proof she was his. She would have pounded back against him had she not been bound.

Her stanchion rattled with his thrusts—she had to lift her head to avoid banging the support bar. What had been as gentle as it could be just to get in became firmer now, as he pounded into her pussy. She molded around him, taking that huge cock like she'd been destined for it, feeling his hips smack against her ass.

Where she'd started reluctant, now she was all welcome. The commentary from the crowd got very far away, lost in the rhythmic tugging at her nipples and the matching rhythm in her cunt. Roger matched the pumps, finding the speed that not only equaled the milkers' squeezing but woke the volcano inside her. It was never quite dormant—every orgasm she'd had in the dairy left her primed for the next, and Roger summoned them all.

"Uhnnn," she moaned, and the audience moaned with her. Clenching around everything that filled her, she would come in a moment. The plug filled her ass enough to rub against his cock inside her— she pulsed, a few flutters that left her wanting. He sped up, his hairy balls slapping against her engorged clit, faster, until he jammed inside deeply, wriggling his hips. If he intended to rub his sack against her clit, it did just what he meant—she came in a shower of rain against his nutsack, with a wordless cry. He froze for a moment, and she could feel hot jets of cum spilling into her. Fuck the prostaglandins; she wanted his dick, his seed, his pleasure.

The audience wanted their spectacle. "One!" they screamed. Ginny could have told them more than the oscilloscope could about what had convulsed them both. He folded against her to press a kiss to the nape of her neck. "You doing good?"

"Fine," she gasped, although if he went limp on her now in spite of his big words, she'd be doing closer to rotten. But he didn't—his rod stayed hard within her, and in a moment he began to fuck her slowly. Long strokes, and if they showed the doubters he was still erect after his climax, that didn't keep them from feeling fine inside her primed pussy.

His hands loosened against her waist, steadying him now more than giving leverage. He seemed to be rocking his entire body to move inside her channel, so wet now with her own natural juices, and some of his. If they were in bed, she'd have turned over to wrap her arms around him while he made his slow thrusts, and kiss him in the lull, but her hands couldn't leave their grips, and the shackles bound her wrists beyond hope of escape. But she didn't want to escape, not with Roger's stiff pole impaling her.

He picked up speed, slowly winding up to a speed she was sure he couldn't maintain, even with that athlete's body, but he slammed into her a dozen times, and a dozen times more. Could he go all night at that pace, pounding against her swollen clit until she exploded first?

Time stopped mattering for her. He was piston to her cylinder, racing like a freight train and her climax hit just as hard. This time she screamed, and she was not alone. "Two!" the audience bellowed, but she could feel Rogers' cock pulsing in her pussy, spraying his milk-giving cum into her.

Reality returned, and it sucked—Roger pulled out. Her pussy gaped hungrily, but there wasn't a thing she could to do recapture him. Had he lost his erection this time? He'd sworn he could come in her five times—he'd made less than half. "Roger?" she mumbled.

"We're good," he assured her, and to prove it, he started to rub his length against her pussy, drawing his cock against her clit. Oh, he was still hard—she hadn't expected him to be a showman and wasn't too happy about being his pretty assistant for sexual magic tricks, but—it felt good and the men watching were muttering to themselves about "fucking show-off" and "How much Viagra did he take?"

"None at all," Roger sneered, and lined himself up with her hole again. Slamming home, he made her squeak with the pleasure/pain of his cock-head against her cervix. His balls thumped her clit with every thrust, and the machines suckled tirelessly on her nipples. Ginny'd swear someone had turned the milkers' suction higher and that her nipples were getting stretched to three times their proper size. The machine should be pulling her milk right out of her—would she get her milk right here? Nothing felt different enough to make her think she'd started lactating, and the audience wasn't commenting. They probably hadn't looked at her collecting bottles once they realized Roger was going to cum again.

Their onlookers shrieked the count, the women with delight and the men with disbelief. Roger jammed his prick into her, giving her almost more than she thought she could take, but the 'scope lit up and the naysayers had to admit Roger'd made good on three of his promised five orgasms.

"Move over and let someone else have a tap on that!" someone yelled. Probably someone who'd expected to freshen her this afternoon, but Roger only suggested, in a perfectly conversational tone, that the heckler go fuck himself. He'd withdrawn from her pussy, but he couldn't be done. She had to believe that.

Just because he'd starting massaging around her clit with that versatile thumb didn't mean he could skimp on two climaxes. Maybe he was tired, but he wasn't forgetting her needs. How did he know she was too sensitive to take the direct pressure right now? And why was he twisting that plug? She managed to nearly forget she had an invader in her ass until he started playing with it. If she could turn around she'd snarl at him, but she couldn't, and um, maybe she didn't want to, it was feeling pretty damned—*GOOD!* The orgasm rocked her, making her pulse under his hand. He slid his thumb into her cunt, rubbing her inner lips on the way in and out, and let her have something smaller for a moment. Only the movement made her forgive the absence of his prick. He'd have to fill her up again, even though he'd been going nearly half an hour and three climaxes. Damn but she wanted to turn over. Maybe get on top. Maybe tease him back hard as he teased her.

And she was still captive in the stanchion. Nothing that happened to her today would be because she did it; everything that Roger got was because he took it. She bucked against his hand and got her butt slapped for it. "Patience." He proceeded to teach her fortitude with two fingers in her pussy, curving down into her G spot. He flicked her clit again and she clenched around him, pleasure blooming through her and rolling up to her nipples. Surely if her milk was coming it would shoot out of her now!

"Damn, but he's hung!" some woman exclaimed. Ginny tried not to place the voice—she didn't want her friends admiring the man who was fucking her.

"Still hard, too," a man said. "Either he's full of drugs or he hasn't really cum."

"Oh, I've cum all right," Roger shot back at the doubter. "Three times, and number four will be along here shortly." He'd withdrawn his hand from her cunt and had started running his fingertips lightly over her butt cheeks. She didn't want him to jostle or twist that plug again.

"How the hell does he do it?" another man asked.

"Natural attributes," Roger informed him airily. "And intensive study of the sensual arts as taught in the *Rahtativad Lingam*. You've all read—no? You haven't?" He chuckled, still drawing tickly lines over her skin. Ginny wiggled under his hands. "I haven't even progressed to the *Khaletipol Yoni* yet, but she's not complaining." He invaded her channel, spreading her wide all over again.

Of course she wasn't, not with that huge stiff cock sliding back into her pussy, a full comfort for the moment instead of a ripe rammer. He thrust slowly into her, his hips bumping against her round buttocks and the head of his dick pressing into her depths. Ginny wanted to say,

"Harder! More!" but she had to trust him to know his own stamina. Another orgasm simmered just below the boiling point, and he prolonged it with every push.

"Rahata—what?" "How do you spell that?" "Where the hell did he find—?" Their audience, or part of it, was diverted away from them. Ginny hadn't opened her eyes this entire time—she didn't want to see how a barn full of men and women stared hungrily at her swollen breasts and juicy cunt being filled with hard cock. She didn't want to see pity from any dairy maid for staying dry even at maximum stimulation, nor did she want to see the lust in all the men who Roger had shoved aside. She wanted to feel that huge cock in her love tunnel, and his hands on her hips, using her for leverage. She wanted her milk, and she wanted Roger.

"Look that up later, or you'll miss his next cum." Fucking Rita! She *would* bring everyone's attention back to Ginny's cunt and Roger's cock.

Ginny wouldn't miss it—if she wasn't shackled to the milking bench he might have shoved her right off the front with his steady hammering. He picked up speed without slacking the distance, forcing a little yip out of her with each thrust. Only her iron grip on the handholds kept her from yelling, and who was she keeping quiet for? Nosy neighbors? Hah! they were all here watching. Let 'em see what a real man could do to a woman—she couldn't unclench her jaw but her cries got louder, matching the rising explosion in her cunt. Oh fuck, she had to come before he did—if he stopped—! "More," she begged. "Don't stop."

"Anything," Roger puffed from behind her, "for a lady." His hips snapped against her ass, his prick a piledriver in her cunt, her overworked clit meeting his ballsack at a frantic pace. *One more! One more!* Oh fuck she needed just that bit more, and he found it by sliding his hand between them. A quick flick to her clit and she screamed—her climaxes were growing stronger, not slacking away, and if she hadn't been supported, she'd have fallen on her face. Only the milking bench kept her on her feet—Ginny went rigid with the waves that smashed her from nipples to clit and back again. Oh fuck he had to stop, just let her feel it—!

She'd worship at his feet for what he did next—stop. Crammed deeply into her pussy, his enormous pole stood stalwart against her clenchings, and pulsed back against them. The 'scope went wild. Her pussy throbbed and grasped his cock, milking the cum out of him.

After an eternity of sensation, Ginny became aware of a warm weight on her back. Roger had lain down atop her, his hands on her shoulders. His dick filled her pussy, hard as before. "You okay?"

"Guh." Had she blacked out?

Maybe he made sense of that and maybe he didn't, but he pressed his lips against her shoulder. "Think it's time to blow this popstand."

He lifted himself upright again to a chorus of whistles and yells. "Give it to her!" "Pound that pussy!" "Fuck, he's still hard!" and other encouragements made Ginny wish she was a million miles away. With this sort of rowdy group, Ginny believed everything Elspeth said about accidental anal, though Roger hadn't lost control of himself to the point of falling out of her. She clenched on the butt plug, a strange comfort.

And give it to her he did—he fucked her hard and fast, as if he hadn't been going for longer than any other man she'd ever met. Never pulling the head of his cock all the way out, he slammed into her pussy, traveling a good seven inches without ever losing contact. Her breath came in fits and starts, his in ragged gasps. His thrusts came faster and shorter, until he rammed in and stuck, and the 'scope chimed for the fifth time. He grunted something that might have been "Five," and panted over her, his hands on her waist.

"Let her up," he said to no one in particular. Jordyn jumped from her bench to release the stanchion, freeing Ginny's wrists. She slapped the switch, stilling the milkers. Jordyn knelt to unscrew them from their clasps. Lord, her breasts had to have expanded another cup size just from the milking. But would they give milk? Were they dripping at last? Ginny put a tentative hand to her nipple. Nothing. Yet. But her last dose of prostaglandins was only minutes old.

Roger pulled out of her, a long journey, and leaned against her rump. "Done. Five."

Someone shoved him out of the way, handling Ginny's over-fucked cunt. "Diaphragm," Elspeth said, sliding something into her. "It will hold the semen against your cervix. Wear it for at least six hours."

As if Ginny would dare reach in there for a long time yet.

"You didn't really cum five times, Styles," a man scoffed from the audience. "You can last a long time and fake it pretty good, but you didn't cum five times. No man can."

"I can," Roger snapped. "I did." He and Jordyn helped Ginny upright.

"You talk a good one, but you're a liar. Throw your money around and your big words, but you did no such thing." The man had one arm around Kitty's shoulders and was squeezing her breast. "You're a fraud." His words echoed in the now-quiet demonstration barn.

"You can kiss my ass," Roger shot back. "She needed five shots of semen, I gave her five, and I can damned well do it again." He grabbed his half-mast cock, which looked like it needed both hands even after what they'd done, and worked it. "I could have given her six." Face wrinkled in concentration, he masturbated his cock to full erection again, and aimed it at the scoffer. Another fast half dozen strokes and he shot a ribbon of cum at the man, splattering his shoes. The 'scope *pinged* Roger's orgasm. The barn went totally silent. Kitty shrugged out of the man's grasp.

"Six." Roger pulled the probe out of his ass and dropped it on the floor. "Fuck you, Jonah. Fuck you all." He cuddled Ginny to his side. "Let's get out of here, babe." He guided her out the barn door; she stumbled on the anteroom steps. Without a word he slid an arm under her knees and scooped her up.

216

Ginny clung to his neck, cradled in his strong arms, and let him carry her wordlessly back to her room. Neither of them had a stitch on, and Ginny's one bit of cover was the wide base of the butt plug. But no one was out and about in the dairy to see her naked pussy—they'd left everyone back in the barn.

He let her slide back to her feet once they were indoors. "Are you all right?" He examined her breasts with their huge nipples, swollen from the milkers' tugging. "Did I hurt you?"

For answer she kissed him. "No. I'm fine. Wonderful. Full of prostaglandins and my milk should come soon." Swollen, tired, adrenaline-hung-over, but fine. Wonderfully fine. Her Roger had fucked her silly. She wrapped her arms behind his neck and kissed him again.

"After that it better." Roger sounded grim. "I was terrified I'd be too late. Don't you dare have any more emergencies while I'm in Paris. I paced the plane all the way across the Atlantic." He hugged her more tightly.

"How did you find out—?" And should Ginny slap or kiss whoever it was?

"India called me."

Nope, not slapping India—Ginny'd get slapped right back. Even if she wasn't too grateful about being saved from a public gang-bang to complain.

He sighed. "I should have known you'd do something desperate if your milk hadn't come in."

All her squirming her naked self against Roger reminded her of something else she was desperate for. "Excuse me a sec. I want to get this plug out of my butt."

His arms went to iron around her. "About that."

"Eep!" What about that?

"We are going to get a few things clear between us before you do anything else desperate." He pulled away and grabbed her wrists in his big hands before she could even drop her arms. Dragging her to the slipper chair, he spun it around so its floral brocade back faced her.

217

He clapped her hands to the top of the chair. "Don't let go." He patted her thighs, slapped them, really, until she scooted her feet back. Ginny wasn't quite as bent over as she'd been with the milking bench, but it was an awkward position, and her giant breasts swayed unsupported. She tried arching her back, but they pulled the arch out of her spine. Damn they were heavy!

"Don't move," he commanded. "And don't speak unless I ask you a question." She looked up at this new, domineering Roger, eight and a half feet tall and made of stone. "This is not a scene. There is no safe word."

Chapter 16 Roger's Displeasure

No SAFE WORD? Ginny'd never been into BDSM, but she knew enough that safe, sane and consensual meant someone had a word to make it all stop. And Roger didn't look like he had stopping on his mind.

"I am most displeased with you."

He'd been cuddling her a moment ago! "What?"

"Eh!" His correction came sharply, as if she were a dog. "That was not a question." He circled her slowly, appraising her.

Nothing held her down except her own will. She could stand up, defy him, make him say whatever came next face to face, and—would he say it? Or would he leave? He'd just walked through fire for her. She stayed.

"Yes, I am most displeased. On account of you, my French employees have been left to twiddle their thumbs. My balls hurt. My ass hurts. And my pride hurts."

Oh shit. His pride must hurt worst of all. Ginny opened her mouth to apologize, but he corrected her again with his explosive "Eh!" Right. That wasn't a question either. She followed his movements with her eyes, bracing herself against the chair.

"I did not expect to have to fly three thousand miles and challenge the entire dairy for access to your pussy." He circled around her again, stopping behind her. He had to be staring at the hole he'd pounded so mercilessly. "At least you took precautions to defend some part of you."

Ginny couldn't take credit for that—but she hadn't fought Elspeth hard enough to find out she'd screwed herself again.

"Bear down." He gripped the handle on the plug. Its wide shoulders stretched her hole when he pulled it out, slowly, making her feel every millimeter of stretch in her ass. The widest part slid through her, letting the narrow end leave easily. He stopped with the tip still inside her hole. She dared not move.

"Never in my life did I expect to shove something up my ass for an audience." Oh but his voice was grim. "Turnabout is fair play." He pushed the plug back into her ass, taking his time, making her feel every millimeter of how her hole widened. Some lube still clung to the toy, but not enough to keep her ring from burning as it expanded.

Roger paused with the widest part inside her rim. Would he finish? Get it over with? Her face heated, but she didn't protest. He was right. He had inserted Dr. Busby's probe, or—the doctor had inserted it. Roger'd tried to talk his way out of it, but he hadn't whined when he lost the argument, and he'd silenced the doubters later. Ginny bit her lip and kept quiet, though a hiss of air escaped her.

He finished reinserting the plug in her ass. Ginny stifled her whimper when the wide part slithered in. This was nothing compared to what he'd endured for her sake. He could have stayed in France. He could have refused the probe, just gotten in line and let the others have their turns with her. He continued his circling.

"Most displeased. You did not wait for me. You concocted this plan, such as it was." His words flayed her soul like a whip. "Why?"

"To bring my milk," she whispered, once she realized this was a real question. "Elspeth and Dirk said it would work."

"No doubt," he gritted. "Consider though, that I have never known you with milk. I have known a great many dairy maids. I have suckled from their breasts, I have drunk their bounty from a cup, and not a one of them has inspired me to fly halfway across the world." He batted her breast, enough to make it sway. It knocked against its partner, making them both swing and thud into each other. "But I came for you, to be rewarded with this—this—debacle."

"I'm—"

"EH!" He chopped off her apology.

Under his savage gaze, Ginny dropped her head between her arms. She couldn't meet his eyes. She could argue nothing of his statements. She could only stay in this uncomfortable position while he pointed out her flaws, and hope for forgiveness. To be allowed to beg for forgiveness.

"Silly Roger," he chastised himself mockingly. "Silly, romantic Roger wanted candlelight and roses for the first time we came together. Champagne even. For you, not for me, but I wanted to watch you drink it and hear you giggle when the bubbles danced on your tongue. I like sappy romantic stuff like walking at sunset and feathery kisses, and undressing each other. Choosing which position to make love in, maybe trying several. I wanted to feel your arms around me and be welcome when I entered your body. Not—" He groped for words. "Not to be the least objectionable source of semen."

Tears pooled in her eyes and overflowed, dripping from her lashes to make dark spots on the rug. How he must hurt from that knowledge, and she'd caused it. If he hadn't arrived in time for her freshening, he'd have been hurt another way, and— He'd called the doctor Buzz, the way Dirk did, and he'd treated Dirk like a friend. Of course, after fifteen years, they'd be— She couldn't ask his friends for prostaglandin treatments. She'd hurt him enough already; she couldn't ask his friends to fuck her, even to treat her stupid, stupid, breasts. Why couldn't she lactate? If her milk had come before she met him, he wouldn't have held it against her how it happened, but after this…. She sniffled, and another tear dripped from her lashes.

She had to make this right! She'd hug him and tell him she was sorry, and when he was ready, she'd give him the romantic stuff he wanted, because she wanted it too, and barely dared hope of having it with Roger. He was a guest at the dairy, not her lover, even if she'd had a little taste of the paradise that existed in his embrace. She started to stand, to go to him.

"*Don't* take your hands off that chair." His words came as a blow. "Stay right where you are. Your submission is all that keeps you safe from me." He paced the few short steps around her again.

"I have no way to cope with this. I can't bankrupt you or buy you out; I don't want to humiliate you. I can't strike you in anger and still count myself a man. I'm not ready to hear that you're sorry because I don't trust that it's not just words." He stopped and fisted both hands in his own hair. "What am I to do with you?"

Ginny decided to interpret his rising tone as a real question. One to which she had the answer. "Punish me."

"Punish you." There was no question in his words—Roger was suddenly eight feet tall again. "How, exactly, then, shall I punish you?"

She'd given him something to hold on to. And a way to begin her penalty; he was making her name her punishment. Too much and she couldn't endure it. Too little and he wouldn't believe she was sincere. But what was too little? How would she find 'just right'? Her torment had begun.

She cast about for the balance. "I should be spanked."

He smiled, if the slight upturn of his lips could be called that—Ginny quailed. Spanking covered a lot of territory. "How should I spank you?" His eyes grew predatory—he knew exactly what she was thinking. He ran his hand over the cheek of her ass, following its curve. "This fine bottom can absorb a lot of punishment."

"Um…" She'd never been spanked, even as a child. She'd been thoughtless but seldom naughty, spending three minutes or five minutes in time out at most. How was it done? "With a belt?"

"You say that as a question." His voice had gone dangerously calm.

"Spank me with a belt." She got the words out with only the slightest quaver. She mightn't sit down again for days. Weeks.

"Interesting choice." Roger gestured at his naked body. "Mine seems to be back at the demonstration barn."

"I have a belt. Closet." A twinkly, fashionable belt. She wouldn't watch him open the door and find the instrument of torture inside.

He rummaged until he found it, hanging by its buckle on a hook. He brought it out into the light to examine. "I don't think so. Unless you mean to take more damage than a mere spanking." He flexed the strip of leather, making the three rows of pyramidal studs twinkle in the light. "I don't think an outright flaying is in order. No." He hung the belt away. "Choose again."

She'd missed on severity, though she couldn't be sorry he'd declined her choice. But what would accomplish only what he intended? "Um, your hand?"

"Ginny, if I touch your skin with my bare hand, it should be for our mutual pleasure." He looked down his nose at her most severely. "I don't wish to see you flinch away from me because you expect pain."

"Um...." She was running out of choices fast, and her back was killing her. Standing up would only bring her another grunted correction. What was paddle shaped? "My hairbrush?"

That got her a sideways look of approval. "That should do. Go get it."

Do—hell, that should hurt. At least she could stand up for the quick trip into the bathroom. "Ginny, girl," she told herself in the mirror while she rummaged in the drawer, "what have you let yourself in for?"

The brush was free of loose hairs; she wouldn't earn any extras by handing him a disgusting object. Its black rubber handle had never seemed so threatening, nor had the vented back seemed sinister in its pinkness. Her ass was about to match.

She returned to Roger, presenting the brush handle first without a word, but with a small dip of her head. Not waiting to be told, Ginny resumed her vulnerable pose, leaning against the chair back. Her breasts swayed, pendulous in their unaccustomed freedom, and very, very heavy. Her nipples were stiff—Ginny tried to tell herself it was from the milkers and the endless orgasms back in the demonstration

223

barn, but she knew that wasn't so—they'd been flat while he'd listed his grievances with her. No, her nipples were stiff again with anticipation. Her pussy's drippiness could be laid at her recent fucking— maybe. The diaphragm Elspeth had slipped into her vagina trapped his semen against her cervix, so no lying to herself that it was his fluids leaking out of her.

She waited for the impact of the impromptu paddle and hated herself for her anticipation.

"So, Ginny," Roger interrupted her thoughts. "How many strokes do you deserve?"

Oh damn, he wasn't finished making her choose her pain. How many did she deserve? How many would she give herself for disappointing him? She hadn't only hurt his pride, she'd hurt his hopes. "A hundred."

"I said this wasn't a scene. That's too many to not be able to stop with a word, and I assure you, Ginny, I do not intend to stop." He turned the brush over in his hands. "Nor do I intend to administer a severe beating." He slapped the brush into his palm, assessing the sting. "Punish you, yes. Get your attention, yes. Make it hurt, certainly." He slapped his palm again; the report was louder. "But not damage you permanently, else I would have used your first suggestion." He trailed the brush down her spine to make lazy doodles on her ass cheeks. She shivered but didn't flinch away. "So I ask again, how many strokes do you deserve?"

What was right, what was right? She groped for the answer that would satisfy him in its harshness. He grew impatient with her dithering and tapped the handle of the butt plug with the brush. The jolt of its movement shocked her into speaking. "Ten."

"Ten it is." He sounded approving. "Count them." The brush cracked against her right cheek, an explosion of pain.

"One." She gasped out the number.

He swung again; pain bloomed in her left buttock. "Two."

Three made her clench her eyes with dread, four made tears trickle from her eyes. Five and six ignited fresh fire on her behind; seven drew her scream. His eighth spank broke her down completely—he demanded she count three times before she could blubber out the number. Nine was a long time in coming—was he rethinking? She clutched the back of the chair hard enough to put a fingernail through the fabric.

Nine fucking hurt! The brush rang off her bruised buttock, every bit as hard as his first blow and no less painful for the familiarity. She choked out the number. The tenth stroke evened out her two throbbing cheeks. But it was the last. Ginny dared not stand up and put her hands to her ass in a useless attempt to put out the blazes. Her tears wouldn't do it.

"Ten, Ginny." He tossed the brush onto the chair. "I'm removing this now for my pleasure, not yours."

The plug shifted in her ass, as if that section hadn't had enough outrages. And of course her traitor body thought it should go straight to her cunt, in a bit of fire that didn't hurt. He didn't draw out the extraction this time, but instead spread her cheeks with one hand and pulled steadily with the other. Her hole felt strangely empty.

And then her other hole felt totally full. Roger had gone hard again, his cock rigid with whatever lust her spanking her had roused in him. "This is a reminder," he told her once he'd buried his immense prick balls deep inside her. "If you want me, there will be no other man, for any reason." His thrusts were the long hard slams of a pile driver. "Even your milk."

Her breasts wobbled and swung with his pounding—Ginny whimpered for the pleasure in her pussy and the pain of her breasts, but she didn't dare move her hands from the chair till she'd been given permission. Roger took mercy, or his own pleasure, reaching under her to grasp vast handfuls of her flesh. "Understand?" he grated. "No other man. Only me."

How could she want any man but him? She struggled to answer between her gathering climax and her weeping. "Only you."

Dairy Maid

"Damn right." He snapped his hips again, pushing all thoughts of other men out of her. "Only me." He doubled his speed, pushing her over the edge into mind-shattering bliss, the throbbing in her pussy matched by the throbbing in her buttocks. He didn't let her fall, nor did he falter and let her cum without movement. She cried out with every thrust, until he spurted into her with a gritted "Me!"

A moment later she felt soft lips on her back, trailing across her spine. "Can you stand up, sweetie?" Roger slid out of her pussy and helped her come upright. He turned her to face him and gathered her tenderly to his chest. "Over. It's over."

"I'm sorry, Roger." Ginny wet his skin with the last of her tears, though fresh droplets threatened to fall.

"I know you are," he whispered into her ear with breathy kisses. "You are forgiven. It's over. Done, and not to be repeated. Any of it." He nuzzled against her temple.

"But—"

"No buts," he interrupted. "Your punishment is complete, you've apologized and been forgiven." He kissed her eyelids and licked away a tear. "And it's done. We don't have to speak of it again."

"Go and sin no more?" In her relief, Ginny found a weak joke.

"Something like that," Roger agreed.

"But—"

"I said we're past it now." A trace of his earlier domination returned.

"What if my milk doesn't come from just today?" she blurted out. That problem hadn't gone away yet, and the proof was plastered against his chest. "Are you staying a while?" He'd said he dashed away from business.

"I can't." He stroked her hair. "And I can't leave you dry." He switched to rubbing the strands between his fingers. "I wouldn't dream of telling you not to make a living or keep trying to get your milk, even with your friends' help, but... Ginny, everything from here down—" He poked her waistline, making her jump. "—is for me." He steered her toward the bed. "Now let me take care of you."

226

She lay on her side while he bustled away, returning with a hot, wet hand towel and a washcloth. He draped the towel over her inflamed buttocks. The moist heat did its work on her bright red buns. The washcloth he used to first wipe her face and then her crotch. "You shouldn't be very drippy," he commented. "I didn't have much left."

"How did you have any left at all?" Ginny dared ask.

He stretched out behind her, applying himself as a huge compress. "Ask the question you really want answered, Ginny." He draped his arm over her chest, beneath her huge breasts. She rested her arm over his, content to be cuddled.

"Okay. How'd you cum seven times in less than two hours?" That would be no trouble at all for her, but for him? Any man? He'd said he wasn't ordinary, and he was right—his feat was completely beyond her experience. "Was that Ratatata-thing for real?"

"Yes and no," he said. "I made up a name to frustrate them when they went hunting, but there are old methods that work and entire shrines to the methods. He rubbed his cheek against her hair. And then Roger changed the subject. "You've probably noticed that I have a very limited diet?"

"White rice and milk," Ginny wound her fingers into his. "I figured you liked it."

"The milk's nice." He pulled her hand along to tickle her nipple. "The containers are nicer. But when I was nineteen, I got very ill. Nearly died. And it's left me with severe food intolerances. White rice and human milk are all I can eat without getting really sick again. Manley Dairy is a haven for me—this is the only place in the world no one questions my food choices. Very awkward for doing business in France, let me tell you, when I have to go to dinner with associates and smell the divine cooking that they make a particular issue of enjoying in front of me, thinking it will put me off-stride." He chuckled grimly. "That tactic ends up costing them money every time."

"You'd think they'd have figured it out the first time," Ginny mumbled. "After you spanked them in the wallet."

"So far they haven't." He chuckled.

She'd enjoyed her meals in his company, eating with gusto. "You don't think I've been teasing you with food, do you?"

"Not at all. I like to watch you eat; you enjoy it so much." He nuzzled her. "The only way I ever get different flavors is if the food gets filtered through a dairy maid, so don't stop. Please."

"I won't." She squeezed his fingers.

"So I've been coming here frequently since then. But not being able to eat freely made me compensate in others ways. Athletically. Business. Sex. I'm a little competitive, you might have noticed."

"I noticed." And also noticed that he tended to win.

"I may not be able to eat all kinds of food, but my body damned well does obey me in everything else. I found the old texts and learned the tantric practices. Good thing, too." She could feel his smile against her head.

"Very." He had to be the one man in the state who could have pulled off today's freshening single-handedly. "Maybe you'll teach me?"

"Gladly." He shouldered his pillow into a better shape. "You still have a prostaglandin problem. How about you pack up your little blue friend and come to Paris with me? I can give you your next application at thirty-nine thousand feet."

"Sounds lovely." Ginny would adore going to Paris with Roger, although she was equally happy to curl up in a local haystack with him. And only one of those was possible during her probationary period. "But I can't leave the dairy yet. I signed a contract."

"There goes that idea." Roger hmm'd. "I'll talk to Buzz and Dirk before I go. We'll think of something. And I'll be back next week." He yawned in the middle of a word. "Sorry, I have to sleep. Even I can't cum seven times without rolling over for a while."

"You did march across the Atlantic too," Ginny reminded him. "And I didn't sleep much last night." She was content to drowse in his arms, but she must have fallen asleep because next thing she knew, he was kissing her forehead.

"Ginny, I have to go. I'll be back as soon as I can, and don't you dare create any more emergencies." He was chuckling, so he meant it but wasn't angry any more. "Good luck lactating." He tickled her nipple, which poked out from under the covers. "Let the other dairy maids help." He put his head to her breast for a quick suck.

She stroked his hair, reveling in the feel of his lips and tongue. "Um, getting anything yet?" Was it too soon to hope?

"Not yet, but it's only been three hours." He licked a circle on her areola. "But soon. Before I get back, I'm sure." Roger came up to meet her mouth. "I still want the candlelight and roses." With a last brush across her lips, he was gone.

Chapter 17 Lemons, Lemonade

JORDYN CAME IN through their shared bathroom at the precisely wrong moment. "Hey, Gin, are you ready for— What the hell?"

The hem of Ginny's skirt had fallen over her face, but everything else was exposed. How was she going to explain standing on her head, with her lower half completely bare, her legs spread, and a shot glass stuck in her pussy? "Um…"

"Never mind. I don't even want to know." Jordyn backed away. "I'll be back in a few minutes. We can go to dinner then. If you can refrain from molesting the tableware."

Ginny came right side up and hurried to place the diaphragm. Jordyn watched her do it. "I was inserting my prostaglandins, if you must know." She wanted to keep Dr. Busby's sample from leaking out. Dirk and the doctor took turns disappearing into the bathroom for a few minutes of solo entertainment and then returning with semen for her. Neither one had suggested applying semen the usual way.

"Had you considered spreading it on the diaphragm and inserting the whole thing while you're right-side up?" Jordyn asked. Her breasts were swollen; she couldn't have pumped or nursed recently.

Facepalm time. Ginny could have spared herself the gymnastics. "It's yoga. I'm multitasking."

They went to dinner, where they were greeted as the charming pair of bookends they were, but while Jordyn knew all the guests and happily made arrangements for feedings and entertainment, Ginny had been spending more and more time on the pump. Every available dairy maid was taking a few minutes from her day to stimulate Ginny, always with one eye on the calendar.

She had two days left of her probationary month.

She still wasn't lactating.

After dinner, Jordyn and Ginny went to the horse barn with a guest. He saddled up a chestnut mare and asked with a wink, "Who's coming for a ride and a little snack?"

Ginny studied the straw on the barn floor. It was nice of him to ask as if Ginny could participate, but they all three knew what that red checked skirt meant. Ginny mumbled, "You guys have fun." She watched Jordyn swing astride the horse behind her cowboy, her skirt rucked up and her arms around his waist.

An hour and a half later, Ginny saw them ride back. This time Jordyn was sitting sidesaddle and her head was on his shoulder.

Ginny missed Roger so badly she could cry, but what would she tell him? "Guess what, all that public display and I'm still dry!" No. She couldn't bear that. She dragged Heidi with her to the spooky barn.

Heidi closed the stanchion for her and placed the silver milkers over Ginny's teats. "I told Elspeth to come get me," she assured her friend as Heidi inserted a well-lubed vibrator into Ginny's pussy.

But she hadn't said a word to anyone. She spent the night in a milking trance. Dirk didn't scold her, much, and he stopped when he found her still empty collecting bottles. He assisted her back to her room and left her in bed with instructions to sleep properly. Ginny toyed herself to three orgasms and fell asleep with tears on her cheeks.

One more day.

Dr. Busby didn't bother taking her temperature or measuring her breast volumes, or even asking her to strip, only dropping the neckline of her blouse. He palpated her enormous breasts and tugged at her nipples as if the milk would come because an expert summoned it.

Not a drop.

She snuffled and tucked her tits away. He put his arms around her, and she clung for the comfort, both wishing he was Roger and glad he wasn't. "I'm sorry it worked out like this, Ginny. You've helped science but at a personal cost."

"They're going to make me leave, aren't they?" Her eyes leaked, staining his white jacket.

"Probably. If you haven't begun to lactate by now, it's not likely that you'll start." He patted her back, but it wasn't comforting. "Your breasts should gradually resume their previous size without the constant stimulation. Or you might remain a cup size larger than when you came."

"Wonderful." It would leave her well qualified for that exotic dancing job she never wanted. Ginny left him and stumbled back to her room, which wouldn't be hers much longer.

The other dairy maids hugged her and commiserated with her, but they all had things to do, people to feed. Heidi and Jordyn stayed with her on the big bed that had been the scene of so many of their adventures.

"At least you guys started to lactate." Ginny tried to find something upbeat about this. "You can be here as long as you want. You're both built for abundance." She hefted Jordyn's breast, lighter than her own, but Jordyn's flowed with sweet milk for anyone who teased it out of her nipples.

"It could still happen, Ginny," Heidi tried to comfort her. "You only just started the prostaglandins."

"Not like I can get more without fucking some random stranger." Ginny couldn't bear that. "And Roger hasn't come back, so I can't even tell him goodbye." Somehow that hurt worse than anything. Ginny rested her head against Heidi's gigantic breast and let her white peasant blouse sop up the tears.

"If he doesn't get here in time, we'll tell him where you went. You have to keep in touch with us," Heidi demanded. "And he'll get here. He got here last time, didn't he?" She rolled Ginny to her back.

"Don't give up yet, Gin-gin." Jordyn pulled down Ginny's blouse and opened her bra. "It ain't over 'til it's over." She put her mouth to Ginny's breast. Heidi sucked in Ginny's other nipple, and together they nursed on their third amiga for an hour. But they got nothing to taste for their efforts, and Ginny was too sad to cum.

Her last day dawned. Ginny was awake for the sunrise; she'd been awake all night. She sat in the Adirondack chair on the porch and watched the sun paint the fields and buildings with rosy slanted light. The conical haystacks cast long shadows pointing to the west, and a few birds twittered. More out of habit than expectation, Ginny twiddled her nipples while she watched the world wake up. A beautiful, fecund world that contained laughing, lactating women and the men they fed. Ginny would no longer be a part of it in a few hours. Crying would only make it harder to see, and she wanted to soak up everything she could, to carry her through the lonely days of searching for a place to live and honest work.

She should have been a part of this world. Her red skirt mocked her: *Dry woman, they don't need you here.*

India tried coaxing her to breakfast, but she didn't want to see the pity in everyone's eyes, and she doubted she could choke down a bite. Instead, Ginny wandered to the cow barn and watched Horace and a guest slide the milkers over the cows' huge teats. Hope they did the cows more good than they'd done her—a dry cow had no place on a farm, and now neither did Ginny. She slipped away before either of them spoke to her. Might as well get it over with.

She found Elspeth in Dirk's office in the big farmhouse, going over ledgers. "Twelve thousand eight hundred sixty ounces shipped last month to seventy-one separate clien—oh hello, Ginny."

"We really aren't ready to meet with you, Ginny," said Dirk. "Please go upstairs to the fitting room and pump until I come get you."

"Really, Dirk, we can take care of Ginny's severance now and not keep the poor girl waiting." Was Elspeth being kind in not delaying or was she just anxious to remove a useless dairy maid?

234

"No, we'll finish finding the discrepancy in the shipping. Ginny should have every chance." Dirk got up and took Ginny's elbow, practically marching her up the stairs. He dug the pump and bottles out from under the bed.

"What's the use? Ginny mourned, but she obediently exposed her breasts to the collectors.

"Humor me," Dirk told her. "Stay on the pump 'til I return for you." He closed the door behind him.

So what else did she have to do? Ginny lay back and let the collectors pull her nipples. Maybe this time, she'd let down?

But no, not even after an hour and a half went by, and then a half hour past that. Pumping would be a thing of the past soon enough. Ginny watched her nipples grow and shrink in the plastic tubes that had gotten nothing from her so far.

She'd pumped steadily but fruitlessly for more than two hours when Dirk reappeared. She was going to miss him, with his jovial smile and broad chest. He'd been kind to her, given her a chance, and if she hadn't had a sideways glance for him since she'd met Roger, she could still appreciate him and his happy dairy.

"Come downstairs. We'll discuss what's next. You needn't cover up yet." He held her arm on the stairs, and she was glad, because she might have taken a header with her shaky legs. Dirk escorted her to the parlor where she and Jordyn first found Heidi. It seemed so long ago.

"Oh, you can cover up, Ginny." Elspeth held a sheaf of paperwork.

"No, she still requires a full assessment," Dirk insisted. "We don't let our dairy maids go lightly." He seated Ginny on the couch.

"If you insist, but I doubt it will make a difference. Did you get anything at all while you were pumping?"

Ginny had to shake her head 'no.' The word wouldn't come past the lump in her throat.

Elspeth plopped down beside Ginny. She reached for Ginny's breasts and began to milk at them. Massaging and tugging, she should have brought gushes of fluid from Ginny's breasts, but not so much as a drop pearled on her nipples. "Still dry, Dirk. Sorry, Ginny." She stopped and reached for her papers again.

"Move over, Elspeth," Dirk insisted. "You know real suckling can get results the pump can't." He knelt between Ginny's knees and lifted one of her breasts. Her immense tit filled his large hand and overflowed. He looked at her quizzically. Ginny nodded. She wanted to feel a man's lips on her nipples once more before she left the dairy. Even if it wasn't Roger.

Dirk licked her stiff and sucked her between his lips. His nursing was strong and steady, and in spite of herself, Ginny felt the pleasure pangs straight to her clit. If she welcomed it, would that make a tiny difference in letting down her milk?

She steadied his head with one hand, and tried to believe she was feeding him. Dirk suckled, trying to offer hope with his eyes, but his mouth had no reason to rejoice.

"Really, Dirk." Elspeth sounded a bit cross. "Do you think anything is going to change now?"

For answer he switched sides, leaving Ginny's wet nipple to chill in the air. He suckled her more, and Ginny began to fear she'd be a nine and a half right there, but she refused to touch herself that last bit. Not with Elspeth watching. It wouldn't matter—Ginny didn't deserve the pleasure now.

At last even Dirk gave up. "I'm sorry, Ginny."

She fastened her clothing and signed papers where Elspeth indicated, and accepted the envelope with a sizeable check. Ginny wouldn't starve right away. But she wouldn't be a dairy maid either.

"Please leave your working uniforms on your bed," Elspeth told her. "The lingerie is yours. I'm sorry your milk didn't come in." Numbly, Ginny accepted Elspeth's hug and well wishes. She tucked her phone into her pocket, now that she was free to use it again.

Dirk hugged her tightly. "There's still a bright future for you," he whispered. Optimist.

Packing didn't take long: she hadn't brought much, and now everything she owned was in this small bag. Jordyn and Heidi kept her company, hugging and handing over tissues every few minutes. "Something will go really right for you, I just know it," Jordyn whispered and Heidi agreed. But nothing had gone right for a while.

If she could slip past everyone and escape, then she could cry as hard as she needed to, but no, all the other dairy maids appeared between her and the door. Taylor, Sailor, Patti, Kitty, Mindy, and more—everyone had to hug her, and from the number of arms she was passed to, some took three and four hugs. Everyone had encouragements for her—the "You'll be fines" and the "Good lucks" ran together in her head.

Her vision had blurred with tears long before the farewells were done, else she would have turned away from Rita's embrace. "I'll take care of Roger for you," she gloated. Ginny ripped away from her, to crash into India.

"I'll take care of Rita for you." India's promise was grimmer, but more welcome.

Heidi and Jordyn walked her down to the driveway. Dirk said he'd bring her car around from the back forty, and the battered little Chevy waited on the gravel. For the first time in a month, Ginny wasn't dressed like her companions. Her jeans felt strange on her legs, and her stretchy lilac shirt had stress valleys between her enormous breasts.

"You can't forget us!" Heidi and Jordyn squeezed Ginny tightly.

"Never," Ginny promised. Her month at the dairy would last forever in her memory, and possibly equally long on her chest. She didn't want to let go of her two friends and get in the car, because that would mean it was all truly over. She didn't look up when a car crunched over the gravel and stopped next to hers. Its deep, throaty roar cut off, and a door slammed.

"Can I get hugs too?"

That made Ginny look up—Roger!

Heidi and Jordyn all but threw Ginny at him. She launched into his arms and crushed her face into his chest. "Oh! I thought I wasn't going to get to say goodbye!"

"Uh, I'm still stuck on 'hello.' What's going on, sweetie?" Roger wrapped his arms around her shaking shoulders.

"M-my m-milk never came and m-my m-month is up, and I have to leave, and I m-missed you so m-much," she wept into his shirt. "And I have to leave the d-airy!"

"Oh my," Roger said. "Ginny...."

Whatever he said after that got lost in her flood of tears. Her nose was probably turning red and her eyes would surely be puffy, and that was just one more reason not to look up at the man who was everything she couldn't have, especially since she was getting his shirt all soggy. But she wouldn't give up her last little piece of wonderful. Not until she had to.

"Ginny," Roger tried again. "None of this is a problem if you'll just listen to me and do one thing." He threaded his fingers through her loose curls and eased her head back, forcing her to look at him.

"What's that?" Ginny gulped. He was getting a good look at her splotchy face, as if she needed more humiliations. At least she hadn't wailed out that she didn't know what to do. Even though she didn't.

"Marry me."

Buh? Her mouth worked but nothing came out. Had she heard right? Her knees started quaking and her heart leaped against her ribs like a mad thing. Had he really—? She gaped up at him.

"Yes, Ginny." He smiled down on her, his eyes crinkling happily and his lips parted in a grin that said he knew her flabber was totally ghasted. "I asked you to marry me. Now say 'Yes, Roger'."

If he'd said, "Paint yourself blue and run through the dining room with a rose in your teeth," she would have agreed to that. But marrying him? "Why?"

"Because that's how you accept a proposal." He tightened his grip on her waist and wiped the last traces of tears from her cheek

238

with his broad thumb. "Why did I ask? Because that's what I want us to do."

"Mmm, okay. Um." What had she said okay to? Her head was swimmy. "Yes, Roger. Yes. But I don't understand why you want to. You barely know me." But the blue sky was six shades brighter, the birds sang from the haystacks ever more sweetly, and his hard body in her arms was too marvelous to try letting go.

"I know you make me see the world as beautiful instead of economic. I know you inspire loyalty in your friends, Ginny, and you're good to them. You're accepting of differences. You throw yourself into a new project headlong. You don't stand around waiting for someone else to solve your problems, and when you're not creating havoc—" The kiss he brushed on her nose took the sting out of that word. "— you're nice to be with. I want to be with you."

Had he really seen all that in her? "But I can't lactate."

Roger raised one dark brown brow. "Have I said you needed to? Besides, it's more 'you can't lactate yet.' We'll see what happens after I put a baby in you."

"Just wait a minute there, mister." Babies were so not part of Ginny's immediate life plans. But then, until thirty seconds ago, neither was getting married. But it confirmed her suspicions that semen had a nine-month lag time in causing lactation.

"I can wait a couple of months." Roger slid both hands down her body to grab her buttocks. "But the lactation isn't the issue, sweetie. I've drunk other girls' milk for fifteen years, I can keep doing it. You can pick which container it comes in." He was going to have her landing flat on her back with that sort of touch—could they at least get inside first?

"I know it seems sudden, Ginny, and I'd planned to just turn up regularly for the next year to woo you. You're honorable about contracts. But now—you're free." He bent to kiss her, red nose and all. "And I want you."

She kissed him back, her lips opening under his. "You really want to marry me? When there's a dozen dairy maids who are equally nice and lactate to boot?"

"You are hard to convince. Hell yes, I want you." Roger snorted. "You got past my defenses. The only one ever. I can fuck for two hours and not cum just as easily as I came seven times in two hours, but you pulled it right out of me with your tits alone. Nobody does that to me. So, Virginia Harper, are you going to marry me? And when?"

"Ginevra," she corrected him. "And yes. Soon. Erm, you don't want a big society wedding, do you?" She had no idea how to arrange an event worthy of paying back a decade of social obligations. "They had a wedding not long ago here at the dairy, they know how to do it."

"Ginevra soon-to-be-Styles, I am going to marry you just as soon as possible! Tomorrow. Here." He pinched her butt hard enough to make her yip. "Just so I can be certain what your name is. Let's go find you a ring."

He swept her into the Boxter, and the afternoon was a whirlwind of dressmakers, phone calls, and jewelers.

"Have to get you a diamond as big as your nipple," Roger whispered naughtily while the jeweler extracted the best stones from the safe. "Better check for size." He stretched out her neckline, pretending to peek, and let go when she swatted him.

"What if I want one big as the head of your dick?" she whispered back, certain there was no such gem in the world.

"The Queen isn't selling the Crown Jewels this week." Roger winked at her and tried to be serious when the jeweler returned with the twinklies, but a "snork!" escaped them both. He picked a gem that exceeded her nipple.

"Roger, maybe this diamond?" She made a smaller stone dance in the light. "That's too big." She didn't want to say "too expensive" even though that's what she meant. "It'll make me walk with a list."

"Guess we need one for the other side!" Roger announced to the stunned jeweler.

"Roger!" Ginny squeaked. "That's—!"

"Hmm. Okay." He dropped one eyelid at her. "I promised you pearls, didn't I? My lady needs a strand for her wedding." The jeweler bustled off for more lovelies. "In fact, I'm going to give you a pearl necklace at least once a week for the rest of your life."

"I can't wear that many." Ginny's eyes were glued to the rock on her finger.

"You can wipe them off."

"Roger!" She smacked his thigh to silence his naughty innuendo. He fastened the pearls behind her head with a smile that promised many things.

They arrived back at the dairy late that afternoon. Roger stopped at the milkhouse for his dinner, draining his portion from a cup. Ginny didn't want anything, fearing she'd drop forkfuls down her front because her hands were shaking from exhaustion. They toddled back to his suite, her arms around his waist. They greeted many guests and dairy maids on the way, not stopping to talk. One was persistent.

"ROG—" Rita shrieked, her arms out. "—er." Her voice dropped eighty decibels when she saw Ginny. Or Ginny's hand, dazzling against his forest green shirt. "Shall I save my morning feeding for you?"

"No need," he told her giving her a bare flick of his eyes for politeness. "My fiancée will take care of me."

Let Rita assume what she wanted. Ginny was done playing games with her.

Roger's suite was bedecked with candles. Pale pink roses in crystal vases cast the flames around the bedroom. So that's what her darling had been doing on the phone while the dressmaker had measured and snipped. Her gown was simple, but had taken enough time that he could indulge his romantic side. Sweet, romantic man. Her sleepless night had to be cast aside—Ginny didn't want to disappoint him. That didn't prevent the yawn that nearly broke her face.

"Poor girl, your bags are fully packed." He traced the dark circles under her eyes. "You didn't sleep last night, did you?"

Busted. Ginny shook her head.

"But you did pump, didn't you?" One hand stole to her breast to cup it and tickle her nipple.

She nodded.

"Still trying. We won't waste the effort." He stripped her overworked shirt over her head and shucked her out of her jeans. "Lie down."

He opened her bra, reverently letting her breasts out. "Do you mind an old fashioned wedding night?"

What did that have to do with him putting his mouth to her nipple? "That's fine."

She ran her hands through his hair, letting him suckle her from above. Oh, his lips hadn't lost a beat in the last week. Was wonderful. Slow foreplay. He could do that all he liked. Oh. Yes.

She fell asleep before he switched sides.

Chapter 18 Festivities and Denials

GINNY WOKE TO stroking on her breast. "Morning, sweetie." Roger placed a soft kiss on her forehead. "Ready to get married?"

"Mmm, yes." She slipped her arms around him. If she stuck her hip under his, she could flip him on top, and they had hours, since she'd been told firmly that everything was under control and she wasn't to worry about a thing. But he wasn't flipping.

"Old fashioned, remember?" Roger stayed planted on the mattress. "I marry you first."

Wow, that was really old-fashioned, considering last week's adventure. She'd take it. Especially since she wasn't going to have to wait—um, how long? "What time?"

"One o'clock okay?" He sounded uncertain. "That will give you plenty of time to get fluffy."

It was eight o'clock now. "Perfect." More than enough. But he'd chosen it with their caterer/venue/planner's coordination. Nobody she cared enough to wait for longer than that.

"Now for your good morning." He put his mouth to her nipple. Wasn't this where she'd checked out last night? She settled back under his talented tongue, grateful to be a nine and a half. If he was too old-fashioned to help her with that last half, she'd just show him what he was missing.

OMG, if this was how she was going to wake up in the future, she would say, "Yes, dear" to whatever he wanted. He nibbled and

243

flicked, and settled down to a good hard sucking, like he expected milk to come flowing out into his mouth. He wasn't saying a thing about yea or nay on milk, but nothing was stopping his nibbles, swirls, and sucks. This was her beloved sucking on her, and playing with her other nipple. Oh, yeah, that hotline from tit to clit was lit up cherry red—with every slurp he sent sparks into her pussy.

He kept her on the brink, evilly refusing to move his hand, no matter how she squirmed and whimpered, and when she tried to reach into her crotch for a couple of clitty strokes, he grabbed her wrists and switched sides. "Old fashioned, remember?" Roger said slyly. Oh that monster knew exactly what kind of torment he was providing!

Now her left nipple was helpless under his tongue! And oh how he was working it! "Roger, please," she moaned, and tried to cross her legs to gain some relief that way. But her wicked man stuck his leg between her knees, and she couldn't even squeeze her thighs for that last half step to her climax.

Ginny fought him, straining to get his thigh up to her needy puss, but he had her overpowered. She couldn't say it was terrible to be kept hovering on the edge of explosion, but if she didn't get one more little touch, just enough to make her cum, frustration was going to kill her dead. Testing his grip and his strength with the thrusts of her hips that just incidentally pushed her tit more deeply into his mouth, she whimpered and cursed, and found no satisfaction. His mouth never left her nipple—his clever tongue danced over her flesh.

"Roger!" she cried again, twisting under him. He vaulted to all fours over her, pinning her wrists and immobilizing her legs with his. She writhed and yanked, but he might as well have been the Brooklyn Bridge for all she budged him. She fell back, panting, and the orgasm receded.

"I can cum the minute you let go," she said, puffing a strand of blond hair out of her face.

"You could," Roger conceded, "But I wish you wouldn't." He leaned down to kiss her, and there wasn't one thing she could have done to prevent her lips from parting under his. "I want you very, very anxious to be married."

"I am," and she was totally truthful. "But do you want me so anxious that I ravish you during the ceremony?"

"Oh would you?" He waved his eyebrows wildly, and she couldn't help it, she busted up laughing. He collapsed on top of her, laughing as hard as she, and they found kisses within their mirth.

She'd let him deny her this time, because trapped against her belly was the rigid evidence that he'd denied himself as much as he'd denied her.

If Ginny showered with Roger, she'd stretch his resolve on being old-fashioned, he swore, and left her sitting on the bed in his bathrobe. A knock sounded on the door. Ginny opened it to a flood of blue and white.

"Roger! We're stealing her!" the dairy maids called.

Roger popped out of the bathroom, a towel wrapped around his hips and a foamy toothbrush in his mouth. "Whah?"

"We didn't have a bachelorette party for her last night, so this is our last chance. We'll bring her back," Jordyn assured him.

"All pretty," Heidi added. The crowd behind her *mmm*'d their appreciation of Roger's bare chest. Ginny wanted to swat them.

"Okay. Uh, did anyone happen to bring breakfast in a bottle?" Roger asked.

The dairy maids goggled at each other. "Oh that was stupid of us."

Ginny would take care of her soon-to-be husband's needs, one way or another. "India, would you feed him, please?" She hugged her abundant friend in dark blue. "He needs his strength." With an arched eyebrow she tried to suggest he might need the energy from three Indias later today.

"I'll take care of him, don't you fret." India kissed her cheek. "Go on now!"

He waved them out the door with a foamy grin. "One o'clock on the lawn!"

"We're going to pamper you!" her friends promised, and shoved her into the bathroom with Jordyn while Heidi and the others rummaged for manicure sets and hairdryers.

Jordyn climbed into shower with Ginny. "Did you even have a chance to think about bridesmaids?" she asked, rubbing a dollop of shampoo into Ginny's hair.

"Not even!" Ginny realized with a shock. "But you and Heidi are the best friends a girl could want, so it should be you two."

Jordyn hugged a squeak out of her. "Sure!" Going back to the mass of suds, she said, "We were all afraid Roger wouldn't get back in time for you to talk with him, but we hardly expected you to get married, and so fast! You never said you liked him that much."

"I couldn't really 'fess up to falling in love with a guest." Ginny put her head under the spray. Ginny yipped when Jordyn aimed the hand nozzle at her pussy.

"This will only do so much." Jordyn spread Ginny's pussy wide, playing the water over her pink parts. "Sec." She found a douche nozzle in the bottle rack. "Is that diaphragm in? You don't want anyone else's prostaglandins in there today."

"EEP!" Ginny stuck a finger in, retrieving the latex disc. "Not any more."

Jordyn slid the fountaining nozzle into Ginny's cunny. "Make you all ready for Roger, huh?" She rinsed Ginny's pussy well, slipping the dildo-shaped sprayer in and out, and tickling her clit with a passing finger.

Ginny clutched Jordyn's shoulders. "Um, maybe that's enough?" Falling in the shower would leave bruises, and besides…

"Hee!" Jordyn removed the douche. "Do we need to do the other end?"

"NO!" Ginny stuck her head back in the spray to rinse away conditioner and avoid any discussion on anal. Honestly, if anyone suggested her ass would make a dandy wedding gift, she'd smack them with something old fashioned, like a crowbar.

Toweled dry, Ginny let Jordyn lead her back into the living room, wrapped in a bathrobe. "It's just us, Gin." Jordyn seated her on the couch. "Mani/pedi time, and all that." Heidi started combing out Ginny's wet hair, while Patti and Brianna buffed her fingernails, and two more of her friends got busy with her feet.

Jordyn brought out a pump and opened Ginny's robe. "Might as well, you aren't moving around for a while." She twiddled Ginny's nipples to stiffness and placed the collectors over them. The familiar pulling of the pump had its usual effect on her pussy. One little corner of her robe covered her crotch—if she didn't wiggle it would stay put, but Mindy ran the buffing pad over the sole of Ginny's foot and it tickled so bad! The fabric fell completely away. Ginny couldn't grab at it fast enough, and her manicurists weren't letting her grab at all.

"It's just us, Gin," Jordyn said over the hum of the hairdryer. "Nothing we haven't seen already."

"Or tasted," Taylor added. She rubbed lightly on Ginny's mons. "Were you planning to give Roger rug-burn?"

Oh dear—Ginny should have shaved her puss along with her legs. "I'll have to get back in the shower."

"No, you won't." Jordyn fetched the trimmer. "Spread 'em."

That trimmer felt as good as it ever did, but with an audience this big, she wanted to slam her legs shut. The pressure on her nipples was making her wet, and now Jordyn was buzzing her. Her pussy clenched, and all the girls giggled.

"We have to explain the birds and the bees to the bride, don't we?" Jordyn inquired, with the trimmer whirring across Ginny's mound. "She has to know her wifely duties, and what kind of 'special hug' she'll get." Jordyn's wide eyes and breathless tone made everyone laugh right over Ginny's protests. Hell, they'd seen her freshening. But this was her bachelorette party and at least no one was giving her tacky lingerie.

"Bees buzz and birds chirp." Would that stop them?

"Yes, they do!" Patti agreed. "Now don't be shocked, but he's going to want to—" her voice dropped into a conspiratorial whisper. "—take your clothes off!"

"Oh horrors!" "Naked!" "Oooh, naughty!" came in choruses around her. Ginny let her head fall back and closed her eyes. They were going to have some fun with her no matter what.

"And he'll want to touch your boobies!" Mindy giggled. "And even suck on them." She did something else tickly to Ginny's foot.

"Watch it with that orange stick," Ginny grumbled. "Okay, he'll want to touch my boobies."

"And you *have to let him!*" Heidi got into the act, and spoiled her advice by laughing.

"I do?" Ginny could play the wide-eyed innocent, even splayed across the couch with girls and devices on every body part.

"Yes, you do!" Jordyn informed her. "And he'll show you his wiener."

What a word. Ginny dutifully gasped with the rest of the girls.

"More like a kielbasa," Mindy considered. "Or a summer sausage."

"Hey!" That was her Roger they were discussing. For the first time, Ginny wondered how many of the experienced dairy maids Roger might have dallied with. But he hadn't flown round the world for any of them.

"Hey what?" Mindy blinked. "It is."

Not going to get into it with them. Ginny was the one wearing the ring. "I suppose he'll want me to touch it too." She pursed her lips in a terribly fake shocked "ooh."

"Oh yes!" came in four-part harmony. "And kiss it." That brought knowing nods and murmured "Kisses, lots of kisses."

"Eek," Ginny said weakly. Spoiling their game wasn't on. She checked her nails. Pale pink on fingers and toes: her friends had done a lovely job and she dared not wreck her manicure. She placed her hands flat to the cushions. Her crotch couldn't have a hair left by now, but Jordyn was still running the trimmer over Ginny's mons. Between the pumps on her breasts and the vibration of the trimmer, even this ridiculous discussion was having an effect.

"It gets 'eekier'! He'll want to touch you *here*." Jordyn demonstrated 'here' with her finger. Ginny jolted with the touch. Her clit had barely relaxed from Roger's earlier teasing, and that trimmer was purring away on her mound. She jerked her leg up, but Mindy wrapped her hands around Ginny's thigh and eased her legs open again. Taylor embraced her other thigh—Ginny wouldn't get away easily. What games would they play with her exposed cunny?

"And do this!" Jordyn slid her finger into Ginny's much too wet passage. "And what else, ladies? Tell her; I don't think she'll believe me." That finger was going in and out, and in, and oh, out, and then started flicking against her G spot on its way by.

"That's where he'll put his winky!" Heidi exclaimed.

Good Lord. Winky? Ginny's laugh was more a snort. "It's kind of big to call a winky." But thinking of him putting whatever it was called into her pussy, just… oh…

"Ohhh!" Her friends vied to sound the most shocked. "She's seen it! Oh, oh, oh." They spoiled their outrage with giggles.

"And he'll have to keep touching your boobies." Patti's wide-eyed, serious face kept crinkling with laughter. She flipped the pump shut and broke the suction on one of the collectors. Brianna released Ginny's other breast, and added, "He'll kiss them, too. And suck. Like this!"

Oh damn, with Patti and Brianna on her nipples, suckling away with their knowing mouths and way more tongue than suction, and her knees spread wide for Jordyn, the trimmer vibrating against her, there was not one sexual secret Ginny could keep. Heidi leaned over the back of the couch to kiss her, and the fragrant waterfall of her hair drowned the scent of roused woman for Ginny, if for no one else.

With a dozen expert hands on her, stroking belly, thighs, and everywhere, Ginny was overwhelmed. These were her friends, her supporters, and they were stirring her to new heights. Ginny bucked against their hands and mouths, throwing Jordyn's hand away from her cunt. But now, Jordyn had only dropped the trimmer and placed her lips against Ginny's needy clit. Suckling to match anything she'd ever done to Ginny's nipples, Jordyn worked her clit with lips and tongue. Helpless under the wet caresses and the dry, Ginny could only feel the heat in her breasts and cunt growing huge enough to combine.

And Roger had asked her not to cum. Not until he'd claimed her as his wife and brought her back to the boiling point. Not 'til later, and her friends were doing her *now*."Guys, stop!" Ginny couldn't push anyone away, helpless under wet nail polish. "Please!"

"Huh?" Every head popped up, disbelief across half dozen lovely faces, some smeared around the mouth.

"It's just—" Ginny struggled to explain without hurting anyone's feelings. "Roger said he wants to be the one who...." She groped for more words. "That feels really good, and any day but today, I'd just go ahead and cum, but he...."

"Ah." Jordyn nodded sagely. "He must be the one to deflower this little virgin passage." Pinching Ginny's labia together, she pretended to work her finger into an impenetrable space. "With his giant winky, he will cause all the petals to fly off your tiny rosebud in a shower of ecstasy..." She spouted fake harem wisdom to a chorus of snerks and snorks.

"I thought 'rosebud' was your ass. Are you gonna give that up?"

Ginny jerked up into a defensive position at the mere thought of Roger's huge cock in her virgin hole. If she could uncoil, she'd find a candelabrum to brain Mindy with.

"That looks like a no." Heidi patted Ginny's shoulders. "Sit up, hon; I need to put some curls into your hair."

Ginny sat up and wrapped her robe over her body. Stopping again before cumming left her with a familiar problem, one the dildo-shaped cold pack might help with. She scooted to the joint of two couch cushions.

Hoping the low spot would take the pressure off her swollen pussy, Ginny submitted to Heidi's brush and curling iron.

If Roger wanted Ginny really, really, anxious for him, then her friends had just given him a wedding gift.

HER NAILS HAD a second coat of palest pink and Patti was tipping Ginny's lashes with mascara when India came in, holding an ankle-length, sleeveless, ivory gown on a hanger. "The dressmaker dropped this off." She surveyed Ginny and the rest, who had scurried about to get themselves fluffy too. "You are one glowing bride. Did I miss the party?"

Heavens, was this a tradition? Although with the dairy maids' cheerful attentions to each other, why wouldn't it be? A lovely send-off. "Kind of. How's Roger?"

"Well fed and restless." India laughed. "If he don't stop jabbing the keyboard, he's going to break that laptop."

Everyone had to have their picture taken with the bride, indoors and out. Ginny got her lipstick kissed off four times by the time Elspeth stole her for a last adjustment before the processional started. What had been a blur of well-wishes became a dizzy prospect of changes, vows, and not falling off her shoes. She hadn't worn heels since her center of balance had altered so radically. Leaning on Heidi and Jordyn, Ginny approached her Roger, a tall, broad-shouldered vision in his light gray suit, with best man Dirk next to him for moral support. She placed her hands in his and made him promises that transformed her future.

A bourbon-scented Horace, of all people, guided their responses and pronounced them man and wife. Ginny melted into Roger's arms, scarcely able to comprehend how her life had turned inside out in less than five weeks. She parted her lips under his the moment "The Rev" instructed Roger to kiss the bride.

"Still anxious, Mrs. Styles?" he whispered into her ear.

"Want to get that suit covered in hayseeds, Mr. Styles?" she shot back.

251

"I'll take that as a yes." He kissed her again, and it was another blur of hugs, congratulations, and toasts. They danced—where had Roger found a string orchestra at a moment's notice?—and cut a cake, though Roger fed her a bite and only kissed the frosting off her lip. He ate some groom's cake, and one had to look hard to see that it was a cunningly shaped pat of white rice. They drank their toasts with crystal goblets, though his "champagne" was white.

Ginny's conversations with guests brought her around to the best man, Dirk. "I didn't know Horace was a minister." Of some very flexible denomination, too. She recalled his worship of Heidi's body in the stanchion.

"Some mail order thing. Church of the Open Bottle." Dirk took a sip of champagne, suavely sipping while Ginny choked. Once he thumped her back enough to bring her coughing under control, he told her, "I'm very happy for you."

"Was this the bright future you saw for me?" Had Dirk known before she did that Roger was so smitten?

"Not exactly. A little," Dirk admitted. "Certainly not this fast, but he's happier than I've ever seen him. He's an old friend. Be good to him."

"The best I can possibly be," Ginny swore, and glanced down at her satin covered breasts. If they'd done their job correctly, she'd be making dinner for Roger in a way she'd never manage in a kitchen, but then, if they'd done their job correctly, she'd be wearing blue checks like the female contingent of wedding guests, not an ivory satin gown and a diamond bigger than her nipple. "You delayed firing me so he'd get here in time, didn't you?"

"Busted." Dirk didn't sound the least penitent. "Had to do something when you showed up bright and early to get the boot. Plus last chance to suckle you." He leaned down to place a kiss on her forehead. "Be happy."

She was. Finding her way to Roger's side again, she slipped under his arm and listened while he discussed something stock-marketty for a few minutes. She considered sliding her hand under his jacket for a bit of groping.

"Toss your bouquet and we'll go," he suggested, just before she dropped her hand to his butt. "And I'll toss your garter."

The cluster of dairy guests Roger shot her garter at parted like baitfish confronted with a shark. The lace and satin band lay on the dance floor unclaimed. Ginny had better attendance for her bouquet toss— Rita nearly trampled her colleagues on her dash to the flowers. India expertly hip-checked the bitch. Sailor ended up with the posies. One of the guests caught her eye—she looked sadly down at her prize. He sidled toward the abandoned garter, and when Ginny and Roger turned to leave, the guest had the garter on one arm and a smiling Sailor on the other.

"I've done all the waiting I can do," Roger told Ginny. "Let's go."

They ran through a shower of birdseed tossed by their laughing guests. Malificent, aka Rita, didn't take hers out of the packet first.

Roger kissed her sweetly outside the door to his suite and slid an arm beneath her knees, exactly as he had after her freshening. He carried Ginny over the threshold, into the only home she'd known with him so far. Setting her down carefully on her teetery shoes, he embraced her tenderly. "I love you, Ginny Styles."

Chapter 19 Old-fashioned Joy

Ginny could barely wrap her mind around her new name, but being loved, oh that she could sink into without any preparation at all. "I love you too, Roger."

"You do?" He sounded surprised. "When did you know that?"

"Wouldn't have married you otherwise." She leaned her cheek against the soft, thin wool of his suit. "I fell head over heels the day you nursed on me in the woods. There's been so much else going on that there never was a good time to mention it."

His hand traveled slowly up and down her back. "Why did you fall for me?"

She could grab his ass now—and have it be the opposite of her words. "You were the perfect gentleman when it would have been so easy not to be."

"Can I stop being a gentleman now?" he wondered. "My inner caveman wants out. Bad."

"Let's please both sides of you." She reached up to kiss him softly. "This room is filled with roses. And candles."

Daylight had yet to fade, and the revelry from their reception could be heard through the glass. Let them party. Ginny drew the drapes. Lighting a match from the book lying on the silver tray beneath a vase of blooms, Ginny touched the match to one candle. The flame rose, flickering, lighting her face. She wanted Roger to see her in the candlelight now, when he'd been denied before. He wasn't silly

Roger, he was beloved Roger, and she would make him happy. Another candle took flame from her match.

She went around the room lighting the candles one by one. Standing between Roger and the flames would make the fire lick around the satin of her gown, touching her silhouette with ivory light. She wanted him to see the narrow span of her waist and the swell of her hips, to let him anticipate the moment when he'd touch her. All candles lit, she turned to him, puffing the match out with pouty lips. She smiled at him and bent in profile to give him a good look at her breathing in the fragrance of the roses. The candlelight painted her enjoying the beauty he'd gone to such efforts to create.

The open admiration in his face squeezed her heart. They'd had a rough start. She'd make it smooth. She came to touch his face, trailing fingers across his cheek and brushing his lips with her own. His jacket slid from his shoulders at her touch.

With caresses and kisses she stripped him, sliding his tie away, opening each pearl button of his shirt. The fine cotton whispered away from his skin. Neither of them spoke, though he shivered when her fingers brushed across his chest. His trousers fell from his hips when she opened his fly, and somehow everything else Roger was wearing disappeared.

He reached for the zipper at the back of her gown, but stopped with his hands on her shoulders when she took his cock in her hands. Her eyes remained on his, her hands independent in their admiration of his rampant organ. Thick, throbbing, his prick filled both of her hands with stiffness and need. She stroked the velvet skin over the hard column of flesh, her mouth touching his with breathy kisses.

Roger moaned softly, the tip of his tongue tracing her lips. A drop of moisture dripped to her wrist, but she didn't look. She knew he wept the first droplets to be ready for her, that more would make crystal beads on the head of his cock. He gasped, but did not move under her hands, letting her stroke his cock to hardness that rivaled marble.

"Ginny—" he croaked, but anything he'd ask her for now she'd preempt. Lifting the meaty weight of his prick against his belly, she came closer, until her breasts were crushed against him, and her tongue flicked against his.

She left trails of kisses down his neck and across his collarbone, over firm pecs and stopping only to flick at a nipple. He hissed. "Does that feel this good for you?"

"Better?" How would she know? But he could nearly bring her to orgasm with his mouth on her breast. She wouldn't take this first time to try the same on him, though he and his Ratatata skills might make that only the first of many orgasms tonight. She bend to kiss her way across his belly, the light dusting of hair at his navel rasping her lips.

Ginny went to her knees before him, ready to press the kisses she'd been teased about onto his swollen shaft. It was Roger engorged to the point of aching tonight—he pulsed in her hands. Precum glittered at his slit, wetting the velvet head of his cock, begging to be kissed away, to be tasted. She lapped at the bitter-salt droplet, and took his cock into her mouth.

"Oh, Ginny," he moaned, but there was no reply to be made—he filled her mouth, stretching her jaw. Her tongue met his shaft, velvet wet stroking velvet dry until he was a pulsing wet column of flesh. Two hands were still needed—she'd take as much as she could, but his length was overwhelming her.

Not that it kept her from doing her best. She swirled her tongue against his cock, feeling the shifting skin and hard core, tracing the curves of its head. This man could cum six times in less than an hour—if she accidentally pushed him into a climax it wouldn't be more than a pause to remove her clothing. Her gown felt suddenly tight around her breasts.

Would she? She pulled it out of him, he swore, but he'd given her as many of his climaxes as she needed. She needed them all. Might take years. A lifetime. She slid her hand down to cup his balls, drawn tight against his body. "Ginny!" His urgency broke into her awareness of how the crisp hairs of his ballsack grazed her palm.

"Come for me." She came away from his cock long enough to tell him what she wanted, or part of it—she wanted him happy, she wanted his climax to shake him to his toes. Diving back onto his shaft, she encouraged explosions with lips and tongue, gripping with mouth and hands to bring him to the brink.

He trembled under her hands and mouth, and held nothing back. Filling her mouth with his semen, he choked out words she couldn't follow, and fisted his hands fisted into her hair. Gush after gush of salty fluid he gave her—she could only swallow and try not to drown. His exquisite shudders lasted past her breath—she had to pull away enough to suck in air, but enclosed him again to catch the last spurts of fluid.

His arms trembled when he raised her to her feet, and his voice caught when he tried to speak. Abandoning words, Roger kissed her, crushing his lips against hers and demanding entrance with his tongue. Entrance she gladly gave him—he wanted to be welcome in her body, and he was, oh he was, starting with the probe of tongue and on to every way he could penetrate her.

"Beautiful Ginevra," he whispered into her hair. The zipper whirred behind her, the fabric falling away from her body. Ivory satin became a shiny puddle at her feet—his wide hands lay hot on her back. "I need to touch you."

Touch her he did, with long strokes against her skin that ended where the last scraps of fabric covered her. He fumbled at the back of her bra, searching for the clasp that lurked between her breasts. She twitched it open for him, but let him be the one to release her breasts from their restraints. As carefully as if he were unveiling a master-piece of art, he eased the lacy cups away from her flesh. Her nipples had gone stiff when she'd sucked him; now they stood in high peaks against the creamy mounds. He drew careful fingertips underneath their bulk, not touching the rosy nubs he'd spent hours sucking.

This time he was intent on the marvel of her flesh, the heft and immensity of each breast weighed carefully in his hands. He bent to her, meeting first her mouth and dropping lower to press his face between her luscious globes. Not rushing on to her nipples, he rubbed his face against her skin, his close-shaven cheeks gliding against her. Ginny ran her fingers through his hair, mussing the perfect waves. For the first time since she'd come here, her twin peaks could just be touched for joy, for comfort, for love, but not for milk. They were huge, they were sensitive, and he was enjoying them just because they were attached to her. He wasn't expecting anything from her tits except pleasure for them both. He licked a line across the tops of her breasts, finding the rise from her chest.

"I'm taking you to bed now." Roger steered Ginny backward to the king size bed. She sat with a bit of a flump when the mattress touched the back of her knees, but scooted back against the pillows. She held out her arms to him. Oh, but he was a fine sight, framed in the glow from the candles he'd wanted. At half mast, his cock pulsed upward, growing firmer with each beat of his heart. He gazed hungrily at her for a moment, and then came to press his length against her. From chest to ankles he lay against her, his mouth devouring hers with ravenous kisses.

Ginny could do nothing but lie beneath his loving onslaught, content to hold him tightly and share in the wet caresses of their mouths.

Again he roamed lower, tugging playfully at the strand of pearls he'd placed around her neck, and she smiled at his teasing. Ginny'd wear any pearl necklace he chose to put on her.

Her breasts became his playground—Roger had to lick and caress every square inch. Ginny had a lot of square inches. He took his time, rubbing his face over her skin, cupping one side while licking the other. Exploring, enjoying—this was nothing like his single-minded sucking of their nursing encounters. Ginny melted under his hands, free from the need to make her tits *do something*. Luxuriate under his attentions, that's all she had to do.

Dairy Maid

He found her nipples in passing, stopping long enough to suck a little moan out of her, but moving on to tracing wet trails to her chest or kiss the flat spot between her breasts, now much narrower than when she'd met him. Sliding his hand down her side reminded Ginny that she had a whole body, not just tits and pussy, and that he liked all of it. Her skin heated under his touch.

Roger pushed her thighs apart and knelt between them. His cock stuck out proudly over her—was he ready to enter her dripping channel? But not yet—he wanted to reach forward for a kiss, and then lift her thighs. Ginny let her knees fall toward her chest, and nearly wept when he put his mouth down to her pussy.

He lapped, he sucked, he nibbled her lips and clit. She was served up like a banquet, one he could eat to his heart's content. Every part of her tender folds was his for the tasting. Probing deeply into her passage with his tongue, or suckling tenderly on her clit, he found a hundred ways to make her moan. She put her hands to her nipples, playing with them in a way that made him open his eyes wide and match the speed of his tongue to her fingers.

Current ran through Ginny's body, and jumped the gap to complete the circuit. Her face went slack with the gathering pleasure—he licked faster, pushing her ever closer to her flash point. "Almost," she panted—he settled to a steady sucking on her clit and reached down to cup one huge breast. His fingers found her nipple, and the spark of his touch ignited her. Ginny convulsed with her climax, crying out his name. Her denials earlier were all made up for now—she clenched and rained for long minutes, with spangles dancing behind her lids.

He stayed with her 'til she went limp, gently uncoiling her to flat. He stretched out beside her to enfold in his arms. Ginny plastered herself against him. "Mmmm."

"Mmm hmm," he agreed, running his fingers through her hair. "You taste good."

"So do you." Ginny resolved to get more of his shaft in her mouth next time.

"Are you ready for me?" Sliding two substantial fingers into her slit, he checked for himself. Scissoring his fingers open found a yes and her G spot—she squeaked and clenched around his hand. "Yes, oh, yes." Roger rolled on top of her and found his destination with the head of his fat cock.

Ginny wrapped her legs around his waist, opening herself wide and welcoming. He reached down to her mouth and worked his way inside.

Oh how he filled her! Ginny lifted her hips against him, inviting his huge prick into her wet pussy—he sheathed himself in her balls-deep. She breathed shallowly, stretching to take him.

"Good?" he asked, and she panted her yes. Then he began to move.

His weight was a joy on top of her, his mouth never leaving hers. And his cock, oh his talented, tireless cock slid inside her, until she thought she might lose her mind. Oh but he could last, and last, even with the long pounding strokes, and when he switched to a tiny, precise movement while fully buried in her, he woke her clit again. A sideways grind of his hips tipped her completely over into a climax. She muffled her cry against his neck, clenching and fluttering around him, sharing her pleasure. She rocked with one orgasm that became two, and then a third wave struck her when Roger thrust deeply and spurted his own climax. Ginny clutched him tightly with her five point hug and thrust against him motion for motion when he did it all again.

He had enough weight on his elbows that he wasn't crushing her, even with her enormous breasts billowing between them—they squashed against his chest. Ginny loved the feel of his skin and muscles trapping her beneath him, and he showed no signs of letting up. A fine sheen of sweat had sprung up between them in their thrusting—they slid against each other in a way her nipples loved. Arching her back to press more closely set her off again in another wave of cumming that he helped along, and then joined.

They lay quietly after that, still coupled. With brushing kisses and sweet murmured words, they explored the joy they'd just shared.

Ginny trailed her fingertips up and down his back, and finally got her long-awaited double handful of his butt. Roger laughed and flexed under her hands. He withdrew, bringing another gasp from Ginny, who squeezed his semi-erect cock on the way out. "Oooh," he groaned. He lay next to her, one hand cupped around her breast, and nuzzled her gently. "Happy?"

"Very." The candles painted dancing shadows on his face. Ginny'd never seen anything quite as wondrous as his smile.

THE SUN WAS long gone and the wedding revelers dispersed to their more usual pursuits when Roger summoned a tray of dinner with a quick phone call. He fed Ginny bites of roast chicken and glazed carrots, and picked at his own dish of rice. A thermos of India's finest went down more quickly.

"Have you ever considered cooking the milk and the rice together for a pudding?" Ginny wouldn't try to rearrange Roger's diet, but surely he'd like a little more variety.

"No." He stared at his forkful of fluffy white grains. "Once I got well, we quit experimenting."

Ginny put cooking on her to-do list. "We can try it."

"At home. Not sure I want to suggest anything to a chef that might make me compete for supply." He took a swig of milk. "These nouvelle cuisine types will try any ingredient once. Speaking of which, do you like French food?"

"Oh, yes!" Ginny's mouth began to water at the memory of her one and only experience of *Magret de Canard au Cassis*. "But it doesn't seem fair when you...." She went silent when he frowned at her.

"You have to eat, I like to watch you, and it makes choosing a restaurant in Paris much easier if I know you enjoy French food." He reached across the table to cover her hand with his own. "You do have your passport?"

Ginny nearly choked on a carrot. "Yes, of course I do. But what...?"

"I mean to take you to Paris for our honeymoon, and incidentally take you to your new home, or one of them. I spend enough time there to maintain a suite at the *Grand Hotel du Palais Royale*, though if you truly hate the idea of being able to see the Louvre from your living room window, we could buy a house. Or an estate." He stroked the back of her hand, which didn't do a thing to make Ginny's bug-eyes go back into her head. "The French government probably wouldn't sell me Versailles, though."

"No, I imagine not. You mean you can see the Louvre, and you've never gone in?" She couldn't keep the squeak out of her voice. He sounded perfectly serious about buying the royal palace, which was shocking enough, but he hadn't visited a museum at his very gates?

Roger shrugged. "Maybe I've been waiting for the perfect companion?" He chased the last of his rice around the dish with his fork, and added impishly, "The Jeu de Paume is a few blocks the other way. If you want to visit."

"If I…!" Ginny dropped her fork. "Yes, of course I want to visit!" Dashing around their tiny table to throw her arms around his neck, she kissed him thoroughly. "And there's nobody I'd rather go with!"

He dragged her into his lap. "Perfect. You can educate the Philistine." He slipped her a bit of tongue and another bombshell. "We'll spend some time on *la plus belle avenue du monde,* too. It's not far."

"The Champs-Élysées?" Ginny breathed. "I've always wanted to stroll down that boulevard." Her head spun from the number of dreams come true he was offering.

"Fair warning, I'm going to drag you into a few of the shops," Roger told her. "Cute as you are in your dairy clothes, my bathrobe, or nothing at all, they aren't really suitable for Paris."

"No, of course not," she agreed faintly. Was there anything in her wardrobe that she'd dare be seen wearing in Roger's company in the most fashionable city in the world?

"How's your French?" Roger wanted to know. "Mine's fluent."

"Mine's rusty." Who would Ginny speak French with in Pennington?

"Not for long." He slipped a hand into her robe, well, his robe, but she was wearing it. "First refresher lesson: *Allons faire soixante-neuf.*"

That she understood just fine. She jumped out of Roger's lap before his rising erection knocked her out of it, and led him back to the bed.

Ginny was able to take more of his cock now that she'd had a chance to learn him a little, but he was so taken with what she was doing to him that he couldn't concentrate properly on her and came soon enough to be shocked with himself. Roger collapsed with his face in her muff. "I gotta turn around and do you right." Good to his word, he sucked her pearl until she exploded.

Once she'd gotten her eyes uncrossed, he asked her a question that had been on her mind since that morning with her friends. "Ginny, are you going to keep trying to get your milk?"

"You're sitting here anyway," Jordyn had said, plopping the collectors on her.

And now—"I'm full of prostaglandins, aren't I." She put her hand down to her pussy, which had received several doses already today. "Do you want me to?"

"It's not me wanting, it's me offering to help if you want it, sweetie." He caressed her breast, so full and hard in his hand. "It's not why I married you; it would be a pleasant bonus, like finding out you speak French."

"I just don't want to disappoint you if it never happens." But Ginny did so love the help he gave.

"Never is a long time." Roger ran his thumb around her areola, bringing the little bumps to prominence. "We'll see what happens when the first little Styles is born. But helping you isn't a chore. Just think, I'm the lucky guy who's got orders to suck his wife's tits."

The first—! Ginny wanted to squawk about how he was planning her life, but who could object when Roger was doing such delectable things to her breast? The stinker was taking a long time to get to her nipple. Just playing with her breast, squeezing and kneading her flesh, but he eventually got down to business with his lips on her bud. And then he suckled. Oh, how he suckled, and if there was any milk to be had he'd pull it out of her. And there were orgasms to be had, which he was quite naughty about, teasing her to the edge and then switching sides. She'd complain if it didn't feel so good, but she tried to control her breathing, letting the lovely explosion bloom in her pussy without him knowing until it was too late, but damn, he switched sides *again!*

"Stay there," she commanded him, and he did, pulling and nursing on her stiff nubbin until she whimpered. Would she be a ten this time? Nine and three quarters was right now—ten was right—right—right—! She squirmed, the *now* being just out of reach.

Roger changed his grip on her nipples, both with his mouth and his hand. Taking more of her in, he squeezed and kneaded, and somehow tickled the tips of her nipples with finger and tongue at the same time.

Now happened—Ginny convulsed under his mouth, her pussy clenching and throbbing without his touch or hers. The shocks rolled through her from nipples to clit, clenching everything in their path. It bowed her back, and thin noises trickled from her throat. Her thighs grew wet with rain.

"Wow!" was Roger's assessment, and then he was in her again, pushing his hard cock into her still-rippling pussy. Overwhelming her, covering her, he pounded into her, bringing another climax almost before the first was done. She clutched him, flinging her hips upward to meet his, swallowing his cock to the hilt with her pussy, demanding that he join her in pleasure.

He came, groaning her name. Ginny held him tightly, focusing his cum, sucking down everything he could give her. One leg twined around his thigh, her other flung over his delectable ass, she clutched him, and she'd never have to let go.

And even if she had to let him up now and then for business—in Roger's hands, she was a ten. Ginny rolled to her side and Roger cuddled up behind her, once he'd blown out the candles. They lay together in the darkness, and in only a few moments and whispered "I love you's," his breath went even with slumber.

Ginny listened to him, reveling in her new lover. Husband. His arms were warm and strong around her, supporting her breasts. Holding her tight.

She roused in the night, only barely aware. His cock had stiffened and was nudging her cunny from behind. Roger didn't seem to be entirely awake. No problem. Ginny reached between her thighs to guide him, slipping him inside. He rocked against her, and in his unguarded state, he didn't last long. He grunted with his orgasm, and sighed back into his dreams.

GINNY WOKE FIRST, in that wonderful beaten-up state hours of good sex and not rolling over provided. She wiggled out from beneath Roger's arm without waking him, and gazed down at him. The man looked beyond yummy in stubble, his dark locks tousled where she'd had her hands in them. She, on the other hand— A quick visit to the shower and her toothbrush restored her to perkiness, and although her pussy and breasts still ached, it was aching in the best way.

He passed her in the bathroom doorway, pausing to greet her with a kiss to her forehead. "Meet you back in bed."

She waited for his return, which involved deep minty kisses. He ended up with his head on her shoulder, his lips to her breast. "Mmm, you smell good." At least a cord of morning wood pressed against her leg. "Did I wear you out completely?"

Rubbing her thigh against his stiffy, she smiled. "You can try." Oops. She'd forgotten she'd married a competitive man. Being suddenly trapped beneath his muscular weight was a good reminder. She opened her mouth under his. Win/win.

"Ready for me?" He bumped against her pussy. "Or we can start over with the foreplay."

"Hmm, the way you do it, it's 'eight-play.' Possibly 'nine-play'." She ran her fingers through the damp waves at the nape of his neck and shifted under him. "Roger, honey, let's switch around. My breasts are a little tender after all." Which was Ginny-speak for "these huge tits are getting squished a lot harder than they were last night." But it left her on top, straddling him.

His erection lay trapped between them, rubbing her damp and rapidly-getting-wetter pussy. She flexed her hips, loving the way the ridge of his glans rolled against her clit. She could slide along his shaft for a long time, especially with his roving hands exploring her. She leaned down to kiss him, sucking his lower lip. Her nipples rasped against his chest hair—she pressed harder against him, stilling the sway of her breasts.

She could enjoy this for ages—but if she rose up enough to aim him, she could be filled with his cock too. "In" was easy, "all the way in" needed small, slow strokes—her channel widened to take his length and girth. She was panting long before she'd taken him fully.

"You okay?" Roger worried. He caught her swaying breasts, stilling their wide arcs.

"Oh yeah." She started to shift her hips, giving him movement. "Hold on to me like that." Or she'd black someone's eye. He decided "that" included rubbing her nipples. Oh. Good call. His thumbs made lazy circles over her nubs, which stood up stiffly for him.

Roger lifted his hips a little, helping her pleasure herself on his hard shaft. He matched her speed, coming up to lick her nipples now and then, to her chorus of "oh, yeah."

They went slow, but her climax built faster—she slammed herself down on his cock, each knock of his dick on her cervix adding to the gathering explosion in her pussy. He might have reached to play with her clit, but he had both nipples instead, and that was just as fine— she'd been a ten last night and she hadn't lost any of that this morning. More and more wildly she bounced, taking his every inch inside.

Ginny came down hard, her ass smacking against his thighs, her clit rubbing against his groin, and it was all over for her in a ball of incandescence. From breast to cunt she flared with her orgasm—if her hair stood out in an electrical halo, she wouldn't have been surprised. Not that she would have noticed. Her pussy clenched around his throbbing shaft, her breasts went nova, and Roger was suddenly sitting up, his face buried in her neck, his own climax shaking him. They clung together until their storm passed.

"Um, Ginny?" Roger's voice was a little muffled. "I'm all wet."

Oops. "Sorry. I've rained all over you." He hadn't commented when she squirted last night; guess this position and his giant cock meant it got all over.

"I don't think it's that." He was staring down at her breasts. "Not up on my chest." He loosened his grip and lay back. "Sweetie, oh, my!" Roger was upright again, lifting one tit, sucking it into his mouth. "Ginny—!"

He suckled on her, harder than he'd ever suckled, with little joyous noises from the back of his throat.

Could it be? Ginny hoisted her free breast. Her nipple felt strange, buzzy, something left from her orgasm maybe, but as she watched, a white bead grew on the tip. It grew larger and burst, rolling in a tiny stream down her areola to wet her hand. "Roger, I'm—!" She was scared to say the word.

"Lactating!" He came off her nipple long enough to say and dove back to suckle more. "Yes!" He worked her breast with a firm, expert latch, swallowing the fluid she'd given up on making. "You're lactating!" He grabbed for the other side, his lips greedy for her.

At last. Ginny could only curve her arms around him, and exult in feeding him. Her milk had come, finally, after she'd despaired, given up, and now he was swallowing her precious secretions down. All for him, every drop for him—she was feeding him from her body, at last. He pulled liquid from her, above, below, middle, both sides. Both eyes. A few tears, this time for joy, trickled down to dampen his head.

Roger suckled her until he got no more—he was still inside her and he'd never lost his erection. Now he flipped Ginny to her back and began to thrust into her welcoming pussy, long and strong thrusts, punctuated with kisses all over her face. She clung to him with arms and legs, letting him take her as he would, not able to do more than accept his ardor. Her breasts had softened from yielding their milk to him—his weight was an embrace and not an encumbrance now.

With each plunge inside her pussy, Ginny's orgasm built until she cried out from the glorious pulsations that built within her. "Roger!" she gasped, and it was enough for him—he stilled and let his own orgasm fill her with the cream she now knew she needed to make him milk.

"Did you get enough?" she had to ask.

"I'm never going to get enough of you, Ginevra Styles." He nibbled her lips.

"I hope not, but I meant milk." She swatted his backside lightly. Damn but he had a nice ass.

"Best breakfast in bed ever," Roger assured her with smiles and kisses. "Not India quantities yet, but soon. We just have to keep at it."

Ginny would keep at it all right—with her Roger to screw her silly and suck her to empty four times a day, she'd soon be able to feed him lavishly. If she ever wore checks again, they'd be midnight blue, almost black—her beloved needed her milk. "Oh, we will."

"Good, because I'm going to want room service in Paris." Roger kissed her again. "The jet's waiting for us."

She'd wondered about that. "A private jet? Just for us?"

"Get ready to join the Mile High Club," Roger assured her. "You're going to go around the world with me on that jet."

If you liked this, be on the lookout for Heidi and Jordyn's training feedings, Heidi and India's milk show, Kitty's adult baby client's visit, and Rita's comeuppance in more Manley Dairy stories, coming soon.

Lacy Tate grew up where the best privacy could be had in a hay loft and started young on her erotic adventures. When not writing, she can be found four-wheeling, dry-walling, or playing with her very own Roger.